Raves for ...
The Thorn of Dentonhill:

"Veranix is Batman, if Batman were a teenager and magically talented. His uncompromising devotion to crushing the local crime boss encourages him to take foolish risks, but his resourcefulness keeps our hero one step ahead of those who seek to bring him down. Action, adventure, and magic in a school setting will appeal to those who love Harry Potter and Patrick Rothfuss's *The Name of the Wind*." —*Library Journal* (starred review)

"Maresca brings the whole package, complete and well-constructed. If you're looking for something fun and adventurous for your next fantasy read, look no further . . . an incredible start to a new series, from an author who is clearly on his way to great things." —Bibliosanctum

"Books like this are just fun to read."
—The Tenacious Reader

"This is hang-on-to-your-toothpicks adventure with a mystery bent as Veranix tries to learn how to control the new magic he has and discover why some powerful people want to kill him for it. It's action-oriented—swashbuckling Indiana Jones meets the burglar Bilbo Baggins of *The Hobbit*—but the characters have a warmth and conflicting goals and attitudes that make them worth following." —Kings River Life Magazine

"I loved every minute . . . this was a great debut novel and I can't wait to see more of Maresca's work"
—Short and Sweet Reviews

"Maresca's debut is smart, fast, and engaging fantasy crime in the mold of Brent Weeks and Harry Harrison. Just perfect."
—Kat Richardson, national bestselling author of *Revenant*

DAW Books presents the
novels of Marshall Ryan Maresca:

THE THORN OF DENTONHILL
THE ALCHEMY OF CHAOS

*

A MURDER OF MAGES
AN IMPORT OF INTRIGUE*

*Coming soon from DAW

MARSHALL RYAN MARESCA

The Alchemy of Chaos

DAW BOOKS, INC.

DONALD A. WOLLHEIM, FOUNDER

375 Hudson Street, New York, NY 10014

ELIZABETH R. WOLLHEIM

SHEILA E. GILBERT

PUBLISHERS

www.dawbooks.com

First Printing, February 2016
1 3 5 7 9 10 8 6 4 2

DAW TRADEMARK REGISTERED
U.S. PAT. AND TM. OFF. AND FOREIGN COUNTRIES
—MARCA REGISTRADA
HECHO EN U.S.A.

PRINTED IN THE U.S.A.

Acknowledgments

Writing a novel is a solitary process, and yet it takes a village. I can't imagine anyone could truly do it alone.

Of course, I couldn't have written *The Alchemy of Chaos*—or any other book—without the support of my wife, Deidre Kateri Aragon. She is the reason I can sit down at the computer, day after day, and putter away until a manuscript is done. She, as well as my son Nicholas, have been a source of constant support and strength. No less important to thank are my parents, Louis and Nancy Maresca, and my mother-in-law, Kateri Aragon, all of whom have contributed in innumerable ways to making it possible for me to write this book.

I also have to thank two of the best beta-readers a writer like me could ask for: Kevin Jewell and Miriam Robinson Gould. Their input helped craft this novel into what it is, even if they sometimes have radically different reactions to certain characters. I also should thank Rebecca Schwarz and Melissa Tyler for their help keeping my plate clear while I was in crunch time for this manuscript.

A huge portion of thanks has to go to Stina Leicht. Stina has been a friend, a mentor, a sympathetic ear, and a good source for the occasional much-needed whap upside the head, which is exactly what every writer needs. Plus, she's the person you want driving the car when you're fleeing from hurricanes and tornados.

I can't emphasize enough how much is owed to my agent, Mike Kabongo. He's handled with grace and humor the arduous task of dealing with my constant harassment while shopping my work. Back when he first responded to an unsellable draft of *The Thorn of Dentonhill*, he said, "Clearly you are a writer I want to watch. Even if you decide I'm not the agent for you, do let me know when you hit the shelves, I want to buy something with your name on it." So far he's continued to show the same enthusiasm for each manuscript I've sent him, and I hope to not let him down.

Further thanks are owed to my editor, Sheila Gilbert, as well as Betsy Wollheim, Joshua Starr, Katie Hoffman and everyone else at DAW. I am deeply grateful for all the hard work they've done to make this the best book it can possibly be.

Finally, there is my dear friend Daniel J. Fawcett, who has been my sounding board and bent ear on everything creative I've done since the seventh grade. Nothing in this book or any other would be what it is without his influence. I wouldn't be who I am today without his friendship.

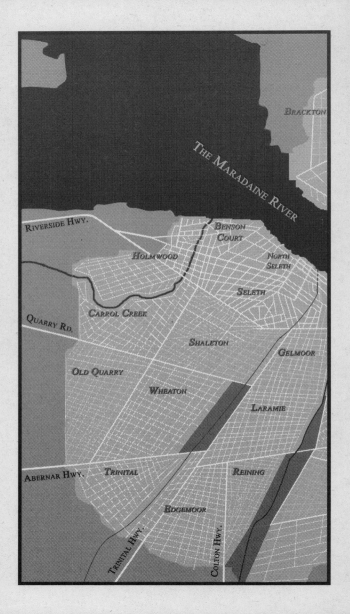

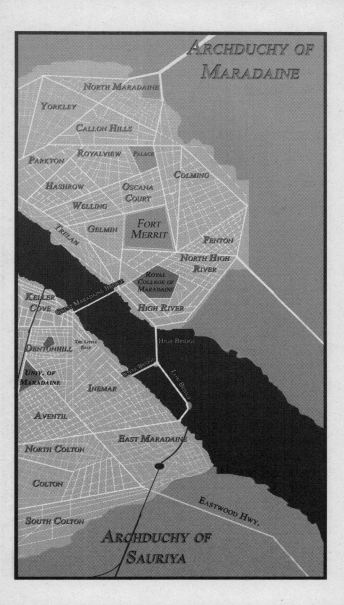

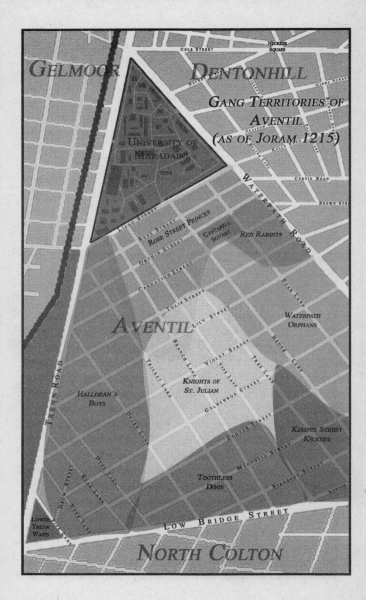

GELMOOR

DENTONHILL

COLE STREET

NICKEER SQUARE

GANG TERRITORIES OF
AVENTIL
(AS OF JORAM 1215)

UNIVERSITY OF
MARADAINE

CURTIS ROAD

BROWN STR

WATERPATH ROAD

ROSE STREET
Rose Street Princes

CANTARELL SQUARE

Red Rabbits

ORCHID STREET

CARNATION STREET

TULIP STREET

AVENTIL

LILY STREET

Waterpath
Orphans

VIOLET STREET

BRANCH LANE

VINE LANE

TREE LANE

THICKET LANE

Knights of
St. Julian

GOLDENROD STREET

Halloran's
Boys

DEANE LANE

CLOVER STREET

Kemper Street
Kickers

PETTY LANE

BARK LANE

MAGNOLIA STREET

PIERROLL STREET

TEENN ROAD

DIRT LANE

Toothless
Dogs

DRUN STREET

FERRY LANE

LOWER
TREHN
WARD

LOW BRIDGE STREET

NORTH COLTON

Chapter 1

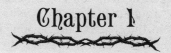

THE DOGS' TEETH PUB was an ugly atrocity of lumber and plaster wedged in the empty space between the row houses at the intersection of Cole and Hester. Bell was amazed that the University allowed such an eyesore to exist so close to their campus, but they never did anything about it. Maybe it suited their purposes, having something so obviously dangerous and disreputable in clear sight. It kept all but the most foolhardy of students from crossing Waterpath.

As far as Bell was concerned, that was just fine. Mister Fenmere felt the same way. Not that Mister Fenmere couldn't handle some heat from University, but if trouble came from there, it was best to keep it to a minimum.

A month ago, of course, Mister Fenmere had been talking about getting a toehold on campus, getting some students to deal for them. Good money to be had there. But Mister Fenmere hadn't been talking about it at all lately.

Mister Fenmere had been pretty blazing quiet for a while, until a few days back. "Nevin's boys have to be brought back in."

This wasn't what Bell was supposed to do, not anymore. But he knew he was being punished for the last month as well. If menial roundup jobs got him back in good graces, he wasn't about to complain.

Dogs' Teeth was the last loose end, the last two of Nevin's dealers. The rest had come back into the fold without any trouble. Blazes, they were eager. They needed the coin, they had people begging for any vial of *effitte* they could get. That was good, drove prices up. People were now paying a full crown for a vial, sometimes even a crown and five. Once things had settled in this part of the neighborhood, they could keep prices right there, and people would blazing well pay. More money for Bell, and more for Mister Fenmere.

That should blazing well make the old man happy again.

Bell went in, the reek of stale beer and filthy people assaulting his nose. He immediately decided this was the first and last time he would come in here. He'd make sure Nevin's boys found somewhere else to meet with him. The place was also extremely dim. Bell wasn't sure if that was an intentional choice, or if they simply couldn't afford the lamp oil to light the place properly.

He went up to the barman, a rotund beast of a man with a bald head and more scars on his hands than Bell had ever seen. "Lendle and Jemt?"

"You mean Lemt and Jendle?" the barman asked. "Who's asking?"

"A man who shouldn't have to come in here to ask." Bell tapped on the bar, making sure his ring was visible enough to the barman. Even a gutter filth barman in a place like this, deep in the mires of Dentonhill, would know that ring, and know that only one of Fenmere's close men would dare to wear it.

"There ain't gonna be trouble here, is there?"

Bell glanced around the place, filled with broken steves and facks, the kind who barely make it through a day's work without a dose of *effitte* and many cups of the Dogs' Teeth's swill down their throats. "You're probably no stranger to trouble."

"There's usual trouble and real trouble," the barman said. "Usual I can handle. I don't need any more real on my place."

"Shouldn't get any from me," Bell said. "As long as I'm not given any."

The barman signaled to one corner, where several tables had been pulled together, and two blokes played cards there, surrounded by what could charitably be called the best-looking women in the place. That meant they were the only women who didn't look like they were a dose away from a life in *'fitte*-trance.

"Gentlemen," Bell said, coming over to the table. "If we could have a moment to discuss matters."

"Who the blazes are you?" one of them asked.

"You Lemt or Jendle?" Bell asked. The two of them were almost the same guy—dark hair, scraggly beards, pocks and scars on their faces. Burly enough to be scrappers, but not the kind of guys you would hire to be muscle.

"Lemt," he answered.

Bell held up his hand to show his ring, and then popped Lemt in the face. "Go roll yourself, that's who I blazing am."

"Hey, brother, there's no need for that," Jendle said. "Everything's cozy here."

"Cozy," Bell scoffed. "The two of you are a couple of fools, you know that?"

"Why is that?" Lemt said, holding his nose. "We were doing fine, and Nevin gets himself killed. We didn't even hear proper. Then we hear nothing at all."

"We figured, you know," Jendle said. "We figured with Nevin gone, you folks were done with us. All clean, you know?"

"I really don't know," Bell said. "Nevin's boys had to sweat for a few weeks. But business needs to get back up, and you two are back in business." He took his small leather journal and a charcoal stylus out of his vest pocket.

"Back?" Lemt stammered.

Jendle leaned forward. "See, we figured . . ."

"Well, stop with figuring," Bell said. "Figuring is for captains, not for toughs and scrappers."

"Yeah, but," Jendle said. "What with what happened and all, we figured we were lucky to be breathing. Thought we should keep our heads low and keep it that way."

"What happened?" Bell asked.

An old man sitting a couple of tables away started cackling. "They mean they're a couple of squealers!"

"Shut it, coot!" Lemt snapped.

"You two," Bell said. Now this made sense. "You're the ones who pointed the . . . who gave up Nevin." He almost said the name. He hadn't said it in almost a month. Nor had Fenmere.

"You didn't know?" Jendle asked. He smacked his partner. "I told you they didn't know."

"No," Bell said. "We knew some of Nevin's boys had, but he protected who it was. So it was you two."

"They sure did!" the old man cackled.

Jendle sneered at the old man, then turned back to Bell. "So, now? You gonna drop us in the creek?"

"No," Bell said. "What happens is you two go back to work. You two are going to sell, and you're going to make sure you bring in a hundred crowns a week."

"A hundred!" Lemt snapped. "Can't be done."

"Each," Bell added. He tallied that amount under their names in his journal and put it back in his vest pocket. "You'll do that, because Nevin vouched for you. Because we need to build up again, and you boys are the ones to do it." He reached under his coat and took out the leather case of *effitte* vials. Not much, of course, just enough to get these two fools started again.

"You're building up here again?" The old man was the one asking.

"None of your business, codger," Bell said. This old man was getting on Bell's nerves. He tapped his fingers on the table, making sure the old man could see his ring. "Best steer clear."

"Oh, fine," the old man said, turning back to his cider.

"You two are back to work, hear? And you answer to me."

"We can't work out of here, boss," Jendle said. "You know he knows who we are."

"We start selling again, he'll come for us."

"You're talking about the—" Bell shook his head. "That ain't your problem, you hear? You do what you're told."

Lemt's hands were shaking. "You say that, but who'll protect us when he comes crashing in here?"

"You know who they're talking about, don't you?" the old man asked.

"Shut it! That's ain't gonna happen."

"I still ain't right when I go to the water closet," Lemt said.

"So what happens when he comes?" the old man asked. He got up from his seat, leaning on a cane, and came over. "What are you going to do to protect your boys here, Bell, when the Thorn comes for them?"

Bell felt his hand shake. "He's not gonna . . . we're gonna . . . nobody's even seen . . ."

"You afraid of the Thorn, Bell?"

"I ain't afraid of anything, I'm . . ." He realized he had never said his name in this place. "How do you know my name?"

The old man leaned in. "Because you're my favorite, Bell."

Bell stumbled back, shoving at the old man, who laughed and melted away, becoming someone else in front of his eyes. Wrinkles smoothed, white beard pulled into a sharp, bare chin. Raggedy clothes became a sharp burgundy cloak and vest. Walking stick changed into a fighting staff. The face was still hidden by a hood, casting an unnatural shadow that had to be magic, but Bell knew exactly who was in front of him.

The Thorn.

"Oh, blazes!" the bartender shouted.

Bell went for his sword, but the Thorn moved faster, and that infernal rope was suddenly wrapped around his hand. With a flick of his wrist, the Thorn then looped the rope behind Jendle's neck and yanked. Bell's fist collided with Jendle's face.

"Son of a—" Jendle managed to get out before he was hit.

The Thorn drew up his staff and jammed it into Bell's leg—right in the same blazing spot he had put an arrow a month ago. Bell crumpled to the floor before he could stop himself.

"Blazes!" Lemt shouted. "Someone get to a blasted whistlebox! Call the sticks!"

"Sure," the Thorn said, swinging the staff around to crack it against Bell's head. "I come in, and suddenly you all want the Constabulary."

Bell tried to grab at the Thorn's legs, but he was reeling from the last blow. The Thorn had jumped onto the table and pinned Lemt to the wall with his staff.

"The rest of you, try to enjoy your beer," the Thorn said. "I've no quarrel with you right now."

"You'll get a quarrel!" the bartender shouted, pulling out a crossbow from behind the bar. He fired, almost wildly, and hit Lemt in the arm instead of the Thorn.

The rope shot out across the room and tore the crossbow out of the barman's hands. "I really loathe puns, sir. You're better than that."

He jumped off the table, landing on Bell, knocking his breath out and forcing him back down to the floor. While Bell was reeling, the Thorn pawed at him for a moment, and then sprung back up. The bastard was already out of the way before Bell could do a blasted thing to stop him.

"As for this," the Thorn said, holding up the *effitte* case, "it's not going to hurt anyone." It lit up in a burst of blue flame, and was gone.

"You're gonna . . ." Bell wheezed out. "You're gonna . . ." He struggled to get up onto his knees. Standing was out of the question.

The Thorn raised up his staff. "You'll let Fenmere know that I haven't forgotten him."

The staff smashed into Bell's face. The next few moments were cloudy and dazed, until he found himself being hauled to his feet by Jendle and the barman.

"I told you," Jendle said, holding a rag over his bleeding nose.

"I didn't want any trouble," the barman said.

The Thorn was gone.

"Blazes," Bell muttered. He pushed them both away and dusted himself off as much as he could. Some small attempt to maintain his dignity. Brushing his hands on his vest, panic rushed through him. He checked both pockets, looked back to the floor, and at the table. Nothing. His journal was gone.

Fenmere was going to have him for lunch over this.

Colin Tyson hated being out of the Princes' territory, out of Aventil completely; the rooftop on the corner of Helter and Necker was Fenmere's territory. Not that they would have spotted him here, especially since he was alone. He couldn't take Jutie or Tooser with him up here, and not just because Tooser couldn't climb worth a blazes. He trusted those two with everything he had, especially since Hetzer had died, but it was exactly because of Hetzer that they couldn't get involved in this. He had already lost one good friend to this business.

The view of the Dogs' Teeth was relatively clear from up here, though Colin wished he had a spyscope or something to get a better look. Hopefully nothing would go wrong, not that he could do anything about it if it did. If Veranix ran into trouble, it would take Colin a few minutes to get on the ground and over to the Teeth. And, of course, someone would wonder why the Thorn was being helped by someone with a Prince tattoo on his arm. That would lead back to Colin.

Blazes, that could bring the whole hammer of Fenmere down on the Princes.

People came running out of the Teeth. Trouble was happening. The only question was, was Veranix in trouble, or was he the trouble?

More people ran out, heading off in every direction. Clearly whatever was happening in the Teeth wasn't something people wanted to stick around and watch.

Then the sticks came running in. That was pretty

damn quick. Sticks must have known it was one of Fenmere's top stooges in there.

Veranix better damn well have gotten out of there before the sticks got there. The last thing he needed was to pick a fight with them.

"Anything good?" The voice was a whisper over his left ear. He swatted backward to hit nothing, and then turned to see Veranix sitting a few feet away. His shadowy cloaked look as the Thorn melted away, leaving only his familiar smirking face.

"How blazing long have you been there?"

"Not long at all," Veranix said. "Blazes, I ran out of there as soon as I could."

"Good. Cover your face back up. One thing if I'm seen with Thorn, another if I'm seen with you." Colin and Veranix didn't quite look like each other, but they both looked enough like their fathers that if anyone from the old guard saw them together, they could easily put the pieces together. The shadow reappeared over Veranix's face.

"So what happened?"

Veranix got to his feet, stretching his neck as he stood. "You were right. Our friend Bell had been making the rounds to Nevin's old dealers. So I gave them a little reminder that I'm watching. Wrecked the supply he was giving them."

"How much?"

"All he had. A pittance. But it was a symbol."

"Symbol," Colin scoffed. "Is that the sort of thing they teach you at the University?"

"Among other things," Veranix said. "What's the time?"

"Somewhere between eight and nine bells. You need to get back?"

Veranix screwed his face up in thought. "Maybe."

"Maybe?"

"First *real* break night I've had since, well, since the warehouse."

Veranix went quiet for a moment. Colin knew why; he was talking about the night Hetzer died.

"So what does that mean?" Colin asked after the pause went too long.

"It means I can stroll into campus at six bells in the morning, and no one would give me any fire for it." Another awkward pause.

"But?" Colin prompted him. "Your professor still grinding you?"

"He wants to see me and . . . it doesn't matter. Point is, I got to look fresh eyed and chipper at eight bells. So I don't have to race back, but I really can't be making this a big night."

"Yeah, I can't hang around here in Dentonhill streets too long, either."

"On the other hand," Veranix said, reaching into his pocket, "It would be a blasted shame to waste the night when we have this." He pulled out a small leather journal.

"What's that?"

"This little thing was where my good friend Bell was recording who he was giving *effitte* to. Plenty of names in here, I would gather." He started to thumb through it, looking far too satisfied with himself.

"You—" Colin started, then realized he was about to shout far too loud, given that he was up on the roof of a Dentonhill tenement. "You go off on 'symbols' when you had something solid?"

"Well, I didn't want to brag," Veranix said. He read in the moonlight, half to himself. "Hockley, Briars, Nennick, Keckin, Sotch . . . Jendle and Lemt, of course . . . who can I give a little hello to tonight?"

"Wait," Colin said. Some of those names bounced in his skull. "Did you say Keckin and Sotch?"

"Yeah," Veranix said. "You know them?"

"Those are Red Rabbits captains, I think." Not that he really knew any of the Red Rabbits. Bastards kept trying to push on Princes' territory, especially around Orchid and Cantarell Square.

"Rabbits?" Veranix's face turned dark, literally. A shadow slowly poured out around him. "It's crossing Waterpath."

"Ease up," Colin said. "I don't need you doing any crazy magic right now."

The shadow snapped away, Veranix getting a grip on himself. He even seemed surprised. "Sorry. I . . . remind me. Rabbits like to gather at the Trusted Friend, right? Carnation and Bush."

Veranix really was going to do this. "All right, hold up. Before you go off half-cocked on the Rabbits, at least give me some cover. There are already too many whispers on the streets connecting the Thorn to the Princes."

"You tamp that down," Veranix said. "If Fenmere really figures out who I am . . ."

"I'm trying." Not that Veranix was a Prince, but in another life he could have been. Colin would have liked to embrace his cousin openly, rose tattoos on both their arms. But he had promised Veranix's father he'd keep him safe, make sure he finished at the University. He had sworn it on Rose Street, and that was something he'd never break. "I can only deny it so much before it sounds like I'm trying too hard."

"Fair enough. What do you need?"

"Give me an hour to get to the Turnabout, get myself

seen having a few beers. That way when you start cracking Rabbit skulls, no one can say I had anything to do
with it."

"I can do that," Veranix said. "Besides, for this, I'm
going to want my bow."

Shadow engulfed him again, blending into the night,
and in a moment, he was gone.

No time to waste getting to the Turnabout. He was
going to need those beers, that was for certain.

"You're back far too early," Kaiana said as soon as Veranix came into her stable house. He had been expecting
her to be waiting for him, but he thought she'd be happy
to see him.

"Why do you say that?" he asked. "Don't I need to get
my rest before end-of-term exams?"

"Very funny," Kaiana said. "You don't have an exam
in the morning."

"No," he said. Though his meeting with Professor Alimen tomorrow was tied to his Magic Practicals exam
somehow. Alimen had been frustratingly vague on how.
"But I really do need to study for my history exam in the
afternoon."

"Don't sell me your sewage," she said. She leveled her
dark eyes at him. "Did it go badly?"

"No, it went wonderfully. Destroyed some *effitte*,
roughed up some boys at the Teeth, and stole a journal
from Fenmere's goon." He tossed the journal over to her.
"Not too shabby, I thought. And normally that would be
enough to call it a night, even before ten bells."

"You haven't been *really* out there in weeks."

This had been Kaiana's argument ever since he
stopped the Blue Hand Circle. That he needed to be out

there, making his presence felt. Doing more. Putting the hammer on Fenmere every night.

"I know that," he said. "You think I don't?"

"You don't seem to care," she said. He knew, intellectually, that she was deliberately trying to irritate him. After all, she knew full well that Alimen had kept Veranix under his thumb ever since that night. She knew that he wanted to crush Fenmere as much as she did. "You have a responsibility now."

"Well then," Veranix said. "It's a good thing that I was only coming back here for my bow and arrows."

She arched an eyebrow at him. "Really?"

He went to the trapdoor in one of the stables, that led to the Spinner Run. "A lot of names in that journal. But two of them—Keckin and Sotch—are captains in the Red Rabbits."

"Red Rabbits?" she asked.

"One of the Aventil gangs," he said. "You really need to learn this stuff." He pulled out his bow—his father's bow, really—along with the quiver, and put them on.

"Fine. So now you're Rabbit hunting?"

"If the Rabbits are letting Fenmere's junk cross Waterpath, then that's something that needs to be handled. Unambiguously."

She gave him the briefest, tightest smile. "That's right."

He went back to the door. "Have you seen Delmin tonight?"

"No, I'm sure he actually is studying. You need him for something?"

"His history notes," Veranix said with a wink. "I really do need to study for that exam."

With that, he was back out into the night.

Chapter 2

CANTARELL SQUARE, specifically the corner of Carnation and Bush, was the place to start looking for Rabbits. The public garden was where their territory bordered with the Rose Street Princes and the Waterpath Orphans. Given their propensity for ridiculous fur-lined jackets, they shouldn't be too hard to spot.

Even still, Veranix wasn't sure how he wanted to go about it. He was of half a mind to kick open the doors of the Trusted Friend and knock a few teeth in until he got the folks he wanted.

That never worked as well in reality as it did in his head.

There also were two real bruisers standing outside the Trusted Friend. Unlike the Princes' favored place, the Turnabout, they weren't willing to let just anybody wander in. And those two guys had their eye on Cantarell Square, almost like they were expecting trouble. Possibly because there were three other guys in the square, hanging out by one of the statues. If Veranix had to guess, they were Waterpath Orphans, but that was only because he knew they weren't Princes. If they were, their sleeves would be rolled up and showing off the tattoos on their arms.

Veranix huddled near the low wall of the square, shrouded by the napranium cloak, with its *numina*-drawing abilities augmenting his own magic. He needed a plan. Could he set the bruisers on the Orphans? Or the Orphans on the bruisers? No, that might start something even bigger, a real battle between the two gangs. That wasn't something he or Aventil needed.

Something simple. Something direct. But that wouldn't, necessarily, involve him having to brawl with the two big Rabbits at the door. Which stymied him. They certainly weren't going to let him in there just because he asked.

Well, they wouldn't let Veranix Calbert, Uni student, in.

The Thorn might be a different story.

So: simple, but with style.

Channeling *numina* through the cloak and into his legs, he leaped up into the air, a bit higher than the Trusted Friend itself. As he came back down, he shed the shrouding and took on his full appearance as the Thorn, making sure to keep the illusion of the hood over his face intact. He landed square in front of the two bruisers.

"Gentlemen, I believe you know who I am. Are Misters Keckin or Sotch available? I would want a word."

The two of them were dumbfounded for a moment, and one recovered enough to go for his cudgel. The other put a hand up to stop his friend.

"Don't think you wanna do that," he said. He gave a look at Veranix. "Keckin? Sotch? What if they ain't here?"

"Then I'll look for them elsewhere. As many elsewheres as it takes."

The smarter bruiser—he at least looked like he had something behind his eyes—gave a glance at the door of the Trusted Friend. "I let you in there, it's my skin, hear?"

"So what do you suggest?" Veranix asked. The guy wanted to help, he could hear it in his voice. Good.

"I don't know if either of those folks are in there or not. But how about I look, and if they're there, I send them out?"

"Fair enough," Veranix said. After all, he really didn't know who he was looking for. But he did confirm one thing: Keckin and Sotch were Rabbits, and this guy knew them. "Don't be too long." The smarter bruiser gave a little nod to his partner and went in.

The dimmer bruiser still had a hand on his cudgel, but he wasn't moving it. He squinted at Veranix, and moved his head from side to side. "Your hood doesn't look normal."

"I suppose not."

The bruiser kept looking on either side of Veranix. "It's like your hood is your face. How does that work?"

"Magic."

The bruiser took a step back.

The smarter bruiser came back out, and definitely not alone. He easily had a dozen Red Rabbits with him, the pair in the front sporting chevrons on their fur-lined coats, as well as tattooed on their necks. They must be the captains.

"And here I thought you were kidding, Binny," one of the captains said. "The Thorn himself, at our door."

"At your service," Veranix said with a small flourish. "Are you Keckin or Sotch?"

"I'm Keckin, she's Sotch," the first captain said. "And these are some of our boys."

Keckin hit the word "some" as if he wanted to make it perfectly clear there were even more inside.

"You'll excuse me that I don't get all your names today," Veranix said. "But let's talk about a mutual friend we apparently have. An overgrown errand boy by the name of Bell."

"What's it to you who we do business with?" Sotch asked.

"You don't even try to bluff," Veranix said. "Have to respect that."

"We don't need your blazing respect," Keckin said. "You can shove off."

"Except if you're doing business with Bell, then you're doing business with Fenmere." Veranix saw a few of the Rabbits in the back twitched a little when he dropped the name. "And if you're moving *effitte* for him . . . then you're going to have a problem with me."

"Oh, you want to talk about *problems*," Keckin said. "Because you've just walked into a whole pile of them."

"Funny, I've just been standing here," Veranix said.

Sotch giggled; a strange, shrill giggle. "Heard tell that Fenmere would be pretty pleased with whoever handed you up to him."

"You're right, Sotch," Veranix said. "You'd become his favorite lapdog."

Sotch gave a little hiss, and on cue the bruiser's cudgel came for Veranix's head. Veranix brought up his staff to parry it, but half a second before it made contact, the bruiser's hand spasmed and the cudgel dropped. The bruiser cried out in pain, which made sense, given he had a knife in his arm.

"Rose Street!" came a young voice from the square. Not Colin.

Veranix flipped backward, away from the crowd of Rabbits, grabbing his rope off his belt. Napranium-laced, like the cloak, easy to draw *numina* through. Easy to control.

Too easy to depend on.

He shot the rope out, wrapping it around the dim bruiser's leg. With a flick of his wrist, he pulled the bruiser over to the side, bowling over half the Rabbits with their friend.

Snapping the rope back, he drew out his bow while the Rabbits were still scrambling. Three shots, fired in quick succession, pinning the stupid Rabbit coats to the front stoop of the Trusted Friend. Another moment before the rest of the Rabbits got into their full senses, he drew in some *numina*, quick and hard, and slammed a couple more against the wall of their clubhouse.

Now the ones still standing had their knives and cudgels out, but Veranix had backed off enough to put several meters between them, and aimed an arrow at Keckin's chest.

"Allow me to clarify my position, gentlemen," he said in his calmest voice. "If you enable Fenmere getting a toehold in Aventil, then you will have a significant problem with me."

Keckin stammered, but before coherent words could come out of his mouth, a shrill whistle from the square interrupted him.

Constabulary.

In the past month one thing had become perfectly clear to Lieutenant Benvin: he was the only person in Maradaine who gave a damn about how he did his job. Captain Holcomb was comfortable in his office, and could care less what Benvin did to crack down on the gangs in the streets. If nothing else, he was grateful that Holcomb's laziness was complete: he honestly didn't care one way or the other what Benvin did. At least the man wasn't obviously corrupt. That couldn't be said for most of the other lieutenants or patrol officers in the Aventil stationhouse.

He wasn't sure any of them were truly getting bribed. From what he had seen of these Aventil gangs, they weren't really in a position to bribe anyone. But something was motivating them to stop him up whenever they could.

People in the neighborhood were no better. There were the gangs, of course. But the rest of the people didn't just tolerate them, they embraced them. Someone had a problem, they didn't call Constabulary. That was the last thing they wanted. No, they called a Rose Street Prince or a Waterpath Orphan or some other damn waste of space.

Some of the patrolmen got on board with Benvin, at first. Though it became clear that for most of them, it was about the thrill of cracking street kids with their handsticks, shaking them for coin, getting kicks off the girls. No better than the gangs, just green and red were the colors they wore. Benvin had no use for those folk.

So he narrowed his squad down to five solid patrol officers and two cadets. The ones he could trust. The ones who did it right. The ones who had been shut out by the rest of the stationhouse. He made them his own.

It wasn't much, but it was all he could get in Aventil. Saints knew none of the district commandants or even Commissioner Enbrain were going to send anything else his way.

Didn't matter. Benvin was going to do his job, and do it right. He'd dismantle every gang in this neighborhood and clean it up. Starting small, with the Red Rabbits, just to show everyone he could do it.

Tonight wasn't for the Rabbits, though, not directly. He planned to shut them down first, but he couldn't make them the only thing he focused on. Tonight they were going to crack open the cider ring the Orphans were running. Sure, it was a tick-and-pence scheme, hardly worth the trouble. But that was why he wanted to crack it. No scheme, no ring, no crime was too small.

So Benvin sat with Jace, one of the cadets, in the wagon on the northwest corner of Cantarell Square, watching with the scope. Arch, Pollit, and Tripper were in the square, waiting for their meet, and the rest of the lads were in place so they could move in. The targeted Orphans were approaching the square with their hand-cart of contraband cider.

And then someone yelled "Rose Street!" and it all went to blazes.

It took Benvin a moment to fully realize what was going on, and by the time he did, the Orphans were clearing out. Pollit and Tripper charged after them, while Arch just looked confused.

But the real action was across the square, where the Rabbits were having a brawl. A full-on brawl. With whom? The Princes? One Prince?

No, it was *him*.

The Thorn.

Benvin leaped off the cart and blasted his signal whistle as he charged across the square.

By the time he was halfway across, Arch had come up behind him, running for all he was worth.

"Thorn?" Arch asked, heaving for breath.

"Thorn," Benvin hissed back. That word was written on the top of their slateboard by Benvin's desk back in the stationhouse, in big letters and underlined several times.

The Thorn disengaged from the group of Rabbits, firing a wild arrow to get them to scatter. He took two steps toward Cantarell Square, but then changed direction as soon as he spotted Benvin and Arch.

Arch drew up his crossbow and fired, but missed wide.

And then the Thorn suddenly faded out of sight as he ran.

"The blazes?" Arch said. "How'd he—"

Benvin spotted a shimmer of something going into one of the alleyways. "There!"

He tore after the shimmer, pulling up his own crossbow. The shimmer was still moving down the alley, as fast as a man running would. Benvin shot his blunt-tip at the shimmer.

The blunt-tip made contact, and with a cry, the shimmer turned back into a cloaked man. He stumbled his way down the alley, giving Benvin a chance to reload his crossbow and close the distance.

"Hold fast and be bound by law!" he shouted, as the Thorn turned on his heel and drew up his bow.

Standing off against a constable's crossbow was not where Veranix had planned to be.

"Bound by law?" he asked the constable—a lieutenant by his collar—while doing his best to maintain his hood illusion. It wasn't easy with the screaming pain in his back. Blunt-tip or not, it hurt like blazes. "I'm not who you want, Left."

"I know who you are," the lieutenant said, steadying his shaking crossbow hand. "You're going to be brought in."

"You go after me instead of a dozen Rabbits?"

"Rabbits are nabbed in dozens," the lieutenant said with a slight smile. "You're something special. Now drop the bow."

"You drop yours," Veranix said. "Mine's not a blunt-tip."

Of course he had no intention of shooting a Constabulary lieutenant. He'd kill Fenmere's men or other *effitte* dealers if he had to. Sticks were another matter. Most of them were good folk trying to do the right thing. This lieutenant probably thought he was.

"I've got three more men coming, and theirs won't be either."

He was expecting friends. Which was why he didn't pay much mind to the person coming up behind him, who was definitely not a stick. Too young and skinny.

"Sorry, Left," Veranix said. "This isn't your night."

The skinny kid brought up a sapper and dropped it on the lieutenant's head. He crumpled to the ground like a sack of rocks.

"Take it!" he shouted with a bit of a laugh.

Veranix wasn't sure if he should drop his bow.

"You can't run that way, Thorn," the kid said. "It blocks off, only a door to a Rabbit clubhouse." He winked and held up his arm, showing off his tattoo. A Rose Street Prince.

"Your knife?" Veranix asked.

"Blazes, yes!"

Constabulary whistles, and the lieutenant moaned and tried to pull himself up.

Veranix put up his bow. "No time for subtlety." Taking out the rope, he shot one end up to the rooftop while he grabbed the Prince's arm. "Hang on."

More Constabulary ran into the alley as he had the rope pull them up to the top of the building.

"Blazes!" shouted the Prince as their feet hit the eaves. "How'd you—"

"Just wait, kid." The Prince was probably the same

age as Veranix was, but no reason to let him know that. He took a moment to marshal up more *numina*—it was going to take a lot of magical energy to pull this off—and half dragging the Prince with him, he made a running leap from the roof.

The two of them sailed across Cantarell Square, landing gently right outside an alleyway off Hedge, halfway between Orchid and Rose streets.

This time the Prince couldn't even muster an expletive. He almost looked like he'd soiled himself.

"All right?" Veranix asked, hiding as best he could how winded he felt. He knew he was pushed past his limit right now. The rope and the cloak, with their *numina*-drawing abilities, could mask those limits, but Veranix had learned how to read his own fatigue through that. He wasn't going to let himself get too reliant on these things.

"Damn," was all the Prince mustered.

"Spread word, kid," Veranix said. "Rabbits might be trying to shuffle *effitte,* let Fenmere bleed across the Path."

"Serious?" the Prince said. Now that Veranix got a look at him, he'd seen this one before, around Colin a few times.

"Let your captain know." He took a few steps away. "And thanks, kid."

He shrouded himself as best he could without exhausting himself further, and slipped off down the street.

"Mister Calbert!"

Rellings, the third-floor prefect of Almers Hall, was waiting at the main door of the Hall, leaning cockily in the doorframe. It didn't suit his large, lumbering form in the slightest, nor did the self-satisfied smirk on his doughy face.

"It's past ten bells, Mister Calbert," he said. "Quite late, indeed."

"It's a break day, Rellings. There's no curfew." Veranix had left his cloak, rope, weapons, and all the rest of his accoutrements of the Thorn back in the tunnel under the carriage house, and changed back into his school uniform. He even had his red-and-gray scarf marking him as a magic student, and the tasseled cap with three pips showing him as a third-year. Rellings's uniform was a few sizes larger, but other than one more pip and a gray-and-white scarf, his was the same.

"But whatever could you have been doing so late, especially when exams are about to gear up? Most of your fellows have been studying."

"That's most of my fellows," Veranix said. "Are you going to give me a hard time?"

"Came in from the southeastern corner of campus. The library isn't over there."

This was what Rellings was on about. He knew Veranix was coming from the carriage house, where Kaiana lived. This had been the scuttle for months, of course. People in Almers figured Veranix was up to something, and it involved the half-Napolic girl. It had been little more than whispers until the month before, when he had been caught in the carriage house with Kaiana half-naked. That only happened because she was protecting the reason why he was really there. Word of that had made its way back to Almers and the whispers had exploded to full rumor and wild speculation. Almost every boy in the dormitory had been giving Veranix nods of admiration, scowls of moral scorn, and, most of all, side-long looks of jealousy.

Not that anything had happened between Veranix and Kai that would have really earned admiration, moral scorn, or jealousy.

The rumors had clearly piqued Rellings's interest.

"No, Rellings," Veranix said. "I was definitely not at the library. Now please let me by. As you might imagine, I'm sore and exhausted. I really need to get to bed."

Nothing he had just said was remotely untrue. Whatever Rellings inferred from that was his own problem.

His meaty face frowning, Rellings waved him through the door. "I'll be doing bed checks later, Calbert."

"If that helps you get through the night, Rellings," Veranix said, and trudged his way up the stairs to the room on the third floor he shared with Delmin.

He came in and dropped onto his bed, ignoring all the glances and raised eyebrows of the rest of the third-floor residents. Delmin was deep into a book at his desk, oil lamps burning hot, and as soon as Veranix was down, he shut the door to their quarters.

"What happened out there tonight?" he asked in a manic whisper. Veranix half opened his eyes, seeing Delmin's skinny face and stringy hair far closer than he wanted them to be.

"I'm fine," Veranix muttered. "Just tired. Had to push a little too hard." He struggled to pull off his jacket and shirt.

"How'd you get that?" Delmin pointed at Veranix's back.

"You don't want to know. How bad is it?"

"It's a pretty horrible bruise."

"Blunt-tip from a crossbow."

Delmin grimaced. "I don't know how you . . . isn't it Constabulary who use blunt-tips?"

"Didn't I say you don't want to know?" Veranix sighed and sat back up. "Define 'pretty horrible.'"

"I'd wait a few days before hitting the bathhouse if you don't want strange questions."

"Like I don't get those already," Veranix said. The scar in his right shoulder was pretty well healed, but it did draw attention.

"All right, I don't want to know details," Delmin said, sitting back at his desk. "But . . . you did good things out there, right? It was worth the trouble?"

"I think so," Veranix said. Certainly Bell's journal had value beyond just the Red Rabbit names.

"Does it make us safer here?" Delmin seemed very nervous to be asking this. Veranix had noticed Del had been avoiding conversations about his outside activities for the past month.

"You mean you and me?"

"I mean, on the campus. All the University." Delmin fidgeted with his pens. "I mean, last time, the professor was taken."

"That isn't going to happen anymore," Veranix said. "That was about the Blue Hand Circle, and they're done."

Delmin looked like he had more to say, but then turned back to his books. "So you need to get on task for this history exam."

"All exams," Veranix said. "Though we don't have a Practicals exam. Just the meeting with the professor."

"Tomorrow's meeting is our exam in Magic Practicals," Delmin said. "I don't know how it's going to work exactly, but one way or another, we're starting that exam at breakfast tomorrow."

"You're probably right," Veranix said. "History in the afternoon, Magic Theory the day after that, and Rhetoric on the last day."

"Rhetoric for you," Delmin said. "I can't help you with that."

"I'll be fine," Veranix said. "It's just writing an argument on paper."

There was a knock on the door. Veranix pulled his shirt back on as Delmin answered it. Eittle, the Naturalism student whose room was the next one over, hovered in the hallway.

"Heard you two talking," he said. The walls of Almers weren't too thin. You could hear that conversations were going on in the next room, but couldn't usually make out details.

"I just got in," Veranix said.

Eittle nodded. He was too polite to ask details of where Veranix had been, and Veranix seriously doubted the young farm boy had any notion of his evening adventures. "Right, I figured. I just ... couldn't sleep just yet. Most everyone is too quiet right before exams. Real quiet, you know?"

"Quiet" had been a word Eittle had been dropping a lot recently, mostly because he was alone in his quarters. His roommate, Parsons, had all but died in an *effitte* overdose. Now he was in a drooling state with other *effitte* victims down at the Trenn Street Ward.

Other victims like Veranix's mother.

Unlike Veranix's mother, though, Parsons was only a victim of his own foolishness. If Veranix had known he was using *effitte* he'd have ... he wasn't sure what he'd have done. But it was too late to help Parsons now.

Veranix had been so lost in thought, he wasn't sure what Eittle and Delmin were talking about. "—and that was the horse's!" Eittle said.

"You aren't going back up for the summer, are you?" Delmin asked.

"No," Eittle said. "I didn't tell you?"

"You've got a plan for the summer?" Veranix asked.

"I'm going in-country with Professor Hester."

"He's your astronomy professor, right?" Delmin asked. "What's in-country?"

"Up in the high hills in Toren, where he and some of his colleagues from other universities have built a series of grand scopes. We're going to be observing the seven planets over the course of the season."

"So this is a good opportunity?" Veranix asked.

"I'm astounded he asked me," Eittle said. He gave a little self-deprecating smile. "I imagine there might be heavy equipment to carry."

"I hear that," Veranix said.

"What are you even talking about?" Delmin asked.

"Do you have any idea the kind of scut Alimen is having me do right now?"

"I'm sure it's not that—" Delmin trailed off. "What is that?"

"What?" Eittle asked, looking around.

"I don't notice anything," Veranix said, but something was making the hairs on the back of his neck stand up.

"Oh, sweet saints!" someone yelled from down the hall.

"What is that?" someone else yelled.

A moment later a stench hit them all like a wave crashing on the shore. Veranix almost fell over from the power of it, like nothing he had ever smelled before. It was as if a sewer had been festering with rotten eggs for months before finally bursting open.

Delmin gagged, and Veranix was barely able to keep his stomach from emptying its contents on the floor.

"Is that the water closet?" Eittle asked, covering his face with his sleeve. "Did it break somehow?"

"Come on," Veranix said, forcing himself to his feet. "Delmin, you all right?"

"That's horrid," Delmin said, stumbling to the window. He pushed it open and gasped deeply.

"Call down to Rellings," Veranix said, tapping Eittle on the chest to follow him.

The stench filled the hallways, the air had turned hazy. Young men were coming out of their rooms, crying and retching. Some were even dropping to the ground.

"Get some windows open!" Veranix ordered to no one in particular. "Where's it coming from?"

The people who were capable of reacting shrugged, looking confused.

"Is it just this floor?" a second-year asked.

"Go check," Veranix said. The boy didn't question him and ran to the stairwell. Veranix followed his first instinct, heading to the floor's water closet. He opened up the door, and while the hazy stench was present, there was no sense that it was any stronger here.

"This isn't it," Eittle said.

Delmin came stumbling over. "Opening the windows doesn't help. I think it's outside as well."

"Blazes," Veranix said. He went over to the water closet window, opening it up. The haze hugged the outside of the building, but the lawn farther out seemed clear. Boys were running away from Almers Hall, pouring out every door. "Let's get everyone out."

Eittle nodded and took a deep breath, which struck Veranix as incredibly bold. "Run the drill! Clear out and hit the lawn!"

Delmin stumbled, and grasped the doorframe to hold himself up.

"This isn't . . ." he wheezed.

Veranix was still quite fatigued from the night's escapades, and the stench wasn't helping, but he got himself under Delmin's arm and hoisted his friend up. "Let's move."

"I've got him," Eittle said, scooping Delmin up. He went to the stairwell, while Veranix checked the various rooms to make sure no one else was passing out. In one room he found a first-year curled up in a ball, lying in his own sick. He grabbed the kid—Benkins?—and pulled him out to the hallway.

"Calbert?" Rellings came down the hallway, his uniform scarf wrapped around his mouth. "Is everyone else out of this?" He got on the other side of the first-year and helped Veranix get him to the stairwell.

"Think so," Veranix said. "Any idea what this is?"

"Some joker's sick idea of a prank, I think," Rellings said. "Get him on the lawn. Air is fresh once you're past the grass." He turned back to the floor.

"Where are you going?"

"One last check," Rellings said, and he went back into the thickening haze.

"Blazes," Veranix muttered. "Come on, Benkins."

By the time Veranix made it to the lawn, almost every boy in Almers was there, gasping and wheezing. Other prefects were making head counts, trying to sort the boys out. The commotion had gotten the attention of the campus cadets, who were scrambling around, attempting to figure out what was going on.

Veranix was finally able to breathe, and two other boys came and relieved him of the first-year. He noticed they were fourth-years, wearing the yellow-and-white scarves marking them as Medicine and Surgery students.

"You all right?" one of them asked Veranix.

"Fine," he said, but his head was buzzing. He glanced back at the door. Rellings hadn't made it back out yet.

"Blasted Rellings," he muttered, and he forced his legs to move back to the door, even though they were feeling like stone.

A hand grabbed his shoulder: Delmin. "Don't go back in there."

"Rellings is still in there," Veranix said.

"Cadets are doing a sweep," Delmin said pointing to the group who were heading up the steps. "I don't think you should go in again."

"I'll be fine—"

"Vee!" Delmin snapped. With an almost flailing hand, he grabbed Veranix by the front of his shirt and tried to pull him close, but all he managed to do was pull himself closer to Veranix. "I really think neither you nor I should go back in there. Understand?"

What Delmin was saying got through Veranix's skull. Something about the stench was magic. "Let's take a walk."

Clear of most of the crowd, Delmin lowered his voice. "All right, tell me straight, Vee. You didn't do this, right?"

"Of course not!" Veranix said. He wasn't even sure how to do something like this. The whole building was coated in a haze, like it was seeping from the bricks themselves, but sticking to it somehow. Even if he could figure out how to do such a thing, even if he had the desire, doing magic on this scale would exhaust him in seconds. "How could you even think that?"

"I didn't really, just . . . right before it hit, I sensed something shifting with the *numina* all around us." One area of magic study where Delmin had a serious advantage over Veranix was in his ability to sense and track the flow of the energy that powered all magic. Veranix mostly only noticed when other mages were drawing on *numina*, but Delmin had a profound skill, a magical bloodhound. Veranix imagined that if Delmin wanted to, he could pinpoint every mage on campus right now.

"Shifting how?"

"It was subtle, I can't quite figure it out. It didn't feel like it was coming from anywhere or anyone in particular. Which is how it feels when you're masking your magic use. And it did happen right after you got back."

"It wasn't me, I swear," Veranix said. He looked back at the building, where two cadets were leading Rellings and another kid out. "Even with the cloak, I couldn't do something like this."

"I didn't think so," Delmin said. "Question is, who could?"

Whatever was holding the haze to Almers lost its grip, and it began to drift away. The smell was still powerful, but not quite as choking as it had been.

"That's not the question," Veranix said. "I want to know why they'd use that kind of power just to prank our dorm."

"A prank?"

"Rellings thought so. I don't know. I don't want to think about it," Veranix said. He lay down on the grass. "Wake me up if it's worth the trouble to go back in."

"You're just going to sleep on the ground?"

"I grew up in a traveling circus. I can sleep anywhere."

Delmin sat down next to him. "What if it wasn't a prank?"

Veranix lay still, eyes closed, trying not to let the obvious thought form. It was no use. "Then someone in Almers was a target."

Delmin started laughing. "Someone in Almers?"

Veranix shrugged. "I'm not so egotistical as to presume it's me."

"Sure," Delmin said. "I'm sure half the dorm has powerful nemeses who want them dead."

"You never know, Delmin," Veranix said wearily. "Everyone has secrets."

Chapter 3

THE TURNABOUT was relatively quiet. Colin's boys weren't even around. There were a handful of folk about, Princes mostly. Colin took his time sipping his second beer. He'd been seen here for a long time, so he was good. All he had to do was wait for news of whatever Veranix did tonight to come through the doors, and everything would be fine. In the meantime, he kept his eye on the main action.

The main action tonight was a table in the back corner, where Hotchins was holding court with a few street-level Princes, mostly birds. Colin didn't really know any of these Princes too well; they were usually working corners over by Branch and Lily, where the Knights of Saint Julian were pushing a little too hard.

Dennick's crew.

Dennick had been a street captain, like Colin, but last week he had gotten too anxious with the Knights, too messy. Spilled a fair amount of Knight blood, which would keep them at bay, but got far too much attention from the sticks in the process.

The sticks had gotten Dennick, but not before Old

Casey and the other basement bosses had burned the captain stars off his arm.

It was a shame. Colin had always liked Dennick. Dennick's pop, he had stood by Colin's father when things went bad in '94. But Dennick was tough. He'd make his way in Quarrygate well enough.

Seemed clear to Colin that everyone in Dennick's crew was vying to get the stars on their arm now, so they huddled around Hotchins, doing their best to sweeten his cream. Hotchins didn't make the call about who got stars, but he had the ear of the men who did. None of those old men spent their nights in the Turnabout.

Colin must have been watching a little too close, because Hotchins gave a whistle and called him over.

"What's on?" Colin said, coming over with his beer, but not sitting down unless explicitly invited.

"You're running light, ain't ya, Tyson?"

"Making do with my boys," he said. Truth was, his pockets had been lighter in the past few weeks. Hetzer had always been the best at working the Uni gates; neither Tooser or Jutie were bringing in as much coin. His death had hit the crew hard in a lot of ways.

"Making do isn't much," Hotchins said. "Things got to move around, and you're the man to help with that."

"Whatever you need, boss," Colin said.

"Good, because we're gonna trade the flop under the butcher shop on Branch to the Knights, and . . ."

"Trade it for what?" Colin asked.

Hotchins scowled. Colin had talked over him, and while Hotchins wasn't that big of a man among the bosses, he still was a boss, and he wasn't going to take any of that. "None of yours to mind. Point being, that was this crew's main crash, and they can't do that no more."

This was really not what Colin wanted to hear. "You

want me to bring them to the crash over Hechie's barbershop?"

"No, Tyson. Your crew uses the one under Kessing's
shop, right?"

"Well, yeah, boss. But that's a pretty small flop."

"And you've only got a small crew," Hotchins said.
"You're not gonna put them all up, so calm the blazes
down." He picked up his striker, which looked like it had
grown cold and greasy, and took a big bite. "Two of this
crew are going under you now. That's how it's going to
be."

None of Dennick's crew looked particularly pleased
with this idea, and Colin couldn't blame them. They had
lost their captain and their crash, and now they were going to be broken up.

"Who?" one of the birds asked. She looked a little
older than Colin, with dark hair cropped real short.
Colin had seen her around plenty, usually at Dennick's
left hand, and she looked like she could scrap well
enough. That said, he couldn't for the life of him remember her name.

"You and Theanne," Hotchins told her. "The rest of
you, go off to Hechie's for tonight. We'll figure out where
you're going later." He slugged down his beer and got up
from the table, clearly demonstrating that he was done
holding court. The bird Colin had just inherited scowled
and stood up as well. Theanne, from what Colin gathered, was the mouse of the girl whose Rose Street tattoo
still looked raw and fresh on her arm, since she also got
up and stood behind the older girl.

"So," Colin said. "I've forgotten your name."

"Deena," she said.

"Right." Now that she told him, it clicked. Dennick
and Deena, they had been together for a while. She

really should have gotten her captain stars now, but clearly that wasn't happening. "Let's take my old table back, right?"

He snapped over to Kint behind the bar to bring over three beers as they sat down.

"So look," he said as they sat down. "I wasn't expecting this, and none of us are going to be too happy about this at first. We're gonna just do our best, hear?"

"Fine," Deena said. "Long as we're straight with each other. Theanne and I aren't going to be rolling doxies for your boys. We'll pull our share, but you best not expect that sort of thing."

"That's straight," he said. "But I wasn't kidding about the flop we crash in being small. We're gonna be half on top of each other as is. But every Prince in my crew respects each other." Kint dropped three beers on the table and stepped away.

"Fair," Deena said. She took a swig off her beer.

"Theanne?" Colin asked. "You fine?"

"Yeah, sure," she said, though her eyes never left the table. Girl made Jutie look old. "We got a hustle going tonight?"

"Nothing set. But the Uni semester is done in a few days, you know? So the Uni kids are usually looking for a big blowout, and we can pump a lot from that well if we're smart about it."

Suddenly Jutie came bursting through the doors of the Turnabout, grin on his face as wide as Rose Street itself. "You should have seen it!"

"What's on?" Colin asked, raising his voice so the whole place would notice. He already had a hunch that this was the news he was waiting for, since Jutie had been working a few Uni boys on an escort right around Cantarell.

"The blazing Thorn, that's what's on," Jutie shouted. "He was knocking down Red Rabbits, and then taking on the sticks, and smacking them all around. It was fantastic!"

"He fought the sticks?"

Jutie shrugged. "Not much. He was tearing on the Rabbits, though. They brought about a dozen blokes out of their club, and he's all 'you don't scare me' and smacked them around."

"Why was he fighting the Rabbits?" Deena asked. "Thought he hit in Dentonhill."

"He, uh . . . hello. Colin, who are these two ladies?"

Colin gave Jutie a quick smack. "They are part of our crew now. Deena and Theanne. Be nice to them."

"I'm always nice to ladies."

"Don't be stupid with them." Colin looked back at the two of them. "This is Jutie, our crew's pigeon."

"I can't be the pigeon if these two are in now!"

"You're still the pigeon," Colin said, and gave him another smack for emphasis.

"Why was the Thorn fighting the Red Rabbits, Jutie?" Deena asked again.

"Oh, right," Jutie said, turning to Colin. "He wanted me to tell you."

"Me?" How stupid was Veranix being out there?

"Well, he said to tell the captain, you know? The Rabbits are moving *effitte* for Fenmere."

"Can't be," Colin said in mock surprise. "That's what he said?"

"You talked to the Thorn?" Theanne asked. "For real, really talked to him?"

"Yeah," Jutie said, trying to play cool. "I was there for him, helped him get away from the sticks, and then he returned the favor."

"So that's what he told you?" Colin said. "The Rabbits are selling *effitte*, working with Fenmere?"

"Yeah, that's what he said."

"All right," Colin said. It had happened, he had heard, and he had witnesses. All good. He even had something he could bring to the bosses. Not too shabby. "That's bad news, for sure."

"Real bad news," Deena said.

"I'll bring this to the basement," Colin said. "You three, sit tight for a bit. Then we'll head over to the flop, and you birds can get settled."

"Joy," Deena said flatly.

Colin went around to the safe house down in the back alley behind the Turnabout, down steps to the basement beneath the Venter Inn. Three quick raps on the door, waited two beats, then three slow ones.

The metal window opened up. "Who's at it?"

"Colin," he said.

"And the word?"

"Open up." The password was that there was no password. That way if you were being held at knifepoint by someone trying to muscle his way in to the boss, you could give the fake password and let them know to arm up.

The door unbolted and the bruiser guarding it let him in, shutting it back behind him quickly. "They ain't in the mood tonight," he warned Colin.

"I just got some news. They won't like it, but I don't need to make a plea or nothing."

The bruiser shrugged. "Your arm."

Colin went down the cramped hallway to the first lamp-lit chamber. It was a taproom of sorts, in that

Hotchins and a couple other minor bosses were sitting around a table playing cards, while two girls — technically with roses on their arms, though Colin doubted they ever worked the streets — poured beers and served the table.

Colin knew all the folk at the table: Giles, Bottin, Frenty, Nints. Most of them had been street captains when he first got his ink. Now they were "bosses," in the most nominal sense. They outranked him, they got to sit in the basement and play cards, but for the most part they simply weren't involved in running things for the Princes. Boss status was a polite retirement for these guys.

"What's on, Colin?" Hotchins asked. "You ain't here to whine about dropping Dennick's birds on you, are ya?"

"Nah, that's fine," Colin said. "I ain't got a guff with that, honest."

"Good," he said. He drew a card he didn't like and dropped his hand. "So what is it?"

"I just heard news that the Thorn started a dustup with the Red Rabbits."

"Did he?" Giles asked.

"Don't sound like our problem," Nints said.

Bottin grunted. "Cards."

"All right, so he tussled with the Rabbits," Hotchins said. "What of it?"

"Well, he also talked to one of my boys."

Hotchins raised an eyebrow. "One of yours?"

"One of mine was in the area."

"Huh." Hotchins got up from the table. "Look, Colin, last month you went and joined in with a tussle the Thorn had in Denton. Lost your left-arm boy. Now he's talking to another of your boys?"

"Like I said," Colin said. He felt like he was going to

break out in a sweat. That would draw questions. "Do you wanna know what he told my boy?"

"I'm just worried you're getting in deep with this Thorn business. You say he's a friend of Rose Street?"

"I honestly think he is."

"All right, so what's he say?"

Colin took a deep breath. "Rabbits are letting Fenmere creep across Waterpath. They're apparently taking *effitte* from him, gonna start selling. In Aventil."

"Saints," Nints said. "Blazing Rabbits. I knew those bastards would crumble if Fenmere pushed them."

"We don't know that's happened," Giles said. "We got the Thorn telling his boy. 'Sides, Rabbits aren't that weak. They just muscled out Jellican from his brewery a couple weeks ago."

"Well, maybe we should look into it," Colin said. "We don't want the Rabbits letting anything creeping across Waterpath, do we?"

"Probably not," Hotchins said. "But we don't want a hammer coming across the Path, either."

"What are you talking about?" Colin asked.

"Real simple, Tyson. The Thorn tussles with Fenmere. The Thorn tussles with the Rabbits. If we join in against the Rabbits, then the idea will get out there that we're with the Thorn."

"And we ain't?" Frenty asked. He was a mousy, skinny guy and Colin was always astounded that he not only made captain, but he survived past it. "I mean, I like the guy. He's fighting our fight, ain't he?"

"Maybe he is," Hotchins said. "Tyson, look, I'll tell Old Casey and the others about this. But maybe the best thing for us is to let it simmer a bit. The Thorn wants to dust up the Rabbits, we let him. Maybe he'll just plain handle it."

"That's how we do things now?" Colin asked, his blood heating up. "Like trading a flop to the Knights?"

"All right, enough," Hotchins said. "Go for a walk."

The bruiser by the door took one step forward. It was subtle, but enough that Colin got the signal. "Walking."

The bruiser didn't touch him as he went back into the alley. That went about as well as he had expected. He shouldn't be surprised, but he had hoped it would have gone better. The Princes were going to let Veranix do their dirty work all on his own. And Veranix would do it, whether Colin helped him or not.

Bell had to return to the mansion after what happened. As much as he would have preferred just to go home, he knew well enough to bring the news directly to Mister Fenmere. It wasn't yet eleven bells; the man would still be awake. Probably awaiting a report from Bell regardless of how things went.

He went to the back door, as he always did. Mister Fenmere always insisted that Bell and people on his level were, for all intents, deliveries, and had to enter the house as such. He was welcomed as warmly as he ever was—which was not at all, but cordial enough—and escorted to the sitting room.

Bell took his pipe out of his coat pocket and stuffed it with Fuergan tobacco. He wanted his *phat*, but he knew Fenmere wouldn't stand for him smoking *that* in his sitting room. Tobacco, though, he was fine with.

He finished two pipes before Fenmere finally came in, with Gerrick and Corman at his side. Two of them carried glasses of Kieran wine. Corman as usual abstained.

"Mister Bell," Fenmere said coldly as he took a seat. "You show up at a late hour looking like a cat ate your shoe. I trust from your expression that this is yet another occasion where you have let me down?"

"I was doing as you said, sir. Going to Nevin's old sellers, bringing them back into the fold. Getting sales going again."

"Good, good. So you've gotten that going? That isn't the problem that's so clearly on your face?"

"One drop didn't go as planned."

"Really?" Fenmere asked. He took a sip of his wine. "Would this be our uncommonly incompetent friends at the charmingly named Dogs' Teeth? What are their names again?"

"Lemt and Jendle," Gerrick offered.

"Lemt and Jendle," Fenmere said. "It really rolls off the tongue, doesn't it? It would be an excellent title for one of those Idiot plays. Do you go to the Idiot plays, Bell?"

Bell wasn't sure where Fenmere was going, and that made him more afraid. Usually when Fenmere talked in circles, it was right before someone lost a thumb. "I've always been more partial to the Romances, myself."

Fenmere stopped his glass an inch from his lips and stared at Bell. For just a moment, the old man looked genuinely surprised. "I would not have guessed that, Bell. I'm pleased that you are not entirely predictable. However, Misters Lemt and Jendle are quite predictable, in that they will fail. They were the ones who betrayed Nevin in the first place, after all."

So Fenmere did know that already. That was a surprise.

"Which made them an excellent lure. That was the only reason you were to include them in your rounds. So answer me, Bell. Is the Thorn still a problem for us?"

It was the first time he had said the name, at least in Bell's presence, for a month.

"Yes, sir," Bell said. "He was there, and he destroyed the *effitte* I was going to give to Lemt and Jendle."

Fenmere sipped at his wine again. "A calculated loss. In fact the vials you delivered today were low-grade dregs. So that, in and of itself, is little to worry about."

Fenmere didn't seem to be angry. This made Bell far more nervous than getting screamed at.

"There's something else," Bell said. "He took my notebook."

"Oh, did he?" Fenmere asked in mock surprise.

"What a shock," Corman said flatly.

Fenmere finished his wine and stood up. "Looking back over his activities in the past months, it became clear that he was looking for any information he could find about deliveries and drop-offs. That led to him stealing the Blue Hand's merchandise from you."

The man really was not going to let that go. Bell didn't care. After that screwup, Bell counted himself lucky to have both his ankles intact.

"You did have your contact with the Red Rabbit patsies in there, correct?"

"I had everything for this week in there," Bell said. "Just like you told me when you . . . gave it to me."

"Ah," Fenmere said, pointing at Bell in mockery. "You see it, Gerrick? That faint light of comprehension in his eye."

"I was your bait, sir?"

"Of course you were, you moron," Fenmere said. "And you handed over to the Thorn exactly what we wanted him to have. A few disposable sellers in Denton-hill, and a target to strike at across Waterpath."

Bell got on his feet. "I was your rutting bait, sir?"

Fenmere's hand slapped his face before Bell even realized he had crossed close to him. "You do not raise your voice in here, Bell. If I want to use your belly fat to make candles, you'll be the one cutting it off. Am I clear?"

Bell sat back down. "Clear."

"Our scouts report that the Thorn has already caused disruption to the Red Rabbits," Gerrick said. "As well as at the Dogs' Teeth."

Fenmere gave a dramatic nod before glaring back at Bell. "Please do not presume I am some idiot waiting for you to report to me, Bell."

The butler came in with a woman waiting at the door. "As you expected, sir."

"Yes, of course," Fenmere said. His whole demeanor shifted to warm and welcoming as the woman approached. She was about Fenmere's age, steel gray hair, dressed like a woman of standing. Even still, there was a quality in the way she held herself, like she was standing on razors. "Laira, it has been far too long."

"Willem," she said crisply. "It is inappropriate for you to use that name."

"Of course," he said, moving in for a polite embrace, which she accepted. "So I should call you Shrike?"

"Please, Willem. I haven't been Shrike in ages. You know I'm Owl now."

"I can't get used to that, frankly. It means we're both too old."

With a signal from Fenmere, the butler had brought over more wine. Fenmere and Owl took theirs, and she took a seat. Who was this woman? Shrike? Owl? Why would she be called those things? It made no sense unless she was—

"Oh, blazes."

Bell didn't even realize he said it out loud.

"Did you see it again there, Gerrick?" Fenmere asked. "It really is amazing when he understands what is happening. But we should be glad; most of our fellows don't even have that."

"I know the type," Owl said. "Fortunately for me, the dull ones do not last long."

"You're one of the Deadly Birds!" Bell blurted out. He had heard plenty about that group of assassins, but he had never met one.

"I was, dear boy," Owl said. "At my age, I just do the business."

"Well, I asked you here for business, old friend."

"Which quite surprised me," she said, sipping at her wine. "Oh, Willem, you do spoil me."

"You are worth it."

"I am," she said. "So, business. You know we do not do a typical assassination contract. If you just want someone in the ground—"

"I know how you work, that's why I called for you. I don't just want him dead. I want him defeated, publicly. I want *showmanship*."

"Then we're your girls," Owl said. "You pay two thousand per girl, per day. You determine how many days they hunt, and payment is based on that term, not when they kill the target. If the term of the hunt expires and the target is never engaged, your money is returned. If your target is engaged but not killed by the end of the term, double your money is returned."

"It's like the best kind of gambling," Fenmere said with a large smile. "I win every way. Corman, what can we engage?"

The accountant bit his lip. "For what we can reasonably spare for this project, I would say eight days total. How you would want to break that up, I couldn't say."

"Two girls for four days," Fenmere said. "That should give all of Aventil an *excellent* show, don't you think?"

"Do you have a preference?" Owl asked.

"If I can't get the Shrike, then I don't even know," Fenmere said with a flirtatious grin.

"She's long retired."

"Then your discretion," Fenmere said. The Owl nodded and took another sip of wine.

Bell sat in stunned silence. He had actually hired the Deadly Birds. Fenmere wasn't just going to kill the Thorn. He was going to *destroy* him.

Chapter 4

AT SOME POINT in the night, after prefects, cadets, and whoever else got involved did what they could to clear out Almers Hall, it was decided that, at least for the remainder of the night, no one should return there to sleep. Boys were gathered up off the lawn and brought to Holtman Hall, where they were bedded down on the floor of the dining hall. Quite a few grumbled and whined as blankets were handed out, but Veranix paid them no mind. He had barely roused himself from his nap on the lawn and let himself be led into Holtman, where he dropped back down to sleep as soon as he was able. A childhood of sleeping in wagons, in tents, on the ground under the wagon, or wherever else had long inured him to any difficulty in falling asleep anywhere.

He felt he had barely fallen back down when he was being nudged. "Wake up, Vee."

"Delmin, it can wait until morning."

"It is morning."

Veranix opened his eyes a crack. Sunlight was already coming through the windows of the dining hall.

"What blasted time is it?"

"Half past six bells," Delmin said.

"I cannot believe that," Veranix said. He got to his feet and started to stretch his neck and shoulders. Around him other boys were rolling up their blankets. "They want us out so they can serve?"

"On the nose." Delmin picked up Veranix's blanket and handed it to him. "You going to be all right?"

"Fine." Veranix rubbed his eyes. "Nothing a strong tea won't fix. I don't suppose they're going to serve us straight away?"

"Don't be absurd. We need to clear out so they can set up. Nothing as sensible as what you're suggesting."

They followed the stream of boys back outside and into Almers. There was no longer a haze of any sort. In fact, other than lingering scent, there was barely any trace of what happened last night.

"Everyone is saying prank," said a second-year at Veranix's elbow. Theology student whose named Veranix never remembered. Oaves? Owens?

"A prank from whom?" Veranix asked.

"Elemental studies?"

"I wouldn't bet," said another second-year stumbling along with them. Prens, who was close mates with Oaks. Oaks! That was his name. "Over in Rentin Hall, it's all elemental and natural sciences and mathematics boys. They could do it."

"Could and would are two different things," Delmin said.

Eittle came up along with them. "Frankly, I'm stumped on 'could.' I've taken three semesters of elemental, and I can't even begin to guess how you would do this."

Prens shook his head. "Rentin has a whole pack of fourth-years, living right on their ground floor. Those troublemakers would have no qualms with such a prank."

Veranix gave a glance to Delmin, who returned a worried look. He was probably thinking the same thing: this wasn't something elemental, it was magic. But what kind of magic, done by whom; these were the big questions they had no answer to. Followed by why.

The idea that Veranix couldn't shake was that there was still some remnant of the Blue Hand Circle out there. If Sirath had recovered, he could do this.

They all made their way back to their rooms. The water closet was crowded with everyone trying to wash up at once, so Veranix gave himself the luxury of taking twenty more minutes with his eyes closed on his own bed.

The scent that remained was faint, just a memory of putrescence, but it was still enough to make serious sleeping almost impossible. Veranix never got deeper than a light doze, roused when Delmin had returned from washing up.

Delmin held his uniform jacket up to his nose. "I can't tell if it infested our clothes or not."

"Most likely," Veranix said. "And laundry service isn't for another week."

"Joy."

Veranix went to take his turn in the water closet. Twenty minutes later, he returned to find Delmin in his uniform, which had turned completely white.

"I tried to clear out the smell."

The rest of the room had not turned white as well, which was Veranix's first instinct to check. "I don't even know how you did that."

"Can you fix it?"

"Maybe," Veranix said. He first went to put on his own uniform. Delmin was right, the stench was embedded into the fabric. Quite noticeable as he dressed.

"Help me," Delmin pleaded. "If I go out there like this . . ."

"Yes, you'll be roundly mocked."

"And Professor Alimen will probably fail me on Practicals."

"Hold on," Veranix said. "I needed my own uniform to give myself a color reference. And to get dressed."

"Fine, just hurry."

Veranix tied on his scarf, then looked at Delmin, all in pure white. He drew in *numina*, and focused on the colors of his own uniform. Then he channeled the energy into Delmin's clothes, hoping that his instincts on matching the two would work.

Delmin's uniform was back to the regular deep blue coat, red-and-gray scarf. It seemed right.

"You're going to have to explain how you did that," Delmin said.

"There's nothing to explain. I just . . . did it." With another draw and release, he purged the scent from his uniform.

"I hate how easy it comes to you."

Breakfast was far more lavish than they were used to for Exams session. Typically at the end of the semester, it seemed like the kitchens were scraping at the edges of their larder. Veranix wasn't sure why—perhaps pity for the stench last night—but they went full out with biscuits and bacon and hotcakes. Veranix greedily ate servings equal to three of his fellows. He was already famished, and the bit of magic to fix Delmin's uniform had pushed him even further.

"The sciences crew over in Rentin aren't denying it," Oaks reported as he joined them at the table.

"That means nothing," Veranix said. "In fact, they

probably are spooking you. They didn't do it, but if you think they might have, that's funny enough."

"You think you know who did it?" Oaks asked.

"I don't, but I think the Rentin crew are just making the most bread from the flour, you know?"

"Maybe," Oaks said.

Veranix downed several cups of tea, which barely pulled the fog out of his head. "Almost eight bells. Time to see the professor."

Delmin scarfed down a few more bites himself, and the two of them headed out across the lawn to Bolingwood Tower.

"You know," Veranix said while glancing at Delmin. "In the sunlight, I wonder if I got the colors right."

"Do not do this to me, Vee."

"I don't know, it just seems brighter on you."

"Well, maybe it's because mine is clean now. Completely."

"It was certainly devoid of color."

"You're impossible."

"All right, something serious before we get in there," Veranix said. "Let's presume that it was a prank and a mage was involved. Who?"

Delmin stopped. "A mage was involved, I'm quite certain. *Numina* was moving, and it was a sudden, subtle change *right* before things happened."

"Fair enough. So who could pull it off? How many magic students are there, in total?"

Delmin thought for a moment. "Let's say around eighty. Well, the kind of subtle work we're talking about, we should probably exclude the first- and second-years. So maybe forty."

"That include the girls' school?"

"You think they would prank Almers like that?"

"I'd say, besides you and me, we can't rule anyone out."

"Probably true. That brings us to, I don't know, fifty or fifty-five."

Veranix nodded. "We should work on narrowing that down."

"We should? Shouldn't we tell Professor Alimen?"

"Not yet."

"You're going to have to give me a really good reason for that."

Veranix sighed. "My gut is telling me this wasn't a prank. And if it was something else, something targeted at *me* somehow, then . . . I don't want Alimen in the mix at all. He was almost killed last time, and I can't have that on me."

"That's why we tell him now."

"Just . . . let's wait. Look into it ourselves. For now."

"In the midst of our exams."

"Or maybe it was just a stupid prank, I don't know," Veranix said.

"The prefects, cadets, and professors will handle it. That's their job. We will take our exams and do our best to pass. That is our job, Vee. Our only job."

"Fine."

"Our. Only. Job."

"I said fine."

Delmin stared him up and down for a moment, appeared satisfied, and continued on to Bolingwood Tower. Veranix followed him up the several flights of stairs to Professor Alimen's office.

When they entered Professor Alimen was behind his desk, leaning back in his chair with his feet up, reading the newssheet. "I made a little bet with myself as to which would arrive in a more timely manner: the morning news or my two appointed third-years. I lost the bet."

"Anything of note in this morning's news, sir?" Veranix asked.

"If you are interested in the minutiae regarding special elections for the Parliamentary seats of members killed during the last session, and the analysis of political partisanship that arises from that, then yes. However, I am not interested in those things." He slammed the sheet down and got to his feet. For an older man, he was wiry and spry. Veranix imagined that he could have been a good acrobat in his youth, with the training.

"We are here more or less on time, sir," Veranix said.

"Mister Calbert, when it comes to punctuality, I have learned to tolerate 'more or less' from you. I will accept that you have both arrived within an acceptable margin of error. Mister Golmin, however, was quite punctual." He gestured to someone who was sitting unobtrusively in the side of the office.

Veranix knew the young man, or, more correctly, knew who he was. He would have recognized the red-and-gray scarf and the four pips on his hat, regardless, but he had seen this fourth-year magic student in various places over the course of his time at the University of Maradaine. Despite never formally meeting, he knew this was Phadre Golmin.

For a magic student, Phadre came off as almost husky. Most of them had at least a lean look, like Veranix or the professor, or gangly like Delmin. Phadre was built like most folks, maybe a little on the soft side. He greeted them with an almost goofy smile.

"Morning, gentlemen," Phadre said. "I, uh, want to apologize in advance to the two of you for what's about to happen."

"That doesn't sound good," Veranix said.

"You are being overly dramatic, Mister Golmin," the professor said. "Are you familiar with the work Mister Golmin has been doing?"

"Afraid not," Veranix said. "But you're about to defend, get your Letters, right?"

Phadre nodded. "That's exactly right."

"I've heard a little about it," Delmin said. "You've been working on external factors that affect *numinic* flow."

"Yes, exactly," Phadre said.

"In final preparation for his defense, Mister Golmin will be engaging in a number of demonstrations to highlight his findings. And I could think of no one better than the two of you to assist him in that."

"The two of us?" Veranix asked.

"I did suggest it," Phadre said. "Delmin, your skill in sensing *numina* is pretty well known amongst the fourth-years."

"Is it?" Delmin smiled brightly.

"Try not to be too proud of yourself, Mister Sarren. The point is, while I understand you have other exams you must focus on, I will require the two of you to use your free time over the next few days to help Phadre prepare for his defense."

"Sir." Veranix's mind was already racing about the Red Rabbits, the prank in Almers, or just hitting more of the dealers in Dentonhill. "I do have quite a few responsibilities to attend to."

"And I am aware of all of them, Mister Calbert. Your History exam is at two bells in the afternoon. Your Magic Theory exam is tomorrow at ten bells in the morning, and your Rhetoric exam at two bells the following day. And this, right here, is your Magic Practicals exam. Assisting Mister Golmin."

"Told you," Delmin said.

"Like I said, I wanted to apologize in advance," Phadre said. "And, Professor, I do appreciate how much you've supported me with this."

"You are my student, Mister Golmin, and I would be remiss if I did not do everything in my power to ensure your Letters of Mastery. In our field it is more crucial than any other."

Veranix nodded almost out of instinct, and he noticed Delmin and Phadre doing the same. For magic students, one had to receive Letters of Mastery—or some sort of equivalent—to be inducted into a Mage Circle. Without a Circle for protection, both physical and legal, it was nearly impossible to be a practicing, professional mage of any sort. Given that their talent for magic was some inherent factor rather than a conscious choice, failing to receive Letters was simply not an option any of them could entertain.

"All right," Veranix said. "So how exactly do we help? I mean, I'm still not clear on what, exactly, your work is here."

"It's fairly advanced ideas in Magic Theory, frankly," Phadre said.

"Advanced and controversial," the professor added. "If you put stock in controversy, which is mostly about old people who don't want to learn new ideas."

Veranix put on his best face. He already suspected this would be a long morning. "Well, let me hear it. I'm sure to understand extremely little."

Phadre got up from his chair and went to a pile of crates that were sitting in the corner of the office. "I'll start simple. Do you remember the Winged Convergence last month?"

All too well.

"What about it?" Veranix asked, trying to keep his voice as innocent as possible.

"Well, there was a marked change in *numinic* flow, quite sharply." He pulled out a metallic device from one of the crates and put it on the professor's workbench. To Veranix's eye, it looked like some sort of spider-legged torture device, with each leg ending in a stylus. He took out a sheet of paper and put it under the machine. "Veranix, could you turn the crank on that? Magically?"

Veranix drew in a small amount of *numina* and started the crank turning. The styluses all started moving in elaborate patterns along the paper.

"Good enough." Phadre pulled out the sheet of paper, showing a series of circles in a variety of colors. "Regular *numinic* flow, as far as we're recording today. Understand?"

"I suppose," Veranix said. "I'm not sure what it means."

Phadre took a piece of paper out of his satchel. "This is what I recorded on the night of the Winged Convergence." The sheet was covered in crazy, jagged squiggles, filled with spikes and jabs.

Delmin was all over the device. "What are you using as vibration catalysts? Gemstones?"

"Very small ones," Phadre said. "Now, I've got recordings like this for the past two years. I've never seen one like the Winged Convergence."

"Yeah, that was a crazy . . ." Veranix started. "I felt something strange that night for certain."

"Right, so the question I'm working on is: why?"

"Because the moons were in a strange alignment?" Veranix shrugged.

"That's lazy thinking, Veranix," Phadre said. "That's *what* happened, but has nothing to do with *why* it happened. There's always a why behind these things, even if we don't understand what those are."

"I never thought about it," Veranix said.

"I'm not sure what he thinks he's going to do for his Mastery Defense," Delmin said.

"And what are you going to do?" Veranix shot back.

"Gentlemen," the professor said calmly from his desk.

"Indeed," Phadre said. "Can we focus on this work here?"

Veranix threw up his hands in peace offering. "All right. Why did it happen, Phadre?"

"That is the central thing I wish to discern. I've been researching into various bi-lunar events, as well as solar events, eclipses, occlusions, alignments of planets. All of these have had reported effect on *numina*. Or the crafts of Physical Focus. You know what that is?"

"I—" Veranix started, trying to wrack his brain.

"It is on the exam tomorrow, Mister Calbert."

"I know," Veranix protested. "Forms of magic—"

"Mysticism." The correction came in triplicate from every other person in the room.

"In which *numina* is not directed through a mage himself, but some sort of physical object. Waish or Bardinic runecasting, for example."

"You might just pass tomorrow, Mister Calbert."

"Thank you, sir," Veranix said, but his thoughts were elsewhere. He glanced at Delmin and silently mouthed, "Almers?"

Delmin shook his head, but the look on his face said that he doubted his own answer.

"So my question came down to isolating what factors with regard to the Winged Convergence—and similar phenomena—are responsible for affecting *numina*. Is it the light? Is it the gravity? Is it some sort of star-based Physical Focus on a cosmic scale?"

"Well, which is it?" Delmin asked.

"I believe it is all, in conjunction. The numbers involved are complicated—"

Delmin's smile widened. "I'd like to see your work—"

"Well, of course, but we need to demonstrate—"

"You've got more devices to do that—"

"Yes, and—"

Delmin and Phadre were bouncing like two actors in the opening scene of *Bears, Bottles, and Wives*, not letting each other finish a sentence but still appearing to understand everything the other was going to say. Veranix sighed and went over to the crate of Phadre's devices. "Not to change the subject, but you've been studying this all year, right?"

"Yes, that's been my research," Phadre said.

"So are Delmin and I going to have to learn it all for your defense?"

"Well, no," Phadre said. "Though I thought it would interest you."

"It does me," Delmin said.

Veranix quickly changed tones. "I'm sorry, it's just . . . it's exams, we didn't sleep well, and we do have History this afternoon. I do want to help you however I can, Phadre."

"Mister Calbert does have a valid point," the professor said. "Time is an essential factor you should consider. Do not waste yours or theirs, please."

"Right, right," Phadre said. "I'm very sorry, it's . . . I'm sure you understand, Delmin."

Delmin nodded vigorously. "It's very exciting stuff you're talking about. I would like to go over your findings at some point."

"But History," Veranix said.

Phadre went over to his boxes. "You're right, Veranix. I apologize. I have several devices for demonstrating effects of light, reflection, gravity, vibration, and many other factors, on *numinic* energy. The key things I need from the two of you are operation and calibration."

"Let me guess," Veranix said, now guessing exactly why he and Delmin were brought in. "I provide the channeling of *numina* around the devices, and Delmin helps you calibrate them?"

"Yes, exactly," Phadre said. "Let's unload the crates, and get started, shall we. This is going to take us much of the morning, just for starters."

"Glad to help," Veranix said, mustering up as much enthusiasm as he could manage. "And while we're at it, Delmin, let's maximize our time. I really get my royal lineages mixed up after the Cedidore kings."

✕✕✕✕✕

The flop under Kessing's shop wasn't too crowded, even with five people there. Saints knew that there were far more packed flops that the Princes held. The one above the barbershop was usually packed across the floor with sleeping bodies on top of each other.

Still, taking in Deena and Theanne was damned inconvenient. Not just because they were a couple of birds, but that didn't help. Two new bodies, folks Colin didn't really know if he could trust, wasn't something he should have to deal with.

He was used to the bosses mostly leaving him alone.

Shortly after they had all arrived the night before, Tooser stepped out and came back with a few blankets and cords. Colin was pretty sure someone would find their washing line robbed come morning. While the girls laid down some bedding for themselves, Tooser hung up the cord and put up a makeshift curtain separating the back room of the flop.

"Fact you even have two rooms is a miracle," Deena had muttered.

Truth was this flop was almost—almost—a place a respectable person could live. Damp and earthy-smelling, but the front room had a stove and a well pump, a few cabinets of larder. Not that they ever had much beyond a few jugs of cider or jars of preserves on hand.

Of course, the other things in the front room were boxes, cases, and crates lining the walls. A boss usually had stuff brought to Colin, and he was told to "hang on to it for a while." In a few months it was taken back. Colin and his crew left those things alone, because they knew this flop was a good deal for them. The only windows were in the back room, and too small for even a kid to crawl through. Only way in was the door, and that was steel-lined with a solid latch. A horse couldn't kick it open. So the flop was secure, ain't no one could second-story it. And if somebody inside closed the double on the door, even the best lockcracker couldn't open it.

So Colin was surprised to wake up and find the door wide blazing open.

"There a reason you showing our business to the world?" he asked Deena.

"Damn right there's a reason," Deena responded. "This place smells like none of you bother to step out to the backhouse when you've got the need. Airing it out is gonna be frightful."

Colin shut the door. "It don't need airing." He shut the latch and the double. "Where's Theanne?"

"Sent her up into Kessing's, get a few things. You have frightful little to eat."

"What, you're going to be cooking breakfast?"

"I'm going to *have* breakfast. What you do is your own blazing problem. Don't think you've gotten your-selves cooks, or maids, or washerwomen, or doxies, or wives."

"Blazing well hope I got a couple loyal Princes."

Deena's sleeves were rolled up as she looked around the front room, and she held up her tattooed arm. "See anything that suggests otherwise?"

"Not yet."

"Good. What's in these boxes?"

"Nothing that's my business or yours. We just sit on them until we're told otherwise."

She nodded. "Fair enough. That included the three kegs of Jellican?"

Colin couldn't remember which boss had stored away the beer kegs, but Mister Jellican had retired and shut down his brewery a couple weeks before. A few more weeks and those kegs would be the last in town. They should fetch a real good price then. Colin would have his stars burned off if his crew drank that up. "Definitely includes that."

She sat down at the table. "Do you even have a ket-tle?"

"Doubt it." He went into the cabinet and pulled out a jug of cider and a few cups. He poured it out for her and himself.

"So what's the word for today, Captain?" she asked.

"A little crowd work in Cantarell Square for you and me. Jutie and Tooser will take Theanne to the Uni gates. Both those things are gonna be pretty light today, what with the Uni boys being on exams."

"How do you know that?" she asked, sipping her cider.

"Because it's our business to know. But you and I will go to Cantarell because I want to get my eye on some Rabbits today." He wasn't about to tell her the real answer, which was that he knew Veranix had a mess of exams in the next few days, so it wasn't like the Thorn could be counted on for anything. The bosses wanted to let him handle the Rabbits, and that probably wouldn't happen in time.

"This business with them letting Fenmere bleed over the Path?"

"Damn right. Look, I'd known Dennick for a piece, and I know you were at his right arm. So I'm counting that I can find you there when I look to my side, hear?"

"Hear." She sighed and took another sip. "We already lost some ground to the Knights, lost Dennick. I'm in no mood to see the Rabbits do any more damage."

Colin held up his cup of cider to her, and she tapped her cup against it.

"Done well, then," Colin said.

"Done well, indeed. Let's get on it."

Veranix was certain half the words Delmin and Phadre were using had been made up. Nothing they were saying made any damn sense. *Numina* was measured in things called "barins"—which was a term Veranix had heard before, though the idea of assigning a numerical value to magic made his head hurt—but the two of them started referring to "centibarins" and "millibarins" and Veranix was sure that meant nothing. Phadre also said something about "luminescent variance" and "prismatic filtration" and a few things that even got Delmin to ask questions.

Veranix turned cranks. He pushed levers. If needed he made *numina* just flow from one side of the room to the other: quickly, slowly, harshly, softly. Whatever Phadre asked for, while Delmin gave him notes to adjust it. The three of them had stripped down to shirtsleeves while working, and even then, Veranix found himself overheated. Professor Alimen read at his desk, though Veranix felt his eyes burning at them. The whole while Delmin was driving him on details about ninth- and tenth-century Druthal.

"So when was Queen Mara deposed?"

"I know this. I know this. *'With battered arm and bloody tears, I've held this throne for seven years.'* So 838 was when Lord Ferrick ousted her."

"Do not rely too heavily on plays to get you through this, Veranix."

"But I know the plays."

"So in whose reign did Monim split into two kingdoms?"

"Ferrick III!"

"Except Ferrick was king of Druthalia Proper, not Monim. Who was the king of Monim?"

"You expect me to remember the Monic kings as well?"

"No, Vee. Professor Besker will expect you to."

Phadre stepped away from a device with the whirling brass cups on the top. "All right, I need a very soft flow, from right to left. Build it up slowly, Veranix, and hold it when you reach twelve centibarins per second."

"Of course," Veranix said, though he had no idea what twelve centibarins per second were or what it would feel like. He drew it in and pressed it across the room without any shaping.

"A little stronger," Delmin said. "Monic kings."

"One thing at a time." Veranix pushed, but the strain was starting to weaken him. How many of these had he done this morning? "Grentin?"

"Grentill. How many of them were there?"

"Eight?" Sweat was forming on his brow, despite the fact that the *numinic* flow he was directing was minor. "How is that?"

"Ten and a half centibarins. And there were only seven Grentills. Grentill the Seventh was king when Monim split in two, and he and his family were all slaughtered shortly afterward."

"Of course they were. Is that twelve?"

"Right on it," Phadre said. "Hold it there for a few moments."

"Who takes the Druth throne in 915?"

A wave of fatigue and nausea hit Veranix. The cups went out of control, suddenly spinning wildly.

"Saints, that was nearly a whole barin! Be careful, Veranix."

Veranix threw up his hands. "Sorry. I think it's time to take a break for lunch."

"It's only eleven bells," Phadre said.

"No, no. I have an exam in three hours. So: lunch. Then some final review until two bells, and then my exam."

"I think Mister Calbert is correct," Professor Alimen said. "Why don't we all go to lunch. I know I could use it as well."

Veranix put his coat back on, as did the rest. "Best thing you've said today, Professor. And it was Gennick the Cruel."

Delmin shook his head. "Kellith the Cruel. Before him was Ferrick the Fourth."

"Right. Then Kellith the Second, and *then* it's Maradaine the VII, and it's all Maradaines from there on." Coats, caps, and scarves on, they all made their way downstairs and out into the hot sun.

"Someone forgot to tell summer it wasn't quite its turn, didn't they?" the professor said, scowling up at the sky.

"Are you joining us in Holtman, sir?" Delmin asked.

"I think it's important to support the fine work done there," the professor said.

"Clearly you haven't eaten there regularly," Veranix said.

"Oh, I do on occasion, Mister Calbert. Trust me when I say that my presence will bring the best out of the staff. Which you should appreciate as well. How is your day, Miss Nell?"

Veranix hadn't even spotted Kaiana, weeding the walking path. She was wearing a heavy smock and a wide straw hat. Veranix was amazed that she could handle this heat. Even though she was born in the Napolic islands, and favored her mother's appearance, she had spent most of her life in Maradaine. She shouldn't be any more used to this heat than any of the rest of them.

"Well enough, Professor," Kaiana said, rising to her feet. She raised an eyebrow at Veranix. "You keeping him in line?"

The professor smiled. "My eternal struggle, young lady."

"Keep it up, sir," she said. "Vee. History."

"I'm on it," Veranix said.

"Good." She gave a slight tap on her nose, which the professor would probably mistake for an idle scratch. But Veranix knew it was a signal to come talk to her after his exam. He had left Bell's journal in the carriage house with her; perhaps she had found something useful.

"We have to get to lunch now," Veranix said. "Busy day."

Kaiana smiled, wide and warm. "Don't let me stop you."

She went back to work as they continued to Holtman. "Who was that?" Phadre asked.

"That's Kaiana," Veranix said. "She works as a gardener here."

"But you know her?" he asked, taking another glance back at Kai. "You just talk to her like that?"

"She's my friend," Veranix said.

"Are you smitten, Phadre?" Delmin asked.

"No, no, of course not," Phadre said. "I just . . . I don't meet a lot of girls."

"There's a whole college of them here," Veranix said. "Blazes, there's a group of them right over there."

Indeed, half a dozen girls in uniform skirts were crossing the south lawn. One of them took note of them and charged across the lawn to approach them.

"Oh my," Professor Alimen said. "Let's hurry along, gentlemen."

"Professor Alimen," the girl called out. Veranix glanced over to her as they moved, finding her almost impossible to ignore. Since she was focused on the professor, he was expecting her scarf to be red and gray, but she wasn't a magic student at all. Instead, she had the green and yellow of sciences.

They were at the door to Holtman when the girl caught up to them. Now that she was close, Veranix noticed her eyes—dark and fierce, with intelligence and fire behind them.

"Professor Alimen, I insist that I speak with you."

"You are not my student, miss," Alimen said with a weary sigh. "I have told you that you should speak to Madam Henly."

"And I've told you that Madam Henly is an idiot," the young woman said. She darted her focus at Veranix, Delmin, and Phadre. "So this is your little club today, sir?"

Phadre and Delmin both looked dumbfounded, but Veranix wasn't going to let her throw any knives at him unanswered. He extended his hand. "Sorry, Veranix Calbert, Third Year Magic."

She took his hand without hesitation. "Jiarna Kay. Fourth Year Sciences. And I need your professor to weigh in on my defense this week."

"And I've told you that is not how things are done, Miss Kay. Now you must excuse us." He went in the door to Holtman, and Delmin and Phadre scurried in right behind him. Veranix gave an apologetic shrug to Jiarna and followed along.

They were just entering the dining hall when her voice cut through the air again. "Don't think you can just scurry away from me, Professor!"

The room went dead silent. The ladies from the girls' college were not supposed to go into Holtman or any of the men's dormitory buildings, and for one of them to charge in and shout at a professor was probably the most shocking thing most of the boys had seen all year. And that included the stench in Almers last night.

"Miss Kay," the professor said with a calm voice that resonated with quiet authority. "You cannot barge in here. It is quite inappropriate."

"Inappropriate?" Jiarna asked, matching the professor in intensity without raising her voice. "The only inappropriate thing I see is that I won't receive my Letters because you people refuse to help me!"

"I have to ask," Veranix said, words coming to his mouth before any common sense stopped him. "What do you mean by 'you people'?" For the past seventeen years he had heard that innocuous pairing of words thrown at his Racquin family with disdain and hatred, and for the past three at his fellow magic students.

"Mister Calbert, do not—"

"I mean foolish professors like him!" She gave a mirthless laugh. "It's all this place has. Can't see a new idea if it hit them in the face."

A prefect had come over with two cadets, who all did their best to look intimidating. "Miss, I'm going to have to ask you to leave here."

"I'm going," Jiarna said. She gave another glance at the professor, and then the slightest smirk at Veranix. "But you'll see. I'll make sure you all see."

One of the cadets had reached over, almost grabbing her by the arm, but she swatted him away as she stalked off. The other cadet snickered slightly, and was rewarded with a smack from his compatriot.

"Well, that was bracing," Phadre said. "Is it quite warm today? I'm rather flushed."

"Quite disappointing," the professor said, shaking his head. He made some signals to one of the kitchen staff, and led them to one of the tables in the corner.

"Forgive me, professor," Delmin said, "but what exactly did she want? She was a science student in the girls' school, right?"

"Once again you demonstrate your gifts of perception, Mister Sarren."

They took their seats, and in moments one of the servers came over with a few loaves of bread, butter, mustard, cold sliced ham and lamb, olives, pickled onions, soft cheese, and cups of cider.

"That never happens," Veranix said. Let alone the quality of the food seemed far better than usual, but the servers didn't typically deliver directly to the tables.

"As I said, my presence would be beneficial," Professor Alimen said. He leaned to the server. "Is there a soup?"

"Onion and wine."

"Very nice, bring us each that." The professor grinned. "Do not stand on ceremony, boys. I would imagine you're all about to faint."

That was all Veranix needed to hear, and he loaded up his plate with a generous helping.

"You dodged my question, sir," Delmin said once he was eating.

"Indeed I did. You are remarkably astute today. That will serve you well on your history exam, I believe."

Delmin frowned and took a few more bites.

"I understand how she feels, though, sir," Phadre said. "I mean, I'm half a step away from a blind panic right now, and I'm getting quite a bit of support on my defense from you and these two here. If her discipline is leaving her in the cold . . ."

"Nothing of the sort, from what I understand," Professor Alimen said testily. "One cannot be left in the cold if they insist on storming outside without a coat. Now I believe we owe it to ourselves to enjoy our meal, and perhaps give Mister Calbert a bit more brushing up on the period of the Shattered Kingdom. I'm sorry, Veranix, but I fear that is going to be your weak point in today's exam."

Soup arrived and they continued to eat, while Delmin quizzed Veranix on the different lineages of the various kingdoms that had formed when Druthal broke apart in the eighth century.

"And the kings of Acoria?" Delmin asked as he took the last piece of bread.

"That's a trick question. Acoria didn't have kings. They had elected presidors."

"But who were they?" Delmin then sat up sharply, glancing around the room. "Vee. Again."

"What?" Veranix asked, but the answer was readily apparent. Smoke came roiling straight out of the tile floor: thick as molasses and an unnatural purple. This wasn't the same as in Almers the night before, no rotten, fetid stench. It was sickly sweet, in a familiar way, and nauseating. So nauseating that several other boys proceeded to retch.

Veranix felt his own stomach twist on him. Instinctively, he created a magic screen over his face, letting him breathe clear air. Professor Alimen must have had a similar instinct, as he was moving freely, going to some of the boys who were falling over. Veranix looked to Delmin and Phadre, who weren't faring as well. Phadre had somehow formed a bright, shining dome over his whole head, and was stumbling toward the door. Delmin was floundering and retching. Veranix got to his friend and magicked a gust of fresh air over his face.

"Come on, Del," Veranix said, putting the other boy's arm over his shoulder. Delmin managed to move with him, but was barely able to keep his feet.

There were at least fifty more students in here, plus the kitchen staff, and he and Professor Alimen were the only ones in a condition to help them right now.

"Professor!" Veranix shouted. "We need to clear this out!"

Professor Alimen looked around, clearly flustered by not being able to help all the falling students. "The windows, Mister Calbert."

The dining hall windows were large installations along the upper half of the wall. They only let illumination into the hall, not ventilation. As far as Veranix could tell, they weren't designed to open.

Veranix's first instinct was to simply blast and shatter the glass, but that might make the cure worse than the ailment. At the very least, he didn't want the cost of the windows being put on his head.

Three large panes, fitted into metal frames. Veranix reached out with his magic, touching the edges of the glass. Letting the energy guide him, he pulled gently and popped one frame out in a whole piece. It was heavier than he expected, and the cost of carefully floating it out of the way while maintaining his breathing filter was almost more than he could bear at the same time.

"Now, Professor," he said through gritted teeth.

Professor Alimen summoned a wave of *numina* so strong that even Veranix could feel it, and with a powerful release, blasted all the purple smoke out the open hole and sent it shooting up high above the building.

Veranix was wavering, about to drop when he felt his burden being lifted off of him. "I have it, Mister Calbert," the professor was saying, his hand gently resting on Veranix's shoulder. The glass lifted away and went back into place.

"Well done," Professor Alimen said in a low whisper. The undertaking had taken a toll on him as well, that was clear. He leaned in with an even lower voice. "Frankly, I would have broken the glass in your place."

"I didn't want the expense," Veranix said, his voice more hoarse and strained than he had expected.

Cadets came rushing in, helping people to their feet and out the doors. One came over to Veranix and the professor. "Are you two all right?"

"Well enough," Veranix said. "Help everyone else."

Delmin had found his feet, looking pale. "Vee, it was the same thing."

What Delmin was saying got through to him. "Same as Almers last night? You felt the same thing?"

Delmin nodded.

"What is all this, gentlemen?" Professor Alimen asked.

Veranix hedged for a moment, but this was clearly beyond the scope of a prank. If he and the professor hadn't acted as quickly as they had, who knows how bad things could have been. "Tell him, Delmin."

Delmin started to explain the *numinic* flow shift he had felt before both events, while Veranix sat down and caught his breath. There was something else familiar about this incident that he couldn't figure out. Looking at his feet, there was a purple residue, a fine dust, still on the floor. Phadre had come over, and taking a leather cloth out of his pocket, collected a small amount of the dust on it.

"What are you going to do with that?" Veranix asked.

"I'm not sure, but it is evidence, yes?"

Veranix got back on his feet and looked closer. It did have a scent, which Veranix knew he had smelled before. He cautiously leaned in and took a sniff. Then it hit him.

That was the scent of *effitte*.

"I can't say I felt the same thing as you describe, Mister Sarren," the professor was saying, "but I will grant you have a greater sensitivity than I do. I appreciate you telling me."

"But what could it mean, sir?" Delmin asked. "I mean . . . oh sweet saints."

Veranix looked back to Delmin, whose eyes were fixed on the ceiling. He followed Delmin's gaze, as did Phadre and the professor.

"Well," Phadre said flatly. "Something familiar there."

Scrawled in purple letters across the ceiling were the words: NOW YOU FOOLS WILL SEE.

Chapter 5

PROFESSOR BESKER—nebbishy, bespectacled man that he was—stalked around the area of Holtman Hall, looking carefully at the boys who were being treated by Yellowshields outside. Eventually he approached Veranix and Delmin, who were camped on a stoop some distance away from the scene.

"Mister Calbert, Mister Sarren, I see you were among those affected by this attack."

"We were in there, yes, sir."

"And the two of you also live in Almers, do you not? So you were affected by both pranks?"

Veranix raised an eyebrow to the history professor. "Is that what they are still calling this?"

"I am not privy to the official reports," Professor Besker said. "However, they were described to me as 'malicious pranks,' so I am presuming that is what they are being considered."

"Malicious is the tune of it," Veranix said.

"That said, as you two were affected by both events, and are scheduled for my exam in an hour, I have been instructed to make the inquiry: have these incidents left you unable to properly participate in the examination?"

The look on his face told Veranix all he needed to know about Professor Besker's question: that he would honor whatever answer they gave as a matter of duty, but he would hold them in contempt should they decline to take the exam at the appointed time.

"I'm fine, sir," Veranix said. "Though Delmin might have been struck worse than me in this last one."

"No, I'll take the exam," Delmin said.

"So I will see you shortly, then?"

"Absolutely, sir," Veranix said, putting on his best brave face.

"Capital." Professor Besker sighed and brushed off his coat. "It really is pointless, you know. Every few years someone attempts some sort of wanton destructive act to ward off exams. As if a cancellation would mean they receive passing marks. Pranks, indeed."

He stalked off to some of the other boys.

"You know," Delmin said, "most of these boys are *not* in any shape to take exams right now."

"We could have weaseled out if we wanted," Veranix said. "But I might as well fail with dignity."

Kaiana approached, changed out of her workclothes into a clean dress. "How bad was it?"

"Very bad," Veranix said. "They're saying 'prank,' but whatever this was, it involved magic in some way, and it involved *effitte*."

"How?" Kaiana's voice dropped to a growl.

"Wait, yeah, how?" Delmin asked.

"The smoke, and the residue it left. Smelled just like *effitte*, same shade of purple."

Delmin's face screwed up in thought, but he said nothing.

"So you're going to do something about it, right?" Kaiana asked.

"Like what?"

"Like find whoever did this—twice now—and stop them."

"No, no," Delmin said. "He has a history exam in an hour. He has another exam tomorrow, and one after that. And when we aren't studying or taking exams, we are joined at the hip to Phadre over there."

Phadre was still shaken up, sitting off in the distance while a Yellowshield looked him over.

"You need to find a way," Kaiana told Veranix.

"I don't know how," Veranix said. "Maybe Delmin's right, and this is something left to the school's officials."

"Magic, *effitte*, and you at the center both times," she said. "Even if that last part is a coincidence, the Thorn protects this part of town from things that cross over from Dentonhill. Or anywhere else."

Veranix didn't disagree with that. In fact, he'd far rather spend the next hour using whoever did this as target practice. "I've got no idea where to start doing that right now."

She glanced around. "Think of a way before someone really gets hurt."

"I'll try."

"Are you crazy?" Delmin somehow managed to yell without raising his voice.

"Rather," Veranix said. Looking back to Kaiana, he couldn't help but notice how uncommon it was to see her wearing a dress like that. The pale yellow of the dress complimented her rich, tawny skin, and he had to admit it looked very good on her. "What are you cleaned up for?"

"I'm going to the church, to drop off your donation," Kaiana said.

"Keep your ears open, then."

"Always do." She flashed a quick smile and went off.

Veranix suddenly found his heart pounding and his face flushed, and he was very glad she wasn't looking at him.

"Tell me you aren't a little bit smitten," Delmin said.

"Shut it," Veranix said.

"Well, if you're not, I can tell who is." He pointed over to Phadre, who now sat alone on the grass, all his focus on Kaiana as she walked down toward the south gate.

"Shut it, I said." Veranix got to his feet. "Let's go take that history exam, get that torture over with."

Deena walked like she expected people to get out of her way. Colin liked that; it was exactly the attitude he needed at his right arm. They walked through Cantarell Square, which was crowded, most people bustling about the makeshift marketplace of carts and stands. None of the companies were performing on the stages today, and a few kids were goofing around up there. Plenty of opportunity for hands to find their way into purses, if that was the intent.

Colin had better things to do, which was a shame.

A small group of Waterpath Orphans were taking the opportunity, mostly young ones. The bird who was a captain—Colin remembered her from the church meet last month when Veranix first started getting noticed as the Thorn—she hung back along one of the low walls, eyes on all her boys. What was her name? Yessa, maybe.

Colin and Deena walked past her, and she hissed.

"Not looking to cause trouble, Orphan," Colin said. "Best not."

Normally he might want to get into it with the Orphans over working Cantarell. Especially with the bosses ceding a block to the Knights. But he had enough on his mind. Clearly one of the other captains could step up and make something happen. They didn't have to leave everything on him.

They walked over to the corner of the square right across from the Trusted Friend.

"How you want this to go?" Deena asked him. "I presume you don't want a rumble."

"No, I don't." A few Rabbits were hanging outside the Friend, sitting on the walkway curb and being the useless layabouts Rabbits usually were. Colin gave a whistle.

"Oy!" he snapped, not moving from his spot. "Any captains among you, or you all too damn lazy to bother being in charge?"

"Gonna eat your teeth!" One of the Rabbits got to his feet and took a couple steps, but still kept his distance.

"Standing right here, no one has made me lunch," Colin said.

"What you say he was gonna eat?" Deena taunted.

"Your teeth," one of the other Rabbits said, cool and calm, sitting on a wooden chair on the small stoop of the Trusted Friend. She slowly got to her feet, and Colin could see the chevrons inked onto her neck. "He still might. You making a rattle here, Tyson?"

So she knew who he was.

"Might be, might be," Colin said. "Word I hear is you've got your hands full of rattle. Someone came and shook you real good, Setch." That should raise her fur up.

"It's Sotch."

"If you say so," Colin said. So easy to hackle. "My boy says the Thorn came and slapped you around."

"Did your boy lose a knife?" Sotch asked. "Maybe he should come and get it."

"I don't know anything about that." Colin rested his

hand on the hilt of one of his knives. Just rested it there. All the Rabbits went crazy, getting on their feet.

"Looks like you want to start a rattle," Sotch said.

"I don't need to start anything with you. The Thorn, apparently, already did."

"What's it to you?" Sotch asked.

Colin pointed down the street in the direction of Dentonhill. "Because the Thorn usually is over there. Other side of Waterpath, knocking skulls owned by Fenmere goons. But then last night he's here, knocking Rabbit skulls. What's that mean?"

"What's it to you?" Sotch repeated. Clever, she was not.

"That tears it!" shouted the one Rabbit who had stepped forward. He drew a knucklestuffer and jumped at Colin. Colin didn't even move, since he saw Deena was right there at his arm. Before the guy even got within five feet of Colin, Deena had the Rabbit down on the ground, face pressed on the cobblestone.

"There's your lunch, Rabbit! Who made you your lunch?"

"Ease it off!" Sotch snapped. "Let him up."

Deena pushed him away, and gave him a kick for good measure.

Sotch chuckled and stepped over, pulling her boy up to his feet. "You seem nervous, Prince."

"Hardly," Colin said.

"You should be, causing a rattle just a few feet from the Friend. With just one bird by your side."

"You won't try anything, Sotch. Even you are smarter than that."

"Won't I? Maybe not right now. But maybe pretty soon, Rabbits are going to own Cantarell. And then what will you do?"

"Rabbits own Cantarell? That'll be the day. Us and the Orphans will push you back, like we do every time."

"Things change, Prince. They might just change a lot tonight. Never know what we'll get."

"Big drop?" Colin asked.

She moved in close, her pudgy face closer than Colin would ever want. "Real big. Right here. Then you'll see, Prince."

"Deena," Colin said curtly.

And then Sotch's face wasn't close at all. Deena peeled the girl off and threw her back to her crowd of Rabbits.

"You're both gonna pay!" Sotch wailed. "Just you wait!"

"It'll be a long wait," Colin said, tapping Deena on the arm. "Always a pleasure, Setch."

"Go to blazes! You'll see!"

Colin went back across Cantarell, Deena at his heels. So they were going to get the *effitte* from Fenmere tonight, most likely. Now that he knew that, he had to figure out what to do with that information.

"Do we get more Princes?" Deena asked.

"Nah," Colin said. "Not yet, not without the bosses signing on to it." There wasn't much he could do without risking his stars, just like Dennick. Only way to stop the Rabbits was to get every other gang to turn the screws. That or the Thorn.

Out of the corner of his eye he spotted someone standing out in the crowd, striding up Hedge Lane. A girl, with honey-dark skin and a yellow dress. She would have caught his eye regardless, but after a moment he knew it was Veranix's Napa girl. Couldn't remember her name, but she had iron and vinegar to her. From what he had seen, she would make a blazes of a Prince, had that been her calling.

She could tell Veranix about the Rabbits drop, get him out here.

All he had to do was figure out how to tell her without letting Deena know.

"Need to clear my head a bit," he said, flashing a wry smile at Deena. "Hey, Napa girl, where you going so quick?"

She spun on her heel, narrowing hard eyes at Colin. He gave her a quick wink, and hoped to the Saints and Rose Street that she would recognize him. She should, she had come to him before, but that didn't mean she still would.

"Don't call me that," she said, looking him up and down. "Not unless you feel like eating the street."

"You think you can make me eat the street?" he asked, half-joking. He needed to make a scene with her, in public, that looked like he was giving her a speck of trouble. Which is exactly what any Prince or other street boy would do if they were hassling her. But he couldn't be sure if she understood that was all he was doing.

"I'd like to see her make you," Deena said, coming up at his elbow.

"Oh, you have a friend!" the Napa girl said. She gave him a flash of attitude. "But you never know who my friends might be."

"Should I be afraid of your friends?" Colin asked mockingly.

"I'm just saying a piece of street trash like yourself might want to think twice before crossing my path and calling me names."

"That's because I don't even know your name, girl. Or how a girl like you walks through here and can call me trash. You come from campus or something?"

"That's right," she said.

"Colin, why are you even messing with this girl?" Deena asked. "Not like you're gonna toss her for her purse. And she sure isn't going to roll you."

"No, I'm not. Why would I waste my time with someone like you? Causing trouble, probably dosed on *effitte*."

She winked, just barely, just enough for only Colin to see. She had given him an opening.

"Hey, now, I don't mess with that *effitte* stuff. That's poison. You want to get that junk, you'd have to bug the Red Rabbits?"

"Oh, would I?" she asked.

"Blazes, they were just bragging to me that they're getting a whole big drop of it tonight. *Tonight*, like they've got no shame about it. Right over at the Trusted Friend."

"You don't say."

"Shameless, isn't it? Looks like they'll be selling plenty soon."

"Someone ought do something about that," she said.

Colin threw up his hands, "You said it, not me. I'm not gonna start a brawl in the street about these things."

"We've got better things to do," Deena said. She was glaring at the Napa girl.

"Well, they better not come near me with that," she said. "Like I said, I've got friends." She started walking back toward the Uni campus. After a few steps she said, "By the way, street trash, next time you see me, call me 'Kai.' Else you will eat the street."

And off she went.

Then Deena's hand smacked him across the back of his head. "Stop your gaping. Do we have a plan?"

"Yeah, we've got a plan," Colin said. "It's called the Turnabout. I need to cool my throat."

The towers were ringing five bells when Veranix stumbled out of the history exam. His head hurt, his eyes hurt, and his hand was cramped up from writing seven essays. He had had no idea, before right now, that he was capable of writing seven essays on Druth history in three hours.

He would rather have spent the time brawling with every single Red Rabbit at once.

Delmin was waiting outside, looking harried but nowhere near as bad as Veranix felt.

"Which ones did you do?" Delmin asked as they started walking to Almers. They had been presented with twelve questions, with the instructions to answer six, and the option of a seventh for extra credit. Veranix knew damn well he was going to need every bit of credit he could manage.

"The one about the Quarantine Wall, since I've actually seen it, that helped. Queen Mara, since I know the play . . ."

"I told you—"

"It helped, I swear. What else? The rediscovery of the Maradaine line, Chamberlain Maxwell, Prince Fultar and Lady Demea, Battle of Fencal, and the Kellirac Invasion in the fifth century."

"You went for the extra credit?" Delmin seemed genuinely surprised.

"I couldn't pass up the opportunity. Am I wrong, or was that uncommonly generous of Besker?"

"I think he was rewarding those of us who took the exam despite the pranks."

"You're calling them pranks now?"

Delmin shrugged. "It's as good a word as any."

" 'Attacks' is a better word."

"Maybe. Anyway, I did most of the same ones you did, except for not Maxwell or Queen Mara. Took River Wars and the Incursion of 1009."

"Saints and sinners," Veranix swore. "Those two made my head spin just thinking about them. Too big, especially the River Wars."

"It's Besker's favorite topic!" Delmin said. "I thought he'd like it!"

"I thought it was an opportunity to make too many mistakes." Veranix didn't mention the question they both passed on, about the initial formation of Mage Circles in 1023. Mostly because how Besker taught it was radically different from how Alimen and the other magic teachers did. Veranix would have written an essay on the early Parliament acts that gave mages protection from unseemly persecution, and allowing for the formation of Circles to train and take responsibility for the mages in their care. While that was entirely accurate, Besker would have given that essay failing marks.

Likely some of their fellows in the exam wrote pieces to match Besker's opinion—that mages of the eleventh century created a system to make themselves immune to any legal action, overcompensating for aggressive, inhumane treatment of mages in the early centuries.

Untrue, but that's how Besker saw it. Veranix could tweak an essay to match a professor, but he couldn't do that, and he imagined Delmin couldn't either.

They found Phadre sitting on the steps to the main entrance to Almers, nose buried in one of his notebooks. "Ah, you've finished," he said as they approached.

"Have you been waiting here for us the whole time?" Veranix asked.

"No, no," Phadre said. "I worked on some of my

calculations, based on our work this morning. I think I've fine-tuned exactly what I need to demonstrate, but we're going to need to finalize the calibrations of the instruments. Quite a lot of work."

"Lovely," Veranix said. "All right, let us go in and wash up, then we'll go to dinner . . . presuming we can."

"Right, no," Phadre said. "At least, not in Holtman. The whole thing is being scrubbed after the attack."

"See?" Veranix said. "Attack."

"Well, that's what the officials are calling it now, after the one up in Faishin Hall."

Veranix stopped. "Where is Faishin Hall?"

"It's one of the buildings of the girls' college," Delmin said. "They're sure it's more of the same?"

Phadre looked surprised. "I'm not sure of the details, exactly. I hear that this time bricks came flying out of the wall. Just popping out and launching across the lecture hall. And then words appeared on the slateboard, like they did in Holtman."

"The same words?" Veranix asked.

"I don't know that," Phadre said. "Though three students and Madam Henly were taken to the hospital ward. Injured by flying bricks."

Something didn't sit right about that at all. Veranix couldn't put his finger on what he was thinking.

"But what about dinner?" Delmin asked.

"Oh, right," Phadre said. "Professor Alimen wanted to make sure we didn't waste any time, so he made arrangements so we can eat while we work. Plenty of food waiting for us in his workroom."

"That's excellent," Veranix said. "Just give us a few minutes, we'll be right there. Come on, Delmin."

He grabbed Delmin by his coat and dragged him into Almers before he could protest at all.

"Were there any taunting words that appeared in here?" he asked Delmin as they went up the stairs.

"I'm not sure," Delmin said. "Not that I heard, but . . ."

"It doesn't matter. We saw them in Holtman. Fools will see, or something like that."

"Right," Delmin said. "This isn't our business."

"Except for the fact we heard someone else say almost the exact same thing to Professor Alimen just a few minutes before that. Jiarna Kay."

"Oh," Delmin said. "I suppose she did. But that would have to be a coincidence."

"Maybe." Veranix reached their room. "Except that she said something else, and I just remembered. Professor Alimen said she should be dealing with Madam Henly, and she said—"

"That Henly is an idiot! Wasn't that who Phadre said was hurt?" Delmin almost squealed. "You don't think she's behind this?"

"Maybe someone should talk to her about it," Veranix said. "Cover for me while I go to the carriage house . . ."

"No, Vee," Delmin said.

"I'll just get the cloak, and pay her a visit . . ."

"First of all, I keep telling you, that isn't your job. School officials, prefects, the cadet squadron. The Th—" He glanced around and lowered his voice. "The Thorn shouldn't show up for something like this."

"Why not?" Veranix asked. "I mean, I said I was going to protect the campus . . ."

"From what's his name and his drug peddlers. This is different!"

"It's a threat."

"Humor me in this. Let's say you get suited up and go traipsing into the girls' college. Do you know how to find Jiarna Kay? Where she lives? Where she might be? Or are you going to spend hours skulking about their dormitories, like some sort of reprobate? And if you get caught doing *that*, you will get kicked out of here."

Veranix didn't like it, but Delmin had a point.

"Fine. What do you think we should do?"

"Get ourselves sorted out right now, and join Phadre so we can help him get his letters, and help *us* pass our Magic Practicals."

"Fair enough," Veranix said. "Let's get moving."

Minutes later they were back outside and walking with Phadre to Alimen's tower. From the walkway, as they approached, Veranix could see the carriage house, where Kaiana was hanging a lamp outside the main door. She only did that when she had news for him. He glanced over at Delmin, but immediately sensed that he would not approve of even going to talk to her right now. This was exam period, time for work.

He certainly couldn't explain it to Phadre, who seemed more than overeager for getting to work.

He had to risk a little magic, even though he had never done this trick with Kaiana before. He breathed in a tight draw of *numina*, grabbing words he barely even whispered, and blew them out across the several hundred yards right to Kaiana's ear.

"Can't get away. What's going on?"

She almost dropped the lamp and looked around confused.

"Just talk, I can hear you." A similar trick would bring her words right to him.

"I saw your cousin in the neighborhood. He confirmed that the Red Rabbits are going to deal."

"He just told you that?" Veranix glanced over to Delmin, who clearly realized that Veranix was doing something magical. His accusatory scowl spoke volumes.

"In so many words. They're getting a shipment of *ef-fitte* tonight at the Trusted Friend."

"I don't suppose you have a sense of exactly when."

"No, I don't."

"So," Delmin said overly loudly. "Plenty of work for us to do tonight, right, Phadre?"

"I think so, yes," Phadre said. "Sorry in advance. We might even have to crash out in the professor's laboratory. Though you might find that preferable to Almers."

"Veranix?" Kaiana whispered.

"I can't get away from this," Veranix sent back to her. His gut twisted. "This is literally part of my Practicals exam."

Kaiana said nothing for a while, and he glanced over to the carriage house, trying not to stumble as they walked. She stood at the door, arms crossed. "I'll think of something."

He took one last look before entering the tower, but she had gone inside with determination. He had a sinking feeling that she was about to do something really crazy.

Chapter 6

THE YELLOW DRESS would have to do. It was all Kaiana had to work with in this situation. Fortunately it was simple enough, lacking the prim complications that a fancier dress might have. It could never be like the dresses the barmaids at the Rose & Bush wore, of course—not that she would ever wear a dress like that.

Right now she needed simple subtlety.

There were only two things she could do: either scout the Red Rabbits herself, and whatever trouble that might land her in, or get Veranix out of the room he was in. The latter was the easier task, especially given the way that fourth-year mage was looking at her. Dressed and ready, she pulled out Veranix's gear and staged it for him to get at quickly. She added a couple apples and some dried lamb to that. Saints knew he would probably need that.

She took one last look in her tiny mirror, seeing a smudge on her face before she realized it was on the glass itself. She wasn't going to manage any better right now, certainly not without looking like she was really trying to look better. She left the carriage house and made her way to Professor Alimen's tower.

Strictly speaking she was breaking the rules by going in the tower. Grounds staff were only supposed to enter buildings in which they had official business or residence. For Kaiana that meant little more than her carriage house and a few of the supply sheds. Out of fear of Master Jolen, Kaiana had followed those rules until recently. Ever since she had been credited with rescuing Professor Alimen from their abduction by the Blue Hand, Master Jolen had almost completely changed his attitude toward her. On campus there had been no acknowledgment that the Thorn had been a part of things, and the common impression had been that she was the unfortunate victim of a grudge against the professor.

Master Jolen would no longer casually threaten her, as he used to. Now he was almost deferential. She had gained the professor's favor. Perhaps Master Jolen feared being turned into a mouse or something.

She wondered if the professor could even do such a thing.

She had mainly taken advantage of her newfound liberty by going to the campus library or the bathhouse. The latter was quite important, for it allowed her to look like a civilized human being in her simple yellow dress.

She could hear the boys in Alimen's office before she was all the way up the stairs. They weren't quite arguing, but their conversation was getting heated. From what she could tell, a mistake of some sort had been made, and they were going to have to repeat earlier work. While no one was quite assigning blame, there was an undercurrent that if one of them—Veranix was implying it was Delmin or the other one—hadn't been careless, they wouldn't have to redo everything they had done in the morning.

That might make what she needed to do much harder, but it gave her an opportunity as well.

By the time she reached the office, the boys had fully escalated, as they were apt to.

"Do you think it's easy for me to do this?" Veranix snapped at the other boy. "You are demanding precision action, and that takes a lot out of me."

"I know, I know!" the other boy said. "Look, there's a lot of factors at play here, and I have to account for every single one. That means we're going to have to repeat ourselves some. I'm sorry."

"By we, you mean me."

They hadn't even noticed her in the doorframe yet.

"Am I interrupting?"

All three of them went quiet as they turned to her.

"No, no, not at all," said the boy she didn't know. He was a magic student by his scarf, but he lacked the absurdly thin look that Veranix and Delmin had. He actually had some fleshiness to his face, which made the awkward smile he suddenly had plastered on his face seem all the more full. "Is there . . . something we can do for you?"

"Me? No, not at all." Kaiana walked over to the worktable, where several brass devices were set out. "I was just curious what this was all about."

"Kai?" Veranix looked completely befuddled. "We really have a lot to do here."

"I know that, Veranix," she said. She turned and stared at him hard, speaking pointedly. "I'm very aware that you have quite a lot of things to take care of right now."

Delmin made a strange noise, like a mouse that just spotted a cat.

"You all right?" the other boy asked.

"Fine, fine," Delmin said.

"I'm being terribly rude," Kaiana said, approaching

the boy directly. Looking him straight in the eye, she extended her hand. "Kaiana Nell."

"Phadre Golmin," he said, taking her hand. Firm grip, but she noticed a bit of tremble in his hand. "You aren't a student, are you?"

She gave him a bit of a smile. "My dress gave it away, didn't it?"

"She doesn't need to be a student," Veranix said. "She's probably smarter than the three of us combined."

"How do I know you, then?" Phadre asked.

"She's on the grounds staff," Veranix said. "Remember, we talked to her earlier?"

"Yes, yes, of course," Phadre said. "You have to forgive me, I've been . . . a little overwhelmed lately. I'm defending for my Letters."

"Oh, how exciting," Kaiana said. She took a seat on one of the high stools by the workbench. "So all this is for your defense?"

"Yes, I've opted for a presentation of theory," Phadre said.

"Really? I'm given to understand that's the more challenging way to defend."

"How would you know that?" Delmin asked.

"Because she pays attention," Veranix said. He looked wary; he gave her the slightest of nods. He wanted to get out of here, go stop the Red Rabbits.

"I'm a very good listener," she said, aiming directly at Phadre. At the same time, she crossed her legs, letting her dress hitch up ever so slightly, now exposing her bare knee.

Phadre took notice.

So did Delmin and Veranix, but that didn't matter.

"Well," Phadre stammered out, "I've been working on how external factors can affect the flow of *numina*. Do you know what that is?"

"I'm not sure," Kaiana said. She might as well have a little fun here. "Is that the ever-present flowing energy that fuels magic?"

She counted the seconds until Phadre's mouth closed. "Saints, she is smarter than us all."

"Told you," Veranix said.

"So, what in all the saints' names were you boys nattering on about?"

Veranix spoke. "We spent all morning calibrating these devices. And now we have to recalibrate them because *someone* seemed to forget that when he'll actually be presenting his defense, one moon is going to be full, and the sun is going to be to the southwest because it'll be two bells in the afternoon, and something else is probably wrong as well."

"And that matters?" Kaiana asked.

"It's actually quite critical," Phadre said. "I thought the effects would be negligible, but when I was running tests myself this afternoon, it seems that time of day, especially, is going to be crucial."

"Well, you can't fix that now," Kaiana said. That seemed obvious, but it also gave her the opening she needed.

"Why not?" Phadre asked. And then it appeared on his face. "Of course we couldn't. We'd need to calibrate in the afternoon."

"Which means you'd have to do it tomorrow. And you boys have your theory exam in the morning, right? And the afternoon to work with Phadre?"

"That's right," Veranix said.

"I suppose," Delmin added, clearly wary about where things were going.

"And I would bet there's work you can do without them, am I right?" Kaiana had him on the line now.

"Well, I do need to finalize the speech of the presentation itself. I mean, I had hoped to hash those details with the elements of the presentation, but if we have to wait until tomorrow."

"Look at these two," she said, grabbing Veranix's face. "They look exhausted, don't you think? One exam today, plus they were in the middle of two crazy pranks, which means they didn't sleep well. Plus they have an exam in the morning."

Veranix did her the service of yawning, almost on cue.

"She's right, Phadre. Maybe we're grinding to the rim on this and need to tackle it in the afternoon."

Phadre looked at her. "But why—"

"Tell you what," she said, talking over him. "These two should go and rest. Really. You, on the other hand, should work on your presentation. So you're going to give it to me. As if I were the professors you're defending against."

"I don't know," Phadre said. But she knew she almost had him. "I mean, this is very advanced theory I'm talking about here."

"True," Veranix said. "But believe me, mate, the presentation is not just what you say, but how you say it. Poise. Eloquence. You want someone to help you with that? Kaiana is who you want."

"Really?" Phadre asked. He was almost there.

"I can be here all night if you need it," she said. She really hoped she wasn't going to regret this, but if it got Veranix to that *effitte* deal, it was worth it.

"Fine, you're right. The calibration is a waste of time right now. Go on, boys. I'll hash this out."

"You sure?" Veranix asked.

"Yeah, yeah. Don't worry, if Alimen gives grief I'll make it clear it was my plan."

"I could stand a bit more study," Delmin said.

"Let's go," Veranix said. "Have a good night, you two." At the door, he gave Kai a glance, mouthing "Thank you."

As he left, and Phadre starting talking about the nature of his defense, all she could think was that he damn well better thank her.

※◇◇◇◇◇◇◇※

Veranix split off from Delmin with a quick word and little argument. He ran from the tower to the carriage house, resisting the urge to strip off his uniform mid-stride. Once he was inside he tore himself out of his clothes as fast as he could without damaging them. Kaiana had secreted his Thorn outfit and gear right under the Spinner Run's trapdoor, so he didn't even have to go down for them. Plus she left him fruit and dried lamb.

She really was too good for him.

Dressed and ready, he double-checked his gear: bow, arrows, staff, and *napranium*-laced cloak and rope. Everything in place, strapped and belted and ready. Time to knock some Red Rabbits around, and whoever Fenmere was sending with the delivery. He had warned them, and if they didn't heed it, they deserved what was coming. After the two pranks and the exam, he was more than ready to work out some aggression on their skulls.

Shrouding himself with the cloak, he slipped out of the carriage house, across the lawn, and over the campus wall.

Two ways to do this. One would be to just kick his way into the Trusted Friend and pound his way through every Red Rabbit until he got their *effitte*. Problem with that was he had no idea when the delivery was, beyond tonight. Or who was delivering it. Or how. They might have it already, or not get it until midnight. So that left the other way to do this: stake out the Trusted Friend, watch for the drop, and then make his move. Or wait until there were fewer people about.

The streets were far from deserted at this hour, still early in the evening. The oil lamps on Carnation Street—the ones that hadn't been broken—still burned strong. No real opportunity to skulk about, and even trying to slip across the rooftops would look strange. Staying shrouded for hours wouldn't work. He needed a quiet place to watch from, where he could keep an eye on everything.

Slipping into an alleyway, he scurried up the back ladders of one of the taller buildings—not that any of the buildings in Aventil were that tall—halfway between Bush and Waterpath. From up there he could see the Trusted Friend, the same two Rabbits from last night were minding the door, along with two more friends. So he had made an impression on them.

He could also see all the way to Waterpath, so anyone coming in this way from Dentonhill would stand out. While the streets weren't empty, they weren't so crowded that he couldn't note anyone out of place.

Drawing his bow, he checked his aim. From here he could hit the door of the Trusted Friend. He couldn't do a precision shot, one of his father's real needle-threading tricks, but that was hardly necessary. He wasn't looking to kill any Red Rabbits tonight, but if he did, he wouldn't lose any sleep over it.

Almost an hour into his watch, two guys caught his eye, coming in from Dentonhill. One of them looked a little familiar, maybe one of the goons he had tangled with in the fish cannery or the warehouse. Definitely one of Fenmere's. The other one didn't seem familiar at all. Maybe Bell wasn't coming for this.

One of them had a heavy leather case strapped over his shoulder.

The two of them went straight to the Trusted Friend and started talking to the doormen.

Veranix didn't need more proof. He nocked an arrow, took aim, and fired, and did it again. Then he jumped from the roof and magicked his way to a soft landing.

Screams confirmed he had hit his targets. When he touched the ground, he saw that one of Fenmere's men was hit in the leg, the other in the back. That one was down face first, while the other—the one with the leather case—was trying to get back on his feet.

Veranix came in, another arrow at the ready, while the Rabbits pulled out cudgels and knives.

"Not so fast, gentles," Veranix said. "I've no qualm with sending you to the sinners."

Fenmere's man turned to Veranix. "I'm gonna tear you apart for that."

"Hardly," Veranix said. With a whisper of magic he opened up the case and flipped it over. Vials of *effitte* came falling out on the street. That was all he needed to see. He sent the arrow into the man's chest, dropping him.

"Oy!" one of the doormen yelled into the Trusted Friend. "Thorn is busting it up!"

More Rabbits came out, including Sotch and Keckin, who looked like they were ready to eat glass. Veranix paid none of them mind, drawing in *numina* and releasing it as blue hot fire all over the vials. In moments the *effitte* was nothing but smolder.

The Rabbits didn't take another step forward.

"So which of you are still in the *effitte* business?"

Before any of them answered, there was a sound whistling through the air. Not unlike an arrow, which triggered Veranix's instinct to jump back.

A spinning blade came flying within an inch of his ear.

Veranix drew another arrow and aimed in the direction that came from, toward Cantarell Square.

"Sweet saints almighty," he heard a Rabbit whisper, and Veranix couldn't blame him.

A woman was at the edge of the square, every other person giving her wide berth for good reason. Her attire was downright scandalous—high leather boots and what appeared to be a matching corset and short trousers, bright blue, with an absurd amount of bare skin showing. Her black hair was schoolboy short and her face was made up with dark eyelining.

Veranix hadn't seen a woman like that since he left the carnival.

Her dress wasn't even the most astonishing element. In each hand she spun a metal-bladed disc, while at the same time she spun two large metal hoops around her waist and hips. Despite the speed she was whipping them around her taut body, Veranix could see those hoops were also razor sharp.

"Did I find the Thorn?" she asked. "Lucky, lucky Bluejay."

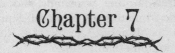

Chapter 7

WHOEVER THIS BLUEJAY WAS, Veranix immediately decided she was not to be trifled with. She had already nearly taken his head off, so there was no need to question her intentions. He sent his arrow straight for the center of her chest.

With an almost imperceptible shift of her stomach, the upper hoop leaped up her body and circled her chest, so the arrow bounced off of that instead of touching her.

At the same moment, she bounded forward, the hoops spinning around her muscular body or in her hands never faltering. She moved with a grace and rhythm that was downright hypnotic. In fact, most of the Red Rabbits were all staring slack-jawed at her, even the women. If she weren't obviously trying to kill him, Veranix might have done much the same thing.

Veranix jumped back, drawing and shooting another arrow, which she again blocked with surprising ease.

"Thorn is in trouble now!" cackled one of the Rabbits.

"Pile it on!" another shouted, and out of the corner of his eye, Veranix saw several of them draw weapons.

The last thing Veranix needed was to have to deal

with Bluejay and a dozen Red Rabbits at once. Time to take them out of the action.

In quick succession, Veranix shot another futile arrow at Bluejay's lethal advance, while channeling *numina* into his legs, flipping over her head. She threw one of her small discs as he went above her, but he gave another swat of magic to bat it away.

On the ground behind her, he did two rapid draws and blasts of magic. The first bowled all the Rabbits off their feet. Nothing that would hurt them, just send them to the ground. The next covered them in a mess of sticky glop, so they wouldn't be able to get back up.

Inelegant, but effective.

Also draining. He could feel he had pushed himself past his natural limits, and magically he was running on the grace of the cloak and the rope and their *numina*-drawing powers. If he could, he'd have to deal with Bluejay in a more traditional way.

"Showmanship," she purred. "I can respect that."

Veranix drew and fired two more shots, risking just a hint more magic to tweak their velocity. Bluejay was fast enough still to dodge and block them, but it was clear from her expression that it was, at least, a little more of a challenge.

She closed in, and Veranix decided it was pointless wasting more arrows on her. She spiraled close to him as he jumped out of the way, dropping the bow and pulling out the rope.

In one fluid motion, she grabbed the upper hoop with her right hand and lifted it over her head. With a twist of her wrist, she spun it around so she could crisscross it back and forth on either side of her body, all while never losing the one she kept spinning on her hips.

Veranix had to admit Bluejay was ridiculously skilled. "Time to clip those wings."

He shot the rope out, entangling the large-bladed hoop in her right hand. Before he could yank it away from her, she sliced at the rope with her small-bladed disc. The rope didn't cut, but a shock flowed up it back into his arm. He instinctively released the rope from her hoop and pulled it back.

That hadn't happened before. It was if being magically connected to it made him feel pain through it.

"Did you see that?" The call didn't come from the Rabbits. Veranix turned just for a moment, seeing that it came from a group of Waterpath Orphans on the other side of the square. Even more audience was forming for this one.

The distraction gave Bluejay the opening to move in. Her large hoop thundered toward him, about to slice his arm when, on instinct, he wrapped the rope around it. It took the strike, but again the full pain of it hit him. He may have avoided getting cut, but it still felt like it. For a moment, he almost let the cover of his face drop.

He sprang back, landing on one of the performance platforms of Cantarell Square. Magic was barely an option, nor was using the rope. Arrows had already proved useless.

Not that there was any need to prolong this. He had stopped the drop, burned the *effitte*, shown the Red Rabbits what for. He had no particular need to fight Bluejay beyond saving his own skin. Running away would do that as well.

"Thorn is getting hammered!" yelled a Rabbit from the sticky mess.

"Get her, Thorn!" That one came from the Rose Street side.

Now he had to at least put up a good fight, move it away from the crowd, before getting the blazes away from her.

"Get her, Thorn," Bluejay mocked. She had taken a few steps back, giving herself a moment to catch her breath. She kept one hoop spinning above her head, the other on her hip, while still twirling the bladed disc in her left hand. She was breaking a sweat, but she still looked like she could spin her hoops all night long if she had to.

"All right, then," he said. Time for nothing but muscle and bone and skill. That meant the staff. Drawing it out, he used just a whisper of magic to encase it, protect it. The last thing he needed right now was for Bluejay to chop it up. "Do you know this dance?"

Feinting a jump, he dropped down low as she swung her hoop above her. He ducked her blade and brought his staff on the hoop circling her hips, knocking it out of alignment. As it clattered to the ground, he managed a glancing blow at her ribs before having to dive out of the way of the hoop in her hands.

Now unfettered except for the one large hoop, she came at him with speed and lethal grace he had no hope of matching. Her relentless attacks kept him on the defensive, his parries doing nothing to diminish her control on the spinning hoop. It took every ounce of skill and effort he had just to hold her at bay.

"I know this dance," she said. "And I know how it ends."

Her attacks were getting harder to block, and she was chasing him backward around the square. She was going to wear him out soon enough.

"Then let's change the music." He dared a quick glance behind him to make sure that he was heading toward the alley—the same alley he and the constable were in last night—and then knocked her hoop upward as hard as he could while spinning around and running to the alley as fast as he could.

Bluejay was right on him, and the onlookers—Rabbits, Princes, and Orphans all—howled and jeered as he tore into the alley. She had almost caught him as he slipped into the alley, sparks flying as her hoop hit the brick walls.

Using the last bits of magic he dared to spare, he threw some bursts of light in her face—nothing more than to dazzle her eyes while he shrouded himself. Then he made a bit of insubstantial shadow fly up over her and out to the roof across the street.

Thankfully she fell for the feint, cackling as she chased the shadow, swearing that she would run him down.

Keeping the shrouding, Veranix slipped out of the alleyway, mouse-quiet. Not that he needed to be quiet. The Princes and Orphans who had been watching the fight were now in the square, shouting empty threats at each other. Some of them had picked up all the weapons that had been abandoned in the fight, including Veranix's bow.

That had been his father's bow.

There was no way to get it back. He had absolutely no fight in him, barely the strength to walk back to campus.

He took one last look. As far as he could see, the person holding the bow was a Prince. If nothing else, that would be something his father could respect.

He walked back to campus, sticking close to the buildings so no one would bump into his shrouded form. Once he was at the campus wall, he climbed over and stumbled to the carriage house. The south lawn was not unoccupied tonight—several people seemed to be scattered around, most with instruments pointed at the sky.

Was there an astronomy exam tonight? Veranix had a vague memory of Eittle saying something along those lines.

Kaiana was in the carriage house when he slipped in, still in her yellow dress.

"How did it go?" she asked as soon as he unshrouded. She didn't even flinch.

"Horrible." He took the cloak off, steeling himself for the hammer to the gut he would feel without its *numina*-drawing powers stimulating him. As he handed it to her, it hit him as bad as he expected, but he managed to keep his knees from buckling. He had pushed himself, magically, way too far again.

"You didn't stop it?"

"Oh, the *effitte*? That, yes. Stopped it, destroyed the drugs, killed Fenmere's two goons. That part was fine. Tell me you have some food."

She went into a cabinet and brought out some dried lamb. "You look a mess. So what happened?"

"A girl," Veranix said. "A very strange girl with spinning blades tried to kill me."

"An assassin?"

"Probably. If she wasn't doing it for money, then it was to make a name for herself. 'Bluejay.' Seriously, that's what she called herself."

"Are you hurt?" she asked, checking him over. "I don't see any blood."

"I think I got very lucky on that score." He looked at his arm, and noticed the rope was still wrapped around it. He willed it to uncoil, but it didn't move. "Something's wrong with the rope."

Kaiana touched it. "What happened?" She tried to get her fingers around it, pry it off his arm, but it didn't budge for her, either. "Why can't you get it off?"

"I'm trying!" he said. Even with it drawing *numina*, he felt drained to his limit. Focusing his concentration, he tried again. This time it suddenly sprang off his arm so quickly it knocked Kaiana off her feet.

"Saints, Kai, are you all right?"

"Fine," she said, picking herself up. Her dress was now quite dusty, and she tried brushing it off, though it seemed futile.

"I'm sorry, I don't know what's going on with it." Though one thing was very strange—he had been expecting to feel even worse in dropping the rope. Instead it was almost a relief, like a weight off his chest. He still felt like he had pushed himself to his limits, but not to the point where he was going to fall over.

"I said I'm fine."

"Sorry about your dress," Veranix said.

"It'll wash."

"When did you get that, anyway?"

"A few days ago." Kaiana gave a bit of an odd curtsey. "Professor Alimen made sure that Master Jolen raised my salary. He also wanted to get me moved out of the carriage house and into regular staff quarters. I graciously told him that wasn't necessary."

Veranix wondered if that was a sacrifice she made for him, so he would have this place. Or perhaps she really did prefer living here alone. He went into one of the stables and started to change back into his uniform. "So how long did you stay with Phadre?"

She shrugged. "Maybe an hour or so. I didn't pay close attention to the time."

"Just you and Phadre?"

"Yes, of course. He's very sweet."

"Is he?" Veranix couldn't keep the ice out of his voice. The memory of Kaiana sitting next to Phadre on the couch, her legs curled under as her yellow dress hitched up suddenly flared in his mind. "He seems all right."

"I stayed and listened to his presentation."

"Did you understand it?"

"What is that supposed to mean?"

"I'm just saying, I doubt I would understand even half of what he's talking about, so I'm sure that you—"

"You know, it's nearly nine bells. You have just enough time to get out of here and into Almers before curfew."

"I was just—"

"Good night." She went into her quarters and closed the door.

Another memory sparked—a month ago, when Lord Sirath and the Blue Hand were searching for the rope and cloak, and Kaiana had stripped off her clothes, pretending to be his lover so no one would suspect why he was really there.

Sometimes the memory of that kiss would hit him out of nowhere. Like he could feel her lips on his as if it was happening all over again. The whole moment—literally just a few seconds before the Blue Hands burst in— happened too quickly for him to process it at the time, but nearly every day since he had relived it one way or another.

Nine bells were going to ring soon, so he couldn't waste time staring wistfully at a closed door. He threw on his uniform coat and left for Almers.

"Oy!" a voice called as Veranix was halfway to Almers. Three cadets came up to him on the path, two of them with lanterns. "Identify yourself!"

They came up close and one shoved the lantern in Veranix's face.

"Veranix Calbert," he said.

"Year and study?" the central one asked.

"Third-year, magic." Anyone could tell that just by looking at his scarf and cap, of course.

"And your residence?"

"Almers."

The one on the right, who didn't have his lantern in Veranix's face, consulted a booklet. "All correct."

"Very well, Mister Calbert. Where are you coming from?"

"Bolingwood Tower." Fortunately the path from the carriage house was right along the way, so that didn't seem unreasonable.

"You live in Almers, you say?" the central cadet asked. "So you were there last night around ten bells when the attack occurred?"

They were now saying "attack" instead of prank.

"I was. I was one of the victims of it."

"I see. And where were you today at shortly after eleven bells?"

"In Holtman Hall. Yes, that attack affected me as well. I was the one who helped Professor Alimen stop it."

"Oh, you helped stop it, hmm? A bit of a hero we have here, boys."

"He probably rescued people from Almers when it happened," the one with the lantern in Veranix's face said. "What a good soul."

It was clear from their tone they were not congratulating Veranix.

"Did what I could," Veranix said. "I'd like to get back home now."

"Home to Almers," the central one said.

"That's right."

"So where were you at, say, three bells this afternoon?"

"An exam. History. You can confirm with Professor Besker that I was there."

"Besker? Take that down."

"Look, are we on lockdown, emergency curfew, or something?"

"Is that what you want, Calbert? Bit of panic, shut everything down?"

Veranix didn't have time for this. "Am I in trouble for being out of doors?"

"We're on an alertness drill, Mister Calbert."

"We're keeping an eye on suspicious behavior," the one with the booklet said.

"What about that lawn full of people?" Veranix asked.

"Those are natural science and astronomy students taking nighttime measurements. Why the concern?"

"All right," Veranix said. He put up his arms, wrists together. "Iron me."

"I'm sorry?" the central one said.

Veranix leaned in. "If you're going to harass me right now, then put me in irons and take me in. Write a formal report. And be specific in your charge."

"Do we have a charge?" the one with the lantern asked.

"We can't even say he's resisting," the one with the booklet said.

The central one glared at Veranix. "Get out of here. Back to Almers."

Veranix took his hands down. "As you say. Good night, gentlemen." He started up the walkway, and after a bit, heard them walking off the other way.

As annoying as that was, at least it was clear that the University was taking the attacks seriously now. As much as he hoped that alone would be the end of it, in his gut he sensed it was far from over.

Chapter 8

MORNING WAS FULL OF PAIN.
Veranix had to remind himself that at no point had Bluejay actually hit him, but given how he felt, it was almost impossible to believe that. Almost everything hurt, and that was even with a proper night's sleep.

He slumped down to the floor, half falling out of the bed, and started in on stretches. There was nothing else he could do.

"Morning to you too," Delmin muttered from his bed.

"*Numina* is more likely to respond to human or other biological intervention than any other source." Veranix parroted one of the key points they studied before finally going to sleep.

"Very good. Unless?"

"Unless the other source is of greater strength. Which makes the whole thing sound meaningless."

"Maybe it does," Delmin said, getting out of bed. He glanced down at Veranix. "Just seeing you in that position makes my legs hurt."

"Stretch through the pain, that's the only way. Grandfather and Mother both swore by it."

"Well, the only way for us today is to take our exam at ten bells. So move along so we can get to breakfast."

Veranix pulled himself to his feet and got dressed, and in a few minutes he and Delmin were both ready to head to breakfast.

The walkway between Almers and Holtman was occupied by a familiar face: Jiarna Kay stood with an arrogant smirk and her cap at an annoying jaunty angle.

"Veranix Calbert, third-year magic student," she said loudly as soon as he stepped outside. "How wonderful to see you up and about so bright and early."

"Morning," Veranix said cautiously as he and Delmin crossed over. "You've trekked down to this part of campus again?"

"I still need some assistance with my defense. Your professor hasn't been of any use, but I think I have the next best thing."

"Good," Veranix said. He tried to walk past her, unsure of what she was about to do. The idea that she had been behind the three prank attacks was still in the front of his mind. "Good luck with that."

"Oh, I don't need luck." She put an arm around his shoulder, and whispered with hot breath in his ear. "I have the Thorn to help me."

It took every ounce of self-control not to yank away from her. "That's a very interesting plan you have. Hope it works out for you."

"Veranix," she said coolly. "Come with me to my workshop. Right now. Or I'll have to let everyone know what you were doing last night."

"I don't know what you're talking about," Veranix said.

"Then let me talk you through it." Arm still around him,

she led him off the walkway so they could face the south lawn. Veranix craned his neck to see Delmin standing petrified in between the two buildings. She pointed to the wall in the distance. "I know you're the Thorn, I know when you returned to campus right over there from doing Thorn things, and I have proof. Proof that my roommate will deliver to the captain of the cadets if I don't explicitly tell her not to in two hours. So be a good boy and come with me."

Veranix looked back over at Delmin. "I'll catch up with you."

"You're very smart, Veranix," she said. She took his arm like he was escorting her to a function. "I think this will work very well for the both of us."

Bell was led in the back entrance, through the kitchen and out to Fenmere's dining room. Fenmere must have been in a good mood, if he was willing to be seen during his breakfast.

"Bell, how was last's night's adventure?" Mister Fenmere was sitting at his long table with Gerrick and Corman, all three having hotcakes and tea.

"It went, well, exactly as planned."

"Excellent." He gestured for Bell to sit down.

Bell took his seat, even though he wasn't as happy with things as Fenmere. "As planned" meant that Hecks and Ferrie were dead, killed by the Thorn. Fenmere had said of them: "The best use they have is bait." Bell wondered when the same would be said of him.

One of the servers poured tea for Bell.

"And the bag?" Fenmere asked.

"He burned it right off, like you guessed."

"That confirms our theory," Gerrick said. "He's not interested in supplanting your business."

"Honestly, I couldn't care what he's interested in. Did one of the Birds find him?"

"One," Bell said. "And I have to say, it was quite a fight."

Fenmere slowly put down his utensils and wiped his mouth. "Could you explain, perhaps, what you mean by 'quite a fight'? Was the Thorn impressive? Did the people of Aventil cheer him?"

Bell tightened his mouth, and decided he needed to choose his words carefully. "You said you wanted a show, and they got one, let me tell you. And, yeah, folks in the street cheered for Thorn. Until that Bird slapped him all around Cantarell Square."

Fenmere smiled and picked up his tea. "Please tell me more."

Bell went through the whole fight as he saw it, piece by piece, blow by blow. Gerrick and Corman both got quite engaged, except for their tangential discussion about possible magical allies to hire now that the Blue Hand Circle were gone. Fenmere just sat and listened, the slight smile on his face as he drank his tea.

When Bell finished, Fenmere put down his empty cup. "This is quite a lovely day, wouldn't you say?" He got up from the table. "I think I'll take a little ride to the apartments today. Bell, keep me informed."

With that, he left the dining room.

"Well," Gerrick said. "I suppose that leaves things in our hands for today. We need to inspect that new chemist, for one, make sure his accounts match his—"

"Hmm," Corman said, moving his eyes over.

They both looked at Bell with no small amount of disdain.

"Don't you have some rounds you should be doing, Mister Bell?"

Bell got up from the table, and nodding to them both, went out back through the kitchen, just as he came in.

Jiarna led Veranix up to the north side of campus, but not quite to the girls' college. Instead she took him into one of the science buildings. The whole walk over she spent talking, almost incessantly, about her classes, her friends at the girls' college, and anything other than the implicit threat she'd made. Veranix didn't listen to what she was saying, but he also had a strong impression that the entire purpose for her chatter was so no one walking past would notice them walking in silence. Given how the cadets were out in force, patrolling the walkways in trios, not appearing out of place was probably a paramount concern. Jiarna had likely noticed just as he had that the cadets were stopping anyone who seemed out of place.

She confirmed Veranix's theory by stopping midsentence as soon as they were inside.

"This way," she said, now all business.

"What exactly do you want me to do for you?" Veranix said. "I've humored you, but I'm not what you think I—"

"Don't insult my intelligence," she snapped. "I honestly don't care what you do outside of campus, but I need a mage to help me."

She opened up a small workroom, with a bench cluttered with devices not unlike the kind Phadre had been working with.

"All right," Veranix said cautiously. "But first let's talk about this proof you have."

She held up a bottle of blackened glass. "This is a solution of dalmatium nitrate. Do you know what that is?"

Veranix knew all too well what dalmatium was—the metal was used in mage shackles and absorbed *numina*. Being in contact with it made performing magic all but impossible. But the rest of what she said had gone over his head. "Not exactly."

She gave him another smug smile. "Don't worry, no one else knows what it is either. I discovered it reacts to shifts in *numina* by changing color. Now why do you suppose that's relevant?"

"I don't know," Veranix said.

"Of course you don't." She held up a device with a lens of some sort attached to the front. "Do you know what this is?"

"Can we skip to the part where you tell me about the proof?"

"If I just told you, Veranix, you wouldn't understand it."

Veranix had no idea why Professor Alimen didn't like this girl. She was apparently the daughter he never had. He sat down on the one clear space in the whole room. "Fine. Illuminate me."

"A fascinating choice of words. Illumination is, in fact, key. This is a camera obscura. Inside here I have a plate that has been treated with dalmatium nitrate. The lens has been treated with a different dalmatium salt solution." With the device pointed at Veranix, she pulled a shutter on the lens. She clicked her tongue a few counts, and closed the shutter. She then pulled out the plate from the back. "And what do we have?"

She handed the plate to Veranix. There was an image on it: shining and sparkling, dots of bright white, but the shape they formed was unmistakable. It was his own face.

"That . . . how?"

"It would only work on mages, and the clarity of the image is mostly due to your proximity. Which is why I was so amazed at the plates I recorded from the south lawn last night, when I was trying to take images of the moons."

She picked up another plate off the table, and again the image was painfully clear. Veranix standing, with the cloak around his shoulders and the rope around his arm. Him, as the Thorn, clear as anything.

"I have more of these."

"That doesn't matter," Veranix said. "Mostly because no one will really understand what these plates mean. Certainly the captain of the cadets won't make any sense of it."

"Maybe Professor Alimen will."

"That doesn't matter," he repeated. "Fine, you figured me out. Do you *really* want to make an enemy of me?"

She raised an eyebrow and chuckled. "Very scary, Veranix. And, no, I don't. We're going to be friends. You're going to help me."

If nothing else, he had to admire her confidence.

"Fine. But I want you to know it isn't the blackmail that's making me do it." He held up the plate. "It's because this is blasted impressive. This alone should get you your Letters of Mastery."

"You would think so, wouldn't you? But that doesn't seem to be the case. The science professors don't understand what I'm doing, and the magic professors don't care."

"Well, I wouldn't claim to understand it, frankly. So you've created a way to capture an image of *numina* around a mage."

"No. Well, yes, but that's inconsequential."

"I think it's—"

"You're easily impressed," she said. "However, the

important aspect of this work is the *numinatic lens*. I need to be able to demonstrate the way *numina* moves, but I don't have a better way to measure it."

"Measure it?" Veranix's thoughts immediately went to Phadre's devices.

"My point is this: the world of science is all about observation, measurement, and evidence. However, it is my contention that we cannot make consistent observations, and all else that follows, without taking the effects of magic or other mystical phenomena—Physical Focus, Psionics, so-called 'miracles'—"

"Psionics?" Veranix asked. "You're talking mind-reading and such? That isn't real."

"You know this for a fact?"

"I know carnival tricks to make you think I know what number you're thinking."

"There are quite a few sources confirming it is a real thing, known privately within Intelligence and selected parts of academia. Professor Jilton—you've distracted me from my point."

"Which is what?"

"That scientific observations aren't useful unless we can take mystical phenomena into account. Be it through deliberate act, such as someone like you doing things to alter the natural order of reality—"

Veranix wasn't sure if that was an insult or not.

"—or the result of ambient *numina* or unobserved phenomena. And *that* is my main point. Take the Winged Convergence last month."

This kept coming up. "What about it?"

"What about it, besides the fact that it should be *impossible*?"

"It should?" That sounded like something Delmin or Eittle would have brought up at some point.

"Of course it should, but no one listens to me!" She grabbed another device off the shelf above the workbench. This was a brass globe with two smaller brass balls attached on thin sticks. She moved the balls in orbit around the globe, putting one inner one in the back and the outer one to the side. She pointed to the inner one. "Namali is full, here."

"That's the blood moon?" Veranix asked.

She looked at him as if his words caused her physical pain. "Yes, that's what some call it. It's full here, with Canus—the sun—coming straight at it from this side. Do I need a lamp to demonstrate this?"

"No." Veranix was getting more than a little annoyed with her attitude.

"Fine. So at midnight, Maradaine is here"—she pointed on the globe—"directly underneath, and you do know that the world is a sphere and the moons go around the world and the world around the sun?"

"I have managed to get slightly educated the past three years here."

"Believe me, Veranix, around here it never hurts to clarify all the facts. But that's good. So with Namali here, we then need Onali over here, in waning crescent."

"How do you know that?"

"Because that's where it needs to be to be in waning crescent. Do you want me to go over all the astronomy?"

"No, this is enough," Veranix said.

"Good. So, let me ask you. If you're standing here, looking up at the moons, how can you possibly see Onali behind Namali, when it's all the way over here?"

The whole business with where moons were and waning crescents didn't make one bit of sense to Veranix, but the archer in him could see a shot that wasn't lined up. "It doesn't work."

"Exactly!"

"But it happened," Veranix said. "We saw it."

"Exactly." She said it like she had just won the argument.

"So it's not impossible."

"No, that's . . . that's not the point." Again, her face made it look like he was hurting her. "If something that should be impossible happens, what does that mean?"

Veranix thought through all the points she'd been making. "Magic was involved?"

"And Almers House makes a point," she said. "Though clearly not through direct intent, but through unobserved phenomena. My *numinic* images on that night were unusable, however."

"Because the convergence made *numina* act wild."

"So I heard. But that meant I had nothing to show Madam Henly, and she dismissed all my theories out of hand, in absolute foolishness."

"Madam Henly, right. She's the main magic instructor for the girls' college? I heard she was injured when a prank was launched at Faishin Hall?" Veranix's suspicion that Jiarna might be behind the attacks was higher than ever, given what she was accomplishing in her work. She was clearly brilliant; brilliant enough to pull it off.

"Was she?" Jiarna asked coldly. "I wouldn't know or care."

That didn't put him any more at ease.

"Look," he said cautiously. "What you've done here is . . . intriguing. But I don't know if I'm the man to help you."

"You *have* to."

"I don't think I know how. I'm not very good at this sort of thing. Maybe Delmin or Pha—"

"They wouldn't help me. You wouldn't if I didn't

threaten you." For a moment, her voice quavered. There was a hint in one of her dark eyes like a tear was about to form, but then nothing.

"I'll . . . do what I can, all right? But right now I will *barely* have time to have some breakfast and then get to my Magic Theory exam, which I am woefully unready for."

"Fine." Her voice now sounded almost defeated. "I will hold you to that."

Someone was pounding on the flop door. Every one of Colin's crew were in, including the new birds, so he had no idea who it would be. It certainly wasn't a boss. If they were calling, the pound would have been accompanied with someone shouting that Colin better answer. There would have been authority to it. Same thing if it had been the Constabulary.

Whoever was on the door, it was somebody young and far too excitable for their own good. Pounding like a blasted dog who smelled a piece of meat on the other side.

"Blazes is it?" Colin snapped.

"Cainey!"

"Who the blazes is Cainey?"

"He was one of ours," Theanne said. Tooser was at the table with her, showing her how to swap dice in a dice game when no one was looking. For a big guy, Tooser had fast hands, faster than anyone expected.

"Good to open?" Colin asked. Theanne just shrugged.

"Cainey's fine," Deena called from the back room.

Colin unlatched the door and let Cainey in. Another young one, same as Jutie and Theanne, with dirty hair and dirty coat. "Did you hear?" he practically screamed as he came in.

Colin shut the door behind the kid. "Hear what?"

"Last night, it was huge! I mean you should have seen it!"

"Seen what, kid?"

"Out there, in Cantarell! First the Thorn came, like, pounding down on the Red Rabbits, right at the Trusted Friend. And there were a bunch of goons, well-dressed nats, who must have come from by the river or something . . ."

"Or just Dentonhill?" Colin asked. Sounded like Veranix had good hunting, and got a fair amount of attention for it.

"Maybe, maybe. These nats came to the Friend, and Rabbits had come out, and then the Thorn swoops in, and he's all bam—down! Bam—down! The Rabbits are all standing around, like, what just happened?"

"I told you!" Jutie called from the back room. He came out, a huge grin on his face. "I knew he'd show those Rabbits whatfor. I would have liked to have seen that!"

"That wasn't all. Just as he has them, there's this bird, see?"

"Really?" Deena leaned in the doorframe from the back room, skeptical eyebrow raised at Cainey. "This ain't one of your stories, Cainey?"

"Not just, Deens, not just at all! This was real, I saw it, other Princes saw it, Orphans and Rabbits saw it."

"Back up," Colin said. "There was a bird? What was that about?"

"Crazy! She's decked out in blue leather, showing more skin than must be legal, and she's throwing blades and spinning blades around her body. And the Thorn, he shoots at her, but she's so good, her blades just knock the arrows away. So the Thorn is jumping around, and she's spinning blades, he can't hit her. He drops his bow, tries to tie her up with his rope, see?"

"So that took her down, right?" Colin asked. He tried very hard to keep his voice level. But there was nothing to worry about. That rope of Vee's was some special magic. He brought that out, any blade-spinning bird would be as good as done.

"No! He wraps it around her, and she's all, 'nope,' and slashes at the rope, and he screams like she cut his own hand! Crazy!"

"Quite." Colin didn't like the sound of all this.

"So how'd he beat her?" Jutie asked.

"He didn't!"

"Liar!" Jutie shouted. "Don't tell me some bird— sorry, girls—but don't tell me some bird with *hoops* beat the Thorn!"

"I'm telling you. He pulls out his staff, and he's all—" Cainey mimed staff fighting, looking more than a little ridiculous. "And this bird—she called herself 'Bluejay,' can you imagine? She's just hammering on him. Wham! Wham! So he runs off, and she chases away!"

"No!" Jutie shouted.

"Calm down, Jutes," Colin said. This wasn't good. If this girl was that good, and called herself Bluejay, then . . . but that was just a rumor. Deadly Birds weren't a real thing, right? "He got away?"

"Far as I saw. Then the Rabbits are all yelling—Thorn did something to stick them all to the ground—and the Orphans and us run into the square, grabbing his arrows and her blades and someone got his bow . . ."

"Someone got his bow?" Colin asked. Blazes, that bow . . . that was Uncle Cal's bow. "Was it a Prince?"

"Why does it matter?" Deena asked.

"We don't want the Orphans beating us on something like that, do we?"

"Yeah, I think so, cap, I think so," Cainey said. "Wasn't no one I really know, but I think it was a Prince who got it."

"That's . . . that could be a problem," Colin said. "The Thorn getting beat out there. He might have cracked on the Rabbits right now, but if Fenmere's taken steps to take him out . . ."

"That's what this bird is, you think?" Tooser asked.

"What dirt is that on us?" Deena shot back.

Colin grabbed his belt, checked his knives. "The bosses didn't want to move on the Rabbits because the Thorn would do it. We can't count on that. So maybe we've got to do something else now."

"That your call?" Deena was a problem. Though he appreciated having someone there who had the good sense to ask questions. Smart questions, even though he didn't like the answers.

"Not sure, but we've got to do something, or we're going to have a real problem with the Rabbits."

"So'll everyone else," Tooser said.

"Good point. Let's taste the cider before we drink it, then. Get the word out, I want a church meet with some folks. Today. One bell after noon. Everyone but the Rabbits."

"Me too?" Cainey asked. Colin had nearly forgotten he was there.

"Yeah, kid. Deena, take him, find some more you trust, take the word to the Dogs and the Kickers. You know anyone you can talk to down there?"

"Maybe," she said.

"Tooser, you and Theanne put out the word to Hallaran's Boys and the Knights. You find Hannik of the Boys, tell him this comes from me. Jutes, you're with me, let's go."

He unlatched the door and let them all out. They went their separate ways and, while Colin latched back up, Jutie waited by the door. "So we're going to get the Orphans?"

"I'm gonna do that."

"You?" Jutie shook his head. "Look, you can't be doing that. You're the cap here. You go around like you're running your own errands, it don't look right. You at least got to look like you've got someone at your arm."

Jutie was right. "Fine. You find that Orphan bird who was at the last church meet. Yessa I think her name is. You know who I mean?"

"Yeah, I know," Jutie said.

"Something else I need from you. This is mouse work, just you and me, hear?"

"Even keep it from Tooser?"

"For now. I want you to find out who's got the Thorn's bow. And if you can, get it to me."

Jutie's eyes went wide. "You think we can get him his bow back?"

"I don't know, maybe," Colin said. "But you and I both know he deserves some respect from Rose Street."

"True, true," Jutie said. "Yeah, I'm on it." He tapped Colin on the shoulder and stepped off.

Now there was only one thing left to do: let the bosses know what he was doing without making them think he had stepped out of turn. That'd be easy enough—he'd just tell them he was gathering information on what everyone else knew about the Rabbits.

Right now, that was all the truth the bosses needed.

Chapter 9

VERANIX USED EVERY MINUTE available finishing the Magic Theory exam. He actually didn't feel like he had done too terribly on the test, but the whole process felt unnatural. Explaining the theoretical aspects of doing magic felt like describing how to make his heart beat. At least part of the exam dealt with Circle history and formation, and the Magic Circle Charters of 1021. Concrete things he could wrap his skull around, even if it only reminded him that next year he'd have to take the course on Circles, Magic, and Law.

He came down from the gallery, exam papers in hand, to find Professor Alimen waiting patiently at the lectern, Delmin and Phadre standing at the ready with him. Veranix had the feeling he was walking straight into a trap. The smiles on their faces didn't alleviate that sense.

"So that was interesting," Veranix said.

"I'm certain you performed tolerably," Alimen said. "And now you three will spend the afternoon focusing on Mister Golmin's final presentation. Isn't that correct?"

"Yes, sir," Phadre said. "I believe we're all set to go. Instruments are ready, my speeches are polished, and we'll be able to demonstrate all my points with clarity."

"Excellent," Alimen said. "However, as it's now noon, I do not expect you to work past five bells."

"No, sir?" Veranix suspected something was afoot. He had never known Professor Alimen to allow such obvious shirking without reason.

"Well, I need to give you time to clean up and put on your dress uniforms."

"Dress uniforms?" Delmin visibly gulped. "Why would we ever—"

"A matter of tradition, Mister Sarren. Simply put, tonight is the final formal professorial dinner at the high service. I have the right and authority to extend invitations to willing and worthy students. Within limits, of course."

"Are you inviting us to High Table, sir?" Veranix asked.

"That is what it's called among the students, yes?" Alimen chuckled.

"You do know how rare it is that third-year students get invited, sir?" Delmin asked.

"Or fourth-year, even?" Phadre said. That was true. Most students only *heard* about High Table, but a great majority went through their entire education without ever being invited. Those who did attend were always stingy with the details, beyond it being an incredible honor. It was a weekly event, every Ghen, yet despite that it was steeped in mystery for the students. It was rumored to be an astounding feast, a towering culinary accomplishment, but also filled with pageantry and spectacle. It was, presumably, everything that students in the School of Protocol lived for.

"Well then, I've accomplished something," Alimen said. "Truth be told, Mister Golmin, for the past four years you've been doing extraordinary work in Mystical

Theory, and I honestly could not be prouder. You two should consider yourselves quite blessed to be given this assignment. And I'm aware that I have placed quite a burden on both of your shoulders—one which I am quite confident of your collective abilities to bear. I realize that such a burden deserves reward." Then he put on an almost maniacal grin. "Not to mention, it will irritate the very blazes out of Professor Yanno."

That may have been the first time Veranix ever heard Professor Alimen say "blazes." He found himself laughing uncomfortably, as did Delmin and Phadre.

"All right, to work, gentlemen. I'll see you tonight." He clapped Phadre on the shoulder and left the lecture hall. Before Veranix or any of the others could gather their thoughts, they heard the professor outside the hall make a few snappish remarks.

Jiarna Kay stepped into the doorframe. "Afternoon, gentlemen."

Phadre suddenly turned into a flustered mess. "You, you . . . you aren't . . . Shouldn't . . ."

"Ease it down, sailor," Jiarna said. "I'm just seeing how my boy here did on his exam." She strutted over to Veranix like she owned him. He suddenly found this far more intimidating than anything that happened with Bluejay the night before.

"I think I did all right," Veranix said. "Now we have to—"

"All right," she said mockingly. She turned to Delmin. "Is he always this humble?"

"Hardly." Delmin himself was half frozen. Jiarna seemed to turn both him and Phadre into morons. Not that Veranix was doing much better.

"I did fine."

"You did superb, my little hero," she said. "You got

invited to High Table. And you know the rules of such invitations."

Veranix really didn't know what she was talking about.

"Do you mean escortment?" Delmin asked.

"He's so bright!" Jiarna said, her gaze fixed on Veranix. "That was exactly what I meant, my little hero. You have been invited to the honor of the High Table, which gives you the right—not merely the privilege but the right—to act as escort to the young woman of your choosing. It's part of the protocol."

"I hadn't realized that," Veranix said. He really didn't have any idea what all the rules of High Table were. Dress uniforms had been mentioned. Did he have a dress uniform? Where was he supposed to get one? Did eating have any sort of ritual?

"Well, now you realize it. And in realizing, I'm sure you know exactly who you should ask to join you. Don't you, my sweet little hero?"

So that's what this was.

"Jiarna," he said, forcing the words through his teeth. "Would you do me the honor of allowing me to escort you to tonight's High Table dinner?"

"Delighted," she said with a flash of a smile. "Now I'll leave you to your work. But, Veranix, I will want to check up on you later."

With that, she was out of the room like a gust of wind.

"What the blazes just happened?" Veranix asked.

"I think you have a date for the dinner," Phadre said. "What is it with that woman?"

"I'm not sure," Veranix said. Did she just want into the dinner because it was an honor? Or did she have some other plan in mind? Veranix still couldn't shake the feeling that there was far more to Jiarna Kay than he could put his finger on. Perhaps it would be best to keep an eye on her for tonight.

"Come on, let's not waste time," Phadre said, walking ahead to Bolingwood Tower.

"This means I have to find someone to escort, don't I?" Delmin groused as they walked, letting Phadre gain a lead on them.

"If you want," Veranix said. "Frankly I would have preferred not to have."

"Then what just happened?"

"My very question," Veranix said. "She found me out."

"Found you out what?" Delmin's confusion then took on a sudden appearance of understanding. "How?"

"She's got some crazy device that can create images of *numina*, or *numinic* flow or something, and so she has an image of me, plain as day, climbing over the wall."

"Wait, wait, she has what? She can—how?"

"I don't know. Something about *numinic* lenses. It doesn't matter. The thing is . . ."

"*Numinic* lenses? I don't . . . I can't even . . ." Delmin apparently lost his ability to speak coherently. "That's extraordinary."

"I thought so, too. I was quite impressed by her savvy. But I was also busy worrying about her, I don't know, exposing me as the Thorn!"

"Right, right. That's bad." Delmin shook his head. "Even still, if she can—"

"My point, Delmin, is that I'm going to have to humor her whim. If she wants to come to the blazing High Table, I'll rutting well take her."

"Fine, fine." Delmin scowled, probably from Veranix's coarse language.

"Sorry," Veranix said. "It's just that . . . look, I'm not

really understanding this stuff that Phadre is doing, or Jiarna for that matter. But it seems like they're doing similar things, and I couldn't help but think of the Prankster."

"The who?"

"You know, whoever is behind the attacks, pranks, whatever. Can we call him—or her—the Prankster for now?"

"If you really want to," Delmin said. "I don't know why we need to give them a name."

"Because it's easier than saying 'the guy.' Anyway, whatever they are doing, it isn't magic exactly, right?"

"Near as I can tell."

"But it also isn't *not* magic, either."

"Yes," Delmin said, his voice stressed. "I think we've determined that we don't understand what this Prankster is doing. At all."

"All right, but is it possible that whatever the Prankster is doing, it has some similarity to the studies of Phadre and Jiarna?"

"Presuming that what Phadre and Jiarna do is, in fact, similar—a dubious prospect considering that you are the only one who has had exposure to both sets of work, and you don't understand it in the slightest . . ."

"Granted."

"Given that, logically, I can't rule it out."

Veranix paused. "Are you endorsing this idea?"

"Not in the slightest."

Veranix stopped walking. "All right, admitting my logic is on loose gravel, do you think it's possible that she's the Prankster?"

"You've already thrown this theory at me, and all I'm going to say is this: it is not your problem."

"It is if she's my escort! And if she knows I'm the Thorn!" He realized he might have said that far too loud, and looked around to see if anyone was nearby on the walking path. "Even if it is someone else, shouldn't I be . . . you know?"

"Shouldn't you what?" Delmin asked. Realization crossed his face. "No, Veranix. You should not. You should do nothing except pass exams. If you've got to do things in the street for whatever reason, that's got nothing to do with what happens in here." He tapped a finger on Veranix's forehead. "Get your Letters, get your Circling, and then beat up drug dealers all night long if you want."

"Maybe you're right," Veranix said, though he didn't believe that at all. "All right, then, what about you?"

"What about me?"

"Escortment, Delmin. Who will you take?"

"I don't even know—"

"Alia Matthin?"

Delmin's ears turned deeper burgundy than any of Veranix's cloaks.

After a moment of sputtering, Delmin looked around. "I don't even . . . we've got to . . . Where's Phadre?"

He wasn't in sight ahead of them.

Delmin smacked Veranix on the arm. "He must have already raced ahead to the tower while we gibbered like idiots. Come on, let's hurry up. Plenty to do today."

When they reached the tower workroom, Phadre wasn't there. He came in just a few moments after them, though. "Sorry, gents. Just needed a moment." He rubbed his hands together with excitement. "Let's get some work done now, all right? Busy day. Busy day, indeed."

Reverend Pemmick wanted every person who lived in Aventil to feel comfortable coming into Saint Julian's

Church for prayer, solace, or even guidance. Closing his doors to anyone was impossible to even contemplate. He would not turn away any of God's children.

Despite that, it was hard to live up to that ideal when God's children took the form of several angry youths, all representing the various bands that tried to wrest control of the streets from the rightful authorities. The past six weeks of serving this community had given him insight into the various groups, especially since they all considered the church a fair, neutral ground for them to meet on. Pemmick did not approve of this idea, but he did appreciate their desire to discuss matters instead of brawling in the streets directly. And it was best they did it in the early afternoon, when only the most devoted of old women were still found praying in the pews.

He had learned about the groups, and the individuals amongst them, as best he could. The ones he saw the most of were the Knights of Saint Julian, which struck him as a woeful appropriation of the saint's good name. The boys and girls made some attempt to dress in gentlemen's suits with vests and tall hats, even if the clothes they wore were ill-fitting, threadbare, and several years out of style. They showed a fair amount of respect for the church itself, and they seemed to hold it with an element of sanctity, even if they rarely came in for services. The group of them—six young men and women—were clustered at the statue of Saint Julian. Their captain, so marked with epaulets on his coat and a yellow band on his hat, was Fortill, though all his people called him "Four-Toe." He left a coin at the foot of the statue, a small token of reverence. He was a good kid at heart, but not too smart. However, his faith wasn't some act of ritual to fit the namesake of the gang. Fortill came in to church every day for early services, his old mother on his arm. Reverend Pemmick was genuinely confused why such a boy would join up with the Knights.

Next a group of Hallaran's Boys came in, notable for the green page caps they all wore, led by their captain, Hannik. They took a place on the far right of the pews. They were followed by the Toothless Dogs, tattooed collars on their necks. This gang almost never came to these church meets, as they were called, and Pemmick didn't know any of them. The Kemper Street Kickers followed, blue kerchiefs tied around their ankles. There was the usual hissing across the church between the Dogs and the Kickers, who apparently were frequently focused on warring with each other over any of the other gangs.

The last two came in together, with smaller groupings than the rest: the Waterpath Orphans and the Rose Street Princes. The Orphans' captain, Yessa, was a young woman who Pemmick felt was far too bright to be part of these groups, and he was saddened that the Orphans insisted on cutting scars into their faces to prove their loyalty. She only had two Orphans with her, as opposed to the five or six that the rest of the groups brought.

The Princes' captain—Colin—also came with only two people. All three of them had their sleeves rolled up, as the Princes would, to show off the rose tattoos on their arms. They strutted as they came in, like they were in charge. In Pemmick's experience, that was how Princes usually walked.

Colin came up to Pemmick. "Sorry to impose on you here, Reverend. But—"

"A safe place for open dialogue," Pemmick said. "I do understand and approve, young man. Far better than you starting fights amongst yourselves."

Colin gave a quick glance to the Toothless Dogs and the Kickers. "I'll try, Reverend."

"This is for peaceful purposes, yes? I won't abide anything else."

"I swear to you, Reverend, on Rose Street itself, that I'm trying to stop things before they go bad."

Pemmick had learned enough about the Princes to know that an oath invoked in the name of Rose Street was a sacred thing for them. "Then let's proceed."

One thing Pemmick had impressed upon all these gangs was that—unlike his predecessors—he was not going to allow a church meet to occur under his roof without engaging in the process directly. In the past weeks they had grudgingly accepted this fact, and Pemmick hoped they would eventually embrace his council.

Pemmick took his place in the front of the pews, gesturing to the rest to join him. "Come now, let's be about this."

"Be about this," muttered the Kicker captain. "What's the hassle, Prince? You called this."

"I don't know you," Colin said. "New cap?"

"Just made. Name's Right Boot. Neary sends his regards."

"'Right Boot' could not possibly be your properly christened name," Pemmick said.

"It's the only name you get, priest, and you'll find out why if you don't respect it!"

"Respect the reverend," Fortill snapped. "You did call this, Prince. What is this? No Rabbits coming?"

"Rabbits are the reason," Colin said. "They've finally caved, breaking the Pact."

This was the first Pemmick had ever heard of a Pact, but the reaction from everyone, save the Princes and Orphans, was so visceral, it must be important.

"No, not even the Rabbits," Fortill said. "I can't believe that."

"It's the truth," Colin said. "At least, I don't know if their bosses are fully in, but at least a couple captains have made some sort of deal with Dentonhill."

"I heard they were sniffing around the Jellican brewery, between Tulip and Lily," Yessa said. "But they haven't been making that much rattle about anything."

Fortill growled. "Blazes, that old brewery is right on Waterpath. That would only help them."

"I'm telling you, they've been making a deal," Colin said.

"So we stomp them!" Right Boot said, using his namesake to demonstrate.

"I do not think that's constructive," Pemmick said.

"But we have to show them that breaking the Pact has consequences," Yessa said.

"She's right," Fortill added. "If there's no Pact, then we might as well all work for Fenmere."

Colin nodded. "So you agree, we've got to do something?"

"I would prefer it if 'something' involved more dialogue and less kicking," Pemmick said. He paced a bit. "This might be radical, but what if I approach the Rabbit captains in question. Try to persuade them."

"I couldn't let you do that, Reverend," Fortill said. Bless him, the boy meant it in all seriousness. "It's too dangerous a risk for you to take."

Pemmick was considering telling these children—it was funny that he thought of them all that way, when some of them were only a couple of years younger than him, if even that—about his mission years in Kellirac. He had a few stories of those days that would make even the most hardened of these Aventil street wretches turn pale. "My job is to minister to the souls of this neighborhood, Fortill. Including the Red Rabbits."

"So wait," Hannik said. "Is this why the Thorn started dustups at the Friend the past two nights?"

"You heard that?" Colin asked. His voice took a prickly edge.

"Heard a lot of things," Hannik said.

"Heard the Thorn got stomped," one of the Toothless Dogs offered.

"Stomped hard," said another. Then they all howled.

"Gentlemen, please," Pemmick pleaded.

"Respect the sanctity of Saint Julian's!" one of the Knights barked.

"That isn't helping," Pemmick said. "How does what the Thorn did enter into things?"

"Thorn's a wildcard," Yessa said. "All we really know is he hates Fenmere more than we do."

"Truth," offered Right Boot.

"He's fighting for us," said the young Prince by Colin's side. "You all know that."

"How'd you know?" one of the Knights shot at him.

"I was there the other night when he dusted up the Rabbits. I heard him. Colin knows."

Colin's face hardened. His man clearly revealed things he would have preferred stayed private.

"What do you know, Prince?" asked the captain of the Toothless Dogs.

Colin sighed. "Not much. But last month I saw some things, crazy things. I got dragged into a merch drop between Fenmere's folks and some mages. Real scary bastards, let me tell you—"

"How'd you get dragged into it?" asked Right Boot.

"That don't matter," Colin said.

"Like blazes it doesn't!" Yessa offered.

Colin looked down to the floor. "My right hand, Hetzer, he snuck his nose places he shouldn't, and I tried to pull him out. And he got killed anyway. Point is, when things went hairy, the Thorn was there. He did right by me."

"And me," said the younger Prince.

"I got a cousin across the 'Path who said he helped her once," an Orphan said. "She's an *effitte*-dosed mess, mind you."

"Fine, fine," said the Toothless Dog captain. "The Thorn has the heart of a saint, and brains of a squirrel."

"Perfect for fighting Rabbits," another Dog said.

"All of you, enough," Pemmick said. "Here is what's going to happen . . ."

"No offense, Reverend, but you don't get to decide what's going to happen." This was Hannik.

Pemmick put on his best beatific smile. "Allow me to rephrase. Here is what I am going to do. I will go to the Rabbits and speak to them about the consequences of their actions. I am willing to be accompanied by one— and only one—member of each of your interested parties. I expect those who come with me to treat my presence with the same respect you treat this building."

"Of course," Fortill immediately offered.

"Stop milking his teat, Four-Toe," Yessa snapped. "You might not respect anything, slan, but the Knights do."

"Knights don't respect corners," said the young woman Prince.

"Don't need to respect when you can't hold them."

"You want to see what we hold?" the young Prince asked.

"Ease off!" Colin snapped. He waved away his two escorts. "Step off, the both of you."

"But, Colin—"

"Not another sound, Jutes."

The boy slunk away to the far side of the church, the girl with him.

Colin held up his hands. "Look, I don't want to start a war with the Rabbits or any of the rest of you. None of us need that. And we don't need Fenmere and the rest of Dentonhill getting a toehold on our side of Waterpath."

"Truth," said Right Boot.

"I think the reverend has a good idea," Colin said. "The Rabbits have to be a little spooked with the Thorn pounding on their door. Maybe a solid talk—from him, but with all of us with him—that will push the Rabbits the rest of the way."

"I'm coming with the rev," Fortill said. "Regardless."

"I'll go," Yessa added.

"In." Right Boot.

"I'll go," the Toothless Dogs' captain said, pointing at Right Boot. "But I won't stand near his stinking feet."

All of them looked to Hannik.

"What, now?" Hannik asked. "You can't be serious."

"It works best if all six of us seem united on this," Colin said. "That might put the fear of God into them."

"Choice of words," Pemmick said lightly.

"Sorry, Rev," Colin said.

"I don't need to do this," Hannik said.

"Of course you don't," Pemmick offered. "Because your gang mostly holds the west side of the neighborhood. You would be least affected by any sort of incursion by Fenmere, yes?"

"It's not like that, Rev."

"Make your choice and live with it," Pemmick said. "I, however, will be at Cantarell Square at six bells this evening. I welcome any and all of you."

He gave them a small gesture, and they began to disperse. And that was for the best. Over by the statue someone was making the show of dropping a token and saying a quick prayer to Saint Julian, but Pemmick saw through the charade. He knew the man was a constable. Specifically, one of the ones loyal to the new lieutenant.

This meeting tonight might have more interested parties at it.

Veranix followed Phadre's instructions, but his mind was on Jiarna, the Prankster, the Red Rabbits, and tomorrow's Rhetoric exam. He needed to clear at least a little of that out of his skull before he could continue.

They finished one instrument, and Veranix used the opportunity. "Quick breather now."

"What?" Phadre asked. "But we've still got . . ."

"I know, I know," Veranix said. "Mind you, this takes more out of me than either of you. Just give me a few minutes to walk it out a bit."

"Let him," Delmin said with a sigh.

"Fine," Phadre said. "But only a few, then we have to pound through the rest of this. Got it?" He was sweating and stressed, that was clear.

"Not a problem." He went to the door. "Hey, Del. Last chance for Alia Matthin."

"Shut it!" Delmin snapped as Veranix went down the stairs.

He bolted across the lawn, about to run to the carriage house, but he spotted Kai pushing a wheelbarrow down a lane near the wall. He headed over to her.

"Hey," he said. "Busy?"

"Quite," she said. "Flower beds need to be weeded, new mulch added. A lot going on today."

"Same here, but I need a few minutes."

"Oh, you need a few minutes." She lowered the

barrow to the ground and took off her gloves. "Since you need it, I guess I can just stop everything. Master Jolen might not threaten to beat me anymore, but he still might fire me. Just so you know."

"Sorry," Veranix said. "I just want to know what you think about something."

Her face softened. "All right. What is it?"

"You know about the crazy, dangerous pranks that have been happening?"

"I'd say 'attacks,' but yes."

"I have a theory who it might be. Just a theory, though."

"So what are you going to do about that?"

"Right now, keep an eye on this person. But . . . that's what I need to know. Do I do something about it? I mean, is that something that the Thorn needs to worry about?"

She frowned, and put her gloves back on. "That's a very stupid question, Veranix."

"It is?" She had picked up the wheelbarrow and started pushing it again. He chased after her. "How is it stupid?"

"How is it—" She shook her head at him. "Look, you may have started doing this to smack around Fenmere and *effitte* dealers, and I am all for that. But you—" She pointed to the east wall of the campus. "Out there is Waterpath. You said that was the line. You were going to hold it. *You.*"

"Right," Veranix said, not sure what she meant.

"So it doesn't matter what it is. *Effitte*, crazy mages, or one dangerous prankster—doesn't matter. When something beyond the scope of what prefects or cadets or Constabulary are capable of handling rears its head, someone has to step up."

"So I should make this prankster my problem?"

"Yes, by the saints, you blazing well should."

He smiled. "That was exactly what I needed to know. You're the best, Kai."

She gave him the barest of smirks back. "Don't you have things to do? I know I do."

"Back on them. Keep my gear where I can get it quick."

"I may have better things to do," she said. "But I'll see what I can manage." She waved him off, and went back down the lane. Knowing that Delmin and Phadre were probably climbing the walls, he ran back. Still plenty on his shoulders, but now, he wasn't worried.

By four bells in the afternoon, the instruments had been recalibrated to be appropriate for the following afternoon, when Phadre's defense was scheduled to take place. They had even had the opportunity to run through the entire demonstration of the defense once. Veranix honestly didn't understand what was going on, but he knew how to follow his cues in a performance, and he hit his timing well enough. Delmin had the unenviable role of having to write down key terms and numbers on the slateboard while Phadre spoke.

As for Phadre's speech, he did have a certain flair in delivering his points, more than Veranix had thought him capable of. Perhaps that had been Kaiana's doing.

When they were finishing up, a knock came at Professor Alimen's workroom door. A female professor was there, in impeccable robes hemmed in blue and violet, valise in hand. Six male students were with her, all with scarves matching her hemming. Three of them stood at attention, while the other three carried several boxes each.

"Can we help you?" Phadre asked.

"Madam Gosalyn, from the College of Protocol," she

said. "Am I to understand that the three of you have been invited to attend the Professorial Dinner of High Service this evening? Misters Golmin, Sarren, and Calbert, yes?"

"That's right," Veranix said.

"Very good," she said. "I have your dress uniforms and your valets for the evening. They will prepare you. I trust you have secured escortment?"

"Not actually," Delmin said.

"Hmm." She looked at him as if he had offended her deeply and personally. "The rest of you?"

"I have," Veranix said, as much as he wasn't pleased about it.

"Very well," she said, reaching into her valise. "If you could inform me—"

Veranix started telling her, hoping to get it out of his mouth before he hated saying it too much. "Jiarna Kay, she's—"

"Do not just blurt it out, Mister Calbert. It's terribly uncivilized." She produced a card from her valise. "Please write it there. Neatly."

Veranix took the card and wrote Jiarna's name, year, and school. He handed it back to her, as she was taking a card back from Phadre as well. She regarded both cards with a raised eyebrow. "Highly unorthodox."

"I suppose so," Veranix said.

She turned to her students—presumably their valets. "Gentlemen, you know your charges. To work."

The Protocol students split into pairs, two coming over to Veranix.

"So what do we do?" Veranix asked.

"Terrible," the unburdened one muttered. He turned to his companion, carrying the boxes. "Meet us at the dormitory and get the uniform unpacked. I'm going to need to take him to the bathhouse."

Chapter 10

THIS WAS THE FIRST TIME in the three years at the University of Maradaine that Veranix had had cause to wear his full dress uniform. He absolutely hated it.

The regular school uniform he had to wear on a daily basis was bad enough, but this was truly an atrocity. It would have been impossible to even get into it without the valets from the College of Protocol. These were clothes that were, in fact, impossible for someone to dress themselves in.

The pants, apparently by design, were tight and restrictive. They were made with wool that was far too hot for this weather and far too itchy for any person to wear for a significant length of time without approaching insanity. The coat had buttoning down both sides, and was also far too tight. It actually made breathing a challenge, which Veranix thought was quite an impressive feat given how lean he was. In addition to the cap—now a short-brimmed velvet one—and the scarf, there were further elements of frippery that boggled his mind. First there was the sash, which appeared to serve the same purpose as the scarf, identifying him as a magic student. But in addition to the colors of the school he was associated with, the sash was covered in badges for each course he had taken.

There was also a capelet. Veranix had to admit, he liked the capelet.

There were also special shoes—hard leather with a complicated series of buckles. "Complicated" was the description that fit every element of the ensemble.

The valets had finished their job, with a minimum of conversation besides sighs of despair. Wordlessly they packed their cases and supplies and left Veranix and Delmin alone in their frippery. Veranix knew he must have looked ridiculous, but at least Delmin did as well.

"Who even has time to make these?" he asked Delmin, looking at his sash. "I mean, do they have them for every student, waiting in boxes for the day they need to wear them?"

"They do," Delmin said. "Because for all of us, at least, that day is commencement. But our invitation tonight means they bring them out of storage."

"Wait a moment," Veranix said. "All of your course badges are lined in white. Mine are a mix of yellow and green and white."

"Mostly yellow and green," Delmin said. "It's noting our marks in those courses. I received top marks in all of mine. You didn't."

"Fine. Let's go."

They left their room to the hoots and calls of the entire third floor of Almers.

"Gentlemen, gentlemen," Rellings said. He stood in the middle of the common room with crossed arms and a strange grin, several of the rest of the third floor fellows gathered behind him. "I must say I'm impressed how well you clean up."

"We live to impress, Rellings," Veranix said.

"Quite an honor you have here," Rellings said. "Up until now, I was the only person from our floor who had been to High Table."

That had been at the beginning of the semester, and it was the only thing anyone had heard about for the month that followed. Never details, simply the vague bragging that it happened. Veranix wondered if there was a secret oath students were forced to take to never divulge what occurred.

"Let's get moving," Delmin said. "Don't want to keep anyone waiting."

They were greeted by a low whistle when they exited the building.

Jiarna Kay stood just outside the entrance to Almers, decked out in her own dress uniform. She looked nowhere close to silly. In fact, the uniform seemed to flatter her far more than the standard uniform, and she was already a fairly comely girl in that.

"Very nice, boys. I am impressed."

"Our valets did a fine job primping us up," Veranix said.

"My compliments indeed." She gave a quick twirl in her skirt. Unlike the typical girls' uniforms, this went all the way to her ankles and was restrictive enough not to rise significantly when she spun. "I wasn't displeased by the work mine did either."

"They paint your face?" Delmin asked bluntly.

"They did," she remarked. It was subtle, but her cheeks were flushed and her eyes lined. Not as heavy as Bluejay's eyelining, but certainly noticeable. She flashed a smile at Veranix. "How is it?"

"It's fine," Veranix growled. "By the way, Delmin knows everything about me, so I'm not going to pretend to like you as we walk over."

She crooked her arm into his. "I don't need you to like me, dear hero. I just need you to get me in the door."

"This smart, cap?" Tooser was asking.

"I doubt it," Colin told him. Hiding two knives in his boots, he went on. "But the preacher set the rules. One person each. I'm the captain, I take the risks. Besides, we need to thicken our grease or the bosses will ask questions. So the rest of you better be busy."

"You want us on the gates?"

"Work 'em smart and clean. Pair off. You and The-anne, Jutie and Deena. At least half the Uni brats are done with their exams and they are going to want to stoke their fires tonight. That's coin we can't pass up."

"No argument, cap," Tooser said, grabbing a hat off the back-room shelf to cover his scarred head. Tooser never talked about what had happened to his head, and Colin never asked, but he had known Toos since they were both thirteen, and he had always had the scars. And no hair. Wearing a hat made him look less frightening, but he only bothered when he worked the gates. "Just wish you were being safer."

"I'll be fine, Toos," Colin said. "But I need you to keep things smooth out there for me."

"So let me ask you, who's your right hand right now? Is it me? Or Deena?"

Colin stopped. "A man has two hands, Toos."

"That ain't an answer."

"You haven't made a rattle over this for the past month."

"Yeah, well, respect to Hetz. It was just the three of us, so it didn't matter. But now you bring in two birds—"

"I was told to take them—"

"I got no guff with that, cap! Theanne's a good kid, and Deena's sharp as any blade I've held."

"She is, and she was Dennick's right hand in his crew. You know as well as I that girl should probably have stars on her arm." Colin was real glad it was only the two of them in the flop right now.

"And not me? My ink is as old as yours."

That was a surprise. "You want your stars? You ready to run your own crew without me?"

"I think I could." Tooser shrugged.

"I tell you plain, Toos. If the bosses ask me who should get them, you're who I'm gonna say. But they don't ask me."

"But for Deena . . ."

"I ain't said anything about either of you yet, and you know why? Because I've been hip deep in sewage from the Rabbits and bosses and who even knows what else. Let things cool, hear?"

"Heard," Tooser said.

Pounding on the door. The sort of pounding that means the person there was sent.

"Who's at it?"

"Bosses want you, Colin!"

"And what's the word?"

"The word is rutting come!"

That was word enough, and Colin knew the voice was one of the bosses' private heavies. "Hopefully this is nothing," he told Tooser. "Run it smooth and clean, hear?"

"Heard." Tooser sounded scared. "Be safe."

Colin gave Tooser a wink as he threw open the latch. "Always am."

High Table was held in Shalinar Hall, the central build-ing in the hub of faculty apartments, near the western wall of campus. This part of campus wasn't off-limits to students, but there was an unwritten code that one shouldn't come over here without a specific request from a faculty member. Most of the professors lived within this cluster of buildings, with the exception of those who held Chairships that included residences. Professor Ali-men, holding the Egracian Chair of Magical Studies, lived in Bolingwood Tower near the southeast corner of campus, far from the rest of the faculty.

Veranix always wondered if that distance was inten-tional segregation of the head magic professor, and who was the one who decided to do that.

Shalinar Hall was one of the oldest buildings on cam-pus, and like most of the faculty-centered buildings, it was very well maintained. The stonework still gleamed white, hardly a crack or chip in the mortar. The high dou-ble doors shone, freshly oiled and still smelling of cedar and citrus.

The two cadets at the doors were dressed in military regalia from nearly a century back, which matched the era and style of the dress uniforms Veranix and Delmin were wearing. The main difference in theirs were the wide leather belts where their swords hung, cinched so tight they could be tourniquets. No wonder these boys were standing at full attention; they probably couldn't slouch if they wanted to.

"Approach if you have invitation," one of the cadets shouted as they came up the wide stone steps.

"We do," Veranix said.

"Then identify yourself!" shouted the other. Both the cadets faced straight ahead, not even looking to the side to properly see Veranix and the others.

"Veranix."

"Oh, saints, do it right," Jiarna said. "There's a sense of ritual to all of this."

"Clearly," Veranix muttered. So he'd do it properly. Matching the cadets in tone and volume, he said, "Veranix Calbert, Third-Year Student in Magical Studies, in attendance by express invitation of Gollic Alimen, High Professor in Magical Studies and holder of the Egracian Chair. I bring in escortment Miss Jiarna Kay, Fourth-Year Student in Natural Sciences."

"Well done," Jiarna said under her breath.

"Um, Delmin Sarren," Del said. "Third-Year in Magical Studies, under express invitation of Professor Alimen. No escortment."

The first cadet pulled a cord, ringing a bell that signaled someone inside to open the wide doors. As they slowly moved, the cadet spoke. "Mister Calbert, with escorted Miss Kay. Mister Sarren, without escortment. Your invitations are recognized, and you may proceed to the hall of the High Service."

They entered the hall, lit with scores of candle-filled chandeliers, following a carpeting path to the dining hall.

"Where did you get that speech?" Jiarna asked.

"You wanted ritual and pageantry? Born and raised in a circus. I may not know all the rules of dining in High Service, but if there's one thing I can give you, it's showmanship."

"Good on that," Delmin said. "Speaking of rules on the dining, I've got some experience. So follow my lead there."

"Will do," Veranix said. They approached the outer hall, where several professors and a few students were milling about, presumably waiting for the moment to enter the dining hall and take their seats. Veranix wondered what would be done to indicate the proper moment.

Among the prospective diners, one person stood out above all others, mostly because she was the only one not wearing a student's dress uniform or professorial robes. Instead she wore a brocade dress of yellow and purple, which looked like it had been made for a baroness. Her black hair had been styled into a cascade of curls down one side to rest on a bare shoulder of sienna skin.

Kaiana was a vision of grandeur and elegance.

And she was standing with her hand on the crooked elbow of the young man escorting her: Phadre Golmin.

"Well," Delmin said under his breath. "That's showmanship."

One of the bosses' goons—a near seven-foot mountain by the name of Hucks—half shoved Colin all the way to the offices under the Turnabout.

"Somebody mad at me, Hucks?" Colin asked once the meathooks the man called hands grabbed him a time too many.

Hucks shrugged. "They sent me to get you. That usually only happens when they don't expect the bloke to come easily."

"Fine, fine," Colin said. "But I'm coming, and unless someone actually told you to smack me around, I'd prefer if you stopped."

Hucks thought about it for a moment. "Fair enough. It was more habit than instruction."

"I respect that."

"Then we'll give each other respect." Hucks placed a hand on Colin's shoulder as they finished their walk to the offices. Not rough, but certainly sending a message.

They were waved through the first door with little

more than a nod from Hucks. Colin was led to the table room, usually populated by the minor bosses wasting time with card games. None of them were there. Hucks knocked on the next door. Gently, with respect. After a moment, the door opened, and a whole passel of bosses filed out: Giles, Nints, Hotchins, Frenty, and Bottin. They all gave Colin a regard that sent a chill up his spine and took seats at the table.

Hucks held open the door and waved Colin to go through, into Old Casey's office.

Casey wasn't the true head of the Princes, but he was the most in charge that a captain like Colin ever saw. Somewhere on Rose Street was a house called the Palace, though almost no one knew which one it was, where Vessrin lived. The King of Rose Street, he called himself.

Colin hadn't seen Vessrin since he was nine. The man had come to give respects to Colin's father on his deathbed. It was the least the man could do. Way back in the day, Colin's father, Veranix's father, and Vessrin had been a tight crew. Before everything went to blazes.

Really, Colin and every other Prince had it only on rumor and Old Casey's word that Vessrin was actually still alive and running things.

Until right now. The old man himself sat behind Casey's desk, Casey standing off to the side like a flunky in his own office.

Seeing Vessrin alive and relatively healthy—he certainly seemed like he could still throw a scrap or two despite his thinning white hair—wasn't the biggest shock. That was reserved for the item lying on the desk, Vessrin's hand casually resting on it.

Veranix's bow.

Chapter 11

CONTRARY TO VERANIX'S EXPECTATIONS, there was not just one table to sit at, but four long tables. One of them was up on a stage—the literal High Table—while the other three completed a square on the floor below. Several table footmen, dressed in old-styled regalia, were at attention inside the square. Veranix wondered where these footmen came from. Were these also students in the School of Protocol, or staff of the University? The High Table was only a weekly event, so what did they do the rest of the time?

They were gently guided to their places on the far side of the square. Veranix was seated between Jiarna and Delmin, with Phadre and Kaiana on the other side of Jiarna. With two people in between, it would be nearly impossible to have any sort of private word with Kai, unless he simply ignored protocol and got up to speak to her. His first attempt to do that was met with a scowl from more than one of the valets, so he let it go and sat back down.

Jiarna, on the other hand, had no such compunction about talking over Phadre.

"You are not a student," she said bluntly. "So where did you come from?"

Veranix couldn't make out exactly what Kaiana said, but it sounded like she responded with good humor. She was smiling at Phadre and Jiarna, that much was certain.

Delmin, on the other hand, was already talking in Veranix's ear. "Do not be freaked out by all the utensils on the table. Each one has a function."

Veranix actually took a look at his place setting. There were three plates—fine porcelain—stacked on top of each other, and a series of forks, knives, spoons, and other devices bordering the plates on three sides. There was a card on the plate, with Veranix's full name written in rich calligraphy, and it was about the only thing he fully understood. Several blank cards were also stacked in a small receptacle at the right side of the place setting.

A small bell on the High Table was rung by an old professor—or perhaps this was someone higher on the academic hierarchy. The various ranks above professor and chair danced around his skull: Deans and provosts, and above them the board of vice headmasters, and finally the headmaster. If Veranix had any clue what the heraldry of the various stoles and colors and badges on the man's robes meant, he could figure it out.

"Who's that?" he asked Delmin.

"Vice Headmaster Ballford," Jiarna answered him. "You really don't know that?"

"I don't have the administration memorized," Veranix said. Until this moment, he didn't think he had even seen any of the vice headmasters before. Up at the High Table he only recognized a few of the faculty. Alimen, of course, at the end of the table, plus a few other professors he had had over the years, including his history professor, Besker, near the other end.

"This is who I need you to know," Jiarna said directly. She was now in mercenary mode. She pointed to the female professor two seats over from Besker. "That's Professor Nontiss. Natural Philosophy. Next to her is Professor Hester."

"Astronomy," Veranix said. "I have a friend who is going on summer study with him," he added upon her questioning look.

"Good for your friend," she said woodenly. "Here's how this works, since you've never done this before—"

"You have?" Veranix asked.

"Of course," Jiarna said, giving him a bit of a sneer. He had a feeling this whole event was going to be excruciating.

Three seats over, Kaiana laughed at something Phadre told her. Veranix's gaze darted over to her, prompting Jiarna to grab his chin and force his focus back to her.

"There will be ten courses served. First the Morsel, then the Mussel, then the Curd."

"What does that even mean?" Veranix asked.

"It doesn't matter right now. The point is, after those three, there is the First Engagement."

"And that matters why?"

"It matters because the professors up there"—she indicated the table—"will come down here and engage with the invited students and their escortment. Three Engagements total. That means you have the opportunity to give me an audience with Nontiss, Hester, and your beloved Alimen. An audience which they, as a matter of tradition, will stay in until Engagement is finished. They cannot ignore me here."

Veranix took a moment. "You've really thought this through, haven't you?"

"Explicitly." A server came and poured small amounts of wine in each glass. Jiarna picked up her glass and took a sip. "Now, that means you need to put in your request for audience, and quickly, please. Those blank cards. You will find that case there is equipped with pen and ink. There, next to the salt box." She simply nodded her head in the direction of the ornate box to Veranix's left.

Another peal of laughter from both Kaiana and Phadre.

"So Morsel, Mussel, and Curd?" Veranix said, desperate to latch on to some element of this experience that was concrete, that he could relish. Food. Meal courses. That was something he could handle.

Delmin interjected. "The Morsel is a small but elaborate dish, which can be eaten in just two or three bites. The tiny fork all the way to your left is for that. Mussel is usually, but not always, some form of small shellfish, most likely Maradaine River mussels. That tool above your plate."

"That's enough for now, Del," Veranix said.

"Pen and ink." Jiarna almost sang the words out. "I would actually like to speak to Hester in the First Engagement. I think he would be most open to the possibilities I'm suggesting."

"What possibilities would that be?" Phadre asked, leaning over to look at the two of them. "What even are your disciplines, Miss Kay? Especially that would be of interest to Professor Hester?"

"I really don't think it's worth explaining my work to you," Jiarna said.

"You'd be surprised," Veranix mumbled.

Phadre shrugged. "Well, I did some consulting with Hester, and he'll be sitting in on my defense."

"Why the blazes is he sitting in on your defense?"

"Well, I will be discussing lunar and planetary positions and their influence on *numina*."

Jiarna quickly turned to Veranix. "Hester, Nontiss, Alimen. Be on it." Then she turned back to Phadre. "I presume you've some way to demonstrate *numinic* flow to professors who aren't magically gifted."

"I've devised several instruments for exactly that purpose," Phadre said. "Veranix and Delmin there have been helping me calibrate them."

"Of course, you would have magical helpers to calibrate instruments, you would get whatever you wanted. I suppose you even have samples of napranium to be sensitive elements of your instruments."

"Napranium, like I could even get my hands on that. I had to use crystals of varying sensitivity and align them perfectly in each device."

"Crystals?" she asked. "I didn't even think of that. I had been concentrating my efforts on aqueous solutions of dalmatium and thalinium salts."

"Dalmatium salts?"

Veranix glanced back over at them, having written his request cards out. Jiarna and Phadre were now nattering away like the squirrels on campus. Off past Phadre, Kaiana watched them both with a smile that seemed more forced with every passing moment.

Steaming plates with a small pastry concoction were brought out and placed in front of each of them. Jiarna and Phadre barely noticed.

"Taste well," the server said as he placed Veranix's dish.

"The Morsel," Veranix said to Delmin, picking up the tiny fork. "One dish down, nine to go. Quite an evening we're having."

Vessrin drummed his fingers on the bow. "Colin, good boy. Look how tall you are."

"Sir," Colin said. He didn't even know what else to say.

"'Sir', he says. This kid, Casey. Can you believe it?" He got up from around the desk and appraised Colin. "Captain stars on your arm. You know those are all yours, right, son? No favoritism got you up."

Colin was well aware of that. If anything, his father counted against him, even if nostalgia for Uncle Cal balanced it out a little.

"All mine, yes," Colin said.

"Because you're smart, ain't you?"

"Do all right, sir."

A light slap hit his face. "Enough with that 'sir' sewage, boy. We're all from Rose Street here."

"As you say," Colin said. "Not to press the issue, Mister Vessrin, but you called me here for a purpose?"

"You got somewhere better to be?" Vessrin asked, slapping Colin on the shoulder, going back to sitting at the desk. "Casey, you got some Fuergan whiskey hidden away somewhere here?"

"I might," Casey said, going over to one of his cabinets.

"Not better, no," Colin lied. "There is plenty going on out there with my crew, and I should have my finger in it."

"Good man."

Casey came over with three glasses and a bottle, pouring for the three of them. "What is going on?"

"Big coin moving around, what with Uni kids being mostly done with exams. There's some rattle with the Rabbits. They . . ." He thought for a moment, not sure how much he should say. But it was one thing handling things on his own; another to lie flat out to Casey and Vessrin. "They might be breaking the Pact, working with Fenmere to bring product across Waterpath."

Vessrin shook his head. "Blasted Rabbits. I told you, Casey, I told you twenty years ago, Reb and his brothers were going to be the death of us. Took a long time, but here we are." He threw back a slug of whiskey. "You have him on it?"

"Not exactly," Casey said, eyeing Colin. "But he's always been a self-starter."

"That he has, indeed," Vessrin said. He filled his glass again. "You on things, Colin?"

"Putting a toe in the water," Colin said. "See, there's a new priest over at Saint Julian's. He's been . . . active whenever a few groups have a church meet."

"What, he listens to you all?" Casey asked. "That ain't good business."

"Listens and takes part. He decided that he's gonna try to talk to the Rabbits himself, tonight."

"Some preacher is going to get the Rabbits to back down?" Vessrin laughed. "He really think it's gonna work?"

"I suppose he has faith," Casey said. "We taking any ownership of that?"

Colin shrugged. "Preacher was willing to have somebody from each gang come with him. I was going to step up."

"When's that going down?" Vessrin asked.

"About seven bells, meet him at Cantarell."

"We at half past six, right?"

Casey looked out the tiny window. "Sounds about right."

"All right, I won't waste more of your time, then. Casey says you've seen this Thorn character who has dusted things up over here and with Fenmere's goons."

"Mostly with Fenmere," Colin said.

"Right, but you say you've actually seen him? Talked to him?"

Colin had to lie now. "He didn't really talk much, you know?"

"But you saw him?"

"Not his face, he keeps it hidden."

"And he shoots a bow, though?"

There was no hiding this one. "Yeah, he does."

"Crack shot?"

Colin shrugged. "Pretty good."

Now Vessrin picked up the bow. "They said this was the Thorn's bow. Dropped it in a big tussle with some bird."

"I heard a bit about that," Colin said.

"Is it really his, though?" Vessrin was almost jittery, sweating beading on his brow.

Colin put on a show of looking at the bow. "It could be. I'm not really sure."

Vessrin put his hand on Colin's shoulder, almost in a desperate, pleading way. "And you never got a good look at him? Nothing . . . familiar, Colin?"

Colin slowly shook his head, keeping his face as neutral as possible. "No, Mister Vessrin. Where are you driving this carriage?"

Vessrin held up the bow. "This bow, Colin. I know this bow."

"What do you mean?"

"This bow . . . I want you to tell me, Colin, I want you to be totally certain here. Is there any chance that this Thorn is your Uncle Cal?"

"What?" Colin didn't have to make much show of shock. That's what Vessrin thought? Didn't he know Fenmere had killed Cal three years ago? He wasn't exactly quiet about that. "Cal is dead, Vessrin. Dead as anything."

Vessrin looked around. "Are we sure? Did you see the

body? Is Fenmere sure? Cal was . . ." Vessrin started to choke up. "Cal was a tricky bastard, right sure he was. If anyone could trick Fenmere he was dead and slip off to start a plan of revenge, it would be Cal Tyson."

"You're saying this bow, it's my uncle's?" Colin reached out to it. Was there some chance he could get his hands on it, get it back to Veranix?

"I'd swear to it. Which makes you wonder, why does the Thorn have it? Why would he have it, unless it was Cal?"

"I don't know what to tell you," Colin said. Which was about as honest an answer as he could give. He had no idea what to say at this point. Vessrin's idea was crazy, but if it took him off the scent of who Veranix actually was, that was probably all the better.

"Well, that's a question he's gonna have to answer, ain't it?" He slapped Colin on the cheek, lightly. "So if you, I don't know, get a moment to have a word with the Thorn, let him know we have his bow. And we'd like to talk to him about it."

"Why don't you go see about that meet with the preacher, Col?" Old Casey said.

"Yeah, sure," Colin said, getting to his feet. He kept his eye on Vessrin as he stepped back to the door, as if the man might suddenly turn into a snake if he glanced away. "I'll . . . I'll be on top of all of that."

"Good kid," Vessrin said, pointing a finger to him as he took another sip of whiskey. "Get on it."

Colin went out the door, making deliberate steps as he passed the other bosses and the heavies at the door. Once he was out in the back alley, he waited until he was out of sight before he stumbled into the closest backhouse to throw up.

He knew damn well that if anyone could stroll onto

Rose Street and steal the Princes away from Vessrin, it would have been Uncle Cal. Veranix could probably do the same just by virtue of being his son. Even Old Casey might have his loyalty tested.

Vessrin wouldn't stand for that. If he knew who Veranix was, and that he was Thorn, there was no chance he would let Veranix survive.

Colin wiped off his face, pulled himself together, and headed off to Cantarell Square. If he could clip this Red Rabbits business before the flower bloomed, then the Thorn wouldn't have to get any more involved.

Arch had stumbled upon some good intel in the church. It wasn't clear if anything was going to happen that would give them an arrest, but that didn't matter. It was time to stop playing games with these boys.

Benvin waited in the alley—the same one the Thorn had embarrassed him in two nights ago. Jace came running over.

"Placements?" Benvin asked. Jace was sharp. No need to mince words.

"We've got Tripper in the square; he's got eyes on the fountain. Pollit is trailing the preacher, block away. Mal and Wheth are up on that roof, with crossbows trained on the door of the Trusted Friend. And Arch, well, he's in position."

Benvin glanced around the corner, and there was Arch. Saints would swear he was an old drunk, stumbling half-blind just far enough from the Trusted Friend for those heavies at the door to pay him no mind.

"Whistle?"

Jace pulled it out of his pocket. "Got it, Left. Ready to make the call when we need it." He pointed across the square. "And Saitle is ready to run for the stationhouse if we need it."

"Good lad," Benvin said. Jace was a real find for this squad, with a sharp eye and a loyal heart. Benvin had to admit, he favored him over Saitle. Saitle was a good cadet, honest to a fault, and he could run faster than anyone else in Aventil. But he didn't have Jace's fire.

Give him a score of boys like Jace, and he'd have the city cleaned up in a month.

He glanced around the square. Mostly empty in the twilight, save a few carts straggling, vendors not heading in for the night yet. Enough crowd so no one would look too strange standing around. In fact, there were quite a few folks milling about, like they were expecting something to happen.

Jace seemed to read his mind. "Thorn had a brawl here the last two nights. Maybe people think there's gonna be a show."

"There's gonna be a show, all right," Benvin said. The preacher was coming into the square. Tripper strolled to a new position, giving two hand signals to the boys on the roof. An Orphan came up to the preacher, and then a Kicker and a Dog followed suit. Each of them had some crew hanging on the outskirts, but all of them were behaving themselves for the moment.

One of Hallaran's Boys came across and joined the party.

Benvin crouched down a little to look Jace in the eye. He was a good kid, Constabulary family going generations back in Maradaine. His father had even died in duty a few years back. "Trust your instincts, Jace. You think it's time to make the whistle call, make it. Even make a Riot Call if you think you need to."

"Riot Call, Left? You think it might come to that?"

Benvin looked back out to the square again. Quite a few interlopers now, and a Knight of Saint Julian had taken a place near the preacher. His crew was at attention, looking ridiculous in mismatched vests and hats, but acting like they were a royal honor guard.

"I'm saying be ready, kid. We're counting on you."

"Aye, Left."

Benvin left the alley and walked into the square. Head high, uniform crisp, hand resting on his stick. Even his brass badge was shining. He wanted to make sure these brats all got the message: the best damn stick in Aventil was coming.

"Oy, preacher, you turned us!" the Kicker said. A captain who called himself Right Boot, even though his parents had named him Reginick.

"Not at all," the priest said. "Though I'm not too surprised that the local authorities have decided to join our meeting. Lieutenant."

"Reverend," Benvin said. "Strange company you keep."

"I minister to every soul."

"You can tend to the sin, and I'll handle the crime," Benvin said. "Well, caps, what's the word?"

"No word to you, stick!"

"I don't know what you all think is going to happen," Benvin said, "But I'm looking around this square, and I see trouble taking shape. I can't abide by that."

"Nor could I, Lieutenant," the reverend said. "My mission is to halt trouble before it starts. I'm certain you understand."

"Reverend, why are you messing with the stick?" the Knight captain—Four-Toe—asked.

"He is a concerned party as well," the reverend said. "Your mission, Lieutenant, is to keep the peace in Aventil?"

Benvin thought for a moment. His mission was to put as many of these self-styled captains and their accompanying menace in Quarrygate, but he did need good cause. His captain wouldn't stand for him just ironing anyone because they had a rose tattoo or a green cap. "I suppose it is," he finally answered.

"Then we might be allies here, Lieutenant. And I wish to help these people settle their grievances without bloodshed or mayhem."

Another person ran over—a Rose Street Prince captain, sweat drenched and out of breath. Benvin knew this one well: Colin Tyson, too clever by half. "Who invited the stick?" he asked.

"I invited myself," Benvin said, stepping up close to Tyson. "You have a problem, son?"

"No problem, Left," Colin said, not giving Benvin an inch. They were almost nose-to-nose.

"Well, this is glorious," the reverend said. "Gentlemen, and lady"—he nodded to the Orphan captain—"I am the one who is going to go discuss matters with the Red Rabbits. I have graciously allowed you to accompany me, but this is my meeting. And since I have nothing to hide, Lieutenant, I will extend my invitation to you as well."

Benvin turned away from Colin. "How gracious."

"And so I am clear, Lieutenant, I told these youths that I would only accept one from each organization. I'm holding you to that same restriction."

With his eyes alone, the reverend showed Benvin he knew exactly where Pollit and Tripper were. Blazes. This one was sharper than he realized. "So be it," Benvin said. "Lead the way, Preacher."

Dinner was three courses in, and Veranix was hungry and sweating. Whoever came up with this whole elaborate multi-course meal of pageantry and elegance and the most uncomfortable clothes in the history of civilization deserved an arrow in the eye. Veranix was quite literally itching to do it.

Every "course" was a minuscule portion of admittedly outstanding food. Veranix was expecting that with the Morsel once Delmin had described it. It had been some absurd concoction involving quail, aged ham, and figs that Veranix had to keep himself from stealing Jiarna's it was so good. Then the Mussel had been only two oysters from the northern coast, followed by the Curd: only a thin spread of a ludicrously fine and sweet cheese on a piece of bread so light it was almost air.

Delicious. Exquisite. And only seven bites of food so far.

Then there was the First Engagement, and Nontiss approached, even though Veranix had almost nothing to say to her. That didn't matter, because Jiarna was on point and ready, as soon as her attention was drawn away from Phadre. Phadre, of course, was completely engaged in the conversation with Professor Nontiss. The entire scope of the conversation went over Veranix's head completely, though the occasional Magic Theory term or Elemental Science phrase made it into his ear.

"Elemental compounds with untapped *numinic* properties?" Nontiss said. "Young lady, you are treading far out on a rickety bridge with those theories. I haven't heard such nonsense for several years, when—"

The vice headmaster rang the bell, and Nontiss made a polite withdrawal.

"Backward thinking," Jiarna muttered.

"It's not uncommon," Phadre said. "I had to dig through so many records and books to get some degree of backing for my theories. Some professors are set in their ways."

"Your friend Alimen for one."

"Professor Alimen? Not at all. He's been the biggest—"

Kaiana got up from her chair. "If you'll excuse me a moment."

Phadre, to his credit, noticed and stood up. "Of course." He quickly skittered to get his chair out of Kaiana's way as she left the dining hall. As soon as she was out of the way, he got back in his chair and engaged again with Jiarna.

Veranix didn't even wait for an appropriate amount of time, or excuse himself properly. He simply got up and left, though Jiarna took no notice of it.

"Kai!" Veranix called as he caught up to her. "You all right?"

She turned to him, her expression completely inscrutable. "I'm fine. Why wouldn't I be?"

"Well, you did storm out of there. I thought perhaps because Phadre was only talking to Jiarna."

"I walked out of there," she said. "And that was mostly to use the water closet. Though I was getting a bit bored by all that."

"Can't blame you there," Veranix said.

"Where did you even find that girl?" Kaiana asked. There was a hint of edge to her question.

"I really didn't, frankly. She more or less attached herself to me."

"You make her sound like an ailment."

"That's not incorrect." He moved in a little closer and lowered his voice. "She knows."

"You told her?" Kaiana managed to yell and whisper at the same time.

"No, of course I didn't. She found out. She has these *numina*-sensing lenses and magically sensitive paper . . . it doesn't matter. Point is, she knows, and she made me take her here tonight. What's your excuse?"

"Phadre asked me and I like a free meal."

Veranix shrugged. "Seems we're getting what we paid for it."

She laughed, lightly. "Are you all right?"

"Just annoyed. Mostly the outfit."

"You do look ridiculous."

"I feel ridiculous, so that's acceptable."

"Good." She waited a moment and added, "And since you failed to compliment me on my dress, I'm now off to the water closet. Which should take me the better part of an hour in this contraption."

"I'll leaving you to it, then."

A sudden burst of light—white and blinding—came out of the dining hall, followed by several screams piercing the air.

Chapter 12

COLIN LET THE RABBIT MUSCLE pat him down, finding six knives on his person. Which meant they missed two of them, though they were the hardest ones to get at.

He had to give good credit to the stick lieutenant. It took some fire to walk in all on his own, though he just glared at the heavies when they thought to pat him down.

"This ali reeks, Prince, and you know it," the captain from the Toothless Dogs whispered. "Ain't nothing right gonna come from it."

"Probably true," Colin returned. Didn't matter, they were in here now, committed to the preacher's plan.

Reverend Pemmick allowed himself to be frisked as well, but they found no weapons on him. He thanked the muscle for their good work, and entered into the Trusted Friend.

Colin had never been in here, as he avoided any place that wasn't Prince territory. That meant essentially the Turnabout, the Rose & Bush, and a handful of pubs on Carnation or Orchid, where he usually only went in search of dice players to fleece.

In all honesty, the Trusted Friend wasn't all that different from any of those, but to Colin's eye the lamps burned a little lower, the place smelled a little more musky, and it all felt too warm for his comfort.

That might have just been because he was sweating. This place was full of Red Rabbits, and they all were staring at the lot of them. Not to mention his guts were still in knots.

Whatever was going to go down next, Colin might not have numbers on his side, but he definitely had an element of surprise, because these Rabbits clearly had no idea what was going to happen.

"Barman," the preacher said. "Is your beer tolerable?"

"It's fine," the barman said, though he didn't sound like he fully believed it.

"Well enough. For myself and my associates." Reverend Pemmick moved over to one of the tables, where a couple of Rabbits stared at him dumbfounded. "My apologies, gentlemen. I need to have a few words with a couple of your associates, by the names of Keckin and Sotch—that is who I should be speaking to, yes?"

He looked at his collected group of Aventil captains for confirmation.

"I think that's it," Colin offered when no one else spoke up. He saw them, half curled into each other in a booth in the corner. "Ayuh, I see you two."

"What the blazes is this, Tyson?" Sotch asked across the room.

"Please, don't blame him for this," the reverend said. He leaned toward the table he had addressed earlier. "I'm terribly sorry, but we are something of a large group. Would you be willing to relocate for our discussion?"

The Rabbits at the table all stared at the preacher, then at each other, and then at Sotch and Keckin. They didn't object; they looked genuinely confused by the unfolding events.

Four-Toe broke the silence, barking out, "Show the Reverend of Saint Julian's some respect!"

That got them moving, on their feet and hands going to their knives. Almost, until they remembered Lieutenant Benvin was in the room. They gave another glance at Sotch and Keckin, who gave them a nod to disperse.

Pemmick took a chair, and the rest followed suit, Benvin taking the seat between Colin and the reverend. Sotch got up and took the last chair, leaving Keckin in the corner. The barman and a serving boy—a boy who surely had a fur coat in his future—brought over the beers and set them on the table.

Sotch was about to pick hers up when the reverend interrupted her.

"Let us take hands and give a blessing," he said.

Slowly, under the reverend's penetrating gaze, each person took the hands of the people on either side, and with the exception of the reverend, they all looked like they were holding a rotting fish. That's how Colin felt, holding hands with a stick on one side and Hannik's on the other.

"Dear God and Blessed Saints, we have gathered at this table in the name of peace. We have gathered so that speaking and understanding can triumph over violence and bloodshed. We are confident that, in your names, we can achieve this. Blessings of the saints upon us all." He smiled at the group. "And now everyone drink, from the glass of the person on your left."

He took Yessa's cup, and each one of them in the circle did the same, Colin taking Benvin's. Sotch looked a little nervous as she drank her new cup, giving a slight eye over to the bar as she drank. But the barman didn't come over to stop anyone, so if he had poisoned anyone's cup, he wasn't worried about it going to the wrong place. Or didn't care what happened to Sotch.

Colin drank anyway. The beer was watery and weak. That didn't surprise him.

"Can we begin this little dance now?" Sotch asked.

The reverend gave a glance to Lieutenant Benvin. "It's come to my attention, Miss Sotch, that you and your associates are considering new business opportunities. Ones that other parties feel might be detrimental to the neighborhood as a whole."

"And these tossers are the other parties?" Sotch asked. "Must really have you all sore, if the six of you are ready to sit with a rutting stick."

"I ain't," Right Boot growled. "This is sewage, all of it." He pushed back his chair and started up.

"Sit down," Colin snapped.

"Don't you tell me what to do."

"Please," the reverend said. "Let's work here. We have a great opportunity."

"Opportunity for what, you demented sod?" Yessa was the one who shouted. "There's only one thing happening here." She got on her feet and leaned in on Sotch. "You and the rest of your bastards do *not* start dealing for Fenmere. You do not give him a toe across Waterpath. You do and the Orphans will tear you up."

"You're welcome to try." Sotch smirked. "You speaking for your bosses when you say that?"

"Your bosses know your breaking the Pact?" Colin asked.

"That ain't your business, Prince."

"But why," the preacher said, raising his voice, "would you choose to ally yourselves in such a way?"

"Ally ourselves?" Sotch shook her head. "The hard boot is coming either way. You all can decide if you want to be under it or not."

"Wait, what do you know?" Hannik was asking. "What's Fenmere got planned?"

"That ain't my worry, Boy. If that's all you want to know, you can piss off. Why don't you all step out, while you still can?"

Pemmick raised up his hands. "Please, we can—"

"Enough of this," Yessa snapped, and then the back of her fist was in Sotch's face.

The tussle only lasted for a moment, as Rabbits came over, and Hannik and the Toothless Dog separated Yessa and Sotch. Blades were coming out.

"Everyone calm," Colin shouted. "Let's take a breath—"

Suddenly the room exploded with a cackling laughter. Lieutenant Benvin, still in his seat, was nearly howling, red-faced with breathless glee.

"You people—you're all so—how is it even—" He struggled to get to his feet. "I've been . . . the last month . . . and you're just petty fools . . ."

The laughter turned to wheezing, and then his red face turned a deep purple. Suddenly his mouth foamed and his whole body started to shudder.

"Poison!" Four-Toe shouted, and he punched the closest Rabbit to him.

The whole room broke out into a scrum.

Then came the smoke, thick and green. At least one server went running out of the hall to the main doors.

"What is that?" Kaiana asked.

"Cover your mouth!" Veranix shouted. He wasn't sure what this smoke was, but in his gut he knew that whoever was behind those first three attacks was hitting again. Instinct with magic formed a bubble around his entire head as he ran in. One step inside, he was surrounded in the green stuff, unable to see past his magical protection.

He also couldn't take another step. His feet were stuck to the floor.

The room was filled with sounds of gasping and choking. A hand groped wildly at him. Veranix grabbed hold of the person, pulling him close. It was one of the servers, screaming in agony, face covered in pustules of some sort. Veranix yanked at him, taking him off the floor and pushing him out of the dining hall.

Kaiana's hands were there, grabbing the server. Veranix realized he had pulled the man right out of his shoes. Also his own hands were being covered in the same pustules. He extended the bubble around his entire body, which caused the man to slip out of his grip.

"Don't come in here, Kai," Veranix said. "Get help."

"But what about you?" she asked.

He didn't answer. People had to be evacuated from the room, but probably all of them were stuck to the floor. The bastard was clever. Veranix tried to magically push away the gas, but it was too heavy, too thick. He could barely get any traction on it. Simple airing wouldn't do the trick.

He sent a blast at his shoes—the things were ruined now anyway—and jumped up to where, in his memory, the table was. He had a good landing, and from his vantage, could see the lay of things a little better. The gas was heavy, holding to the ground, so standing up on the table let him see above it. The lower tables were en-gulfed, and most of the people completely gone — except three on one side. Delmin, Jiarna, and Phadre were all standing up on a table near their seats, encased in a magic sphere of sorts. It looked like both Phadre and Delmin were holding that up, but it took every ounce they had. Sweat was pouring off their brows.

It was worse at the High Table. Everyone up there was stuck: the sticky substance on the floor coated their bodies completely. The smoke was only around their legs, but this wasn't any comfort. All of them were howl-ing in pain, unable to move.

And the smoke was rising.

Veranix ran on the table, almost slipping before he remembered his own protection also gave him little trac-tion, knocking over dishes and plates as he went, until he reached the three of them.

"Are you all right?" he called out.

"For now!" It was Jiarna who replied — the other two were too occupied holding up their sphere to even speak. The bubble must have also blocked sound, because he could barely hear her. He more read her lips than any-thing. Now that he was close, he could see the three of them had the pustules all over their faces and hands.

"I need to get Alimen. Maybe he can undo this!"

"No time!" Jiarna said. She pointed to his coat. "Brass buttons, salt and water!"

"What?"

"Quickly!"

Salt and water. There had been the salt boxes on the tables, as well as water glasses. Veranix dove into the swamp of smoke and groped around until he managed to find both. He came back up. "Now what?"

"Put the salt and all the buttons in the glass! Hurry!"

He had no idea what he was doing, but he knew that Jiarna was much, much smarter than he was, and his suspicions of her being the Prankster had completely evaporated. He dumped the salt into the glass, and pulled off the buttons from his coat and dropped them in as well. Nothing particularly interesting happened.

"Now what?"

"You need to activate their intrinsic properties *numinatically*."

Veranix would have hit her if she wasn't in the sphere. "How the blazes am I . . . what does that even mean?"

Phadre spoke through gritted teeth. "Flow *numina* through the cup, raw and unfocused. But lightly. Start at eight centibarins and raise it slowly to twenty-five."

Veranix had no idea how to reach eight centibarins, certainly not with any precision. "Delmin, can you feel me?"

Delmin nodded, but he looked like he was going to pass out. He was barely able to keep his eyes open.

Veranix held out his hand and started a light flow of *numina*. "You tell me when I hit eight!"

Delmin's eyes opened, his jaw clenched as he stared at Veranix's hand. Veranix nudged a little more *numina* moment to moment.

"Now!" Delmin screamed, sounding like it was the last thing he would do.

Veranix swung his hand at the cup, and began to raise the flow.

Something definitely started happening in the cup. The brass buttons rattled and turned white, and then bubbles formed in the glass. White gas began to seep out the cup, just wisps at first. Then it poured over the top of the glass, in absurd amounts, and as it came out, the green smoke dissolved. In moments, there was a clear circle around them all. Delmin and Phadre dropped their spheres, both nearly collapsing as they did. Jiarna caught Delmin before he dropped off the table.

The white gas spread further, and soon the green gas was gone.

The damage was done.

Servers and students, stuck to the ground, moaned in agony, their dress uniforms burned through. Their bodies covered in sores and pustules. Some weren't moving at all.

"Vee," Delmin wheezed, pawing at Veranix.

"I got you, Del," Veranix said, grabbing his friend. "You did good."

"No, Vee," Delmin said, forcing the words out. "I felt him this time. I saw him."

"What?"

"The server who ran. That was him."

Veranix looked to Jiarna. "Are you all right?"

She nodded, and Veranix passed Delmin over to her.

Delmin looked back up at Veranix, and a moment of understanding flashed in his eyes. "Go."

Veranix gave a last glance to the High Table, where all the professors were still trapped, including Alimen. He was moving, though his legs were horrifically damaged.

Veranix sprang across the table and out the door. Kaiana was still there, tending to the server he had pulled out.

"What—" she started.

"Call for all the help," he said. "I'm going to get that bastard."

Chapter 13

THIS WAS NO TIME to be wearing a dress uniform, even one that had already been half dissolved. Veranix charged out the door, down the stairs, and across the walkway, all the while drawing in *numina* for controlled use. He couldn't afford burning himself out, not now. He had to find this guy, catch him, and enough time had been wasted.

A server's coat was discarded behind a bush on the south side of the apartment park. Veranix took that as clue enough, and went in that direction.

Despite the urgency, despite his anger, he held a tight rein on the *numina* he was shaping, shifting his clothing as he ran. By the time he was past the faculty apartments, he was no longer in dress uniform, but full in aspect of the Thorn, including hiding his face under a shaded hood.

That cleared most people out of his way in a damn hurry.

A trio of cadets spotted him coming up, and drew their weapons. Veranix didn't break pace, instead leaping over the three of them—sweetening his jump with a hint of magic—and landing behind them without a missed step.

"Get him!" one of the cadets yelled, and then whistles were blown. Veranix was about to curse his luck, but it gave him exactly what he needed. Up ahead on the walkway, a figure turned in surprise, and then started running.

Veranix had him now. Even with the cadets hot on his heels, he was gaining ground on the bastard. All he needed was a way to deal with him once he caught up.

The solution presented itself as they approached the south lawn. The tetchball squad, in preparation for the Grand Collegiate Tournament this summer, had been practicing every chance they could this week. Under the light of the two moons and the oil lamps of the walkway, the squad was cleaning up their gear. That meant that a couple tetchbats were lying out on the grass.

Veranix darted right to snatch one, confident he could still catch the bastard. At the same time the guy reached into a vest pocket and threw something onto the ground behind him. Crystals of ice formed on the walkway, and Veranix felt a slight *numinic* buzz coming from the ice itself, not the runner.

In moments the walkway was covered in ice, and the cadets giving chase slipped and crashed over each other.

Veranix came at him from the lawn, and the man—Veranix could see now he was a man of at least twenty, maybe a bit older—threw something else from his vest. Instinctively, Veranix knocked it away with the tetchbat. Whatever it was, it burst in a ball of flame and smoke some distance away.

The guy was almost to the gate and threw down something else in front of him as he ran. This also formed ice crystals, but unlike the cadets, he jumped onto it and slid out the gate like a hawk on a fell swoop.

Veranix instead leaped up to a tree near the wall, grabbing a branch to swing over the wall of the campus.

This man, this waste of skin, was about to run down Hedge, perhaps hoping to get lost in the crowd. Veranix wouldn't let that happen. Drawing just a hint of *numina*, he hurled a blast of magic at the man. Not very strong at all—Veranix almost didn't want to even waste magic on him—just enough to make him stumble. Just enough to lose his lead.

Veranix was on him, bringing the tetchbat down on the bastard's right arm before he got the chance to pull any more surprises out of his vest.

The man screamed.

"No more tricks," Veranix said, raising up the bat again. This one was going for his face.

The bat didn't move. Veranix looked up, and saw a rope had wrapped around it, and was being held taut. Ten feet behind him was a girl—tall and muscular, dark hair and eyes, creamy brown skin, and a dark gray mask around her mouth and nose, matching the rest of her outfit.

"Even that one?" she asked.

Benvin's limp, shaking body fell on Colin. He caught the stick before the man hit the floor, more out of instinct than anything else. Was it poison? He felt fine—or as fine as he could—and no one else looked like they were succumbing to anything. Blazes, they were fighting like anyone's business. Four-Toe had grabbed Pemmick by the arm and kicked and gouged his way toward the door, while the rest were beating their way through the crowd of Rabbits.

Colin had a dying stick on his hands.

Blazes.

There was no way Benvin came here without backing

of his own men, and as soon as Four-Toe got out that door every Prince, Dog, Kicker, Orphan, Boy, and Knight in the square would probably descend upon the place, and if there was a dead stick—a stick lieutenant, no less—in the center of that mess, the rest of the sticks would probably burn it to the ground, and then do the same all over Aventil.

Colin grabbed Benvin by his green-and-red coat and hauled him over the bar, then jumped over it himself.

"You can't . . ." started the bartender. Colin shut him up by punching him the throat.

"What'd you give him?" Colin asked.

"Not . . . not . . ."

Right, it hadn't been Benvin's drink. Colin had drunk the lieutenant's beer, and the stick had drunk . . .

The reverend's.

"You poisoned the blazing priest?"

The bartender was too busy gagging to give any response.

A sudden slash of a knife got Colin's arm. Not too deep, but it hurt like blazes. The damned kid was trying to have a go. When he made another slash, Colin snatched his wrist and took the knife away. "None of that." He smacked the kid across the head for good measure on top of that.

"There a back door through there?" he asked the kid, pointing toward the kitchen.

"Ain't talking, Prince!"

Two more smacks.

"Door?"

"Rot in blazes!"

Colin threw the kid over the bar and grabbed Benvin's nearly still body, dragging him back to the kitchen.

"Think, Tyson, think," Colin muttered. What would

Vee do? He was so blazing smart. How would he save a poisoned man?

Get out the poison. Make Benvin sick.

Colin looked around the kitchen. A greasy little hole with a stove and pots and racks of supplies. Colin grabbed one jug off the rack and sniffed it. Vinegar.

Over by the stove was a dish of salt. Colin grabbed it and dumped it all—surely five crowns or more worth of salt—into the vinegar jug and shook it up.

Colin propped Benvin's body up, tipped back his head and poured the salty vinegar down his gullet.

If that wouldn't make a man empty his stomach, Colin didn't know what would.

In a matter of seconds, Benvin reacted, and everything came back out of his mouth in a violent eruption.

"Wha—wha—" he sputtered.

Colin hauled him up on his feet. "Come on, Left." Halfway out the back door, Benvin threw up again, and then again in the alley. Colin tried to get him moving after that, and found a hand on his throat for his trouble.

"The blazes you trying to pull, boy?"

"Saved your rutting life, stick," Colin said. "Rabbits poisoned you."

The stick loosened his grip. "Not me. I drank the rev's."

"I know."

He looked back to the door, where the sounds of the fight could still be heard. "We need to slam this down."

"We, mate?" Colin snapped. "Am I a deputy now?"

"Shut it, Prince." He let go. "I've got work to do." He stumbled to the mouth of the alley.

"You're blazing welcome!" Colin snapped.

"Be glad you aren't in irons," Benvin said. For a moment he stopped and looked back at Colin. "You'd do

well to get any Princes out of the square, if you can."
Then hand pressed against his stomach, he lurched into
the street.

Colin went out after the stick, though he could tell by
the shouts in the air, as well as the whistles of the sticks,
that it was probably too late to take Benvin's advice.

Kaiana had gotten the server Veranix had pulled out of
the dining hall sitting and awake. His face was a mess,
but he was alive, and if he was in pain, he was bearing it
well.

Veranix was out the door, chasing the man responsible. That was what Veranix had to do, of course. Which
meant cleaning this up was her job. No one else was going to do it. For all she knew, everyone else in the dining
hall was dead.

She looked into the dining hall, steeling herself for
the horror she was about to see.

The floor was littered with people—moaning, wailing,
covered in boils and pustules. The only people on their
feet were Delmin, Phadre, and that girl—she the best off
of the three of them. She helped prop Delmin up as they
gingerly walked on the table toward the door.

"Kai!" Phadre said. "Don't step on the floor. You'll get
stuck."

She looked down at the floor. Some substance—thick
like tar—was covering it.

"What do you need?" she asked.

"Cadets and Yellowshields, fast," the girl said. "But
they won't be able to do much without getting rid of that
tar first."

"You have any ideas?" Delmin wheezed out.

"I've used up most of mine," she admitted.

The moans and wails started to change into cries for help.

"We need to do something," Kai said. She looked down at the one server. He was barely able to move. "I'll be right back."

She ran over to the main doors to find the cadets wandering inside, looking quite confused. "Is something going on?" one of them asked.

"There's been an attack," she told them. "Many people are hurt, possibly dead. We need as much help as you can get."

"Yes, my lady," one of them said, saluting her. He nodded to his friend and ran off.

Kaiana could get used to that.

The other one followed her back to the dining hall. "Saints and sinners all," he muttered. At this point, Veranix's escort—Jiarna, that was her name—had gotten Delmin off the table and to a safe part of the floor. Phadre had made his way back toward the High Table, all the while calling out toward the kitchen. No one seemed to be answering back there.

"How much damage did this fellow do?" Delmin asked, as Jiarna nearly dropped him on top of Kaiana. He draped over her, and she dragged him out onto the floor.

"Veranix chased after him," she whispered. "Is he out of his league?"

"I have no idea," Delmin said. His eyes barely focused on her. "Kai? I may have found my limit for magic tonight. Or wine. Or the two combined."

"Yes, I think so," she said. "But what about Vee? If he magicked the fog away, he's probably already weak. Can he—he wouldn't have had a chance to get his weapons."

"He didn't magic it away," Delmin said. "Well, he did it, but Jiarna knew what he needed to do."

"How?"

Delmin shrugged. "She knows things. I need to close my eyes." He did just that.

Jiarna was moving about the table, checking each seated person as best she could from her vantage.

"You," Kaiana said, pointing to Jiarna. "Come here."

"I'm busy," Jiarna said. "If you didn't notice the crisis . . ."

"I noticed. I noticed you came out all right. Unlike the rest."

Cadets and Yellowshields came pouring into the hall. Orders were shouted, and they got to work getting the injured off the floor. Two helped Jiarna off the table, despite her mild protests, and put her at the door by Kaiana.

"I also got real help," Kaiana said. She grabbed Jiarna by her sash and pulled her out into the hallway.

"What are you—let me go—stop it!" Jiarna struggled, but couldn't break Kaiana's grip.

"We are going to talk, you and I," Kaiana said.

"Look, I'm sorry your escort found me more interesting to talk to . . ."

"Saints, I couldn't care less about that," Kaiana said. It had stung while it was happening, but her perspective had shifted since then. She pushed Jiarna to the floor next to Delmin. "He says you knew how to make this mess go away."

The girl managed to jut out her chin proudly, despite being on the ground. "That's right. I knew how."

Kaiana knelt down close so she could get in this girl's face. "So let me understand something. You bully my friend so he takes you to this event. An event that happens to be attacked by this prankster, and you just happened to know exactly how to deal with this thing."

"I wouldn't have known how," Delmin mumbled.

"Right," Kaiana said. "You knew, though. That seems very convenient to me."

"Convenient? What are you talking about?"

Delmin opened his eyes a little. "It was weirdly specific."

Kaiana had enough of this smug girl's attitude, and grabbed her by the chin. "Very simple. Did you have a hand in this?"

"What? No!"

She looked genuine, not that Kaiana completely trusted that. "So that guy who ran out of here, the one Veranix went after, he's not your accomplice?"

"No, he's not—and get your hands off me." She batted Kaiana away. "Why are you even—why would Veranix chase after him?"

"Because that's what he does," Delmin said. He chuckled weakly. "Give him a test to study for and he freezes up. But if he can solve a problem by punching it in the face . . ."

"Wait, wait . . ." Jiarna said. She looked hard at Kaiana. "You mean you . . . of course. The carriage house girl. Well done, miss. You fooled me."

"If you're fooling me," Kaiana spat out. "If Veranix gets hurt out there, I will take it out on your bones."

"Fine, fine," Jiarna said, pushing her way back up on her feet. "Really, he just ran out after the . . . remarkable."

"That still doesn't explain how you knew how to fix it."

Jiarna looked down to the ground sheepishly. "I didn't really know *how*, not exactly. But copper has magiochemical properties of dispersal, and salt for cleansing, and water is a universal medium for *numinic* activation."

Delmin was on his feet, popped up like a weed. "What

did you . . . how do you even know that? I've never even . . . magiochemical properties?"

Kaiana was glad that she didn't have to feel dumb on her own there.

"It's what I've been researching. Among other things. The research on this stuff is minimal, frankly, but I've managed to figure a few things out."

"Research?" Kaiana asked, though it was less a question and more a random thought. "So you've found some information about this . . . this sort of thing. Yes?" She looked to Delmin. "I mean, what she came up with and how these attacks were done involve the same principles, right?"

Delmin screwed his face in thought. "Well, I'm not sure. But it might be a start."

Phadre came out the door with a pair of Yellow-shields, who were carrying a stretcher with Professor Alimen on it. The poor man, he looked awful. His legs were covered in burst pustules, and he looked like he could barely keep his eyes open. Despite that, he reached out toward her and Delmin.

"Children, you're well? So much . . . I don't even . . ."

"We're fine, sir," Delmin said. "Fast thinking on Phadre's part kept the three of us safe."

"Well done, Mister Sarren. I might just pass you on your practicals. And I could see that Mister Calbert took extraordinary measures, but . . . where is . . ."

"He went for help, sir," Kaiana said. "He's fine."

"Good, good." He rested his hands on his chest. "I'm so sorry this evening was a failure for you, children."

Phadre looked to Alimen and back to Kaiana. "I'm going to go with him to the hospital ward. Is that all right?"

"It's fine," Kai said. "Take care of him."

"Thanks." He gave a glance at Jiarna, holding it just a bit too long. Eventually he just said, "Copper. Brilliant."

"I think the brilliance can spread around," Jiarna said.

The Yellowshields carried Professor Alimen away. Phadre gave a quick wave and followed after.

"Well, that saves us that trouble," Kaiana said. Best Phadre goes off so she didn't have to plan this behind him. "Delmin, go with her. Go through her research—"

"Hold on a moment!" Jiarna said.

"Go through her research," Kaiana emphasized. "I'd bet crowns against horse teeth that our prankster read the same books. Maybe you can get a clue who he is."

"How would that work?" Jiarna snapped. "For all we know he's from the other side of the country."

"No, Kai's right," Delmin said. "This is something personal. Whoever this fellow is, he either studies here now or used to. Come on."

Jiarna cocked her head at Kaiana. "And what are you going to do?"

"I'm going to see if I can help Veranix before it's too late."

Jutie knew Colin was keeping quiet about something. He'd only been a Prince for about a year, but that year was by Colin's side, sleeping just a few feet from the man. Colin had plenty of secrets, plenty of fingers in stews all over town. That was clear. And that was his business; he was the one with stars on his arm, after all.

For the past month, though, at least part of what he was hiding was the Thorn. Ever since Hetzer died, Jutie had on more than one occasion entertained the idea that Colin actually was the Thorn, and even considered that it was Hetzer, having faked his death or something.

The Thorn certainly seemed like a Prince, as far as Jutie saw. Thrashing with Fenmere, thrashing with the Rabbits. But he was also shorter than either Colin or Hetzer, so those theories were out.

"Where's your head?" Deena asked.

Jutie looked over to her as they walked back to the Uni gates. They had done quite a few walks, made some coin; it had been a good night so far. She was looking at him with concern, so it wasn't a rebuke. He must have been staring off.

"Stupid stuff is all," he said.

"What's the stupid?" she asked.

"Thinking about the Thorn. Like, what's he up to right now?"

"No clue," Deena said. "Maybe he's going to join Colin's chat."

"I doubt that," Jutie said. "I don't think he's the meeting type."

"You've seen him, right?" Deena asked. "Like, been right next to him."

"Yeah." Jutie shrugged, trying to play it off like it wasn't anything special.

Deena pointed to the gates, where a couple of Uni brats were walking out. "They look ripe enough. Should I take the lead?"

"By all means," Jutie said, offering them to her. Out of the corner of his eye, he saw a couple green caps of Hallaran's, and a brace of Knights, but they were working the gates cautious. Taking whatever pickings weren't first swept up by Princes. Jutie wasn't happy with that, but there weren't enough Princes working the gates to get it all. That was a mistake, but he wasn't a captain, and the other caps did what they pleased with their crews.

Deena put on a big smile and strode over to the two

brats: bloke and a bird, looking like they were ready to stoke a fire or two before finding a quiet corner to hide away in.

"A beautiful night to you both," Deena said, arms wide. "Finished your exams, did you?"

"That's right," the bloke said cautiously.

"Well done, well done." She leaned in, lowering her voice to speak more intimately. "You did pass them all, you think?"

"Think so."

"Then it's cause for celebration. Wouldn't you agree, my dear?" She addressed this to the bird.

The Uni bird was a little more game than her companion. Matching Deena's smile, she said, "I think I've earned it."

"I bet you have, dear." Deena wrapped an arm around the bloke's shoulder, giving Jutie a sign to come a bit closer. Now the bloke was flanked by Deena and his bird, and he looked like he didn't know if he should be enjoying this or not.

"So, mate," Deena said to him. "You want your lady here to have an excellent time tonight, I would hope."

"Of course," the Uni brat said.

"That, my friend, will take knowledge and coin. Now, you're quite fortunate—"

Deena wasn't able to move to the next part of her pitch, because a series of bursts and pops came from the gates. A sheet of ice appeared on the ground, followed by a tosser sliding on the ice. He reached the end and kept running without a stumble.

"The blazes?" Jutie said, only to see another figure leap over the wall.

He didn't have his usual gear, but Jutie knew the Thorn when he saw him. And the Thorn was going after the tosser.

That meant the tosser was bad news.

Jutie jumped and put himself between the tosser and the two Uni brats. They may not have agreed to a safe walk yet, but they had already engaged with them, so Jutie would keep them safe.

The Thorn came down on the tosser, with only a tetchbat as a weapon. The Thorn was able to knock the tosser down with the bat, but things went to hell when a new bird came into the picture.

Jutie hadn't seen her before she made her move—astounding, given that she was dressed to be noticed. Dark gray, almost black, shockingly enough. Mouth and nose masked. Sleeveless shirtwaist and buttoned vest, so she wasn't showing skin except her arms. Her arms were pure muscle, and she had gotten a rope around the Thorn's bat.

Jutie went for his knife, throwing true at this bird. The Thorn also let go of the bat, and it went flying at the bird.

She leaped into a backspring, never losing grip of her rope, and dodging the knife and bat completely. When she was on her feet, she sent the bat flinging toward Jutie. He didn't get a chance to dodge it; he took it straight in the chest.

"Saints, Jutie!" Deena said. She went charging over, fists up, swinging at the bird like a bruiser. The Bird blocked each punch with absurd grace and speed, and then delivered a kick to Deena's chin, getting her leg up impossibly high.

The Thorn had pinned the tosser with a foot on his neck, but now the bird was coming back at him.

This wasn't just a bird—this was a Deadly Bird, like the one Thorn must have fought last night. The Thorn must be doing something right, if someone paid that kind of coin to kill him.

Jutie glanced back at the Uni brats, frozen in place.

"Run!" he snarled at them. They were gone in a trice.

He didn't have a scrap against this bird, but he could still help the Thorn. One of the corner shops had a bit of awning tented up with a pole. That would work. He darted over to it, grabbing the pole despite the protests of the shop owners.

The bird had gotten the Thorn's arm wrapped in her rope, and was launching a series of furious acrobatic attacks on him. He blocked and dodged, but he kept himself pinned in place, trying to keep the tosser from getting away.

"Thorn!" Jutie ran over and threw the staff to the Thorn. As the Thorn caught it, Jutie tackled the tosser and pressed his face to the ground. "Get the Deadly Bird! I got this!"

"Obliged," the Thorn said, stepping off the tosser and spinning the staff around. Now armed and unburdened, he launched at the bird with a flurry of attacks.

The tosser struggled, but he didn't have much strength in him to get Jutie off.

She met the Thorn's attacks, dodging the staff and further entangling him with her rope. Despite getting his left arm and leg tied up, he managed to land a hit, knocking her to the ground near Jutie.

Still keeping his weight on the tosser, Jutie grabbed at her wrist. Maybe he could buy the Thorn a moment to get untangled.

"You're quite the nuisance," the masked bird said, and swung her legs around, wrapping them around Jutie's neck.

Before he knew what had happened, he was yanked off the tosser and dropped onto the cobblestone headfirst.

Jutie's whole world went gray and spinning. The last thing to go before he went black were his ears; a Constab whistle shrill blasted through the air.

Chapter 14

N O MORE GAMES. This Deadly Bird had made short work of two Princes, including Colin's boy Jutie. She was going to have to be dealt with, but he wasn't going to let the Prankster get away. He couldn't afford to underestimate either one. The woman was clearly as skilled as Bluejay, in her own way, and the Prankster had more than one magic-but-not-magic trick up his sleeve. Or in his vest, as it were.

Free of the bird's rope, and seeing that the Prankster was about to get back to his feet, Veranix needed to deal with the both of them quick.

He charged at the bird, planting the makeshift staff— again thanks to Jutie, bless that kid—on the Prankster's back to launch a kick at her. She dodged, which he expected her to do. She could move, that was certain. Like Bluejay, much about her reminded him of his circus days.

He had planned to swing up the staff after she dodged his kick, knock her down so he could dispatch her quickly, and give his full attention to the Prankster. But she adroitly flipped over his staff, landing between him and the Prankster.

She moved . . . she moved like his mother. She even had his mother's coloring.

Veranix only knew a smattering of Sechiall, the Kelli-rac dialect that elder Racquin used liberally around each other yet rarely passed on, but it was worth trying.

"Vek se sheel." Your feet work well.

She winked at him.

"Khe ni ra." They keep moving.

That confirmed it. Racquin and, with her moves, prob-ably a circus girl at that. Not his circus, he would hope. That would have been impossible, unless she joined in the past three years

She laughed and shot out her rope again. Veranix ducked to avoid it, only to earn a well-placed kick in the chest. He still managed to sweep the staff at her legs, which she ably jumped over. That didn't matter, because he struck true on his real target: clocking the Prankster across the head as he tried to stand back up.

That should keep him from running away for another minute or so.

The bird launched a full series of flips and kicks, and Veranix matched her moves to stay away. "So who are you? Thrush? Kingfisher? Crane?"

A fist landed dead center in his sternum, knocking him back and off his rhythm. Veranix stumbled and fell.

"Blackbird," she said, and pulled back on her rope. Ve-ranix hadn't even noticed that she had gotten it around his staff and his body, wrenching it and his right arm behind him before he was able to spin around and right himself.

She hadn't been able to get the staff out of his hands, though.

Constabulary whistles filled the air. They had been going for some time, but Veranix wasn't letting himself hear them.

She still pulled on the staff, and Veranix used her strength to augment his own, using a hint of magic to push himself even faster. That was more than she could successfully dodge, and he struck her clean in the chest.

Blackbird on the ground, at least for the moment, Veranix untangled himself from her rope and turned back to the Prankster. He was already on his feet and starting to run down Hedge Lane, toward Cantarell Square. Veranix gave a quick glance at Jutie and the girl Prince. Both were still breathing, and Veranix didn't have time to give them further aid. He only hoped when Blackbird got to her feet, she didn't take any revenge out on them.

Hedge was crowded, far too crowded for this hour, and there were now Constabulary whistles coming from all directions. Something was happening, screams and shouts ahead. Veranix tried to pay it no mind and focus on the Prankster, but the next block was filled with stopped carts and pedalcarts, and teeming with Constabulary trying to force their way through.

Whatever was going on, it meant the Prankster had nowhere to run. He scrambled up on a carriage, giving Veranix the chance to jump up after him. Both of them stopped in their tracks as soon as they saw the commotion: a full on brawl in the square of every damn Aventil gang, and a handful of Constabulary desperate to pull them apart.

"Blazes," he muttered.

He saw the Prankster, though, clear as anything. The man was chuckling.

Veranix jumped on him, wrapping the Prankster's arms behind him in a hold. He couldn't let him reach into his vest again. "You're not going anywhere."

A moment later, a rope found its way around Veranix's neck. "I was thinking the same thing," Blackbird cooed.

"Ah-ah," the Prankster said, showing off a vial of some liquid in his hands. He must have grabbed it from his vest before Veranix had him. "Best let me go, or this hits the ground."

Veranix tried to get a hand under the rope, while not letting the Prankster go. Especially challenging once Blackbird pummeled him in the back. He spun around, knocking her with the Prankster's body. Free to breathe, he said, "You'd kill yourself?"

The Prankster, in a strange moment of solidarity, delivered his own kick to Blackbird, knocking her down into the carriage bed. "This wouldn't affect you or me, boy. But it has a unique effect on horses."

And with that, he threw it into the square.

No fog or smoke came from the glass, but a fine mist. And as soon as it hit the air, every horse on every cart or carriage in the vicinity of the square looked up and made a very unhorse-like scream.

And then they all started to run. Including the ones hitched to the carriage Veranix stood on.

Colin didn't dare leave the alley. If there was another Rose Street Prince in this scrum, he didn't have an eye of them. He took out his last two knives. He might not be in the brawl yet, but the brawl was gonna come to him soon enough.

Constab whistles were blowing like crazy. The Riot Call. This certainly warranted that, but it meant sticks from every part of Aventil—maybe even Dentonhill and farther—would come running here.

Cantarell Square was a dangerous place to be, especially with ink on his arm.

The front of the fight was mostly Knights of Saint

Julian, having gone full force at the Rabbit heavies at the door. The street right there was the bloodiest, but everyone else was having a go. Dogs and Kickers were clearly using the whole thing as an excuse to be as brutal to each other as possible.

Colin glanced up at the alley wall. The back was blocked off, so up and over was his only way out. He didn't know the rooftop tricks of this part of the neighborhood, and he didn't see a good climb yet.

A hand grabbed his shoulder, and he almost put a knife in the throat of its owner, until he saw it was the reverend.

"My boy, is the lieutenant all right?"

"He's alive, at least he was until he went into all that," Colin said. The reverend's head was cracked open, blood running liberally down his face. "Let's get you someplace safe, Rev."

"Very little is safe right now," the reverend said. "And what about those people there?" He pointed to the square, where several neighborhood folk—not gang or Constabulary—were cowering near carts and the stage in the fountain.

"Blazes," Colin muttered. "You'll probably want something done about that."

"It would be the right thing to do."

The blazing right thing. He might as well be the Thorn.

"Fine. But I can't do it alone."

"None of us are alone, son."

"Do what I do," Colin said, hiding his knives again. They had to be gone for this plan. Not that he was sure what he was about to do would work. It depended on everyone brawling out there not only recognizing what he was about to do, but respecting it. He wasn't convinced anyone would do either.

He raised his arms above his head, crossing them at the wrists. An old sign, going back to the street wars in '94, and later a sign of the Pact itself. Hopefully these folks would know what it meant, that he was unarmed and not fighting.

He stepped out of the alley, the preacher by his side. He hoped that would make difference. One guy doing the Pact Sign was a loon. Two folk doing it, though . . . that might just get noticed enough to keep them safe.

Five steps in, no one had attacked them yet. In fact, a couple of Orphans gave them some berth to move.

"Shouldn't we tell them to cease their brawling?" Reverend Pemmick asked.

"Let's not push our luck here."

They were about halfway to the stage when Colin glanced behind him. A handful of other folk had joined in with the action. Mostly Knights—bless them and their strange loyalty to the church and Reverend Pemmick— and a few others who probably just wanted to get the blazes out of there. Not that Colin blamed them.

Pemmick moved out ahead to the first group of folk, helping them to their feet and encouraging them to take the same pose. Now they were a small island of calm in the crowd.

"Take them out down Bush," Colin said. It wasn't the clearest route out of the square, but it was the closest. He reached the stage, and keeping his arms locked in position, climbed up on it.

"Princes!" he shouted. "Pull out!"

Only a few people noticed him, and most who did were Orphans or Rabbits who used the moment to get a cheap punch in.

Someone else jumped up on the stage. A young guy, like Jutie or Veranix, except he was wearing Constabulary green and red. Armed with nothing but a whistle, he pointed a finger firmly at Colin.

"Stand and be held!"

"I ain't fighting, kid!" Colin shouted.

Whatever argument the Constabulary cadet was going to counter with was interrupted by a sound; a horrible cry piercing the air that no human throat could make. The noise was so strident, so disturbing, all the brawling just stopped. After a moment, Colin saw the source. Every horse in the area—attached to carts, carriages, and cabs—held their heads straight up in the air as they howled.

Howled like wolves.

Then they all ran, a stampede through the square, smashing everything and everyone in their path.

A path that led straight to the stage.

Horses, carriages, and carts surged forward. Veranix lurched back, and his grip on the Prankster slipped before he righted himself. As he tried to grab hold of the bastard again, the rope around his neck tightened. Blackbird was back on him, and the Prankster leaped from the moving carriage. Veranix could have sworn he was laughing when he went.

Veranix ducked and rolled back, forcing the rope to slacken and knocking into Blackbird. She hit him with a knee in the back, then two hard strikes in the shoulder that left his arm suddenly numb and useless. He tried to strike back at her, but all he managed to do was flail his arm in her general direction. She grabbed it and twisted him around.

The carts thundered through Cantarell Square, and people screamed as wood and metal and flesh crashed together. They plowed through the wooden stage in the center of the square, and for a brief moment Veranix saw Colin up on the stage, leaping out of the way of the onslaught of horses.

Someone else on the stage—Constabulary green and red—jumped onto a horse. Veranix didn't have a chance to see much more before Blackbird shoved him down to smash his head onto the seat rail. He brought up his good arm to stop himself, jarring his wrist. Blackbird switched her hold to get an arm around his neck, and pulled him into a tight choke.

Head spinning, barely able to breathe, Veranix drew in *numina* and burst it back out of his whole body, hard and fast. Ugly, sloppy magic, but it knocked her off him. Before she could recover, he turned over and hit her again with a focused blast, knocking her over the tailboard.

He pulled himself up, finally taking her rope off his neck. His right arm still wasn't any good, but he was starting to get feeling back, even if that feeling was pain. But he finally had a chance to get his bearings.

The cart he stood on was one of nearly two dozen, all thundering together in a stampede of mad horses that had already reached Waterpath. He glanced around and saw he was not the only one in this predicament. Three other carts were occupied. No—four, as Blackbird was hanging on to the shaft of the cart behind him. She seemed to be too concerned with staying alive to give him any trouble for the immediate future.

A young tradesman's family was on a shopcart close up ahead in the stampede, with the father desperately trying to get control of his beast, while the mother held on to their child with one arm and the cart's rail with the other. Another had an old cabbie and a young woman, screaming like crazy. And up near the front of the mess, the kid in the Constabulary coat—probably a page or a cadet—holding on to the horse he had jumped onto, trying to force it to stop.

Then there were the horses themselves. Veranix had spent enough of his youth around them to know that he had never seen anything of this sort. Whatever the Prankster did, it drove them mad. Wild frothing mad, and running together at a pace no horse would ever maintain without a rider giving them every bit of spur and whip they could muster. And yet they ran, ran like every sinner was at their heels.

Veranix's own cart was shuddering, the wheels about to fly off their axles. The thing wasn't built to handle this kind of abuse, nor were the rest of the carts and carriages in this mess. It wasn't long before all of them would be mangled in a mess of wood, metal, and horseflesh.

He picked up Blackbird's rope and willed it to coil at his hip, forgetting for a moment it was just a regular rope. It took more magical effort to control it than he was used to. No napranium rope or cloak, that meant no extra magic to pull from. Just his own strength, which he had already been pushing hard. The smartest thing he could do right now was jump clear and get out of this mess.

The wheels of two carts knocked, and in a moment they tore each other into shards. The wheels gone, both carts dropped and crashed, their horses slowed slightly by the drag. The horses behind them plowed into the smashed carts, one of them getting slaughtered by the wooden debris.

The woman in the cab screamed in terror.

No chance for the smartest thing.

A breath of magic to aid him—he had to use each

ounce sparingly—he jumped to the next carriage. He slipped, and his instinct to catch himself went to the wrong arm. He recovered with the good one, grabbing the side handle before his legs went under the wheels. A scramble to get up on the running board kept him from getting himself killed.

He went through the carriage to the other side, glancing back at the cart he just came from. No sign of Blackbird. She probably got off this stampede deathtrap while she still could.

While he was getting up on the dashboard, suddenly the carriage jerked to the left. He caught himself before tumbling off—something the cabdriver wasn't quite as lucky with. He went flying off, colliding with a lamppost.

The whole stampede had turned, now sweeping down Lowbridge. They crashed through shop stands and pedalcarts and anything else that got in their path, but fortunately people in the street had the sense to clear out. At this speed, they had about two minutes before they hit the bridge itself. That is, if they didn't go into the water.

No more time to waste. Veranix shook his bad arm, forcing feeling into it. His shoulder made a loud pop— audible even over the roar of the stampede—which hurt like blazes. Whatever he did, though, got his arm moving again. He got back up on the dash, ran two steps, and leaped to the occupied cab.

"Ma'am," he said as he landed. The young woman screamed, which he expected her to do, followed by senseless gibbering. She was clearly frightened beyond any capacity for speech, which he could hardly blame her for.

"Let's get you safe, hmm?" There wasn't much else to say. Not that he was sure how he was going to be able to do that.

He had a flash of an idea, which might do the job. At least part of it. Bracing himself on the cab, he gathered *numina* as carefully as he could. He couldn't risk burning himself out, but there wasn't time to waste. At least he was going to do something he was familiar with, which helped. Energy built up, he shaped it and filled the road behind them with the same sticky substance he had trapped the Rabbits in the night before.

The stampede behind them stopped dead when it hit, crashing spectacularly, horses breaking their legs as they went down headfirst. If anyone had been left in those carts or carriages, they would have been killed horribly, but the only one who possibly could have been was Blackbird. Veranix wasn't about to shed a tear for her.

"How—how—" the woman sputtered out. At least she could form coherent words.

"Stay safe, ma'am," Veranix said, jumping onto the horse pulling her cab. Two more bursts of magic snapped the harness, and the horse surged out ahead of the cab. He turned back, and gave one last gentle push of *numina* to slow her and the cab down to a stop.

Next, the family.

The stampede crossed Dashen. One minute to the river.

He threw himself, magically, off the horse and into the merchant cart next to it. It, at least, was filled with flour sacks, so there were worse things to land in. He got to his feet, ready to figure out the best path to get to the family.

Blackbird had beaten him there.

Chapter 15

V ERANIX HAD TO RISK MORE MAGIC, powering a targeted, stable leap over to the cart. Blackbird had already shown the lengths she would go to to get him—Fenmere's contract must be lucrative—so using the helpless family as bait was a perfect ploy. They were already huddled in fear, the husband clutching his wife and child.

Veranix landed on the cart. "Don't even—" was all he got out.

Blackbird's hand shot out, snatching her rope off his hip. In a moment she was winding it around the family, though her eyes were locked on Veranix.

"Pantix Throw on three," she said.

"What?" He couldn't believe what she had just said.

"Pantix on three," she repeated. Not that she actually needed to explain what she meant—he could do a Pantix in his sleep, and she clearly realized that. But why she was telling him that made no rutting sense. She finished tying the family up and glanced up ahead. The Lower Bridge was coming up impossibly fast. Veranix was about to strike when he noticed what she had actually done.

She hadn't tied up the family. She had strapped them in a Hesker Saddle. They were afraid, but not cowering. At least, not from Blackbird.

"One!" she shouted.

Veranix braced his feet, more than a challenge in this rickety, racing cart on the verge of collapse.

Blackbird turned to him. "Two!" He could have sworn when she said that, she threw a wink to the little girl wrapped in her parents' arms.

"Three!"

She jumped at him, and he got his hands up to push her feet up as she came at him. If it had been a show, it would have been sloppy as blazes. A throw like that one would have earned an hour of screams from his grandfather.

But it did its job, in that Blackbird went up in a high arc, her end of the rope in hand. Veranix had to admire her timing, because she hit the zenith just as they had reached a warehouse with a loading hoist. With grace that astounded him, Blackbird lashed the rope to the hoist's hook. As she dropped back down, the rope around the family went taut, and the three of them launched off the cart. Blackbird knocked into them as they went up, souring her landing. She hit the cart floor hard on her knee and shin.

Veranix glanced back for a moment, and the family hung safely from the warehouse hoist, while a whole crowd of Constabulary, Fire Brigade, and Yellowshields were following far in the distance.

Blackbird lay on the floor of the cart, clutching at her leg. "I guess you won," she forced out through obvious pain.

"Not yet," he said. The stampede was seconds away from crashing into the stands and displays around the bridge causeway. And the Constabulary kid was still hanging on to his horse. Now Veranix could see what he was doing, besides trying to get control of the mad beast. He had been blowing his whistle like mad, a warning for everyone up ahead.

Veranix bent down and picked her up.

"What are you doing?" she shouted.

"Something very stupid," he said as he got her into his arms. "It's been my theme tonight."

She had her arms around his neck, but this time she wasn't trying to choke him. Pushing *numina* through his legs, he wasted no time jumping off the cart as it crashed through a newssheet stand. He touched ground like a feather, a short distance from chaos, and lay Blackbird down.

If she had said anything, he didn't hear it over the horrible crashing and screeching as the stampede smashed through the Lower Bridge causeway.

Veranix drew in every bit of *numina* he could and shunted it into raw power and speed. The whole horror of the crash—everything around him—slowed to a crawl, each shard of wood or metal almost frozen in the air as he dashed around the bits of destruction. He only had moments, the magic wouldn't hold, he couldn't maintain it. It was like trying to hold on to an angry cat.

He only needed ten more steps. The lead carriage, the one with the Constabulary kid on the horse, had gone up the causeway, the mad horse had leaped over the railing of the bridge and was starting to plummet over the edge. Five steps, but it wasn't going to hold. Veranix jumped at the carriage and grabbed hold of the side handle.

A moment later, all his magic was gone. The regular speed of everything hit Veranix with a wrench as the carriage went over the edge. Its back wheels caught onto the railing, jarring for a moment as the rest of it dangled over the edge. Veranix hung from the side handle with one hand—the hand that three minutes ago hadn't been working at all.

Benvin was still hazy and nauseous. The past few minutes had been a blur, every moment since getting sick in the Trusted Friend a series of disjointed memories that had no connection to each other. The Rose Street Prince, grabbing one of the Rabbits, screams, horses. Only now were events flowing together in a constructive form.

Which meant he had no idea exactly how he ended up leaning against a lamppost with Arch pressing a cloth to his bloody head, with the square filled with casualties and destruction. There were quite a few Constabulary and Yellowshields, tending to those in far greater need than him.

"Should we have that?" he found himself asking.

"Have what, Left?" Arch asked.

"I—I can't remember."

"Maybe we really should have a 'Shield on you. Or take you to Lower Trenn."

"No, no," he said. "Where's Tripper? Pollit?"

"Pollit's taking command of organizing the lockwagons. Plenty in irons, gonna take a few trips." He lowered his voice. "I told you this once already."

Benvin had a vague recollection of that. Other bits were coming back. "Yeah, right. And Tripper got walloped by the stampede? Yellowshields setting his leg?"

Arch nodded. "He won't be on the streets for a while."

Wheth came running over—even in Benvin's state that young man couldn't be missed. Dark skinned, Ch'omik descent, the only one in Aventil's Constabulary. Perhaps in all of Maradaine. No one else in the station gave him time of day, but Benvin saw right away Wheth had a good eye and was hungry to prove himself.

"You all right, Left?" he asked.

"Arch thinks I should see a proper doctor, but I'm fine." He put on a brave smile for Wheth. "You and Mal get any shots off in this mess?"

"Hard to know what shots to take, frankly," Wheth said. "But we had a clear view of the whole thing."

"Good, because I have no clue what happened here in the thick of it. What can you tell me?"

"Well, as soon as the preacher and the Knight came out of the Friend, things exploded. The Knight yelled something about betrayal, and the Knights tore through the square at the place. Then the Dogs and Kickers got into it, but as much with each other as anyone else. Soon everyone out there was in it, and Arch made his move to get in the door."

"Plain lot of useless that was," Arch said.

"Jace and Saitle started up the Riot Call, and that was just about when you came out the alley."

"Right, right." He remembered a bit more about that. "We've ironed any of the Princes? The Prince captain?"

"A few, I think," Arch said. "But I don't think he's in the mix." He looked to Wheth.

"I spotted him for a bit, sir, after he came out of the alley; somehow he was with the preacher. He ran out to the stage, yelled something, and then Jace jumped up on him."

"Jace?" Benvin shook his head. That kid always took on more than he should. No fear in that one. "Did he iron the Prince?"

"No, sir." Wheth looked stricken. "That's when the stampede started. Crashed right through the stage."

"Jace!" Benvin pushed past them both. "Where is— Arch, you should have told me he—"

"I didn't know, boss," Arch said.

Wheth spoke up. "Left, that's just it. That stampede crashed through, and Jace, he . . . he jumped onto one of the horses. Maybe he thought he could stop the whole thing."

That crazy kid. "He thought he—" He looked around the square. "Do we have a horse? A pedalcart? Anything?"

"I'm on it," Wheth said, and he ran off.

"Come on." Benvin started walking in the direction the stampede went, Arch on his heels. If nothing else, this would be easy to follow. "Looks like this went into Denton, or even Inemar. We got anyone we can trust out there?"

"Not sure about trust, but . . . Jace's family is old guard Constabulary. I think his sister is on horsepatrol in Inemar."

Blazes. "He's got a brother out there, too, doesn't he?"

Arch shrugged. "It's a pretty big family. They're all over south side."

Benvin stepped up his pace, his stomach turning sour again. "Then let's hope we don't have to give them bad news."

Hanging on to the carriage door, Veranix could see the horse and the kid. The kid, every saint bless him, was clutching on to the harness shaft on the other side of the horse. The horse was madly thrashing the empty air, as if it was still trying to run to the water. Down in the dark river, Veranix could see at least three other horses had succeeded at that.

The carriage creaked. Those back wheels weren't going to hold very long.

"Kid!" Veranix shouted. "Can you reach me?"

The kid looked up at Veranix. Veranix realized he had absolutely no magic left, nothing. That included shading his face, a thing that was usually instinct. This kid had to be seeing him clearly.

He shook his head, "I couldn't stop it."

"Nothing could, kid."

He looked back up and scowled. "You're no older than me!"

Veranix pulled himself up, so he could get his feet on the running board, give himself a little more stability. Another groan from the wheels above told him they wouldn't last long. "How about we both live to be quite a bit older? Climb up that shaft."

The kid—definitely a Constabulary cadet, now that Veranix could see the details of his coat—tried to move, but almost got clocked by the horse's wild hooves. "I can't get up."

The groans were turning into creaks. Soon they'd become cracks, and then everything would plummet to the water. That horse was going to be the death of them.

"Kid—"

"It's Jace!"

Now he had a name.

"Jace, we've got to release the harness. I can reach the release, but you're going to have grab ahold of the carriage dash before I drop it."

Jace tried to pull himself up, but he couldn't manage to hold on with one hand well enough to reach the dash. "Can't." He looked down again, at the dark river and thrashing horse. "This is really it, ain't it?"

A loud snap came from above. Veranix didn't dare look to see what it was.

"Like blazes it is." The main thing preventing Jace

from saving himself was that wild horse. If Veranix couldn't release the horse from the carriage, he'd have to stop it some other way. "This is going to seem stupid."

"What?"

Veranix let go, dropping off the door down to the horse, grabbing part of the harness as he fell. He now hung right to the side of the thrashing beast.

"Are you crazy?"

"Quite," Veranix said. Holding on to the harness straps, he delivered a kick straight to the horse's head.

It didn't seem to have much effect.

"What are you doing?"

"Only idea I have left," Veranix said. Another kick. It didn't change the horse's behavior in the slightest, or knock it out. Not that he thought he'd have much luck in that regard. "You'd think Constabulary or someone with a rope would have shown up by now." Another kick. "Come on, Saint Senea. I don't ask too many favors from you."

A crossbow bolt went into the horse's head. Its thrashing stopped instantly. Veranix looked up to see a woman in Constabulary uniform dropping her aim. She turned away and shouted. "Get some rutting help! We got two people here!"

Jace was able to pull himself up, now that the horse stopped moving. "Corrie!"

The stick looked back down. "Jace?" She bent over the rail as best she could while screaming, "I need some blazing help right blasted now!" She leaned over the railing and reached out, though from her position she wasn't anywhere near close enough to grab either one of them.

Veranix managed to pull himself up enough to get his feet onto the harness assembly. From there he could

climb the rest of the way. Jace looked like he was about
to do the same, straining to reach the stick's hand. They
were still a few feet away from each other.

Another horrible crack, and the wheels snapped off.
The carriage dropped.

Veranix jumped on instinct, like every trapeze drop
he had ever done as a kid. He crossed past Jace as the
carriage fell, and grabbed his arm with his left hand.
Eyes still on Jace, he slapped his right hand into the
stick's.

A perfect drop catch, to make up for the sloppy Pantix
earlier.

The stick was screaming, in both terror and joy, as
more hands came down. A whole group of Constabulary
men got hold of them and hauled them back up onto the
bridge.

The Constabulary woman grabbed Jace in a heavy
embrace as soon as he was over, swearing the whole time
in ways that astonished Veranix. Suddenly the woman
grabbed Veranix by his shirt and pulled him in as well.

"Corrie, Corrie, don't crowd him," Jace said, pulling
Veranix out. "Blazes, he should probably have a Yellowshield look at him."

"Yeah, blazes, right," Corrie said. "You too. Go over
there, we got work to do."

Jace put an arm around Veranix's shoulder, leading
him down the causeway through the crashed carts and
carriages to the area where the Yellowshields were as-
sessing injuries. Veranix couldn't help but notice the
firmness with which Jace was holding him.

"My sister, she works nightshift horsepatrol," Jace
said. "She probably didn't get a good look at you."

"Why would that matter?" Veranix tried to sound unconcerned.

Jace stopped, and looked Veranix in the eye. "I should tell you, I think I got hit on the head out there, so I didn't get a good look at you either. You understand?"

Veranix nodded, though he wasn't sure if this Constabulary cadet was on the level or not.

Jace put a coin in his hand, and pointed down Dockview. "You slip off down that way, you should be able to take a tickwagon back to Aventil. But you better move quick."

He clapped Veranix on the arm, and walked off toward the Yellowshields.

Veranix didn't waste any time taking his advice.

Chapter 16

IT WASN'T NINE BELLS YET when Veranix got back to campus, but the gates were already shut, cadets on duty outside. That never happened. Of course, multiple assaults involving magic and whatever else didn't usually happen either, so Veranix wasn't surprised. Lilac Street outside the gates was similarly shut down. Shops had their doors barred, iron trellises pulled down. More Constabulary were walking the street as well. No sign of Princes or any other gang.

Over the course of the tickwagon ride, he had recovered enough to magic his clothes to a regular school uniform. He had no idea if he'd be able to re-create his dress uniform, but he decided it wasn't worth trying. If he tried to get through the gate wearing it, questions would be asked. Questions that would be awkward to answer.

Blazes, he just charged out of the dinner disaster to chase the Prankster. If anyone other than Kaiana really registered that, and connected that to the events in Aventil tonight . . . there'd be no more hiding his life as the Thorn.

Better to be an unremarkable student needing to get through the gate. He made his scarf white and blue:

Philosophy, the most populous field of study. He also gave himself four pips. Nothing more unremarkable near the end of exams than a fourth-year Philosophy student wandering up to the gates in an inebriated state.

Fortunately there was a drunk on the tickwagon who had thrown up on him, giving his ploy that extra bit of authenticity.

He stumbled over to the gate, walking past the cadets as if he didn't see them. He grabbed hold of the shut gate and tried to open it. There was the off-chance that it would be just that easy. "Blazes is this?" He threw in his best flat-voiced North Maradaine accent.

A hand grabbed his shoulder. "We're on lockdown. No one in or out."

"Well, that's absurd," Veranix said. "Gates stay open until nine bells."

"Do you have any idea what's happened tonight, friend?"

"Oh, I know," Veranix said. "I know I gave one of those Rose Street Princes a few crowns for a good time tonight, and, by every saint, did they deliver. I don't know where the place was, but the girls—"

"Please don't tell me any more," the cadet said.

"But you really should hear it."

"Stop." The cadet punctuated his order with a tight grip.

"Fine, fine," Veranix said, throwing up his hands. "Look, I don't know what's going on, I just know that when I left here, gates were to close at nine bells. It's not nine bells yet."

"Look, buddy," the other cadet said. "I know you probably finished exams, went out for some fun, but real trouble happened tonight."

"Let me tell you about real trouble," Veranix said. He

added some exaggerated finger pointing, which might have been a bit of an overembellishment. Not that he really needed to be examining his craft at this moment.

"Attacks, buddy. People hurt. Maybe dead."

"Dead?" Veranix almost broke character.

"I don't know, I just heard it was bad."

"Fine, fine. What does that have to do with keeping me out?"

"Keeping everyone out. There's a lockdown protocol."

"Yeah, yeah, but ... really, guys, I need to get into campus. Help a guy out."

"Can't be done," the first cadet said.

"Ain't fair, guys," Veranix said. "Really, I followed the rules."

"Look, you've just got to wait for the captain—"

"Wagon." The second cadet pointed down the street.

Indeed, one of the University's wagons was approaching. Veranix noticed there were several students piled in the back of it. A cadet—no, a cadet captain—was driving it. Clearly he had gone out to collect students in the position Veranix was pretending to be in.

And he hadn't gone out alone.

The yellow dress stood out like a beacon down the street.

"See," one of the cadets said. "The captain is here, and he'll check you out."

"Check me out?" Veranix asked.

"Look, the whole point—just wait, all right?"

"Fine." All this wouldn't have been necessary if he just had his cloak. He wondered if he should start carrying it with him everywhere.

The wagon pulled up. "Another straggler?" the captain asked.

Veranix shrugged. "I hadn't planned on the gates closing early."

"None of us did, son," he said. "Saints, boys, it's worse out here than in there."

"So we've heard," a cadet said. "But this one had a good time."

"Did you?" Kaiana finally spoke. "Captain, this is the one I was sent to find."

"Oh, is he?" The captain's voice had an edge of bemusement and scorn to it.

She came down from the wagon, her face unreadable. "Indeed." She walked up to Veranix, and before he even realized it, she threw a backhanded slap across his face.

That stung like blazes, but even through that he could tell she had pulled her hit. This was performance.

"You're a stupid lucky bastard, son," the captain said.

"Blazes, what is wrong with you?" Kaiana asked. "Saints, you stink of beer and sick. Did you vomit after your whoring? Or during?"

Veranix fought the urge to applaud. At the very least he needed to match her level. "Well, it may have been both. I lost track, frankly."

She grabbed him by the ear, and faked twisting it, which he played up for their audience.

"Captain, may I bring him to the Master of Protocol now?"

"Of course, good lady," the captain said. "Rest assured that I, at least, found your company worthwhile this evening."

She gave him a slight curtsy while holding on to Veranix's ear. "I'm so glad there's still decency on this campus. And I can trust in your discretion?"

"Of course, Miss Nell."

He gave a whistle, and the cadets opened the gates.

Kaiana led him in while the wagon started up behind them.

She didn't let go of Veranix's ear as they walked, but as soon as they were far enough away she reduced the force of her twist.

"I don't know what you did, but that was brilliant," Veranix said, still walking leaning to one side. "I presume we have to stay like this as long as we're in sight."

"Damn right we do," she said. She might have been enjoying this too much. "Briefly, when I realized that they were locking down the gates and sending out wagons to collect students, I knew I might have to do something to get you back in. This was after I had noticed the trail of destruction you left in your wake."

"That was the Prankster."

"Did you get him?"

"No." On her raised eyebrow he added, "Between the second assassin coming for me, and the stampede he caused, I was a bit busy."

"Fair enough. Anyhow, I told them a story of a boy who was invited to High Table, invited me as escortment, and then skipped to go carousing. Naturally they fell over themselves to help me find this terrible boy."

"Me."

"No names," Kaiana said. "That was the clever part of my plan. Because I didn't want to bring embarrassment on the professor who invited this deadbeat student, I asked the captain to keep this as quiet as possible." She glanced back and let go of his ear. "Are you hurt?"

"Nothing that will kill me," Veranix said. "But I'm probably bruised all to blazes." He remembered what the cadets had said about the attack. "How bad was it? The cadet said someone might have died."

"I don't know," Kai said. She anticipated the thing he

most wanted to know. "Last I saw, the professor was hurt, but alive. Phadre stayed with him."

"Good. And, how much story are we going to have to come up with about where I went off to?"

"Not much, I would think. It's not like anyone was asking. People were more concerned with the injured."

"Fair enough." They kept walking in silence for a while. "You were right, you know."

"Of course I was," she said. "About what, exactly?"

"That I have a responsibility to deal with things like the Prankster. He's going to do more, I can tell you that much."

"I know. That's why we're going to the library right now."

Colin got back to the flop to find it far more crowded than usual. Must have been almost twenty Princes in there, including two other street captains: Arrick and Grint.

"What's the buzz in here?" He threw the double once he was inside. "Nobody told me we were having a party."

"I didn't know you liked to be told everything," Grint said. "I like to be told what's going on, don't you, Arrick?"

Arrick nodded. "I find it quite helpful."

Colin sighed. That's how this was going to go. He went over to the table where some kid was sitting down. "Get out of my chair."

The kid vacated and Colin sat down. "The meeting was for one captain from each gang. That was me."

"Who decided that was you?" Arrick asked.

"Oh, you thought it should have been you, Arrick? Were you bothering to give a damn about Red Rabbits letting *effitte* and Fenmere across the Path? How about you, Grint?"

"I didn't know a damn thing about it!" Grint snapped. "What I hear is you took it upon yourself to hold a church meet. You decided that it was more important to tell Orphans and Boys than your own fellows!"

"Fair point."

With a whistle, Grint got one of the other chairs evacuated and sat down, and Arrick did the same.

"Glad to hear you admit that. The rest of this mess your fault?"

"I ain't owning it. Hell, I told the bosses—I even told—" He almost said Vessrin, but he knew to keep that to himself. Vessrin had crafted the mystique around himself; it wasn't Colin's place to diminish it. "I even told it straight to Old Casey. They thought it was a good idea for me to go. And things turned left, turned hard to the left, but that was on the Rabbits. Bastards tried to poison the priest, but ended up getting the stick."

"That lieutenant who wants to knock us all into Quarrygate? He's dead?"

"Couldn't be," some Prince in the background said. "I saw him out in the streets, after Colin there called for Princes to clear out."

"Yeah," Colin said. This he ought to fess up. "I . . . I saved the stick."

The room exploded in shouts and yells.

"Hey, enough!" Tooser was in the thick of it, having come out of the back room. He hit a couple of the kids with large-handed slaps. "You show some respect!"

The room quieted down. Arrick leaned in across the table, almost spitting in Colin's face. "You're telling me that that bastard Benvin was dying at your feet, and you *rutting well saved his blazing life?*"

"I made the call, it's what captains do. Tooser, we got anything to drink in here?"

Tooser scowled, but went to the pantry.

"Listen," Colin said. "Way I saw it, things were already going bad, and a dead stick lieutenant would have made things even worse. Instead, you know what that bastard Benvin knows? He knows he owes me. He knows he's still walking because of a Rose Street Prince. Tell me that won't burn him up."

Grint gave a slight nod, but Arrick didn't look happy. "A few of my crew still got pinched by the lockwagon."

"I'm sorry about that." For all Colin knew, so did his own crew. Tooser put out cups and a jug of cider. Clearly not enough for every Prince in the room. "Toos, are we—"

"We're all here," Tooser said quietly. "But there's stuff you should know."

"Well then, share with us!" Arrick snapped. "Because we're all Princes, and we shouldn't have rutting secrets here!"

Tooser sighed. "Jutes and Deena, they had some sort of run-in, involving the Thorn and another one of those Deadly Birds. They both got pretty well beat."

"What?" Colin was on his feet, his chair hitting the floor, and pushed his way through the crowd.

"We ain't done!" Arrick shouted.

Colin didn't pay him any mind. He went into the back room, where several Princes were dozing, most of whom looked like they had been hurt. Most not too much, but Jutie and Deena were both lying up in one corner. They were both bruised all to blazes. Deena's eye was swollen, and Jutie had a nasty gash across the top of his head. Despite that, he was grinning from ear to ear, talking to Theanne as she changed his bandage out.

"Blazes happened to you two, Jutes?"

Deena spoke. "We were at the gates when the Thorn showed up, trying to grab some other tosser. Then this lady—dark gray from head to toe, starts up with him. Next thing I know, this one here gets into it to help the Thorn."

"Damn right I helped the Thorn!" Jutie said it loud enough for everyone in the flop to hear. "You said it yourself, Colin. Hetzer died helping him. If he's good enough for Hetz to die for him, I'm getting in there."

"That doesn't matter," Deena said. "What matters is this lady cleaned the streets with our faces."

"Sorry about that," Colin said. "And the Thorn?" Veranix was out in the thick of it. Again. He knew that. Blazes, he saw it when the stampede started. That blasted Constabulary cadet had more stones than he did, jumping on the stampede. Veranix just went right past him and he did nothing.

Right past him, with a masked girl right there with him. Stupid, blazing stupid. He could be dead.

"Thorn was trying to stay on the tosser, Bird was on him, we did our best, but she was damn good."

"Course she was damn good, Jutes. She's a professional assassin!"

"I got some swings in."

"He got no swings in," Deena said. "To be fair, I got fully trounced by her."

"Hey!" Colin called out to the rooms. "Anyone know if the Thorn got killed?"

"What the blazes does that have to do with anything?" Arrick snapped. He had come into the doorframe. "Our folk are laid up like this, some are probably in the lockwagon, and you're asking about the Thorn?"

"Thorn is a friend of Rose Street, idiot," Jutie said, pulling himself up to his feet.

"You talking to me like that, scrap?" Arrick shouted. "You got stars on your arm?" He came in and took a swing at Jutie. Colin caught Arrick's arm before he connected, twisting it behind his back.

"Ease down," Colin snapped.

"Get off!"

A few folk—Arrick's crew, likely—all drew knives and knucklestuffers. Jutie and Tooser went for their blades.

"Hey, hey!" Colin shouted. "All of you, bring it down."

"Get off me!" Arrick shouted.

Colin shoved him to the floor and held up his arm. "Whose stars are the oldest here? Yours, Arrick?"

"You know they ain't," Arrick said, still on the ground. The fire seemed to have been knocked out of him, at least for the moment.

"Grint, how about you?"

"I'm not in this, man." He stayed in his chair, sipping his cider.

"We got any bosses down here? No? Then who is the blasted captain in charge down here?"

"You are," someone mumbled from the corner of the room.

"Anybody here *not* a Rose Street Prince?" He pointed to one guy who still had his knife out. "You saying you don't have ink on your arm?"

"Of course I do!"

"Then put the blasted knife away, idiot! We're all damned Rose Street Princes, and we don't need to be cutting each other!"

For a moment, no one did anything.

"Now!"

Knives and knuckledusters went away.

"Blazes, folks," Colin said, walking back out to the

table. "Look, we did not have a good night out there. And I mean all of us in Aventil. You want no secrets, Arrick?"

"It'd be a start," Arrick said, finally getting up off the floor. "That and keeping your crew in line."

He had a fair point there. "Jutes. Respect the man's stars."

"Will do," Jutie said. "He's not an idiot."

That kid, he'll probably be running the Princes when everyone else was in their graves.

"All right, then. Listen up, folks."

The whole room was on him now.

"It's possible that the Pact is dead. If so, Fenmere will get a foot over Waterpath, and it'll be the Rabbits who gave it to him."

"Then the Rabbits need to get knocked down," Arrick said.

Grint shrugged. "Looked like they got a good knocking tonight."

"Which is why I only said possible, folks. Might be tonight smacked some sense in to them. We gotta see, let the bosses know what's going on out here."

"You mean you tell the bosses," Arrick scoffed.

"Blazes, Arrick, if you wanna be the one who tells them, or you wanna come with me, I'm fine with that."

Arrick paused. Clearly he thought Colin was trying to trick him, and wasn't sure which way to go. "We go together, then."

Colin gave him that. "You wanna go now, or wait a bit? Sticks are out in force, let alone whatever else is going on out there."

"I suppose we need to let them know what's happening."

"All right. Rest of you folk, you're welcome to stay or

go as you see fit, this is a Prince flop after all. Most of you ain't spent much time here, so look to Tooser and the rest of my crew for the rules. Two big ones: do not touch the crates, and do not open that door for someone who isn't a Prince. We clear?"

There were general nods.

Colin knocked Grint on the shoulder. "That means you, brother. Look to Tooser in here, get?"

"Got."

"Good. Last thing, folks. I've told you all the Thorn is a friend of Rose Street. I want to know what's going on with him, and so do the bosses. Anything you hear, I want to know about it."

The faces around him looked confused, but people nodded.

"All right. Come on, Arrick."

Two steps into the alley they were treated to the sight of a stick getting his teeth knocked out in the middle of the street. At least a dozen Rabbits were doing the honors, right there in the middle of Rose Street.

That wouldn't stand. Not for one blasted second.

"Princes!" Colin shouted. "We've got a row!"

As his folk poured out of the flop, Colin drew out his knives and set his sights on the Rabbit captain.

"Isn't the library closed right now?" Veranix asked as they got closer. "And shouldn't the whole lockdown thing be a problem?"

"It is closed at this hour, yes. However, if one is friendly with Missus Heldivale—"

"Is that the head librarian?"

"Yes it is. You have stepped inside there, yes?"

"I've entered the building."

"As have I, quite a bit in the past month. She's a lovely woman. Do you know who else she's fond of?"

"Delmin?"

"He's astoundingly popular with her, as a matter of fact. So he is over there with your escorted of the evening. You do remember her, yes?"

"Jiarna? I was just glad to know that she's not the Prankster."

"She was your suspect?" Kaiana shrugged. "I suppose she's got the knowledge."

"And the anger."

"Did you listen to her conversation with Phadre?"

"Honestly, no. I lost track of it after they got technical."

"I'm not surprised."

"Shut it."

"You realize she's brilliant, but none of her professors want to even look at her work?"

"Yes, I know that. Really, she showed me her work this morning, and I can't imagine why they aren't throwing Letters of Mastery at her. Or Phadre, frankly." He thought about it for a moment. "Their work is almost the same, so why are they giving her a hard time?"

"I think it's because he's doing magic, and treating it like it's science. She's doing science, and bringing magic into it."

Veranix stopped in his tracks. "All right, how the blazes are they not throwing Letters of Mastery at *you*, by every saint?"

"Do you see a lot of Napolics going to school here?"

"I don't see a lot of Racquin either, but—"

"We aren't even going to get into that." Her face went tight and she kept walking toward the library steps. "This is not the time for this conversation."

"Of course it isn't," Veranix said. "There's no conversation beyond mission, is there?"

"What does that mean?"

"I mean . . . I mean, what are we doing?"

"We are going to the library to find out what, if anything, Jiarna and Delmin had discovered."

"That isn't what I mean!" He could jump into a fight or over the side of a bridge without a care, but trying to actually talk to Kai about . . . anything other than doing that would make his courage fly apart. "Look, when the Blue Hand came into your carriage house—"

"Are you kidding me?"

"I need to know what you—" was all Veranix got out when the library doors opened, and Delmin stuck his head out.

"Oh, you're here. I thought I heard you."

Veranix really wanted to knock Delmin in the teeth right then.

"Prankster got away from me," Veranix said. "Another assassin got in my way."

"Another?" Jiarna stuck her head out the door. "As in, a different assassin from some other occasion with an assassin involved. You've had call to deal with more than one assassin?"

"Welcome to the world I'm in, Miss Kay," Veranix said with a flourish.

"As in, just now, tonight, someone was trying to kill you."

Veranix went into the library. "Well, she was trying to kill me, and then our friend started a stampede of every horse in Cantarell Square, and she actually helped save people." On the shocked looks of the other three, Veranix shrugged. "I was as surprised by this as anyone, frankly."

"I don't think this is something I can be involved with," Jiarna said, striding down the hallway.

"You are involved." Kaiana went after her. "In case you forgot, someone tried to kill you tonight."

"That's not true," Jiarna said. "He tried to kill everyone in the room I happened to be in."

Veranix jumped in front, startling Jiarna. "And now you're on the team. What have you and Delmin found?"

"You do this—the three of you do this—on a regular basis?"

"I do not," Delmin said.

"Yes, I do," Veranix said.

"Why, by Saint Jesslyn? No, don't tell me. I do not want any part of this. All I wanted was to get the professors to agree to adjudicate my Letters Defense."

"You involved yourself, Jiarna. Now you're in. Fortunately, I do the heavy lifting, and take the heavy beatings."

"How heavy?" Delmin asked.

"I'm probably bruised all to blazes right now." Veranix opened up his shirt to show them.

"Blazes, Vee," Delmin said. "You're going to get killed doing this."

"Not tonight, though. And if I can help it, no one else here will. So what did you two find out?"

"That he—the Prankster, if that's what you want to call him—came through the library in the past few days and took things from the archives," Delmin said.

"What sort of things?"

Jiarna spoke up. "Part of the archives—the deep stuff, not the regular books—involve records on every Defense of Letters for the past fifty years. Even the defenses that failed. The defense packet gets meticulously copied—the defense, the rebuttals, the critique. Even research and correspondence."

Veranix wondered who would have the time to do that sort of thing. Maybe that's what the librarians did. "All right. And this matters why?"

"Because my research has brought me through many of these files, trying to find anything I could that had covered the same ground. I didn't have access to the failed defenses, but I found reference to a student from a few years ago whose work caused an accident at his defense."

"Work like this Prankster's?"

"I'm not sure. It was definitely along the lines of the integration of science and magic. I discovered them going through the correspondences of Professor Jilton."

"Who is Professor Jilton?" Veranix asked. She had mentioned him the other day.

"Probably the foremost expert on Integrated Mysticism in all of Druthal, who teaches at the Royal College of Maradaine. He's studied all of it—magic, miracles, Psionics—"

"Not real!" Delmin immediately said.

"Kept quiet by the government, suppressed by their own secret Circles."

"You're giving those theories credence?" Delmin asked, incredulous. "Secret circles of telepaths and psionicists working for Druth Intelligence?"

"If you've read the testimonies—"

"Not the time for this," Veranix interrupted. "You were talking about Professor Jilton. He teaches this stuff over at RCM?"

Jiarna made a meek shrug. "Or taught, since he's gone on a long sabbatical. He had exchanges with the failed student, because in the other letters I read he made reference to him."

"By name?"

"I think so, but I don't particularly remember."

Veranix wanted to scream. "You don't remember?"

"Yes, I'm sorry I didn't memorize the name of a failure who was mentioned in passing in a handful of hundreds of pieces of research I did, Veranix. Which was why I came here to look for those letters *right rutting now*."

Delmin audibly gasped.

"Can we not be so dainty when lives are at stake?" Kaiana asked.

"I know lives are at stake, but I do not understand why it is on *us* to deal with it!"

"Is someone else in a position to take care of it?" Kaiana looked at Delmin, and then the rest of the group. "I mean, let's not fool ourselves here. This Prankster, though he may have failed his Letters Defense, clearly has an impressive set of talents. Is there anyone more qualified to take care of him besides Veranix?"

"I'm not saying that at all," Veranix said.

"I am. He is beyond the campus cadets, he is beyond Constabulary or the Aventil street gangs. And we've seen the lengths he'll go to. We're only alive because the two of you were fast thinkers a few hours ago."

"I suppose that is true." Jiarna took the compliment with a slight smile. "But there's nothing else we can do right now. As I was saying, the letters from Professor Jilton are gone."

"So the Prankster stole them?"

"Perhaps. We've gone through some other materials, and there are pieces missing throughout the library—including several defense packets. All of which tie to my research topic."

"All things that might have given us a tie to who is he, in other words?"

"Essentially. I don't know what else I can do."

"I might know how," Delmin said quietly.

"Sorry, what?" Veranix asked.

Delmin swallowed hard. "I think I know how to figure out who this guy is."

"All right, then, let's have it."

"Well, I don't have it right now. It's also kind of a long shot, and it's going to take me a little time."

"How long?"

"Let me think, all right? I need to do some research. But we probably should not forget that tomorrow, you have an exam, I have an exam, and we need to be on hand for Phadre's defense."

"Where is that, exactly?" Jiarna asked, feigning a casual interest.

"I don't know right now," Delmin said. "When I have more information, I will share it with you all. But you'll have to excuse me that I place not failing out of school at a slightly higher priority. And so should you."

That was aimed with a stern finger at Veranix's chest.

"That's fair," Veranix said.

"Glad you think so." Delmin paced a bit around the library antechamber. "Look, we've all had a ridiculously hectic night, and maybe we should all just go to our respective beds and figure things out in the morning."

"Presuming our bed hasn't been gassed out." Veranix chuckled.

"Yes, presuming that."

"Mind you, I'd like to think I've given this Prankster at least a bit of pause before he strikes again," Veranix said. "I mean, for the most part, I didn't embarrass myself out there. I did give him something of a walloping when I was able to get a shot in."

"I'm sure you did," Kai said, though she sounded rather patronizing. "Though I'm surprised no one from Protocol has hunted us down for our clothes."

"Clothes!" Veranix almost shouted it. "Del, let me get a good look at you." Using Delmin's clothes for reference, he magicked his outfit back to a dress uniform.

"You can't use my courses sash!" Delmin said as soon as Veranix finished. "You did not make those marks."

"Fine," Veranix said, making the sash vanish in a whiff of magic. "Mine got destroyed in the attack."

Jiarna shook her head and made for the door. "I'm deeply regretting getting involved with you people."

Veranix followed after her. "Hey, listen, I . . . I want you to know I really appreciate how you've helped. Things in the dining hall would have gone a lot worse if it weren't for you."

"I knew what to do, that's all."

"I know. What I'm trying to say is . . . you made me take you here tonight to get your Letters Defense the support it needs. I don't know what I can do now to help you with that, but if you need anything, just ask."

"I will, don't doubt that."

"I don't. Just now I'll help you because I want to, not because you're blackmailing me."

She gave him a slight smile. "Good to know." With a tip of her cap, she left.

"So now what?" Kaiana asked from over his shoulder.

Veranix held the door open so they could leave. "That depends. Delmin, when can you get me that name?"

Delmin sighed. "Our exams are in the morning, and Phadre's defense is at two bells. Add in the legwork I'll have to do, let's say I can have it by six bells."

Veranix nodded. "Kai, I need a favor. I presume you

still have a stash of the money we've taken from Fenmere's dealers."

"The expenses fund?"

"I'll need a new bow by midday. Arrows as well. There's a bowyer up in Keller Cove on Craskin Street—"

"Keller Cove? There and back by midday as well as *doing my job*?"

She was right, it was too much to ask. He would have to do it himself, between his exam and Phadre's defense. It'd be tight, and he'd not have a chance for lunch, but he needed a bow out there. If he ran into Bluejay or Blackbird or anyone else, he needed to be fighting at full capacity. "You're right. Just leave the money at the bottom of the Spinner Run. I'll take care of it."

She sighed. "How will I know what to get?"

"I don't deserve you."

"No, you don't."

As the three of them walked through to Almers Hall the various patrols of cadets occasionally stopped them, but let them go just as quickly. Their dress uniforms probably contributed to that. Veranix gave Kai a quick crash course of what she'd need to know. The bowyer he was sending her to made a high quality product, so the main thing he was worried about was pull strength. Knowing Kai's arms were probably stronger that his own, he advised her to pick something that she could draw and hold for several seconds without pain.

She left them as they reached Almers, where the prefects let them in with little problem.

"You boys weren't hurt too bad?" Rellings asked them as they reached the third floor.

"It could have been worse," Veranix said.

"It was worse for plenty of people," Delmin added.

"Just glad you two are safe. Been through enough."

They went into their room and shut the door. "Is it my imagination, or is Rellings turning into an almost decent person?"

"Well, in two days, he won't be a prefect anymore. So he needs something to fall back on."

Delmin started to take off the layers of the dress uniform. "Is someone going to come get us out of these?"

"Honestly, if they try tonight, I'm going to thump them soundly across the head."

"I like your plan. But I'll need your help."

"Likewise." Veranix came over to unclasp things on Delmin's back. He had some difficulty raising his arm to reach things at the top of Delmin's shoulder. "In fact, my right arm isn't exactly cooperating anymore."

"How bad?"

"Well, I don't think anything's broken, but it's very stiff and twitchy right now. Help me out of these clothes."

Delmin started, and gasped more than once. Veranix was starting to realize how bad it was. "You're sure nothing's broken?"

"I'm in a considerable amount of pain, but broken bones tend to be a couple notches past 'considerable.'"

"This is a very strange scale you use."

"Life on the ropes, you learn to live with pain." A thought occurred to him. "Is there a circus playing somewhere in the city?"

"I really wouldn't know. Why?"

"Because these two girls who attacked me—assassins, really—I think they're circus girls. I mean, Blackbird, definitely, but probably Bluejay as well."

"Their names are Blackbird and Bluejay?"

"Swear to the saints."

"Well, they blackened and blued you up pretty damn well," Delmin said. "If I felt like your body looks, I'd be a weeping ball."

"I kind of want to be. But I'm going to have to push through, do my stretches before going to bed, or it's going to be worse by blazes."

"I don't even want to know."

"What's worse is, I am *famished*." It really was a miracle he wasn't falling down on his face at this point.

"That meal was a lot of nothing, wasn't it?" Delmin laughed. "I mean, delicious, every bite. All eight bites."

"Please tell me you still have a secret stash of apples in your wardrobe."

"Apples, dried lamb, mustard, bread, and cheese," Delmin said. He opened up the wardrobe and pulled out a crate. "This wasn't my first formal dinner, you know." He opened up the crate and displayed the bounty.

"Thank Professor Alimen and every saint watching for blessing me with the smartest man on campus to share a room with."

"You're quite welcome."

Chapter 17

FENMERE WALKED INTO his sitting room to find
it more occupied than usual for first thing in the
morning. Corman and Gerrick were on hand, as was
Mister Bell. The true surprise was Laira—Owl, as she
preferred now. Such company before breakfast might
indicate good news, but the looks on their faces did not
portend that at all.

"Things went wrong, I presume."

"Putting it mildly," Gerrick said.

"Well, it depends on your perspective, for some of it,"
Corman offered.

"How is there anything bright in this?"

"A few ways, actually, if you look at numbers . . ."

"Gentlemen, please, I haven't had any breakfast yet. I
presume there are multiple points of failure here to be
presented?"

"Then let me speak," Laira said. "So far my girls have
had two unsuccessful encounters with the Thorn. The
fight with Bluejay made quite a commotion—"

"I had heard about that, actually. I was quite amused
by the whole thing."

"But he got away from her before her partner could

close in. As can happen. Then last night he engaged with Blackbird. Circumstances were . . . different."

"Different how?"

Bell interjected his opinion. "There was a whole stampede through Cantarell Square—"

"Mister Bell, kindly keep your thoughts to yourself until I actually ask you to speak."

Laira cleared her throat and continued. "Briefly, due to other parties, the situation put innocent lives in danger. Blackbird abandoned her mission to save those people."

"Why would she do that?"

Laira shrugged. "My primary concern when I bring a new girl into my fold is skill. That means I will occasionally find myself with girls whose moral foundation isn't ideal for this work. Blackbird has no trouble killing her assigned target, or even those who interfere with her assignment—"

"She thumped some Princes who jumped in."

"Thank you, Mister Bell." Fenmere gave him a look that he hoped would put the man in his place. Surely Bell knew how precarious his position was since the Thorn kept embarrassing him? He must realize his main value was as bait at this point. Perhaps he did, and that's why he was being more brazen. Fenmere had to admit, he could respect a bit more spine in the man. That didn't change things, though.

"The point being, Blackbird is the type who takes action if innocent lives are in danger. As is the Thorn, apparently . . ."

"Are you about to tell me they *worked together* to save a little girl and her puppy? Some honey-sweet story like that?"

"No," Laira said, biting her lip. After an awkward

pause, she sighed. "It was a family with a little girl. I've heard nothing about a puppy."

"I paid you for this?"

"I am fully reimbursing you Blackbird's portion of the fee, regardless of the rest of the outcome."

Gerrick spoke up. "I presume you have taken steps to prevent this sort of thing from happening."

"Steps?"

"Removed this Blackbird from your employ, perhaps with some permanence?"

"I'm not one to waste resources like that. However, she is currently incapacitated from her encounter. So, in addition to your reimbursement, I will keep Bluejay on the hunt for the remaining two days, as agreed, and at no further cost, I will assign Magpie to join her."

"Magpie?" That didn't sound especially lethal.

"Don't worry, Willem. She doesn't have any moral code at all."

"I trust in your judgment, Laira. I wished everyone in this business handled failure with your grace and professionalism."

"Then if I have your leave?"

Fenmere gave a signal to Thomias to take her to the door, and gave a final exchange of pleasantries before she went.

"Can someone tell me why this isn't a disaster?" he asked as soon as she was gone.

Bell trepidatiously raised his hand.

"Yes, speak already."

"The whole business did create a mess in Aventil, including a near riot among most of the gangs. Knights and Rabbits, mostly, but everyone was in the mix. Plus that stampede. People are saying the Thorn caused it."

"He caused it?" Fenmere asked. "I mean, we know

he's a mage, but he caused a stampede? I've never heard of such a thing. Is it possible?"

Gerrick and Corman shrugged. "I suppose when magic's involved, anything is," Corman offered.

"Even magic has its limits, Corman." Fenmere made a mental note to look into the options for new magical allies, now that the Blue Hand were gone. Preferably some who didn't have the same mad agendas as the Blue Hand. Pure, boring mercenary mages-for-hire were all he wanted. The Firewings were looking promising.

Bell spoke up again. "That's just what some people are saying. Including the sticks in Aventil."

"Well, that is some good news. Whatever happened, his support there is wavering. Anything else, Mister Bell?"

"Yeah, well, between the two events with the Thorn, no one from the Rabbits has delivered on the money they owe us. I thought I should pay them a visit now, perhaps with some additional muscle."

"Agreed," Fenmere said. The whole business with the Rabbits was little more than ruse, but even as a ruse, appearances must be maintained. The last thing he needed for that was for anyone, especially the Rabbits, to think they could get away with skimping him. "Take a few of the boys from the cannery. But be discreet. No need for a big show of crossing Waterpath this time around."

"The open glove before the knucklestuffer?"

"This time, yes."

"Like the sound of that," Bell said. The man was probably frustrated with his role of watchdogging the Thorn. Baiting the Thorn.

"Well then, be about it." Fenmere waved Bell away, who wasted no time making himself scarce.

Thomias returned with tea. Fenmere sat back and sipped at it while looking at Gerrick and Corman. "So, what else is there to worry about? I'm not thrilled about the failure of this—Blackbird?—but we're getting our money back, and it sounds like a fair amount of chaos was wreaked throughout Aventil."

"And Inemar," Gerrick said.

"Sorry, what?"

"The stampede went through Aventil, down Waterpath, then along Lowbridge until it crashed into the bridge itself. Fatalities were surprisingly low."

"And the Thorn is being blamed for this?"

"Not in any official capacity that I can tell," Gerrick said. "We don't have many contacts in Constabulary offices outside the neighborhood, but from what we've determined, it's more whispers and implications. Mind you, outside of Aventil, most authorities are unconcerned if the Thorn is a real person or not."

Corman added, "In Aventil there are at least a few on the Constabulary who wish to throw the Thorn in Quarrygate."

Fenmere mused. "I can't decide if I would find that satisfying." There was something pleasant to the idea of the Thorn being captured, unmasked, and thrown in a deep hole. It would certainly break the spirit that had been building in Aventil since he emerged. "I wouldn't be surprised if he was connected to the Rabbits, and all this action against them is so much theater."

"There is another matter," Corman said. "It ties to the new chemist."

"Is he asking for more time and materials again?" After months of searching they seemed to have found someone who could master the Poasian process of distilling the sap of the *effitssa* plant into *effitte*. If it wasn't for the processing aspect of the drug—a secret his Poasian contacts kept tight—he would have been growing *effitssa* in hothouses right here in Druthal, and been able to make *effitte* without having to worry about further smuggling operations. Not to mention, there would be no need to keep playing nice with his Poasian partners over in the islands.

This chemist—a wiry nebbish named Cuse—seemed capable enough, though he kept making excuses and delays. In his favor, he had been able to make a version of *effitte* that Fenmere's experts agreed was high quality, even if the color was wrong. Unfortunately, making it also cost ten times the amount he could sell it for. Cuse swore that with a bit more time he could get the cost down, but he needed further raw materials for his research.

"No, he is not. In fact, he's gone."

"He's what?"

"Gone. Missing. It looks like the lab we set him up in had been wiped clean. Nothing left in there at all."

"We had four men keeping watch over him!"

Gerrick nodded. "And they're dead."

"How the blazes could this happen?"

"We're still trying to determine that."

This was wholly unacceptable. "When did this happen?"

"We last checked in with them a week ago," Gerrick said.

Corman added to this, "I went there last night. Near as I could tell from the bodies, they've been dead several days at least."

Several days. Which meant someone was able to stage a quiet attack on his property, steal equipment and a person away, and not even get noticed. In his neighborhood.

No one, not even the Thorn, had managed something that audacious.

"For future reference, gentlemen, this is the sort of thing you wake me up for."

"Of course, sir. I've put people on it, trying to find out just what happened. I did consider involving Constabulary, even. At least, specific people."

"No, I don't want that. Keep it with our own. Tight circle. In fact, let's keep it as need-to-know as possible."

Gerrick raised an eyebrow. "You think this was something internal?"

"I can't imagine something like this could happen without someone turning on us." He didn't need another complication. There was enough iron in the forge right now—Red Rabbits, Thorn, new mages, opportunity to move in on Tyne's operation in Keller Cove, more special packages the Poasians wanted to send in. He shouldn't have to flex his own authority in his Dentonhill. "In fact, is there anyone who needs a good lesson right now?"

Corman nodded. "Allsairs has been coming up short. Only marginally, but still."

"Good. Let's make a point of not letting that slide anymore. Our boys shouldn't ever be too comfortable."

"We'll take care of it," Gerrick said, picking up his valise. "We'll leave you to your breakfast, then."

The two of them left.

Fenmere went off to the dining room. Maybe this afternoon he'd personally visit some of the other captains. Remind them who the blazes was in charge of this neighborhood.

In morning light Colin was finally able to get a look at himself in a shop window reflection. The new cut on his face was going to scar badly, that was clear. He'd almost look like a Waterpath Orphan. Of course, he was lucky. Once things had turned left, at least three Princes— Arrick included—had gotten killed. None of his crew, thank the saints. Tooser had had the sense to keep the rest of them in the flop and throw the double. It probably had broken Tooser's heart to do that, but he had made the right call. Fighting Rabbits on Rose Street was one thing. If the Rabbits had gotten into their flop, that would be the worst breach possible, save getting into the basement of the Turnabout.

Colin had knocked down at least three Rabbits. Maybe dead, he didn't check. Constabulary whistles sent everyone scattering, and Colin found himself crashing in a flop he'd never been in before. It was a Prince hole, but a real slop of one. The kind of place where folks rarely bothered to find a backhouse when the corner of the room will do just fine. The Princes here were . . . not the type who were ever going to make captain. But they had roses on their arms, so they were his brothers and sisters. Some of them had been hurt in the fight, and one bled out before the night was over.

The streets were pretty damn quiet when Colin came out. Shopfolk were at work, but everyone went about their business with their heads down. No chatter, no laughing, no friendliness.

It was like walking through Dentonhill.

Sticks were on the corner, but their attention was on the bodywagons, still cleaning up the mess from last night. They didn't waste time with him, didn't even look twice.

First he checked on his folks. They were fine, thanks to Tooser, but Jutie was chafing to get out on the streets. The rest of them had the sense to stay in. Colin took

Jutie with him to the Turnabout, though. Easier than arguing with him.

The Turnabout was near empty. Hotchins sat alone, at the only table not knocked over. The only other soul was Kint, behind the bar, making a futile attempt to clean up the mess back there.

"Saints, Colin," Hotchins said as they came in. "The blazes went on out there last night?"

"All kinds of madness," Colin said, sitting with him. "What have you heard?"

"Heard? I didn't have to hear nothing. A whole passel of Orphans and Knights came in here, ready to crack skulls. They did a damn fine job of it, too, until sticks came pouring in. They dragged near everyone in the place out the door in irons. So what the blazes did you do?"

"What did *I* do? I didn't do anything but follow the preacher to a meeting to keep the peace."

"Well done, Tyson. A wondrous peace we have here."

"This isn't my fault! The Rabbits brought this down, poisoning the Constabulary Left! Everything went to blazes from that!"

"The lieutenant? You mean Benvin?"

"Yeah, Benvin!"

"He ain't dead, I can tell you that! He's the one who dragged everyone out of here."

Colin shut his mouth. No need to share that he saved the stick's life. After a hard stare from Hotchins, he said, "Maybe it wasn't a great poison, but it was enough to blow up the peace table."

"So why are Orphans and Knights coming after *us*?"

"I ain't got a reason for you, boss, other than the whole Pact seems to be torn to ribbons."

Hotchins turned to Jutie. "You got an idea, kid?"

"I don't know much, boss," Jutie said. "I wasn't in the mess at all."

Hotchins pointed to the bruise on Jutie's head. "How'd you get walloped like that, then?"

"That was from the bird who was trying to kill the Thorn."

"The what?" He shook his head, and then signaled to Kint. "Beers and bread, now."

Kint sighed and got to work, despite his bar being in shambles.

"All right, lads, you two are going to tell me *every damn thing* that you know happened on the streets the past couple nights, and we're going to go over it again. Then we'll all go talk to Casey, and you're going to tell him everything exactly like you told me. Got it?"

"Got." Colin grit his teeth. Kint came over and dropped beers and biscuits in front of them.

"Good. Now, kid, let's start with you. Tell me about birds going after the Thorn . . ."

The main problem Veranix had during his Rhetoric exam was that every ounce of his body ached. It took all his willpower not to moan and whine while he wrote argumentative essays on how building war-effort factories and workhouses in Maradaine's underserved western neighborhoods was ultimately detrimental to the quality of life for Maradaine's impoverished. Strictly speaking, the terms of the exam allowed one to make arguments on either side of the debate, but Veranix was familiar enough with Professor Chentlan's personal politics to know what arguments to make to stay on his good side.

Veranix finished the exam with only a few moments left on the clock, and after a hardy shake of thanks from Professor Chentlan—a good, jovial fellow if ever there was one, and Veranix was glad he hadn't been present at the dinner the night before—he made his way out of the exam hall without letting anyone see how much pain he was in.

Kaiana was waiting outside the hall.

"What are you doing here?"

"I'm in an oddly unique situation today," Kaiana said. "Campus has doubled their efforts at security, including employing professors, prefects, and university staff to safeguard against strangers infiltrating the campus."

"And this means you—"

"Being as I am highly recognizable by, frankly, everyone on campus, I am more or less trusted without question. Come with me."

"Why . . ."

"Watch." They walked just a short distance before two cadets and a prefect approached them.

"Where are you coming from, student?" the prefect asked.

"Exam," Veranix said.

"I've been given special escort assignment," Kaiana said. "He's involved in a defense presentation later, and Professor Alimen wants eyes on him."

"Carry on, then, Miss Nell," the prefect said, and then three of them walked off.

As soon as they were out of earshot, Kai said, "Everyone is calling me 'Miss Nell' today. It is bliss."

"Professor Alimen wants you to watch me?"

"No, I made that up," Kai said. "But they don't know that. Let's go."

"Have you heard anything about Alimen?"

"They let him out of the ward this morning, walking well enough. And Phadre says his defense is still on for this afternoon."

So she had already talked to Phadre today. "Do we know where that's supposed to be now?"

"I don't know about that; maybe Delmin does. He's at the carriage house already."

"That's where we're going?"

"I have a new bow for you. I presume you're planning on using it this evening. I figured you'd want to at least get a feel for it for a bit."

"I do," Veranix said. It was almost noon bells. Phadre's defense was at two, so an hour with the bow, lunch, and then the defense. And after that, Delmin would have the name.

"How are your bruises?"

"I've been hurt worse."

"When?"

"I think you underestimate the level of beating a life on the high ropes actually is," Veranix said. What he went through last night, Grandfather would have called "warm up stretches."

"I just want—" She faltered, her voice cracking. She stepped off the path, going under the shade of a tree.

"Kai, what is it?" He approached cautiously, not wanting to make too much of a scene in the middle of the campus, certainly not when it was in such an intense lockdown.

"Last night, I didn't even realize until I went to bed that you just *ran* out there without even a thought to your own safety. No weapons, no cloak, nothing. What were you thinking?"

"I was chasing the Prankster! I didn't have time to gear up and stay on him."

"I'm sure it made sense in the moment, but . . ." She turned back to him, tears in her dark eyes. "God dammit, Veranix, I can't have you getting yourself killed out there."

Veranix couldn't stop the smile that came to his lips. "Good, because I can't either."

"Don't make a joke—"

"I'm totally serious. Last night I was ... stupid. But part of that was because I was just chasing this guy. Tonight—tonight, saints willing, I'm going to be ready to hunt him."

"Good." She held her lips tight. He could see in her eyes that she wasn't telling him something.

"What happened?"

"While you were taking your exam, there was another attack. In the Deans' Tower. Some kind of smoke that then turned into fire—"

"How bad?"

She choked on her words for a moment. "At least four dead. One of the vice headmasters—Ballford—and an underdean and two secretaries. A lot more injuries."

He knew why she didn't tell him right away. Because he would run off, all rage and no plan, to punch anyone he could in a futile attempt to find the Prankster.

"Let's go see this bow."

They reached the carriage house, where Delmin was crouched on the floor, the napranium rope laid out on the ground in front of him.

"Why is that out like that?" Veranix asked. One of the most dangerous, valuable things in Maradaine, and they had it just lying around in plain sight.

"I put it out so Delmin could look at it," Kai said. "You know he can't touch it."

"Yeah, but—" Veranix reached for it.

"Don't!" Delmin snapped, grabbing Veranix's hand. "Something isn't right."

"What do you mean?"

Kaiana spoke up. "Like I said, I want you to be at

your best out there. I remembered the rope acting strange the other night, and that's why I wanted him to look at it."

Delmin pointed at a part of the rope. "Right there the *numinic* flow is all over the place. It's pouring and looping around and . . . I've never seen anything like it."

Veranix could at least see part of what Delmin was talking about—at least, he could see how there was a hint of fraying, scratches from where Bluejay's blades sliced the rope. "It got cut the other night."

"Well, it's—I didn't realize how delicate the weaving work was. It's far more intricate, and the slices caused damage in ways I can't even understand."

"I suppose asking if you can repair it—"

"Is utterly ridiculous, yes."

Veranix knew he should have expected that answer.

"So he shouldn't use it?" Kaiana asked.

Delmin shrugged. "Near as I can tell, it won't work the way it's supposed to. Instead of drawing *numina* to you, it'll just clog up the flow of it. You probably felt that."

"Kai's right, something was wrong with it."

Kai scooped up the rope. "Settled then. Neither of you touch this thing right now." She almost laughed when she looked at Veranix. "You look like you're about to cry."

Veranix didn't want to admit he almost felt that way. "I had gotten accustomed to it."

Kai went down to the Spinner Run, leaving the rope behind, and came back up with a bow and quiver. "Well, get accustomed to this, now."

The bow she had bought was a thing of beauty—he could tell just by looking at it that it was of finer craftsmanship than either of his old bows. He almost hesitated to touch it.

"Kai—how much money did you spend on this?"

"Ninety-three crowns, with the arrows."

Ninety-three crowns was more than Kai had been paid all semester. "We had that much in the—and you just keep it here?"

"Most of it goes to the church and the ward." By which she meant the Lower Trenn Ward, half hospital and half sanitarium, where the half-dead victims of *effitte* overdoses were cared for. People like her father and his mother.

He took the bow and quiver, slinging the latter over his shoulder. The weight was good, balance was perfect. Wood was likely yew, from northern Druthal. Taking position on one end of the carriage house stable, he drew an arrow and pulled it back. Draw weight was ideal.

He took the shot at the far wall. Then another, and another. Walking to the wall, he had put them in a tight grouping, right where he wanted.

"Good?" Kaiana asked.

"Perfect," he said.

Her smile lit up the stable.

Pulling out the arrows and replacing them in the quiver, he went back to take more shots. "Tell me about getting that name, Delmin. Because I'm told there is now a death toll."

"I don't know the name yet. But I know who does know it, and where that person is. I can go after Phadre's defense."

"Will it take long?" Veranix kept shooting.

"It's a bit of a hike, and then however long it takes there, and then back. I don't even know."

"I'll go with you, then." He knocked out arrows as fast as he could. "This is really excellent, Kai."

"Good," she said. "So, I don't think you should start

your hunt from here. Especially if you still have assassins after you."

"Right. Blackbird already saw me come from campus, so I should at least not take any more chances along those lines."

"I certainly would appreciate not having assassins or anyone else come *here* looking for you. I live here. There's a flop for rent above a laundry and press shop on Tulip." She took the bow and quiver from him. "I'll have your things squared away there by this evening."

"You've enough money still?"

"Enough for that," she said. "But you might need to get back to smacking around *effitte* dealers this summer."

"I do not want to hear this," Delmin said. "Aren't you going to have other duties over the summer?"

"Whatever Professor Alimen wants," Veranix said. "He's been hinting about me doing something for the Grand Tournament of High Colleges."

"Hinting what? We can't compete." Rules about magic students competing in any athletic competition were almost absurdly strict.

"I just do what I'm told," Veranix said.

"That is the opposite of truth."

"So," Kai said. "Bow, quiver, arrows, staff. Cloak, boots, vest, and the rest of the outfit. No rope."

"No rope," Veranix said, more than a little worried. The rope had literally saved him from Bluejay. If he was really going to go out there to get the Prankster, risk Bluejay or anyone else after him out there, he'd have to be in top form. No room for mistakes.

"All right, then," Kai said.

There was a knock on the door.

Kai quickly put the weapons under a tarp, and then went to answer it.

Phadre was there, with a paper in hand.

"Oh, morning, gents," he said. He clearly wasn't expecting to see Veranix and Delmin, and Veranix was nearly certain he was covering up his disappointment in not getting Kaiana to himself right now. "Good to see you. Will save me the trouble of hunting you down later. How are you feeling, Veranix?"

"Well enough."

"Right, well, I didn't see you after the whole . . . well, you know. Really well done in there, implementing Jiarna's idea. You saved a lot of people. The professor noticed."

"I trust he's fine."

"Well as can be. He can walk, but his legs did get . . . I can't rightly describe it. There were nasty boils, and . . . it was quite unpleasant, but he's bearing it."

Veranix was glad to hear that. "Well, we'll see him at the defense. Two bells?"

"Yes, and it's in the lecture hall, where Alimen teaches his theory classes." He chuckled nervously. "Presuming nothing else happens. We've had quite the poor luck, eh, gents?"

"Quite," Delmin said. "Maybe we should all have lunch, then? Leave Kai to her work?"

"Yes," Veranix said. "Capital idea."

"Right, yes," Phadre said. He gave another uncomfortable laugh. "But, well." He fidgeted with the paper in his hand.

"Is that something you need to give me?" Kaiana asked.

"No. Well, yes." He held it out to Kaiana, extending his arm as far as possible, as if he were afraid she might hit him. "I know it's an imposition, but if you could . . ."

She opened up the paper and gave a quick look. "I

can take care of this." Her tone was guarded, neutral. "You're sure?"

"Positive."

"Don't worry about it, then."

Kai's tone of voice left Veranix nothing but worried.

Phadre, on the hand, seemed relieved, exhaling deeply before clapping his hands together. "Yes, then. Lunch, indeed."

"Go, all of you," Kai said. "I've got plenty to do."

Veranix tried to hang back and get one last word in. "Kai, I just—"

"Go."

The carriage house door slammed behind them, as the three stood out in the hot spring sun.

"Come on," Delmin said. "We stand out here too long, the cadets will get suspicious of us."

Chapter 18

BELL HAD BEEN TOLD to take a few boys and figured four qualified as "a few." He brought his cannery overseers, the guys who went about on collections in the blocks around Necker Square. Good lads he trusted, but not ones he would ever bring directly to Fenmere. These guys, they would never talk to anyone higher than Corman, and that would only be if they were in trouble.

No strutting going into Aventil. It didn't suit them to look like a passel of Fenmere's heavies crossing Waterpath. No need to call attention to themselves, not until they reached the Trusted Friend. Just five guys walking along with the regular foot traffic of Carnation. They didn't even walk together, Bell letting the rest take the lead. Each would go into the Trusted Friend on his own—it was a Rabbit hangout but they would serve any folk who came along, as long as they weren't from another Aventil gang.

When Bell got there, the place had fewer Rabbits than he was expecting. Blazes, with his four guys, they were pretty evenly matched.

And Keckin and Sotch were nowhere to be seen.

"Where are your captains?" he asked the two Rabbits nursing ciders at the closest table. "Keckin and Sotch, or any others."

"Ain't any captains here right now," the Rabbit said. "Maybe a few over in Quarrygate. Some . . . elsewhere."

"I didn't ask who was here," Bell said, coming over and leaning on the table. "I asked where they were."

"Blazes, I don't know."

"Keeny, check his memory."

One of the boys came and grabbed the Rabbit by the scruff of his neck. Before Keeney could do anything, the Rabbit twisted out and jumped away from the table.

"Hey, hey, what the blazes? You ain't gotta give me hassle. We've been through some stuff here."

"Been through, been through," Bell said. "And yet your caps, Keckin and Sotch, they made deals. Money is owed. Do you have our money?"

"Hey, I don't know about that." The Rabbit held up his hands. "You can't put it on me." His friend also got to his feet, backing away.

"Why?" Bell asked. "Deal was made with the Rabbits. You two have fur coats. Maybe we should take what we're owed from you."

"Leave 'em be." From the door, an older man with four chevrons on his fur-lined coat. He was flanked by four of his own men. This wasn't a captain. A boss above them.

"So you're the one I should talk to." Bell flexed his fingers and sat down. "Glad to have you here."

"I got no cause to talk to you," the Rabbit boss said.

"No, I think you do. See, I'm just here being courteous. Money is owed to us. So I'm asking nicely for the folks under your charge—namely, Keckin and Sotch—to make good on that debt. Or you do it yourself. I really don't care how it's paid. The important thing, to me, is that this doesn't have to move beyond a courteous request."

"You want courtesy?" The boss sat down opposite Bell. "Then, *please*, forget about any money, any *effitte*, any deal you feel might be in existence with Keckin and Sotch. It's dead. Take your friends and go home now. While you still can."

Bell was almost impressed by the audacity. "Maybe you don't realize who you are talking to when you are talking to me. Right now, I'm not the man sitting in front of you. I'm not merely one guy here with four other blokes who could slap you around. Right now, you're talking to *Dentonhill*. You are talking to Mister Fenmere. Do you grasp that? And if Mister Fenmere says there is a deal with Keckin and Sotch, and they need to make good, then it's something you need to listen to."

The boss reached into his coat pocket and pulled out a vial. He placed it on the table. It looked like the typical *effitte* vial, except the liquid inside was bright red instead of lavender.

"That is why you're wrong."

This boss seemed so blasted sure of himself. Bell was almost impressed. "And what is that?"

"We're calling it 'the Red.'" He shrugged. "Not the most original name, but it works. It's as effective as *effitte*, more addictive, cleaner bite. Less trance with this stuff."

"Of course there is." Bell had heard this sort of talk before. Everyone wanted to believe there was a "safe" *effitte*, or some other sewage.

The boss clearly didn't care what Bell thought. "And we don't need to smuggle in a damn thing to make it. And we're the only one who has it."

"You really think so?" Bell asked. "Even if that isn't a

vial of sewage, how long do you think you'll have before Fenmere—"

"All right, we're done."

Just as he said that, his boys jumped on Bell's blokes, fast as anything, and pummeled them with thin dirks. Bell didn't even have a chance to grab one of his own knives before his men were down on the ground. Hands came out of nowhere, grabbing Bell by the wrist and neck. His face was pressed onto the table.

"You are so stupid," Bell said. "Do you have any idea what kind of fire you're going to get?"

"I can imagine," the Rabbit boss said. "Now, since I'm talking to *Dentonhill*, since I'm talking to *Mister Fenmere*, let me make something very clear. The Red Rabbits are through being kicked around by him. He comes for us he's gonna find more of this. If he thinks he's going to bring fire, we'll *burn him to the ground.*"

"You all are crazy." Bell grunted, struggling to lift his head off the table. "You really think you're going to stand up to him. Better tried and were buried."

"You have no idea what we've already done, or what's coming." The Rabbit boss walked out of Bell's sightline. "Put him somewhere they won't find him, until we're ready. And clean this place up."

Bell was ready to scream obscenities at them all. They weren't going to get away with this.

A hood went over his head, and before he could pull away, his hands were bound behind him. Hands yanked him to his feet and dragged him out the back.

Fine, let them have their moment right now. Before this was over, Fenmere was going to grind them up and paint the walls of Aventil with the paste of their bones.

Phadre was a sweating, distracted mess as they carted his equipment from Bolingwood Tower over to the lecture hall. Every few seconds he glanced over his shoulder, as if he expected someone to jump out at him.

Not that Veranix could blame him. Defense of Letters was stressful enough, add in how he had been in the middle of at least two of the Prankster's attacks, anyone would be an explosion of nerves. He was amazed that Phadre could even walk straight.

"How long do we have to set these up?" he asked for the seventh time.

"Twenty minutes," Veranix said, again. Which should be fine. They were all assembled and calibrated. Perfect. "You've got this."

"So it's twenty to two bells."

Veranix was about to say it was thirty minutes to two bells, but a glance from Delmin told him to be quiet. Fine.

"Where do you want us to place what?" Veranix asked as they reached the lecture hall.

"Line the instruments up on the display desk," Phadre said, eyes darting all over the room. "This is really it, hmm?"

"You'll do fine," Delmin said.

"Blazes, you've nearly got me understanding this," Veranix said. "That, my friend, is an accomplishment."

"I just hope we've accounted for all the variables. Positions of the moons, the sun."

"Did you chart each of the inconstant stars?" a voice called from the upper galley. "Though I haven't been able to isolate their individual gravity in terms of *numinic* shift." Jiarna leaned forward out of the shadows.

"I could probably point to each one right now," Phadre said. "Enevium and Kioxu are probably in a different place from our calibrations, but I think the effect would barely be in microbarins."

"Eight point two microbarins, actually," Jiarna said.

Phadre's face went pale.

"I'm only joking," Jiarna said suddenly. "Really, I have no idea."

"Let him be, would you?" Veranix said. "Poor guy is about to—"

"It's fine, Vee," Phadre said. "I'll . . . it'll be fine. Just help me get the instruments in place."

They placed each device—Phadre had names for each one, but they all went over Veranix's head—and Phadre double-checked that they were set up to his liking. He then rolled out the slateboard and placed it to the side of the desk. Veranix and Delmin stepped back as he paced back and forth between the board and the desk.

"I think that's it," he said. "You know your parts?"

"I do," Delmin said, taking a piece of chalk and standing at the ready by the slateboard.

"I've learned my cues," Veranix said. "Promise I won't improvise."

"Good, good," Phadre said. "Because I'm going to."

Before Veranix could ask what he meant by that, a few professors came in the room. At least three of them were in the attack the night before, and they were being helped by some of the others. Professor Alimen came in on his own, though walking slowly.

"Mister Calbert," he said hoarsely. "I'm gratified to see you are well. I'm given to understand we owe a great debt to your quick thinking last night."

Veranix offered his arm to the professor. "Quick action, perhaps. I left the thinking to people much smarter than me."

Alimen waved off his help. "And that alone is showing growth in wisdom. But you weren't to be found immediately afterward."

"Yes, well," Veranix said, "with so many people in need of care, I thought it best just to get out of the way."

"Still, I'm glad to see with my own eyes that you are unharmed."

"I'm glad to see you on your feet, after . . ."

"Yes, well, it was an unpleasant experience." Alimen leaned in and whispered, "Confidentially, I am cheating a bit with magic. Mister Sarren is surely aware. I may need all summer to truly recuperate. I will be counting on you, Veranix."

"I'll be here, sir."

"Good. I should sit and stop drawing *numina* to hold myself up. I would sully Mister Golmin's results. We can't have that."

He and the other professors took their seats at the front of the lecture hall.

"At your convenience, Mister Golmin," Alimen said.

"Thank you, honored sirs," Phadre said. Clearing his throat, he launched into his preamble. "*Numina*, of course, is the great mystery of magic and mysticism. We sense it, we use it, we manipulate it, but we are still baffled at understanding what it is, and what controls the way it affects the world, and how the world affects it." All of sudden, the nervous, sweating wreck was gone. Phadre spoke to the group like he was born to it.

"Only recently have we learned how to chart and measure *numina* with any degree of reliable quantification. We can measure its concentration in *barls* and its movement in *barins*."

Delmin started writing the vocabulary on the board, while Veranix took his cue and shifted a flow of *numina* at the barinometer, or what Veranix had been calling the barinometer in lieu of its proper name.

"Of course, how can we know that what we are

reading here is truly a measurement of *numinic* flow?" Phadre said, gesturing to the device. "Mages, of course, can sense it to varying degrees, but that is subjective. How can we show it in an objective manner consistent with the scientific methods of Natural Philosophy?"

This was a change from the script. Veranix didn't know what to do beyond maintain the flow he was providing, while Delmin looked completely confused.

"The best way might be an independent form of observation. Miss Kay?"

Jiarna came down from the upper balcony, already in position at the top of the metal spiral stairs. She was carrying her invention with her. Despite the shocked gasps from the professors, she spoke fiercely, not giving any chance to be interrupted.

"Combining a camera obscura with a lens treated in *dalmatium* salt solutions, the flow of *numinic* energies can be observed by the human eye." She held her device and opened the shutter. "With a plate treated in dalmatium nitrate that effect can be recorded."

She removed the plate and handed it to Professor Alimen.

He glanced at it. "Mister Golmin, I must say, people rarely take such risks with their Letters Defense. I am quite put out by this brazen behavior."

"Sir, if I could— " Phadre started.

"That said," Alimen added, holding up the plate, "you and Miss Kay have my curiosity piqued. Pray to your saints you maintain that. Continue."

Giving the slightest smile to Jiarna as she came over to the slateboard, Phadre continued with his speech.

The holding cells of the Aventil Stationhouse were overflowing. Benvin literally had nowhere else to put another prisoner. Cells were packed, and the injured prisoners were over in the ward under custody. No one was going to be moving for a while, at least not until he could get charges laid and bodies put in front of a jurist. The representative from the City Protector's Office was taking his time getting down here.

Which meant the patrolmen were all grumbling at having to deal with actual work. Saints forbid they have arrests, they clear the streets. Right now, every gang in Aventil was hurting, a situation which pleased Benvin to no end. The patrolmen didn't like it, and neither did the other lieutenants. A few of them had been getting some kind of butter to look the other way, most likely.

Benvin didn't give one blaze about that. Last night he cracked the window, and soon he would shatter it.

"We got numbers and names yet?" he asked as Arch approached.

"Getting there," Arch said. "We're still sorting things out."

"I wanna start having sit-downs with captains, if we have any. Do we?"

"At least a couple. I know that Waterpath Orphan captain is in there, since she gave me this gift." Arch pointed to a gash stretching from chin to cheek. "That's gonna leave a mark."

Jace limped over from a back room, carrying a sheaf of papers.

"I told you to take the bleeding day," Benvin said. The kid had been through enough, barely surviving the stampede that the Thorn had probably caused.

"Did you take the day, sir? Your night was worse than mine."

"I've got too much to do," Benvin said.

"Then I'm here to work. I'm not going to let a few broken ribs stop me."

"Kid," Arch said, "you almost died last night."

"So did the Left, and so did Tripper. Yet they're both on duty. I'm not shaming myself by not doing likewise."

Benvin didn't let a smile show on his face, but he was proud of the kid. With most of his family sporting the green and red, Jace wasn't about to let anyone say he wasn't worthy of it. That was why Benvin had chosen Jace for his team.

"Fine, then. Run through the names and numbers with Arch. The City Protector's office is going to want to know who we're gonna charge with what, and if we don't have the lines all crossed, half these folks are gonna get turned back out on the street."

"Captain is of half a mind to do that already," Arch said.

"Can't blame him. Blazes, I'd bet half the folks in there will claim they were just defending themselves, and they'd probably have a point."

Mal came up from the stairwell. "Hey, Left? One of the Orphan captains apparently wants to talk."

"Wants to?" That was a first.

"Only to you, though."

"Is it the girl who was at the meeting? What was her name?"

"Yessa, or something like that."

That sounded right. He didn't have all the various bosses and captains of the seven gangs memorized. That's why he had files and slateboards in his task room.

He made his way to the interrogation room, noting how

empty the rest of the stationhouse was. Captain Holcomb was fuming mad about how crazy things were on the streets last night, putting just about every body he could on patrol. He had even forced Wheth and Pollit out there, and only didn't do the same to Mal and Arch because of all the folks in the lockup. Holcomb was aching to crack apart Benvin's team. "Your little task force has done enough."

The girl—the Waterpath Orphan with her captain's scars across her cheek—sat in irons at the desk. "Not bad little flop you have here, Left," she said as he came in. "Me and my Orphans got a decent breakfast for once."

"Glad to oblige," Benvin said, sitting across from her. "You have something to say?"

"Well, as much as we've enjoyed it, me and the other Orphans would like to get back to our business."

"What business is that? Another row out there with the Rabbits?"

"Rabbits will get theirs, but that's not our problem. None of this is our problem, and you know that."

"How do you think that?" Benvin asked.

"Look, stick. Whatever is happening out there, whatever happened last night, Orphans ain't a part of it. All I did last night is fight back when a fight started on me. Ain't that my right? You were there. You were poisoned, and the Rabbits jumped. I didn't even want to be there."

"So why were you?"

"Other gangs sitting down, with the reverend mediating, and no Orphans at the table? That ain't good for us, either. But you got to ask, stick, why'd we have the sit down?"

"Rabbits looking to deal in *effitte*, I thought."

"Are they? That's what Tyson said, but I didn't see none of that."

"Tyson. Colin Tyson, the Rose Street Prince?"

"Yeah. He called that first church meet to bring in

the rest of us. But all we had was his say-so about the Rabbits turning on the Pact, letting Fenmere cross the 'Path."

Fenmere. The captain had made it perfectly clear that Fenmere, over in Dentonhill, was not Benvin's problem. The Constabulary force at that stationhouse was more than capable, according to Holcomb. Benvin had done some digging around, and as far as he could tell, the only sticks who weren't hopelessly corrupt had been killed on duty last month.

"So what are you saying?"

"Tyson started this whole row with the Rabbits, and where is he?"

He was still on the street, which Benvin regretted. The kid had pulled him out and saved him, but Yessa was right. Was he trying to play some long game to get everyone else to take out the Rabbits? "You think this is all his ploy?"

"I've known Tyson a while, ain't his style. But the one I don't know is this Thorn."

"What about the Thorn?"

"Near as I know, the Thorn is the one who told Tyson about the Rabbits selling *effitte*. And the Princes listen to him, for some reason. Or, at least, Tyson does."

"Why?"

"You've got me there," Yessa said. "So the way I figure, the Thorn has his whole thing with Fenmere. Uses that to get the Princes to listen to him. Once he has them, he uses that to set them on the Rabbits, and with that, the rest of us on each other."

Girl had a point. That whole stampede business could have been the Thorn trying to cut down all the gangs at once. Blazes, for all they knew, the Thorn's whole "war" with Fenmere might be some crazy show.

"You know the streets are a mess right now, hmm? I let you and yours back out there, what do I get?"

She leaned in over the table and smiled in a way that would be seductive if the girl didn't have a cut-up face. "What do you want?"

"Safe streets."

She smirked and leaned back. "You think I can pull that off?"

"I think you can call a church meet or something. I think you can get people talking. If nothing else, you can get Orphans off the street. One less random factor in all this."

"Maybe."

"And maybe you'll keep talking to me once you're out there."

"Now you're crazy, Left."

"Maybe I am. Maybe I'm so crazy I'll swear to the City Protector and the magistrates that you started the brawl in the Trusted Friend."

"Blazes, that's a lie!" she snapped. "You couldn't have even seen how things started!"

"You think? Possibly. But the word of a Constabulary lieutenant means a lot in court if it isn't gainsaid. And who is gonna do that for an Orphan captain? The Rabbits?"

"The preacher would, and you know it."

"Maybe he would. Provided he survives this."

"I ain't turning on the Orphans."

That gave him just enough to work with.

"Then don't. Get me word on what the rest are doing. What the Thorn is doing. Because, believe me, I want to put *him* in Quarrygate far more than any of your Orphans."

She sat silent for a while. He had seen enough to know she was on the hook.

Someone pounded on the door. Arch popped his head in. "Boss, we've got a huge row on Waterpath and Lily."

"What?" That was Yessa. Didn't surprise Benvin one bit. Right there was where Orphan and Rabbit territory met. "They fighting with Orphans?"

"I don't keep track of all that, bird," Arch said. "Riot Call is out, and we've got to get in there."

Benvin got up. "Think on it, girl. When I get back, tell me where you want to sleep tonight."

He left the room, and found himself going down the hallway with Arch and Mal flanking him. "Let's go in hard on this, boys. I want riot coats and helmets, and I want lockwagons loaded up with every blazing ganger we knock down."

"Running out of space to put them, boss," Arch said.

"Cram the bastards in." At this point, he couldn't give a damn about Orphans or Rabbits or Princes—though he'd lock them all up if they gave him the excuse.

But he'd be damned if he wasn't going to take in the Thorn before the week was out.

Words and numbers and terms Veranix didn't understand flew back and forth. Professors asked question after question, and neither Phadre nor Jiarna faltered in response, though they often tackled opposite sides of the question—Phadre the magical theories in scientific terms, Jiarna talking the scientific analysis of magic. Delmin scrawled on the board when requested, and it struck Veranix that he had long since lost his footing in this presentation.

Veranix struggled to keep up with the aspects of the demonstration that still applied, and followed instructions when told to channel *numina* toward one of the devices.

"Which leads us to the inevitable conclusion," Phadre said, though he was saying something Veranix had never heard before in rehearsing. If anything, it was a conclusion he was reaching at this very moment, fueled by his own back and forth with Jiarna. "That there is a cosmological body that affects *numinic* flow which we have yet to account for."

"Presuming that, how could such a thing exist?" asked one of the professors—an astronomy one, if Veranix were to guess. "I can accept there are things we haven't discovered, but where might it be found? Or are you saying it can't be seen?"

"It can't," Jiarna said. "But its effects can be. Namely, in the Winged Convergence, which is an impossible event."

"A Winged Convergence is clearly not impossible, young lady, as we've seen it," Professor Alimen said.

"Poorly phrased, sir. It ought to be impossible, but as it clearly does occur—"

"And has a profound influence on *numina*—" Phadre added.

"This *numinic*-influencing body must also affect the light of Onali and Namali, refracting them to appear to converge at a time when they ought to be in completely different places in the sky."

Veranix added his own contribution, magicking up a visualization of Jiarna's model, floating in the air next to her. She glanced at it briefly, and then gestured to the two moons on the model.

"This is a radical theory," the astronomy professor said. "Though, to be honest, no more radical than several other popular theories regarding Winged Convergences."

"True," said another professor.

"Hmm," Alimen said. "Are there further questions for these two?"

"Endless questions," the astronomy professor said. "But in terms of our session, I am satisfied."

"I have one more," Alimen said. "Should you—you both—be presented Letters of Mastery, what would your next intentions be?"

"Further scholarship," they both said in unison. For a moment, they glanced at each other and grinned, maniacally. Phadre gave a small bow to Jiarna, yielding to her.

"As Professor Kellian said, these are radical theories we've presented, sir. What we've presented here is only the beginning of what could be a lifetime's worth of study."

"Two lifetimes," Phadre said. "I would . . . I would relish that opportunity, sir."

Alimen pulled himself to his feet, "I put it to the call, then. Are there denials? Are there objections?"

The professors gathered stayed silent.

"Then it is done. As high proctor, I then declare that this Letter—that these Letters of Mastery, to be bestowed on Phadre Golmin and Jiarna Kay, are defended, and their validity to be backed by the authority of the University of Maradaine."

The professors all applauded, and Jiarna cheered, wrapping her arms around Phadre. Phadre almost collapsed, knees buckling.

"Gentles and ladies, I thank you for your participation," Alimen told the professors, and they all filed out, each offering a final congratulations to both Phadre and Jiarna.

"Miss Kay," Alimen said. "I must apologize to you for my earlier dismissals of you. I will be honest, I am still skeptical of your theories, but perhaps that is because I don't fully understand them. However, it is clear that you have shown yourself to be a scholar of unique insight."

"Thank you, sir," Jiarna said.

"And Mister Golmin, I am quite pleased with the courage you showed here. I might not have been so forgiving of your stunt to include Miss Kay."

"I believed in her, sir," Phadre said.

Alimen grinned. "Well done, Phadre. Both of you. However, I'll impose upon the both of you to clean up after this. Mister Calbert, Mister Sarren, with me."

Veranix offered his own congratulations to the two of them and followed the professor out.

"You both acted quite admirably," Alimen said, allowing them to assist him as he walked. "I presumed from your reactions that Phadre surprised you both."

"Quite," Delmin said.

"I'll have to confess, sir, I still am not sure what happened in there," Veranix said lightly.

"Given your scores on your theory exam, Mister Calbert, I am not surprised."

"My scores, sir?" Veranix didn't even bother to hide his concern.

"Don't worry, you passed, with sufficient margin for further advancement."

"And I, sir?" Delmin asked.

"You know you are receiving full marks, Mister Sarren, let's not belabor it."

"So I presume next year we are both to be in the next level for theory and practicals?" Veranix asked.

"Yes, indeed," Alimen said. "At least, as far as I'm concerned, you both receive full marks in Practicals. I cannot speak toward your other exams."

Veranix laughed nervously. "In theory, sir, how poorly

would I have to do on History or Rhetoric to be threatened with dismissal?"

"I'm not sure, exactly," Alimen said. "I highly doubt it would come to that, Veranix. But should it, rest assured that I would engage in a full inquiry to prevent it."

"So are we done for the semester, sir?" Delmin asked.

"Officially, yes. Though I would appreciate it if you both attended the Ceremony of Letters tomorrow, for Phadre's sake, if nothing else."

"We'd be honored," Delmin said.

"Of course," Veranix added, even though that was the last place he wanted to be. "And then, sir?"

"If you are asking if I am engaging you this summer, then yes, Mister Calbert. You as well, Mister Sarren, if you have not made other arrangements."

"Nothing formal, sir."

"Well, it is a discussion for a few days from now. Consider yourselves at liberty until, let's say, the twenty-eighth."

"Thank you, Professor," Veranix said.

"Yes, well, I'm sure there is plenty of trouble you can get into in that time," he said. "However, I will press on the two of you to help me to my tower before you engage in debauched revels."

"Anything you need, Professor."

The professor smiled and cupped one hand around Veranix's head. "It's probably pointless to tell you not to do anything too wild, isn't it?"

Veranix looked away as he took some of the professor's weight onto his shoulder. "I suppose it would be, sir. Especially tonight."

Chapter 19

VERANIX WAS IN A HURRY to get wherever it was they needed to get to for Delmin to find out the name they were looking for. Delmin was being more than a little bit coy about it, which annoyed Veranix to no end. But he insisted that they return to their rooms first and change out of uniform.

"Why are we doing this?"

"Well, for one, we have now both finished our final duties as third-year students, so as of right now, this is inaccurate." He pointed to the three pips on his hat. "We are either fourth-years on summer break, or we will be thrown out of gates for poor marks."

"You wouldn't."

"I was making allowances for you. Either way, it's probably appropriate, given where we are going, that we not necessarily announce ourselves as University students."

"Where are we going, exactly?"

Someone knocked on the door. Veranix was annoyed by the interruption, but let that go when he opened it to find Eittle, dressed in regular street clothes

"Finished up, lads?" he asked.

"Done with all, now we wait," Delmin said, putting on a rather smart vest and suspenders. Sometimes Veranix forgot that Delmin came from a decent amount of money. "Though I'm pretty confident in full marks all. You?"

"Finished with the last. I'll be heading out for the observatory tomorrow."

"Good luck with that," Veranix said. "It sounds like it'll be quite a time for you."

"Yeah," Eittle said, looking to the ground. "I know you fellows are both busy and all, but I was wondering . . . I thought I'd go down to the Lower Trenn, give Parsons a visit before I left. Thought you two might want to come along."

The idea hit Veranix like a slap in the face. Go visit Parsons? On the fifth floor of the Lower Trenn Street Ward, where all the mindless *effitte* victims were tended to? Including Veranix's mother? He couldn't go there, couldn't see her, it wasn't possible. Not even—

"Of course," Delmin said. "That's a perfect idea. Just give us a click."

"Sure." Eittle nodded and went off.

"Are you crazy? We need to—"

"We need to go to the Lower Trenn Ward, actually," Delmin said. "That's always where we were going and now we have a better excuse to go down there."

"I cannot go to the Lower Trenn Street Ward, Delmin! Fenmere has eyes everywhere, and . . . and . . . I can't . . ." The words wouldn't come out, tears coming to his eyes. "I don't . . ."

"Hey, hey," Delmin said, taking Veranix by the shoulder and sitting him on the bed. "If it's too much for you, I'll go alone. You stay here. I've got this."

Veranix's heart ached. "No, I . . . more than anything,

I want to go down there, but . . . if I do the wrong thing, if I reach out, then maybe . . ."

"I've got you, Vee." Delmin gave him a big, stupid, toothy grin. "No matter what, you're gonna be all right."

"I don't deserve you, buddy."

"No, you don't. Come on."

The walk out the western gates and down Trenn was relatively sedate, filled mostly with Eittle talking about his summer program. In a way Veranix envied him getting out of the city, being able to just study the night sky in the quiet and open air. He still wasn't sure what his summer was going to be, though it involved staying on campus under Professor Alimen's watchful eye. Hopefully not too watchful, since he had every intention of gumming up the Fenmere *effitte* machine at any opportunity.

The ward was an enormous stone monstrosity, a blight squatting like an ugly toad at the corner of Trenn and Lowbridge. A grand fortress centuries ago; now a crumbling, impoverished hospital for the hopeless.

They entered to find a grimy desk manned by a white-and-yellow coated elderly woman. "Can I help you boys?"

"We're here to see Kandell Parsons," Eittle said. "He's on the fifth floor."

She arched an eyebrow over her spectacles. "Not much need for visitors on the fifth."

"Even still," Eittle said.

She shrugged and pointed them in the direction of a stairwell. She gave them no further mind as they went over. Was this old woman one of the sets of eyes Fenmere had, reporting to him anyone who might go to the fifth floor? She was writing something, perhaps "Three young men, possibly students, visiting Parsons."

Veranix shook it away as they went up.

When they reached the fifth floor, the thing that took him by surprise was the moaning. Moans, sighs, and groans echoed from all around them as they emerged. The rest of it was exactly how he expected: dankly smelling of human filth. There were windows, at least in this large antechamber, where the afternoon sun still found its way in, casting rose light and gray shadows from the iron bars. Attendants carried and wheeled patients around, moving them from the side rooms and down the hallway.

"Saints, that's disturbing," he muttered.

"What did you expect?" Eittle asked.

"I don't know, I . . . I thought they'd sit silently or something."

"It's not exactly like that," Eittle said. Veranix wondered how many times he had already come out in the past month. A nod of recognition from one of the attendants as they crossed the floor confirmed it had been more than once.

"Your man's in the parlor," the attendant said.

"Appreciate it," Eittle said.

"The parlor?" Veranix asked.

"They have names for all the parts of the floor. The parlor is where they have them sit during the day between meals and other treatments." He led them down the hallway.

"What other treatments?" Delmin asked. Veranix was only half listening as Eittle explained about bathing and enforced movement, attempts to keep the body healthy in case the mind ever healed itself.

"That ever happen?" Veranix asked, making sure he looked at every patient they passed. Dead, vacant eyes every time, mouth half open. A man with an army tattoo on his arm was wheeled past them in a rolling chair. That could be Kaiana's father. Did she ever come out here?

The army man moaned, and then made some gibbering noises.

"There have been . . . hopeful signs." Eittle's voice didn't sound very hopeful. "That, for example."

They entered the parlor, where several of the patients were seated in a semicircle, while a young attendant read from a book of poetry in the center of the circle. Veranix didn't know the poems, but she read them well enough. She'd never make it in the Cantarell Players, but she understood what she was saying.

Most were seated. A few, Veranix noted, were standing. Same dead, vacant look, but on their feet.

"They can walk?" Veranix asked Eittle.

"They can be led, and stand," Eittle said. "But they don't move around on their own. Parsons, though, he's not there yet."

Parsons was in a rolling chair on the edge of the group. He sat motionless, head lolling to one side, eyes not even focused on anything. Eittle gave a small nod to the poetry-reading attendant and pulled Parsons's chair away from the circle. He brought him over to a small wooden table in a corner of the room, and sat down.

"Hey, man," he said. "Look who came with me today. Calbert and Sarren. They wanted to see how you were doing."

Veranix wasn't sure what the blazes he should do. "Hey, Parsons," was all he could muster.

What else could he even say? If anything, he'd want to scream at him for being so stupid to even take *effitte*. Taken it completely willingly, paid for it. He didn't have it forced down his throat like Veranix's mother, or even get hooked while fighting in the Napolic islands like

Kai's father. There was no excuse at all. If there was anything of Parsons still in there, clawing to be let free, Veranix almost felt he deserved to be trapped inside his own body.

Instead he said none of those things.

"You've missed quite a bit," Delmin said. "End of term exams were downright dangerous this year."

Eittle started talking, telling Parsons about the Prankster attacks, giving a lot of detail about the one in Almers.

After a bit Delmin stood up. "Be right back."

He got a few steps away before Veranix popped up and grabbed him by the arm. "What is on? Why are we here?" he whispered.

Delmin lowered his own voice, flashing his eyes over to Eittle for a moment. "Not everyone on this floor is here because of *effitte*. Stay put." And then he winked.

Delmin blazing well *winked*.

He was enjoying this a bit too much.

Veranix turned back to join Eittle when he bumped into a patient being led into the parlor by an attendant.

"I'm sorry, I—"

Veranix's throat closed up.

The patient standing in front of him was his mother.

Her hand jutted out, pawing at his face. "Suh suh suh suh suh." She started twitching her head.

"Miss Ayxa, you can't do that," the attendant said, pulling the hand away from Veranix. "Ayxa" was the assumed name she had used when his parents were in Maradaine. When Fenmere caught them. A false name used to keep Veranix safe. "I'm terribly sorry, sir."

"I thought—" Veranix could barely form words without tears coming to his eyes, without his voice shattering. "I didn't know—she—"

"Sometimes they have flashes of reaction," the attendant said. "Spontaneous movement or articulation. But then it passes, see?"

Veranix's mother was silent again, except the low moan, and her dead eyes stared at nothing in the far distance.

"That was very good, Miss Ayxa, but you shouldn't spook the nice young man."

Eittle's hands came on Veranix's shoulders. "We're very sorry for any disturbance."

"Quite all right," the attendant said, and she led Veranix's mother away.

Veranix wanted nothing more than to pick her up and carry her out of this horrific place.

"Hey, Vee? It was nothing, all right?"

"Nothing," Veranix whispered. Every organ inside his body was rebelling. He could barely breathe, and the bile was creeping up his throat. He wanted Eittle to take him out of there. He wanted to run out.

If one of Fenmere's spies were in there, they would report how someone made a scene after bumping into Miss Ayxa. That might be just enough to put him and his mother in danger.

With every ounce of will, he forced a grin on his face, forced his stomach down.

"Yeah," he said as lightly as he could manage. "Just spooked me, having that lady paw at me. That happen a lot here?"

"Not that often," Eittle said. He leaned in. "I really get it, how spooky it is in here. Don't think I don't. I just . . . I think it matters that Parsons has people who do this for him."

"What about his family? Don't they—"

"They've shut off from him." Eittle's jaw tightened.

"Look, this isn't my field, but I look around here and see a tiny spark behind the dead eyes in here. These people, they're still *there* inside their skulls."

"You think so?" Veranix felt his voice tremble.

"I do. Thing is, most of these people, they're alone here. But maybe if friends, if they come here, they engage, then maybe . . . that could give a chance of coming back."

"I get it," Veranix said. "Most of these folk, they . . . they probably need someone."

"Look, I . . . I know this a lot to ask, but . . ."

Veranix could see where Eittle's hedging was going. "You want me to come visit Parsons over the summer?"

"I think it would be good for him. Maybe you and Delmin both?"

"Let me find Delmin," Veranix said. "And we'll see what we can work out."

Veranix stepped away and went searching down the hallway for Delmin. He wasn't sure where to go, but then he felt something. Even with his underdeveloped *numinic* sense, he could tell there was some magical activity going on in one room. Not actual shaping, but pulses and waves.

He looked in to see Delmin standing over a patient in bed. The man was completely still, eyes wide open, and horribly scarred. And the pulses of *numina* were coming from him.

"All right," Delmin said, giving Veranix a gesture to stay put. "I appreciate it. Is there . . . anything I can do to help you?"

More pulses came. Delmin cocked his head like he was listening, and then chuckled.

"I'll see what I can do about that. And, really, thank you."

He left the room, grabbing Veranix by the crook of the arm and pulling him along.

"What was that?" Veranix asked once they were a bit away.

"Like I said, not everyone up here is an *effitte* victim. That was Illian Groat, a magic student from about six years ago."

"Student?" Veranix clarified. Delmin saying that implied that Groat never received his Letters or Circling.

"He was in an accident—a magic-related one—during a failed Letters Defense. It left him like that."

"You were talking to him?"

"In a fashion. His body is completely damaged, but his mind is intact. Wide awake there, but can't move."

Veranix shuddered. He thought the state his mother was in was damnation, but being awake and aware in an immobile body would be unbearable. "But he can still channel *numina*."

"Roughly. And he knows Riverboat Signals, like most young boys who grow up in North Maradaine do."

That made it clear. "So he can spell out words, and you can read it."

"Precisely. One moment." Delmin crossed over to one of the attendant's desks. "Ma'am, I was visiting my friend in that room, and I'm pretty sure he's in need of a full body wash."

The attendant sighed ruefully, and then put on a fake smile. "I'll get on it."

"Was that what he wanted?" Veranix asked as Delmin returned.

"I could hardly say no to that."

"So I presume that his accident—"

"Was caused while working with a student delving into the magical nature of elemental science. He had developed a *numinic* battery, which . . . didn't work. The resulting explosion left Groat like that."

"The same accident that we think is tied to the Prankster?"

"Caused by one Cuse Jensett. Who lived in Almers, ate in Holtman, was advised by Madam Henly and—"

"Expelled by Vice Headmaster Ballford."

Cuse Jensett. That was the man.

"Why didn't we hear about this? Why hasn't his name come up?"

"I don't know, everyone thought Jensett was a lunatic who failed. He did fail, quite spectacularly. Maybe no one who remembers him thought him capable of this."

"But you did," Veranix said.

"I remembered reading about the incident, but didn't think anything of it until Jiarna reminded me of it. Then I remembered that Groat was out here, and . . . frankly, I hoped that I'd be able to communicate."

"Brilliant, Del. Rutting brilliant, we've got the name."

"Of course, you still have to find him. I've been thinking, he can't have done all of his work without proper equipment. He'd need a workspace."

"Like what?"

"Something sizable, where he can mix his chemicals, where the scents of it won't stand out. He'd need to house the equipment, he'd need to have a powerful heat source. There's not a lot of places that could fit that. If he didn't have a university laboratory, then maybe a tannery, or a brewery, something like that. But he'd have to be able to take it over, since what he's doing couldn't escape notice. Maybe one of the abandoned factories out west?"

"Right." Veranix looked around, the empty stares and mindless moans now digging into his skull. The thought of his mother sitting in all this every day was making his stomach rebel. "Can we please get out of here?"

"What about Eittle?"

"He . . . he wants . . . look, I need to get out." He leaned in and whispered. "I literally bumped into my mother. I don't think I . . . I can't handle any more of this place."

Delmin's eyes went wide, and he nodded in understanding. "Get out," he said. "I'll take care of Eittle. You go. You've got a man to catch."

Veranix managed to get three blocks away from the ward before he surrendered to every emotion cascading through him. He staggered into an alley and vomited before he could get to the backhouse, then collapsed to the ground in tears.

She must have recognized him. Some spark, some awareness in the back of her destroyed mind, knew exactly who he was and tried to reach him.

He didn't know if that was horrible or beautiful.

She was walking. She touched him. She tried to speak.

Maybe she could get better.

Maybe someone there saw what happened, one of Fenmere's spies.

He didn't want to think about what that might mean. Probably nothing would come of it. As far as anyone knew, he was just someone visiting Parsons.

Parsons. Stupid Parsons. One thing he didn't want to do over the summer was to go to see Parsons. But it meant something to Eittle, and if he had an excuse to come in, he could see how his mother was doing.

All too much to think about.

"Oy, you drunk? Or on something?"

Stick at the mouth of the alley.

"No, sir," Veranix said, pulling himself to his feet. "Just . . . got some bad news is all." There was no hiding the tears on his face, so he just wiped them away.

The stick looked him over with a discerning eye, just a hint of compassion. "Eh, well. This is no place for that. Find a proper pub to drown it in, or go home. But back alleys ain't a safe place for decent folk to be. Not here, not tonight."

"Right, thanks," Veranix said. He had seen more Constabulary on the streets today. Maybe what happened on campus was also affecting the neighborhood. Of course, the gang fights in the streets and his own scuffles the past few nights were nothing to ignore. "On my way."

"Be quick about it."

Veranix made his way to the laundry and press, on a part of Tulip Street that could belong to the Princes or the Knights of Saint Julian, depending on who you asked. Storefronts were closing up, shuttering iron gates. It seemed too early for that. Sun hadn't even set yet. But then Veranix noticed a pack of Knights walking up the other way, knives on their belts, and blatantly resting their hands on the hilts.

Spoiling for a fight.

He reached the laundry and press, where the owners nearly turned him away. He asked about the rented flop, and they groused that it had been taken. He ended up arguing with them for several minutes that the room had been rented for him to use, and they insisting he couldn't rent it, because it had already been rented out.

Finally he snapped. "The girl who rented the room. Half-Napolic, came over from the University? She is my friend. She rented the room *for me*."

"I don't need no doxy work done over my shop!"

"Nothing of the sort, ma'am. I . . . I just need a room for the summer. She was kind enough to procure it for me."

"If I hear doxy work, you're going to feel the back of my hand, you get?"

"Got."

Veranix took the side stairs—wrought-iron steps in the alley—up to the rooms, following the matron of the laundry and press while her husband finished closing up. She led him to the hallway, and pointed out the door to the rented room. She then noted where their own apartment was, and how easily they could hear anything that went on in there, as well as notice if many people were coming up and down those stairs. Veranix had noticed they squeaked and groaned with every step, so he had to admit it would be hard to sneak in from there.

He went into the flop, which was just a single room. It was a serviceable enough room, which was good, since he had more or less committed himself to renting it for the whole summer. Clean and bright, if simple. A bed, table and two chairs took up most of the room—functional looking, nothing more.

Kaiana sat on the bed, thumbing through a book, barely noticing his arrival.

"Do you have a name?"

"Cuse Jensett. Which means nothing to me."

Kaiana stood up. "Or me, unfortunately." She pointed to the pile on the table. "All your things to be the Thorn are here. Except the rope."

"Except the rope." Veranix had to accept that couldn't be helped. He went over to the window. It looked over the alley and the back of some other buildings. It didn't look like anyone could see it from the main street. He opened it easily enough. So he could slip in and out through here with little difficulty.

"Anything else?" Kai asked. "I really should get back to campus."

He went over to the table and sat down. "You've been fantastic, Kai. I . . . I couldn't do all this—"

"I know you couldn't."

"I was at Trenn Street Ward just now. On the fifth floor."

She quickly sat down. "You . . . but . . . why?"

"That was where Delmin needed to go, and Eittle wanted to go see Parsons, and . . . I saw my mom. She . . . she recognized me."

"That's impossible."

"I'm telling you, Kai, she touched my face and started trying to speak."

Kai sat in silence for a while. "I really should visit him."

"I get why you don't. That place is . . . harrowing." The image of blank faces, standing and staring—that wasn't leaving his mind any time soon.

"I have tried." She sighed. "I've actually walked down there and stood outside for . . . hours. I just can't get myself to go inside. If I did, it would be like . . ."

She trailed off.

Kai sat silently for a moment. "Do you know what's strange? I was three when my father brought me here, but I have some very vivid memories of Napoli. The hot sun, the bright blue water, smelling so strongly of salt, a little boy with . . ." She trailed off for a moment in reverie. "The taste of *pahapa*. The word *pahapa*. But my mother? Just a blur of some vaguely maternal presence. No face, no voice, just . . . an idea of a person."

Veranix kept quiet. She had never spoken about her mother or Napoli before. Only her father, and usually with a bitter tone of barely restrained disdain.

"I wonder sometimes if she's still alive, or . . . if she thinks about me. And if somewhere, in the depths of his damaged, broken mind, he's thinking of me at all. Because he certainly wasn't in the end."

Veranix found her hand tightly gripping his own. She said nothing for a while.

"How was Phadre's defense?"

"He passed quite handily," Veranix said. "As did Jiarna. Was that what he asked you to do, with the letter?"

"That's me, everyone's delivery girl."

"I've never—"

"It's fine, Veranix. Yes, he asked me to get her over to the defense. Did she get to present?"

"They did it together, like they were in each other's heads," Veranix said.

"Yes, I suppose that makes sense," Kaiana said, just a hint of glumness in her voice. "She is pretty damn smart."

"True," Veranix said. Then an idea hit him. "Could you do me another favor?"

She sighed. "What is that?"

"Show the rope to Jiarna. She might be able to figure something out that Delmin couldn't."

Kaiana gave a halfhearted nod. "I suppose that makes sense."

"Kai," Veranix said. "I would never be able to do any of this without you. You know that, don't you?"

She smiled but didn't look up, though she squeezed his hand again. "We're quite a pair, aren't we?" she finally said. "You need to get ready, I need to get back. You have a plan?"

"Contact Colin, see if 'Cuse Jensett' means anything to him. Failing that, finding some other kids to knock around until they tell me something. Leaning toward Red Rabbits."

"You really think he's in Aventil?"

"He went south when he left the High Table. He didn't think he was being chased at the time. And I can't imagine he'd want to be too far from here."

"All right." She got up from the table. "Stop by the carriage house on your way back. If I don't see you by dawn, I will do something drastic."

"Define 'drastic.'"

"People will get punched in the face."

"That is my favorite definition of that word."

She laughed and suddenly took him in a quick embrace. "Be safe and smart out there."

"Why change my style now?" he joked.

She sighed, and, after patting his cheek, left without another word.

Veranix stripped off his clothes and went through his equipment. He was surprised to find that Kaiana had included the jar of his grandfather's muscle ointment with his gear. Still bruised and sore from the past three nights, he liberally applied it on his arms and shoulders.

Satisfied that he had done as much as he could to ease his aching body, he got dressed in his Thorn outfit. Once he had the vest on, he strapped on the quiver and hooked his bow and staff to the bandolier. He checked that all the quick release clasps were working, able to draw bow and staff at a moment's notice.

Finally he put on the cloak, immediately feeling the rush of the influx of *numina* into his body. He took a moment to relish that, to sense where his own magical strength ended and it began. If he had to, he would push himself to the very limit tonight. Cuse Jensett was out there, and he was going to pay for what he had done on campus. And if Bluejay or any other Deadly Birds got in his way, he would waste no time trifling with them.

The sun had nearly set. Veranix put his hood up, magicked the shadow over his face, and went out into the night.

Colin needed many beers, and fortunately the Turnabout was providing that in spades. The whole day had been spent in going up and down to the basements, telling the same damn story over and over. Every boss had questions, and then split up him and Jutie and asked more questions.

Fortunately, the one thing he wasn't going to tell them—who the Thorn was—was something they didn't even question him on. They asked about the Thorn plenty, and they clearly thought Colin had been duped by the Thorn one way or another. They never seemed to suspect Colin was working with the Thorn with his eyes open.

The whole blazing thing was exhausting.

Colin nursed his beer, hoping to have satisfied the bosses. Jutie stayed at his side, having clearly been turned out by the whole process. He hadn't said much all evening, just drank his beer.

Hotchins came over and sat down. Looked like it was about to start over again.

"Rabbits just knocked the stuffing out of the Orphans over on Lily," he said. "You were right about one thing, they're looking to step up."

"I told you."

"Something else." He put a vial of something on the table. It looked almost like *effitte*, but it was bright red. "Some of Rencie's crew had a thing near Cantarell with some Rabbits. They found these on the bodies."

"What is it?"

"Rencie and her folk didn't leave any of them able to answer questions, so we don't really know. It ain't *effitte*, but if I were to guess, it ain't *not effitte* either, if you get me."

Colin took the vial and opened it, just letting the scent hit his nose before shutting it again. "Color's wrong, but the scent ain't."

"That's how I see it," Hotchins said. "No matter what, Rabbits are making a play, and this stuff is at the center. I don't want them to get any traction on that."

"No, sir," Jutie said. Colin glanced at him, noticing the kid was all but dead-eyed.

"All right," Colin said, turning back to Hotchins. "I take it you want me to handle it."

"It's in your lap, boy. Might as well see it through." Hotchins sighed, looking out at the street. "Course, the sticks are giving the full show of color tonight. They're liable to crack your skull if you so much as step out there."

Another voice, a faint whisper, invaded Colin's ear. "Need to talk."

"Right," Colin said, glancing around the Turnabout. That was Veranix, but he saw no sign of the boy. Of course, he could damn well be magicking himself up again, looking like any other bloke. Not that he saw any strange blokes in the place. "We can't just charge at the Rabbits and crack their skulls. We need a plan."

"Then make one," Hotchins said. "Get some folk together, and figure something out. But tell me what the blazes you're gonna do before you run off. I want to know if your plan is blazing stupid."

"Fine," Colin said, getting to his feet. Raising his voice a bit louder than he necessarily needed to, he added, "I'm going to hit the backhouses. Then I'll get on that."

"Do what you need to, boy," Hotchins said. "Just be about it."

He went out through the alley door, and hoped Veranix got the message.

Veranix watched Colin come out the back alley, and whispered some magic to his ear. "Come up to the roof."

Colin glanced up, scowling. He checked that no one was watching, and then jumped up to the iron back ladder and climbed up on the roof.

"I don't know if you were listening to what's going on—"

"I wasn't."

"Well, I don't have a lot of time. Things are going bad out there. I need to take care of my business, hear?"

"Heard." Veranix wasn't going to push, even though he would want Colin by his side, if possible. "This is different business for me. There's been attacks on campus—the guy I chased after last night. I need to stop him."

"Why do you—" Colin stopped himself. "Never mind. If you do, you do, I get that. It just seems like . . ."

"I know how it seems. But if I'm going to draw a line and tell Fenmere he can't cross it, then I can't let anyone else run all over it. This guy has hurt, and he has killed. And on top of that, he is smart, he can do things that . . ." Veranix didn't have time to go into it. "The point is, he has to be stopped, and as cocky as it might sound, I might be the only person capable."

"But you're going to be careful about it. I cannot come and back you up. The Princes need me."

Veranix clapped his cousin on the shoulder. "Hey, I understand. I'll be fine."

"Fine." Colin sighed. "So what do you need?"

"I have a name, and I just need to find him. He must be in Aventil . . ."

"Why do you even think that?" Colin shook his head and sat down on the roof.

"This is where he ran to. From the center of campus, where he could have gone anywhere, he went to the south gates."

"I suppose that's a fair point. I don't know what good it'll do, but if you have a name, I can see what I can find out. But, really, enough is going on that I don't think I can do much for you."

"The guy's name is Cuse Jensett."

Colin's face went white. "Did you say Jensett?"

"That mean something?"

"Does it—don't you know?"

Everyone in Veranix's life seemed to berate him over things he was supposed to know. "Whatever it is, I don't."

"Look, our dads, when they tried to bring together the neighborhood, they had a bunch of guys working with them. Guys like Vessrin, who called himself the Prince of Rose Street back then, and Charn Hallaran . . ."

"Who ran Hallaran's Boys, all right. And?"

"Yeah, one of those guys was Reb Jensett. But everybody called him . . ."

Veranix was able to finish the sentence. "The Red Rabbit."

"I've never heard of Cuse, but Reb had two brothers. Maybe he's a nephew or a cousin or something. I mean, the name is too much of a coincidence."

Veranix couldn't quite wrap his head around this. "No, this guy, he's got a vendetta with the University. That's what he's been doing."

"Yeah, I've heard some of it," Colin said. "Blazes, I saw what he did with the horses. But this isn't a guy who is on his own, you know? He's got to have some kind of support. He'd need crowns, right? Somebody is being his bank. Maybe it's the Rabbits. Maybe they're holing him up somewhere."

Veranix nodded. "Delmin says that he would need some kind of large place to do his work. Raw materials, mixing, heat. Special equipment as well."

"Like a brewery?"

Same thing Delmin had said—that got Veranix's attention. "You know something?"

"Might be nothing, but a few weeks ago this brewer over on Tulip and Waterpath—they just stopped making any beer, and the folks who ran it left town. I didn't think much of it, but I heard the Rabbits were sniffing around the place."

"That could be it," Veranix said. "All right, I'll take a look."

"There's something else, something I just heard. The Rabbits, they . . . they're starting to put something out there. Like *effitte*, but different."

That fit in the whole scheme. "Something new like that would take a real genius, right? Someone who could do real magic with chemicals, you think?"

"You think it's from your guy?"

"I think it's one more reason to take him down." He had caused nothing but pain and fear on campus, and he was going to add to the misery that was the *effitte* trade. Veranix was more than ready to pay all those things back to him.

Colin stood back up. "You be careful out there, hear? Every gang is rowing tonight. I don't know what's going to happen. Sticks are out in force . . ."

"Not to mention the Deadly Birds. At least one is still out there."

"What are you going to do about that?"

"This." Veranix shrouded himself. He pushed his voice so it turned into whispers that swirled around Colin. "The last thing I want is for Jensett to see me coming."

"Saints," Colin swore, spinning as if to find exactly where Veranix was. "That's just unsettling."

"You be safe out there tonight, too," Veranix said. With that, he leaped off the roof of the Turnabout, into the night.

Chapter 20

"SO, COLIN, you piss out a plan?" Colin had returned to the Turnabout to find Hotchins and several other Princes staring at him. Time to spin something to turn the heat down.

"I've been thinking," Colin said.

"What about that brewery they've been sniffing around?" Jutie asked. "We could hit it hard."

Colin was tempted to hit the brewery, but that could make things worse for Vee. And for all he knew, the Rabbits weren't even around there. Could be an empty hunt.

"Too big, too deep into Orphans' territory. We go in that far, we could get cut off." Colin sat down trying to buy another moment to think of something. "Orchid Street."

"What about it?" Hotchins asked.

"We make sure the Rabbits know that Orchid, between Bush and Waterpath, is pure Prince territory. They've done a bit of creeping onto one side of that street. I bet there's a couple flops that are Rabbit holes. So let's get a few tight crews together, head over to Orchid, and flush them out."

Hotchins shrugged. "It's a start."

"What's a start?"

Colin looked up to see Lieutenant Benvin at the doors of the Turnabout, with two of his men at his elbow.

"You locking up Red Rabbits for peddling *effitte* and the like, that's what," Colin said. He grabbed the vial of Red still sitting on the table. No point trying to hide the thing from Benvin, better to take control. "Look what they've got out there." He threw it over to Benvin.

Benvin caught it. "This supposed to be *effitte?*"

Hotchins looked at Colin like he was ready to punch him in the neck. "Something like it, Left."

Benvin held up the vial to a lamp, while the two other sticks chuckled. "Wrong color, but it does have the look of it. But how can we prove this is something the Red Rabbits are peddling?"

"I just told you, Left," Colin said.

"You told me this came from the Rabbits," Benvin said, crossing over to the table. Every Prince in the place—not that there were many—tensed up as Benvin sat down with Colin, Jutie, and Hotchins. "But who the blazes are you, Tyson? Just some gutter-born Rose Street Prince. A thug and a cheat. Why does it matter what you tell me?"

"I ain't—"

"A liar?"

One of the other sticks looked around, "Like there's a Prince who isn't a damn liar."

"Hey!" Jutie was on his feet. "You can't come in here—"

"Pardon me?" Benvin snapped. "Is this some sort of private club? Is your name on the lease, boy?"

Jutie was silent, hard-eyed at all the sticks.

"What is your name, boy?"

"Juteron Higgs, stick. And I live on Rose Street."

"Sit down, Higgs. Don't give us a reason to drag you in the lockwagon tonight."

This was clearly happening, so Colin waved to the barman for a few beers. "So what are you here for, if not to lock up Princes? You drinking?"

"Is it smart for me to drink?" Benvin asked.

"Up to you. You and your men can have beers and strikers like anyone else. Ain't a private club, after all."

"I'm trying to figure out why I'm here, Tyson." He held up the vial of Red again. He noticed that one of Benvin's men stayed at the main door, and the other wandered over to the back. No way out without kicking through one of them. "Why'd you target the Rabbits?"

"Me?" Colin didn't know what the left was on about, but he got a raised eyebrow from Hotchins.

"Near as I can tell, this whole business about the Rabbits being in league with Fenmere, dealing *effitte*, or whatever this junk is—that all came from you. You roped the rest of the gangs in, and the reverend. And me. I almost swallowed it."

Colin leaned in and lowered his voice. "You know what you swallowed, and who gave it to you. And who saved you."

"Right." Benvin's voice boomed. "Let's none of us forget, the Rabbits poisoned me last night. Everyone here clear? They meant to poison the reverend, saints know why, but they got me. But your man Tyson, he pulled me out of there." He grabbed a beer away from Colin as the bartender delivered it. He got on his feet and addressed the room. "So raise your glasses, Princes. Because when this lieutenant is there to lock each and every one of you away, you can thank Colin Tyson for saving his life."

"You did what, boy?" Hotchins asked.

"Made sense in the moment," Colin muttered.

Benvin gulped down the beer and sat back down.

"So you start the rows, you save a stick, you get the neighborhood in a state, and I'm still trying to figure out why."

"You've got quite the imagination, Left, if you think I've got that kind of power." Colin now felt the heat of the Princes staring at him, especially Hotchins. There wasn't much to do besides laugh it off. "I'm just a Prince."

"You're geared, if you think Colin started this, Left," Jutie said. "I told him about the Rabbits."

"Did you? Well, now, Mister Higgs, how did you know about it?"

"Heard it from the Thorn himself, right after he skirted you in the alley."

"Right after he —" Benvin's eyes went wide. "You!"

Benvin lunged at Jutie, but Colin kicked at the stick's chair, knocking him over. Jutie slipped out of his grasp and jumped to his feet, drawing out his knife.

"Jutie, run!" Colin shouted.

Jutie made a line for the door, but Benvin's man drew his handstick and came at him. In a flash the two of them collided, falling onto the floor. Jutie cried out, but before anyone else could move, he was back on his feet. Two steps and he was out into the night.

And the stick was on the ground, blood pouring out his chest.

"Arch!" Benvin shouted, going to his man. The stick was convulsing, far too much blood already on the ground for him to live.

The one at the back door came running over. "I'll call the Yellowshields!" he said, going out the front. Whistles cut through the air.

Then the stick was still.

Benvin turned, red-faced, to Colin. "You are going to pay for this, Tyson."

Colin held up his hands. "I didn't touch anyone. You can't lock me up for being in the room."

"I will get you, boy. I will haunt you until you are in Quarrygate for life."

Two footpatrol sticks ran in, and their faces dropped when they saw the dead man.

Benvin was up, all business, "One of you, put out the call to the whole stationhouse. Every man on foot, horse, or wagon is to go All Eyes for Juteron Higgs, Rose Street Prince. Arrest on sight for the murder of Officer Arch Nathons."

Colin felt a meaty hand grab his shoulder. Hotchins. "Get down in the basement, Tyson."

"But, Jutie—"

"Get down there, now, and stay there. He's in the wind. And you're in the hole."

Sotch found this evening to be truly lovely, despite the unpleasantness of the past few days. Her Red Rabbits had held their own against bastards from every damn gang in Aventil. The Thorn had tried to rattle them, even. But she and Keckin kept their folk together. Even when skulls were getting cracked and sticks were throwing folk in the lockwagon, they got their people out of there and back to the brewery.

The place made for a good flop, better than the last few places they had used. Cuse, the boss's nephew, was put out by having twenty-some odd Rabbits crashing down in the place. His work had been cordoned off, mostly in the basements and the vats. He insisted the crews keep away from his stuff, and Sotch and Keckin made sure they complied. As long as they stayed away from the windows, since the fact they were crashing down in the brewery had to stay quiet. Surely some Orphans knew, of course, but it was crucial word didn't get back to Fenmere. Not yet.

And it wouldn't for a while, not with Bell tied and bagged like a hog in the corner of the office. He had long stopped struggling and grunting, but Sotch could still hear him breathing.

As she lay on the bedroll, Keckin's warm body her pillow, she had to admit that having Fenmere's man just a few feet away, powerless to do anything, gave her a blazing rush that beat anything *effitte* or the Red could do. The only reason she wasn't pouncing back onto Keckin was that she had already exhausted him.

"Should we feed him?" Keckin asked idly.

"I'm not in any rush," she said. "He's a bit of a doughy man, don't you think? Easy living, suckling off Fenmere's teat. Missing a few meals won't hurt him."

"Go roll yourselves," Bell grunted.

"Already did."

"I heard."

There was a knock on the doorframe—the office didn't have a proper door, of course—and Cuse stepped in. Thin little weasel with thick spectacles and greasy hair. It was a good thing he was so blasted clever. He'd never last a night as a regular Rabbit. Sotch shifted the blanket to make sure she and Keckin were covered. "What do you need?"

"I'd like to grab a few of your boys for tomorrow," Cuse said. "I need a bit more raw muscle to finish the project."

The project. Sotch didn't like this personal sewage Cuse was reveling in. He was being given a blazing lot of latitude, on his uncle's orders. But this thing of his drew too much heat their way.

"We talking smack around muscle or lift and carry?"

"Mostly the latter," Cuse said. "But, frankly, if the cadets or the Thorn get in my way, I wouldn't mind a few boys with knives in my pocket."

"I thought your pockets were full of tricks," Keckin murmured.

Cuse grinned, far too proud of himself. "Last night's was pretty good, but that was over two hundred crowns' worth of material in one vial."

"You're a little loose with Rabbit crowns, Cuse," Sotch said, getting to her feet. She grabbed her trousers off the floor and put them on.

"None of you will be lacking in crowns in a few weeks. Most of those vats are brewing the Red. That will more than pay off my other materials."

"So you keep saying."

"And after tomorrow, my project will be done. So you won't have to worry."

"What's his project?" That came from Bell in the corner.

"Don't mind him," Keckin said. He grabbed his boot off the floor and threw it at Bell's head.

Sotch had her vest on. "Let's get you some muscle, eh?"

Sotch led him down the office steps to what had been the brewery's warehouse and dock. Most of the crews—hers, Keckin's, and anyone else who was hiding from the lockwagons—were crashed out in there. About twenty Red Rabbits in all.

"All right, Rabbits," Sotch called out to them as they came in. "Cuse here needs, what, four or five of you?"

"Four or five, yes." Cuse's attention was on one of his own boxes by the warehouse door. His supplies were all over the blasted place. "Strong lads, preferably."

"Strong lads," she echoed. "Any of you want it?"

Cuse was now completely enthralled with the contents of the box, and Sotch could hear something rattling in there.

"Is that supposed to do that?" she asked.

"Only if—" His eyes darted around the room. "The Thorn!"

Sotch turned in the direction he was looking, but saw nothing. "What are you—" was all she got out before an arrow went into her arm.

She fell down. Cuse had already leaped behind a crate as another arrow struck the ground, hitting exactly where he had been a moment ago.

"The Thorn is here!" she screamed out, flailing to get her hand around the wound, blood gushing everywhere. "Get him!"

"Where?" Someone shouted, only to get an answer in terms of an arrow in his knee.

"Somewhere up there!" another Rabbit said, pointing up.

Twenty-odd Rabbits drew weapons—blades, darts, and knucklestuffers—but none of them really knew where danger was coming from other than up. No person, no bow, no anything to be seen as the source of the arrows.

Suddenly the crate Cuse had hidden behind slid away, crashing into a couple Rabbits. Cuse was exposed, and another arrow flew down from somewhere in the rafters. It missed him by hairs, and he responded by throwing a bottle up, up to the roof, which burst into purple smoke.

"Are you stupid?" Sotch yelled at him, as she tried to stop the bleeding. The damn thing hurt like blazes; she could barely lift her fighting arm.

"It's fine," Cuse said, and as he did, a figure—no more

than a shadow—dropped down from the purple smoke. It was almost insubstantial, like a shimmer in the air, save for the fact that the purple smoke seemed to stick to it like tar on the fingers. It landed like a cat in the middle of the warehouse floor.

"Get him!" Sotch shouted, and the closest Rabbits converged on it—on him, the Thorn.

One immediately had his knife knocked from his hand, and then went down like he was hit across the head. From the shape of the shimmer, it was clear the Thorn was armed. A staff.

Two more Rabbits were dropped.

The Thorn moved through the crowd of Rabbits, making a line toward Cuse.

Cuse threw something else at the Thorn, who knocked it away easily, sending it at a far group of Rabbits. They screamed as it burst in a ball of ice and snow, trapping them.

Cuse ran out of the warehouse. "Hold him off!" he shouted.

"Rolling saints, stop him now, you bastards!" Sotch yelled. She could barely manage to get on her feet, her arm in agony. The side of her body was covered in blood, but she wasn't going to let her Rabbits get beat. A few more jumped at him, one getting clocked down to the ground. The rest managed to grab hold of something, even if it looked like so much smoke and haze.

A wave of something purple pulsed off the Thorn, knocking those Rabbits off of him. Sotch felt it herself, a slam to her chest, bowling her back off her feet.

Whatever the Thorn did, though, changed him back from haze and shimmer into a man again. He swung the staff around in a wide arc, putting down the next closest Rabbits.

"I'm going to eat your bones!" Keckin shouted this, running in with nothing but trousers and two long knives. Keckin knew how to use those knives, though; that's why he was a captain. Hard, fast slashes, aiming for the Thorn's arms and legs. The Thorn jumped and flipped out of the way, barely staying away from Keckin's lethal assaults.

"Get the bastard, baby!" Sotch shouted, pulling herself over to the crates to give her something to hold on to as she got on her feet.

The Thorn leaped up high—higher than a man possibly could, but he clearly had sorcery on his side—and hurled something at Keckin. More magic. Keckin parried it with his off hand, but it must have still hurt him. He cried out, the knife flying out of his hand. It skittered onto the ground a few feet away from Sotch.

The Thorn landed on the ground, slamming his staff into the chest of the Rabbit closest to him. His hands like lightning, he put the staff up and drew his bow again.

"Give up, Jensett!" the Thorn shouted, an arrow aimed at Keckin. "I've no quarrel with the rest of you."

"You've a quarrel with me, Thorn," Keckin snarled. He held up his knife, ready to strike. Even from that distance, Sotch knew he could do it: dodge the arrow, step in close, and cut his enemy. Keckin was one of the best knife fighters on these blocks.

The Thorn fired, and Keckin moved like a viper. But the Thorn hadn't aimed at him, it was one of the other Rabbits coming up on his flank. The Thorn slid out of the way of Keckin's attack, but Keckin managed to get a piece of him. It wasn't much, little more than a scratch, but it was enough to make the Thorn cry out.

"You still bleed and scream like a man," Keckin taunted. He spun on his heel and made another strike, right for the Thorn's heart.

The Thorn just flicked his wrist, and Keckin stopped dead in the air. With a dismissive wave, Keckin went flying against the wall.

Sotch glanced around the warehouse floor. Nearly two dozen Rabbits, and every one was on the ground. Moaning, wailing, or utterly out of their senses.

She let herself drop back down to the ground and stretched with her good arm to get Keckin's knife. It was pointless, as the Thorn just strode past her, kicking the blade away as he went by. "Stay down."

Sotch wasn't about to do that, forcing herself to follow him into the brewery.

"Cuse Jensett!" he shouted, his voice echoing throughout the place unnaturally. "No one left to save you!"

Cuse, for his part, stood at the far end of the brewery, the cockiest of grins on his face. "Then I'll have to save myself." He held up a metal ball in each hand.

The Thorn had another arrow nocked, but before he fired, Cuse knocked the two balls together.

The response was like lightning, leaping from the balls and hitting points around the brewery. The whole place lit up. Lightning danced around the whole room. The Thorn took his shot, and as the arrow was released from his bow, the lightning all converged on the Thorn. He screamed out and dropped to the ground.

The lightning dissipated, and the Thorn was still on the ground.

Cuse was also on the ground, an arrow protruding from his leg. He was swearing and screaming, while the Thorn was completely silent.

The Thorn was still breathing, though. That should be corrected.

"Leave him, Sotch," Cuse snapped as she approached. "How bad off are you?"

"Quite," she snarled back. "So is everyone else."

He tried to get himself up. "I have something in my lab downstairs that'll help us. Can you get there?"

Sotch felt like she would fall over any moment. "What is it?"

"A green leather case. It's right on my table."

"I got it." Keckin came over, clutching his chest. He was wheezing, like he could barely draw breath, but he was moving faster than the rest of them. He touched Sotch softly on her back. "You'll be fine."

Cuse crawled over to the Thorn. "Thought you were so very clever, didn't you? Didn't think that being the biggest source of *numina* would make you a target, did you?"

Keckin returned quickly with the case, kneeling next to Sotch. She still had the arrow in her arm, and only now did she realize the amount of blood she had trailed across the room. "What do I do, Cuse?"

Cuse looked over at them, and his face fell slightly. He probably presumed he'd be treated first, but wasn't going to argue. "Get the arrow out of her arm. Then put the orange powder in the wound and touch it with the copper strip."

"Hold still, gorgeous," Keckin said. She braced herself as best she could while he yanked the arrow out of her. She didn't let herself scream as more blood trickled out. She probably didn't have much to spare. Keckin followed Cuse's instructions, and when he touched the powder with the copper, it was like fire in her whole arm.

But then it passed, and the wound was closed.

"Blazes," she muttered. She still felt weak as a baby, but she could move her arm again.

"Do the same for me," Cuse said. "And hurry, before he wakes up."

"Why don't we just kill him?" Keckin asked.

Cuse smiled and sat up. "Oh, no. That would be a terrible waste. Believe me, I have a very good reason to keep him alive." He chuckled quietly. "So many things still to do. Such a big day tomorrow."

Chapter 21

DAWN CAME without Kaiana getting a moment of sleep. Dawn had come, but Veranix never had. There was no way that could be for a good reason.

Just as she got off her cot and put her boots on, there was a pounding on her door. Veranix never would do that.

Delmin was at her door. "He isn't back."

"Then something has gone badly," she said. "Let's go."

"Go where?"

"Into Aventil, to find him," she said, grabbing her coat off the peg. Delmin stood there, dumbstruck. "You coming?"

"Are you sure it's wise?"

"It's incredibly unwise, I would imagine." She grabbed one of her hand spades and put it in her pocket. Not much of a weapon, but it was the best option she had on hand. "And he'd come for you without hesitation."

"You're right," Delmin said. He glanced around the room, as if trying to find something he could arm himself with. "I probably shouldn't even embarrass myself if things get violent, should I?"

"If things come to that, run for a whistlebox."

"What about the rope?"

Kaiana paused. "You can't use it. Blazes, Vee can't use it right now. It's . . . broken."

"It is, but . . . it's still napranium. It and the cloak are the same, and . . . I've been thinking about some of the things Phadre and Jiarna were saying last night . . ."

Phadre and Jiarna. Kaiana wasn't surprised their names were now said in tandem. She should have expected that when Phadre had her invite the woman to his defense.

"The two things might have some affinity for each other. We might be able to use it to find him."

Kaiana didn't have an argument against that. She went down into the Spinner Run and grabbed the rope, putting it in a satchel that she hung over her shoulder. "Let's go find him, then."

They went out to the south gate. At this hour, of course, there were cadets on guard, but they gave no trouble to anyone leaving. They were questioning every person entering, and there were quite a few, even this early. The daily deliveries were greater than usual, with the commencement ceremonies occurring. The wagons were backing up down the street, while the cadets argued with drivers who insisted that they made the same deliveries every week, and the cadets should recognize them and stop causing trouble. In the midst of shouting drivers and a crowded street, the cadets let Kaiana and Delmin out with just a friendly wave.

"Do you have a plan?" Delmin asked once they were on the street. The neighborhood was quiet once they were away from the gate. A bit of early activity in the shops and a few Constabulary walking around. Despite that, there were plenty of signs that things had been hectic the night before. Windows broken, garbage in the street, and the occasional smear of blood on the wall.

"First, we go to the flop I rented. It might be that Vee just went there, unable to get back to campus."

"Maybe he's there, too hurt to get help."

Kaiana didn't respond, but that had been exactly what she had been thinking. And even that would be one of the better scenarios she could conjure in her imagination.

But Veranix wasn't there when they arrived, and there was no sign that he had been back in hours.

"Next?" Delmin asked.

"Can you, I don't know, sense anything? I'm not sure how it all works."

"Nothing too specific, at least here," he said, looking around the place. "I mean, there's some strange pooling and swirling of *numina*, like the cloak had been here, but it's because it had been here for a while. There's not much trail for me to follow."

"And with the rope?"

"There's . . . resonance? Maybe that's the best word. It's like the energy of the rope is reacting to the fact the cloak was here, but . . . again, it's nothing I can follow."

"But if we get closer to him, you might be able to tell?"

"Might." He didn't sound very confident about that at all. "Maybe we need to think about where he might have gone. The potential places Jensett is working."

"Like?"

"I was thinking like an abandoned factory or tannery— some place where he can work with chemicals and not be noticed. I told Vee there's plenty of those out in the west side of the city, but I don't know about here."

"Then let's find someone who does know."

She already knew who: they were going to have to find a Rose Street Prince.

"The hole" wasn't strictly speaking a punishment, as much as a preventative measure. Colin knew this. Jutie had killed a stick, with plenty of witnesses, and that wouldn't go away easy. Surely the sticks had turned out the streets for him.

As his captain Colin would have Jutie's back out there. Any captain worth the stars on his arm would knock the skulls of every stick walking Rose Street to save his crew. Hotchins and the rest of the bosses knew that, which is why they dragged Colin down to the basement offices for the night. He couldn't be trusted out there, not tonight.

Colin had understood this when other captains had to spend the night down there. He knew it had to have torn them up, but it was the right call.

This was Colin's first time. First time one of his crew was in the wind. And it tore his gut the whole night long.

Jutie wouldn't be left to swing, of course. Other Princes, other captains—ones who could have a cool head—they'd be looking for him. Hopefully, they'd find him and keep him hidden and safe.

Nobody told him a damn thing all night.

To be fair to the bosses, they didn't keep him actually locked away in a closet or anything. He stewed at the card table with Nints and Bottin and Giles, while Hucks stood in the doorway. Beers and strikers were brought, enough to keep him calm. Not so many beers that he might try something crazy.

Not that Colin had had any doubt Hucks would have clobbered him if he had tried something.

Hotchins and Frenty eventually showed up with some boiled eggs, hard biscuits, and tea, letting Colin know it was morning. Nints, Bottin, and Giles took their leave, probably to finally get some sleep.

"We know anything about Jutie?" Colin asked.

"We know the sticks don't have him yet," Frenty said. "But that's about all we do know. Kid went into the wind well, I'll give him that. Best kite job I've seen."

"Nobody's seen him? What about my—the flop my crew crashes at?"

Frenty nodded. "Checked there. Credit to your boy Tooser, he kept it locked tight, and when we told him you were in the hole and he and your birds needed to sit it out, they took it well."

"Tooser's a smart one, really," Colin said. "You all should start looking to him for stars."

"One thing at a time, Tyson," Hotchins said. "We've got a dozen messes going on right now, and all the sewage seems to flow back to you."

"I can see that," Colin said. No point trying to deny it.

Hotchins pushed a plate over to Colin and sat down. "Let's start with Jutie. Where do you think he'd go?"

"If he didn't crash in a Prince flop? I'm not—" He remembered the incident in the street a month before. "He's got a brother. Narrow walker, this guy. Works tannery or something clean, you know? Wettle, or Whenton . . . Wylon, that's it."

"Wylon Higgs," Hotchins said. "You know where they live?"

"Not on Rose Street. Maybe not even in Aventil."

"You think they'd hide Jutie?"

"From the sticks? I—I'll tell you, I only ever saw this guy once, and like I said, narrow walker. He really didn't like that Jutie was a Prince. But blood is blood, you know?"

As soon as he said that, Colin's stomach twisted. No

telling what happened to Veranix last night. Rabbits or that Jensett might have killed him. Deadly Birds might have killed him. "Any other news out there? Streets still rowing? Rabbits still acting up?"

"After our ugliness, it all got quiet, to tell the truth. Mostly because the sticks really were out in force. Like I ain't seen in *years*, let me tell you."

"I suppose that's Jutie's fault."

"He didn't help," Frenty said.

"So am I still in the hole?"

"You should be," Hotchins said. "But Casey says we need to move on this Rabbits thing, and he liked your idea of hitting Orchid Street."

"He did?"

"And you are blazing lucky he did, too. That's the thing that kept him from ordering your stars burned."

Colin swallowed hard. He knew things had taken a real left turn, and he was certainly in the middle of it all, but he had no idea that it was even coming close to that.

"He was . . . he wanted . . ."

Frenty's hand dug into Colin's shoulder. "Hotchins really hit the tetch for you, so don't forget it."

"No. Not at all, Hotch. I 'preciate it."

"Good." Hotchins sat back and sipped at his tea. "So in a bit you're gonna take some muscle—none of your crew, mind you—"

"Sure, fine, good idea."

Hotchins paused, clearly not thrilled about being talked over.

"You'll go and clear any fur coats out of Orchid. You handle that, things should be calmer for you."

Colin nodded and took a bite of the food. He had no appetite at all, but the last thing he could do was let Hotchins see what a state he was in.

Silently he prayed to whatever saint might listen to him that Veranix was all right.

Veranix found awareness coming at him like a buzzing fly, in fits and starts that were impossible to hold on to. There were light and shadows, there were voices, none of which he could make any proper sense of. He became more aware of a pain in his head that throbbed and pounded, and then realized that something metal was pressing against the back of his neck. He tried to touch it, push it away, but his arms wouldn't move.

Arms wouldn't move because they were bound.

Veranix forced his eyes open.

As his vision focused, he saw how he was held, as bizarre as it was. He was bound by coils of metal that spiraled around his bare arms.

His arms were bare. Looking down, he saw the rest of him was as well, save the cloak still over his shoulders. He was propped up on his feet, with the same metal coils around his legs. And he was kept upright by whatever was resting against his neck.

He pulled in *numina* to knock all these bindings off of himself, but as soon as he did, it was yanked right back out of him. A second attempt yielded the same result.

"Oh, what was that?" one voice said. Veranix became more aware of the voices near him. He couldn't see much of anything, partly because he was facing a wall. Footsteps approached, and two figures stepped into view.

One was Cuse Jensett, the Prankster. He looked grubby and disheveled, deeply tired around the eyes in the way a lot of students did right around exams. But he also had an ebullience in his demeanor, like he was deeply pleased with the results of hard work.

In fact, he looked much like Phadre did when he passed his defense.

The other was an older man, nearly bald save a few wisps of white around his ears. He looked Veranix over with shrewd eyes.

"I'd like to lodge a complaint," Veranix said weakly. "These beds are horrible."

"Well, that settles it," the old man said. "You're exactly who I thought you were."

That brought Veranix sharply into the moment. "You think you know me?" He pulled at his bindings, but they didn't yield even an inch. And magic, he had already determined, was useless.

"Oh, I don't know your name, Thorn," the old man said. "Any more than you know mine. But those eyes, that voice, the cocky jokes? That I know all too well."

Veranix took a guess. "I take it you're Reb Jensett."

The old man chuckled. "Reb was my brother. Died a few years ago. Did you know there were three Jensett boys back in the day?"

"I didn't know there were Jensett boys at all until yesterday, frankly."

"Typical," the unnamed Jensett said.

"So who is he, Uncle?" Cuse asked.

"Do you want to tell him, Thorn?"

"Honestly, I'd rather punch him in the face, but given that you've put me in this contraption . . ."

"Contraption," Cuse said contemptuously. "Come now, is that the best you can manage for this triumph? A synthesis of magic and science? I may not know who my uncle thinks you are, but I recognize you from the dinner. I know you're a magic student. Surely you can appreciate craftsmanship."

Veranix rolled his eyes. "Yes, you have me bound in dalmatium, so I can't do any magic. Bravo."

"Dalmatium!" Cuse was incredulous. "You are a simpleton, Thorn! Mere dalmatium, as if all I cared about was blocking your magic. That would be useless." He stomped out of view.

"Cuse, boy, there's no need—"

"No, no, Uncle," Cuse said, coming back over. "I want him to know what I have been the architect of. He may be a fool, but he can at least *comprehend* the magnitude of what I've done." He returned with what looked like a crystalline jar, glowing faintly blue. "You know what that is?"

The term Delmin had mentioned the other day sprung to Veranix's mind. "A *numinic* battery?" For some reason, that made sense, even if Veranix still wasn't sure what it meant.

Cuse seemed honestly impressed by the answer. "Spot on, Thorn. Full marks. A source of stored *numina* to fuel my project. The raw background flow can be enough for some effects, but to do something really impressive, it must be gathered and stored. And as I'm not a mage, I can't do that with my body. Not like you."

"Fascinating," Veranix said. "So that's how you hurt and killed people."

"And now I'll do so much more, thanks to you." He admired the jar again. "You see, for what I've planned for today, I was originally only going to be able to use background flow to charge up three, maybe four of these. It would be a fair amount of *numina*, but now . . ."

Veranix suddenly understood the bindings. He was the source of the *numina*. Him and the cloak. "How many did you charge?"

"Twenty-seven," Cuse said gleefully. "I could have done more, mind you, but there are interesting dynamics when these are arranged in triads that I've never been able to exploit to this degree. Yes, twenty-seven will be quite intriguing."

Veranix gave the old man a glance. "Pride of the family, is he?"

"I could ask you the same, Mister Tyson."

Veranix chuckled, trying to cover the sudden shock of hearing that. "My name isn't Tyson, friend."

"Maybe that isn't your name, boy. But I'll be damned all to blazes if you aren't Cal Tyson's son."

Cuse gave a lopsided smirk. "And that, dear Thorn, is why you're still alive. Well, that and using you to fuel production of the Red."

Chapter 22

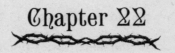

"**W**HERE ARE WE GOING?" Delmin's voice was in full whine as he followed behind Kaiana. But he had probably not ever delved into one of these side alleys, so she could hardly blame him for being apprehensive.

"There's a room down here where some of the Rose Street Princes sleep. Including the one we want to find."

"Right. I forgot we wanted to find one."

"Found the wrong one," a voice hissed.

Kaiana turned to see a Prince—not Colin—behind Delmin with a knife at his throat. This Prince was young, though, a few years younger than Delmin or her. And she had seen him before—he brought her to this flop when she went looking for Colin.

"Easy, easy," she said. "You don't want to do that."

"Really don't," Delmin squeaked out.

"Why are you snooping around here, Napa?" he asked.

"Looking for your captain," Kaiana said.

"Right, right," he said. "I remember. Why I been trailing you. You got another delivery for him or something? Bringing this skinny rat to him?"

The blade was pressed onto Delmin's skin—just enough to let him feel it, but not enough to cut. Delmin looked terrified beyond all capacity for speech or thought.

"Ease off, Prince. We're not your enemies," Kaiana said.

"You ain't my friends." He looked around, like he was making sure no one else was watching. "And none of mine can help me. But I think you know who can, don't you?"

Kaiana decided she needed to take a chance. "You mean the Thorn."

The tension in his knife hand eased just a bit. "I knew it! You know the Thorn! You're his contact, ain't you?"

"It was his stuff I brought here last month," she said. "That's why Colin and the other Prince went to help him."

"Hetzer," the kid muttered. "So what's it about now?"

"Kai . . ." Delmin gasped out.

"Easy, Del. We're all going to keep it easy," she said. "You're the Thorn's friend, right? You too, Uni? What do you do for him?"

Delmin squeaked out. "I was there that night. Your friend—Hetzer. He tried to help me. One of those . . . one of those mages, they came for him and me. He stood his ground. Should have run, but he stood."

The kid turned a bit. "You were there that night? Then where was it?"

"Warehouse, way up in Dentonhill. One of Fenmere's."

"All right, all right." He looked hard at Kaiana, keeping the knife on Delmin. "I'm in some real fire here. Can Thorn help me out?"

Kaiana had to be honest. "No, kid, he can't."

"The blazes?" The knife came tight onto Delmin's flesh.

"I think the Thorn's in trouble," Kaiana said quickly. "He went hunting someone last night. Someone causing a lot of trouble on campus."

"The bloke he was trying to get the other night?" His hand pulled away again. "I owe that guy a bit of blood, I can tell you that."

"That's the one."

Delmin suddenly reacted, a burst of wild magic, splitting him and the Prince apart. The Prince stumbled, but Delmin went flying to the ground.

"What—"

"Hey, Prince," Kaiana said, directing his attention to her eyes. "Keep on me, all right? That guy, we're pretty sure the Thorn got in trouble going after him. So we're trying to find him."

The Prince shrugged, put the knife back down, and slinked back into the shadow a bit. Kaiana noticed his hands and coat had a fair amount of dried blood on them. "So who's this guy? You got a name?"

"Cuse Jensett," Delmin said from the ground.

"Jensett?" the Prince said. "Blazes, that's a Rabbit name."

"White Rabbits?" Delmin asked.

"Red Rabbits," the Prince said, a bit put off. His eyes narrowed. "I know one place where I think there's a bunch of them."

Kaiana nodded. "I'll take it. Where?"

"Rabbits have been pressing their chins, you know? They recently pushed into an old brewery."

"A brewery?" Delmin asked. "That would . . . that could be exactly the sort of place Jensett would need to do his work."

"Where's the brewery?" Kaiana asked.

"Tulip and Waterpath."

"Thanks, Prince," Kaiana said. She grabbed Delmin's hand and pulled him up onto his feet.

"Hey, wait," the Prince said. "If the Thorn needs help, if this guy took him down, then . . . I want a piece. Blazes, I owe him a piece."

"You look like you've got enough trouble right now, kid," Delmin said.

"Damn right I do. If the Thorn can't help me out of it, then . . . might as well do something to make it worth it."

Kaiana looked him over again. "Delmin, give him your coat."

"Are you crazy?"

"He puts your coat on, hands in his pocket, and he won't stand out."

"How can we trust—"

The kid flipped his knife around and offered it, hilt first, to Kaiana. "If you two are really friends with the Thorn, I've had his back twice this week. I'm not going to quit that now."

"Good enough for me," Kaiana said, refusing the knife. "Right, Delmin?"

Delmin groused but handed over the coat.

Cuse and the old Rabbit had stepped away, conferring with some of the other Rabbits out of Veranix's earshot. Veranix took the opportunity to determine how deep in the blazes he really was.

For one, he was nearly naked, so no weapons. He was bound in the metal coils, and attempts to move his hands proved fruitless. Magic equally so. Anything he pulled in was yanked out of him, presumably by the coils. If he understood that stuff better—like Phadre or Jiarna did—maybe he could at least come up with a way to circumvent that.

He laughed to himself. More likely, he'd simply understand what was happening.

"I honestly think it's foolish," the old Rabbit was saying.

"I don't care. You have your plan, which I've done plenty for. Your revenge is no less petty than my own."

"Fine, fine," the old man said. "When will you be back?"

"No later than noon bells. The ceremony starts at eleven bells, and I'll trigger things shortly after that. I'll watch the carnage for a while, but from a respectable distance."

"How far is that?"

"Honestly, Uncle, with this many *numina* batteries, it might just be that the whole campus is affected."

At that, Veranix couldn't hold back. The dam burst open. "I am going to tear you apart, Jensett! I will make you eat those batteries."

"He is a little firefly, isn't he?" Cuse asked idly.

"Like his father," the old man said. "Cal wasn't the brightest, but he could talk up a storm."

"Well, you can reminisce with him. I'm off to destroy the University."

"Good luck with that."

The old man came back in Veranix's line of sight. "Look, son, I don't blame you for not liking the Rabbits. Reb was one of the first to turn on your father and your uncle when things went left."

"I really don't know what you're talking about."

"Do not insult me, all right, kid? Let me tell you, you've got a beef with Fenmere, well, so do we all. And this stuff here, that my nephew cooked up? It'll take down Fenmere. Blazes, he tricked the man into giving him the starting funds. So we—the Red Rabbits—we're going to make him suffer. Don't you like that?"

"It's not the worst thing," Veranix admitted. "But I could use a better view."

"I get it, kid. Your pop was a good man. I liked him. You want to do right by him. This'll do it."

"Humor me and define 'this.' Besides Cuse destroying the campus."

The old man waved that off. "That's his thing. *His* revenge on the University. You understand, I'm sure."

"Understand?" Veranix said, feeling his anger flow through him. "I smack around *effitte* dealers and scum who work for Fenmere. Your boy there has been hurting and killing innocent people."

"Eh, it makes him happy. And we want to keep him happy right now. He's the one making the Red."

"The Red?" Veranix asked. That was mentioned before. Cuse said he'd be fueling it, whatever that meant.

"We'll take Fenmere's whole market. The Red is better, and we can make it cheaper."

"The Red is like *effitte*? And you're making it? Here?"

"That's right," the old man said. He said it, pride filling his face, which then fell. Maybe he could tell by Veranix's expression that he had just said the wrong thing.

Veranix slammed as much *numina* through his body as he could stand. The coils were sucking it away, growing hot around his wrists and ankles.

"What are you doing?" the old man asked.

The room was humming.

No matter how much *numina* he pulled, Veranix couldn't beat the device.

But maybe he could break it.

The crew Colin had been given were older, tougher brutes. Tough enough to live as long as they had, but none of them particularly blessed with wits. If they had been, they would have made captain, given the time they had put in the streets. They were good for this job, though: bruisers who could crack skulls with the best of them.

Orchid Street was a pretty typical collection of shops for the neighborhood: a general store, a secretarial and post, a cheese maker, bakery, so forth. The north side of the street was clearly Prince territory; they had a storeroom and a couple flops over there, nothing that mattered too much. On the south side they hadn't bothered holding any flops or shops.

Rabbits had been seen on the corners on Orchid for the past few weeks, marking territory. The lines were fuzzy, and for the sake of the peace, the Pact, the Princes hadn't made much noise over Rabbits making the south side of Orchid their own.

Now it was time for a racket.

"Oy," Colin called as they approached the cheese shop. The shop owner—an older man with a thick mustache—was sweeping his stoop. He started to wave them off as they came over.

"No trouble, please."

"No trouble," Colin said. "We're just here to help our neighbors."

"Help?" the man asked cautiously, backing into the shop. "I don't need anything."

Colin moved into the doorway. "No? Because if you had, say, a rodent infestation, me and my boys could help you chase them out."

"Rodents?"

"Rodents," Colin said. "You know, furry troublemakers? Maybe in your basement, or one of your rooms upstairs?"

"No, no," the cheese shop man said. "I got none of that. None, you hear?"

"Fine," Colin said. He pulled a few ticks out of his pocket and handed the coins to the man. "You wouldn't happen to know anyone who does have such a problem?"

The man glanced out the door and down the street, checking to see if any of his neighbors were watching. "You didn't hear this from me, hmm?"

"Of course not."

"Bennim, the sew-up, he's got a problem in his place. A bad one."

"Anyone else?"

"Gawkins." The secretarial and post. "And I know he'd like some help with it."

"You're a good neighbor, friend." Colin slapped him on the shoulder and led his boys down to the sew-up's shop. "We'll do right by him, eh?" he said to them. "Buy some cheese, bring it to Casey and the rest."

"If you want," one of the heavies said. Ment was his name. Big guy, no real imagination.

"Do people right, live like Princes," Colin said. If nothing else, that was something his father had drilled into him. Vessrin, Jensett, Hallaran, the rest of his old friends . . . they never understood that. Colin wondered what the neighborhood meant to them at all.

The sew-up—a cheap doctor who asked few questions—was probably the main reason the Rabbits had moved in over here. Colin didn't know Orchid as well as Rose Street, but if Bennim was any good, the Princes would have already locked him down as one of their own. So he was likely a drunk or clod with shaky hands.

Colin knocked on the door, but didn't wait for any call from inside. The door wasn't latched, so they just went in. The front parlor was a shabby sitting room, and a boy sat at a little desk.

"Hey, whoa!" the kid said. "You can't come barging in here."

"Sure we can, kid," Colin said, and no one was going to argue much with him and five bruisers. "We've got a bit of business here."

"Doc is with a patient, eh? You'll have to wait."

"Not right now," Colin said, pushing through the next door.

The doctor might have been with a patient, but the only treatment he was giving involved them both being naked. They screamed and jumped off each other.

"What . . . what the blazes are you doing here?" the old man shouted.

"Sorry to interrupt your . . . session, Doc," Colin said. He glanced at the bird's clothes on the ground, and noticed the fur-lined coat. So she was a Rabbit. "We heard you had an infestation of Rabbits, and we thought we'd clear it out for you."

"Now wait just a moment—" the doctor stammered.

The bird wasted no time grabbing one of his instruments off the table and leaping for Ment like she was about to plunge it into his eye. Ment didn't even blink, grabbing the bird's wrist and snapping it before she even touched the floor.

"Now you might have some real work," Colin said, wrapping his arm around the naked old man. "Look, I don't mean to mess things up for you. I can see the appeal of whatever deal you've cooked up here." That said, this Rabbit bird was an older, scrawny thing that probably hadn't been a real source of honey for the Rabbits in a while. "But it ain't any good for my friends here. You can see that."

The girl was shaking on the ground now, like she wanted to scream but couldn't.

"Ment, cover her with something, hmm? A little respect."

"Let me help the girl, please," the doctor said.

"In a moment, all right," Colin said. "This is how it's going to go. First we're going to clear out your infestation. Then we'll keep some boys here to make sure it doesn't return."

"Just boys?" the doctor asked.

"I'll see what I can do," Colin said. "We don't really deal in that sort of thing, or turn out our own." He threw that at the girl on the ground, though she didn't seem in the mood to listen to anything.

"I don't see much point in arguing," the doctor said.

"Capital," Colin said. "Ment, stay with our new friends. The rest of us, let's go clean out the warren."

"Something is happening," Delmin said as they approached the brewery. "Oh, saints, something is really going on." He stopped walking in a straight line, spinning wildly.

Kaiana grabbed him by the shoulders. "Del! You're drawing attention to yourself."

"Sorry, sorry, it's just ... I don't even know ..." He grabbed onto his head, like he was trying to pry it open.

"What's wrong with him?" the Prince asked Kaiana.

"He can sense magic," she said. She grabbed Delmin by the front of his shirt and pulled him out of the walkway.

"What, really?"

"It's there!" Delmin shouted, pointing simultaneously in two directions.

"Where?" Kaiana looked at both places he pointed. One was an old building. The other was a wagon rolling down the street. "Is that the brewery?"

"Yeah," the Prince said. "But the two guys driving that wagon were Rabbits."

"Damn it," Kaiana said. "Del, is it Vee . . . is that what you sense?"

"Maybe. I don't . . . I can't . . ."

"What does that mean?" the Prince asked.

"You think he's on the wagon?" she asked.

"Something is on the wagon. Something is in the brewery." He covered his eyes. "Too much, too much."

"Do you feel him?"

"They're both him," Delmin said.

The Prince looked back and forth. "Is that possible?" He shrugged. "I don't know how this magic stuff works."

Delmin's hands crossed back and forth. "It's all too . . . no . . . that is . . . that one . . ." He pointed to the wagon. "That's just a hum. A very loud hum."

"What does that mean?"

"The other is a scream. A living howl of *numina*. And it—it—"

Delmin fell back against the shop front, pressing his palms against his eyes.

"This don't look good, bird," the Prince said.

"No," Kaiana said. She looked over to the brewery. "Watch him."

"Whatdya mean watch him?"

She grabbed the Prince by the front of his coat. "Does he look like he can fend for himself? You. Watch. Him. I'm going in."

Kaiana didn't wait for the Prince to respond, going toward the brewery while shoving one hand in her coat pocket. She wrapped her fingers around the handle of her spade.

The main door was open, just a bit. So there was no need to force her way in.

As soon as she looked inside, she saw only two people — Red Rabbits by their coats. They weren't paying her any mind, and it was easy to see why.

They were far more focused on the fact that the building was vibrating.

Chapter 23

"CORRECT ME IF I'M WRONG, Uni," Jutie said to the skinny kid, "but something tells me that wagon is nothing but bad news. Rabbits and magic, right?"

The poor guy looked like he'd been hit by *effitte* and a swift kick to the head. "Yeah. Something—a lot of magic, but sitting, not focused. Not a person, you know?"

"I really don't know, Uni," Jutie said. "But there are people on it."

"There are," the Uni said, and he stood up in a jolt. "It isn't Vee—err, the Thorn—it's *him*."

"Him who?" The kid was already striding after the wagon. "Blazes."

"Him, and he's doing something so big it hurts me from here," the kid said. "The guy the Thorn went after."

"You know what he's going to do?" The Uni kid was a mage, who knew what they could do.

"Not what, but I can feel the power levels." He stopped in the middle of the street, and then pulled Jutie to the corner walkway. Jutie didn't make a thing of it, the kid was a mage, and a friend of the Thorn. "That's the problem, see? Whatever is on that wagon, I'm too sensitive to it. I get close, it's like a knife in my skull."

"Got it," Jutie said. He didn't get magic, but the idea that some sort of big magic could mess up a mage's head made a certain amount of sense. "So what do we do?"

"Wait for the Thorn?"

"Won't he be all knife-to-the-skull over it?"

"No, he—we're different kinds of mages, let's leave it at that. But . . . blazes, if he—he might not be able to do anything about it."

"And you can't either."

"No, but . . . I might know someone who can." His face got very serious. "If I can get ahead of it, maybe I can warn them."

This was something Jutie understood. Safewalk to the Uni gates. "All right. We're going to take the fastest route I know to get ahead, and saints help whoever gets in our way. Can you run?"

The Uni kid nodded.

"Then let's go."

"You stop that right now, Thorn!" the old man was shouting. The room was vibrating, making the old Rabbit's voice tremble.

"I'm the Thorn again?" Veranix asked, forcing the words out through short breath. "I thought you wanted to call me Tyson."

"Saints, what is that?" someone shouted in the distance.

"You've got me hooked up to those tanks of the Red, hmm?" Veranix said. "I bet that's some sensitive cooking. How much of me do you think they can take?"

Now the *numina* was a torrent pouring out of his body, wave after wave. The coils felt white hot on his skin, but his whole body was heat and fire and magic.

The old man pulled out a knife. "You stop that now!"

"Or what?" Veranix shouted. Dust and debris started to fall down from the ceiling, and the walls were shaking. "What about this whole old building? How much could it handle?"

In the distance something burst, like a blast of a tea-kettle.

The old man ran out of sight.

Veranix's heart was pounding. He didn't have much more to give. More bursts and blasts. Veranix hoped those were the vats of the Red, whatever the stuff was, boiling over, useless.

Then something above them cracked—a horrible sound of wood breaking apart, and then a collapse. Maybe he had broken the building.

Which was good, because he couldn't push himself anymore. There was nothing but pain and heat, like his body was an ember of a dying fire.

"You will pay for that with blood, Thorn! I'm going to cut you open and wear your stomach as a hat! You'll—"

Then there was a thump and the solid sound of a body hitting the floor.

Footsteps approached slowly. Then a very familiar voice spoke.

"Do I even want to know what happened to you?"

"Kai?"

She came into view.

"I did tell you I would punch people in the face."

"Please tell me you can get me out of this contrap-tion."

"At least this time you ended up the naked one." She looked far too amused by this.

"Kai!" There wasn't time for this.

"Sorry," she said, examining the coil around his arm.

A bit more urgency came in her voice as she worked her fingers under the metal. "I shouldn't joke. I knocked out the old man, but there're still a couple Rabbits upstairs. Of course, part of the roof collapsed."

"Only a couple?" Veranix asked. "Cuse was here, but . . . he's going to the campus."

With a grunt, she pulled the coil and it moved far more easily than Veranix thought it would have. "Soft metal," she muttered.

"I couldn't move it from in here," he said defensively.

"Wasn't judging," she said. "He's got another prank planned?"

"Beyond anything else. He used this—used me—to charge up the *numina* for his plan. So this will be bigger than all the others put together." Veranix worked his hand free. "It'll be my fault."

"No," Kaiana said, moving to the other hand. "You can't think that."

"If I hadn't gotten captured . . ."

"Then we stop him, Vee." Her eyes went wide. "The wagon!"

"Wagon?"

"There was a wagon, and Delmin felt something on it, and he couldn't move, but I came in here . . ."

Veranix got his other hand out. "Delmin is here?"

"On the street," she said. "With some Prince who wants to help you."

"My gear, find it," Veranix said. He bent down and got his legs free. "Not Colin?"

"No. A kid, really," she said, going off out of sight.

"I know who you mean." Jutie—the kid who had been there for the past few scrapes. Veranix appreciated the loyalty, though he wasn't sure he deserved it.

Kai came back with his clothes. He had now gotten

out of the contraption, and as soon as he was free, he felt a shift in his magical energy. The cloak was charging him again, but it was the false strength the cloak gave. His own energy was still quite depleted.

"Weapons?" he asked as he got dressed again. "With the noise of the collapse, it can't be long before the Constabulary show. I'm not their favorite person, either."

"I probably don't want to see them either," Kaiana said.

"Worry more about them seeing you," Veranix said, finishing doing up his vest. "In fact, get out ahead. I'll find my stuff."

"You think I'm leaving you?"

Veranix should have expected that. "No, but—"

"But nothing." She produced his bow and quiver. "You're pretty light on arrows."

"I only need one good shot." Veranix strapped them on. "'Cuse couldn't have gotten very far."

"Except he's on a wagon with several Red Rabbits."

Veranix spotted his staff lying in a corner. "I'll think of something." He grabbed it and went up the stairs.

Kai was right on his heels. "That got you into this mess."

"But this time I have you here." He shaded his face—not that it really mattered, given what the old Rabbit said—as he reached the main brewery floor.

The place was in shambles—vats fallen over, smashed open. The red poison pooling on the ground, draining off to the sewer grates. One of the support pillars had broken, and the roof had collapsed there.

And on the far side, Keckin and Sotch were limping out the door, half carrying each other.

"You're letting them go?" Kaiana whispered to him.

"They aren't worth wasting an arrow on."

"Am I?"

That question was asked just as something whistled past his face, far closer than he would have liked. It hit the wall—a razor-sharp disc, sticking where it struck—but Veranix's attention went to the source. The dark-haired woman in the scandalous blue outfit.

He snapped an arrow into the bow and took aim. "Now's not playtime, Bluejay."

"But it is," she said, swirling her bladed hoops on her arms.

"That's Bluejay?" Kaiana gasped.

"And since you broke Blackbird's wings, I had to bring a different friend."

Veranix barely saw the flash of blonde hair before she was right next to him, releasing a flurry of punches at him. He dropped back to dodge, releasing the arrow in a wild shot. Before this new girl could get a solid hit, he grabbed Kai's arm and forced some hard magic into his legs, jumping over several of the large vats into a far corner of the warehouse.

Kai screamed, half fear, half joy, as they landed.

"Is this what it's always like?" she asked.

Veranix grabbed another arrow, taking a quick count as he drew it. Five left. "Kai, don't argue."

"About—"

"You're going to run while I keep these two busy, hear?"

"But—"

"I need you to stop Cuse, Kai. Clear?"

"Thorn, we know where you are," the blonde bird called in singsong laughter. "Come on, come on."

"Ready," he whispered. "Now!"

He spun from behind the cask and fired at the blonde, who dodged out of the way. The shot would have been true to her heart, but a second after he released, he sent a wisp of magic into the arrow, curving it toward Bluejay.

She wasn't ready for that, and didn't get her hoops up in time to block it. Of course, his aim was atrocious, and only grazed her bare arm.

But that was enough to get her attention while Kai went for the door. Good use of an arrow. Only four left.

"The Napa!" the blonde one shouted. She made a run, drawing out three darts from a bandolier. Without breaking stride, she fired them off in rapid succession.

One hit Kai in the arm, which caused her to cry out and stumble. Veranix instinctively shot out a burst of magic to knock the other two off course.

"She's not our game, Magpie," Bluejay said. "Let her run."

The blonde—Magpie—chuckled. "Fine. I get to kill a mage." She turned on Veranix, who had swapped out the bow for the staff. Both these ladies could dodge and block him all day, so there was no sense in wasting arrows on them. Or the day. If his magic was at full strength, he could have stuck these two to the floor and been on his way.

But magic was in tighter reserves than his arrows. Just knocking the darts off course made him lightheaded, and that was with the cloak.

So his staff and his wits were the only things left to hold off these two Deadly Birds. Hopefully he could keep them at bay long enough.

No one had been in the room for hours as far as Bell could tell. Something had happened after the noise and shouting that had taken their full attention. That was for the best, as he wanted no further part in having to listen to Sotch and Keckin act like the proverbial rabbits.

Then the walls shook apart.

Something had fallen on Bell, but he couldn't tell what with the hood over his head. It was heavy, but only heavy enough to be annoying. It was clear that no one was bothering to check on him. That gave him all the reasons to pull and strain at his bonds with no worries about being caught. They had tied him tight, and he tore up his wrists working his way loose, but after several minutes he got one hand free. He pulled off the hood and saw that he was in an abandoned office of some sort. A bookcase—thankfully empty—had fallen on top of him.

It took several more minutes, but eventually he pulled his way out from under the case.

He looked around the room to see what he could use as a weapon. The best option was the rope he had been tied up with.

A commotion came from outside the office, somewhere on the brewery floor. Grabbing the rope, Bell slipped out cautiously to see what was going on.

The first thing he saw was the girl—the assassin Bluejay, specifically. He had seen her the other night, half in the dark, but in the light of day she was astounding. The bladed hoops spun on her hips effortlessly, to mesmerizing effect. Bell could watch her spin all day if he had the chance.

Of course, she was using those blades to try to slice up the Thorn, who was fighting like blazes to hold off her attacks, as well as another bird, a blonde one. Bell didn't know that one's name, but she was clearly tough and fast, blocking the Thorn's staff attacks with just her arms. Bell didn't know why her arms weren't broken from that, but she kept at it.

For both the birds the fight was fluid and easy. They seemed to be having the time of their lives.

For the Thorn it was anything but effortless. Every move was desperate, a last-second block or dodge to avoid being sliced or punched. He was losing ground, backing away with every attack the girls made.

Bell almost felt bad for the guy. At least he would, if the Thorn didn't deserve such a thorough beating.

But after a bit it was clear they were just playing with him, wearing him down.

Bell could have stayed up on the office steps, and had a grand view of the whole thing. But he wanted to be closer. He wanted the Thorn to know he was there. After all the taunts and jibes, Bell wanted the Thorn to see his face when he died.

Coming down to the brewery floor, he could see that the Thorn hadn't been so lucky with those last-second dodges and blocks. He had more than a few cuts on his arms and shoulders, but despite that, he was still fighting like blazes.

As Bell got closer, the Thorn took a punch from the blonde, but managed to feint and pivot, using the blonde's body as a shield from Bluejay's strike. She took a bad hit, crying out, and right at that moment, the Thorn slammed his staff into the ground, and the room shook. A blast of something burst away from the Thorn, hitting the two birds and Bell, knocking them all to the ground.

They all dropped, and he dashed. Bell pulled himself up on his elbows, but by the time he could see, the Thorn had made it out the door.

"You let him get away!" he yelled at them.

"Who the blazes are you?" the blonde asked.

Bluejay hopped to her feet and stepped into the center of her fallen hoops. "He works for the client." She hooked her feet under her bladed hoops on the ground, and in a moment got them spinning around her body again, as easy as breathing. "Don't worry, friend. His death is supposed to be public."

Her hips still swaying, she dashed after the Thorn, far faster than Bell imagined anyone could be while keeping those blades spinning.

The blonde wasn't quite as quick. Her vest had taken the brunt of the slice, but blood was oozing from it. "She's right," she said, walking after them. "And he's not going far."

Bell was about to follow when he heard another noise from behind him. He spun around and saw an old man—the Old Rabbit who had killed his boys and taunted him. Before he even realized what he was doing, Bell's hand was around the old Rabbit's throat.

"Wait—" the old man gasped.

"Oh, now you want me to wait?" Bell spat at him. "I told you who I was. I am Dentonhill. I am Fenmere." He squeezed tighter.

"But—I can—I can tell you—who he—"

Bell didn't bother to find out what the Old Rabbit could tell him as his hands tightened. There was nothing that man could say that he cared to hear.

The old man could tell his secrets to whatever sinner found his soul.

Chapter 24

THE PRINCE LED DELMIN through a maze of alleys, shop hallways, and one family's kitchen, running so fast Delmin's heart threatened to burst through his ribs. But the pain in his chest was nothing compared to the tearing in his skull, the shredding power coming from that wagon. He couldn't see it at any point in their mad dash, but he always knew exactly where it was.

And then there was a change, a pulse of power, almost imperceptible. A wrong note in an orchestra of agony. But it forced Delmin to stumble and fall in the alley. The Prince was right on it, grabbing Delmin by the arm.

"Come on, Uni, not far now."

"Already at the gate," Delmin said, forcing the words out. "I don't think anything is stopping them."

The Prince hauled Delmin over his shoulder and dragged him along. "You're telling me that a wagon full of blazing Red Rabbits could get through the Uni gate? You can't sell me that."

They came out of the alley with a clear view of the gate, and there was no sign of the wagon. There were the fading remnants of a bluish mist and a scent of magic lingering. But more disturbing was how the cadets, the rest of the wagoneers, and several folk on the street stood completely still.

Like statues.

Delmin instinctively covered his mouth and nose with his shirt, not that it would do much good.

"Blazes is this?" the Prince asked.

"Stay back," Delmin said, forcing himself to pull in *numina* despite the screaming in his head. It was there, all around, he just needed to claim it.

This was the hardest part. As well as he could see it, drawing in *numina* and keeping it always felt like holding boiling water in his hands. Even if he could force himself to stand it, it would still seep through his fingers.

He had to hold on to it, had to build up enough. Even though his body scorched, joints on fire, he held that power in with every ounce of strength he had.

How did Veranix do this so effortlessly?

He had drawn in more than he could ever stand, more than he ever had before, and then forced it to become breath. His breath, the only way he could visualize it, which put that fire and energy into his own lungs.

Then he opened his mouth and let it come out of him, a tremendous gust of wind through the street.

He hadn't even realized he had shut his eyes.

He opened them to find himself on his knees, leaning on the Prince, who took it with grace.

"Blazes, Uni, what did you do?"

"I'm not sure, but that was all I had," Delmin said. The mist was all gone, though. The people in front of the gate were moving now, at least starting to.

"Well, that was a damn thing, all right." He pulled Delmin onto his feet. "Come on."

They only made it two steps before they almost

collided into Kaiana, running like a madwoman. Her arm was sliced open and bleeding.

"What are you doing?" she demanded.

"The wagon, it was him," Delmin said.

"I know, we have to stop him."

"What about the Thorn?" the Prince demanded.

Kaiana faltered. "He told me to run. Two—two assassins were on him, and he made me go ahead."

The Prince looked back at the people by the gate, who were now falling over, heaving and convulsing. Whatever the Prankster had done didn't kill them, but coming out of it looked horrifying. "Because that guy has to be stopped."

"Right," Kaiana said.

The Prince pushed Delmin onto Kai, and she barely was able to grab him before he fell to the ground. That act of magic had left him with almost no strength in his legs at all. "He thinks he knows what to do. So you better get on it."

"What are you doing?" Kaiana asked. The Prince had stripped off Delmin's coat, tossed it to them, and drawn two knives.

"I'm going to go help the Thorn, because I bet you're going to need him."

Then he went back in the alley.

"Delmin, you're a mess," Kaiana said. She didn't even bother trying to help him walk, instead throwing him over her shoulder.

"So are you. Your arm—"

"Worry about it later," she said, carrying him past the people retching on the street. "How can we stop Jensett?"

"I don't know how, exactly," Delmin said. "But I've got a very good idea about who."

Running was pointless. Veranix had almost no lead on the Birds, and he had no doubt that either Bluejay or Magpie could catch up to him in his current state. He might have wounded them both, but he was hurting on every level. The blast of magic that gave him his opening to escape had taken him too long to build up, and hadn't been strong enough to do much besides buy him a few moments.

Moments he was surely losing. He didn't even dare glance behind to see if they were on his heels. No strength, no magic left to shroud or jump away. His best hope was to get some open space so he could make a clean shot. Maybe if he took one of them out of action with an arrow, he'd stand a chance against the other.

If the other was Bluejay, at least. She was ridiculously talented, but it was clear that she was a lot like him—a performer with skills that could be used in a fight. She had showmanship in spades, but enjoyed the show more than the kill. He could use that.

Magpie was a different matter. She was a killer, and her skills were in fighting. She might look like a woman from northern Druthal, but she didn't fight like one. She had moves the like of which Veranix had never seen, and strength to match it.

If she got in close again, he was dead.

The whistling of Bluejay's blades let him know they were approaching. Veranix forced himself into a sprint, around the corner, into Cantarell Square.

There had been no final number, from the Constabulary or the Yellowshields, of the injured and dead in Cantarell

Square from the other night. Reverend Pemmick wanted to light a candle and give a prayer for each one, but he had no numbers, no names. The authorities had kept him out of the square the previous day, but he would see to it today.

A handful of the Knights of Saint Julian stood watch at a respectful distance, and more than a few of the stalwart old ladies from the congregation joined in the observance.

"Saint Julian, bless these unnamed souls," he said as he lit candles on the stage, which had been hastily reconstructed by the local players. "I have no words, no comfort, as their lives were lost in senseless tragedy." He lowered his voice to a whisper, and he was grateful that the old ladies were far more invested in their own prayers than listening to him. "What role I might have played in sparking that tragedy, I am not entirely sure. For these unnamed souls and their delivery into blessing, I will dedicate myself to further penance."

A sharp whistling sound cut through the air, followed by a sharp impact. A bladed disc—a Kellirac *dektha*—imbedded itself into one of the wooden posts of the stage.

Pemmick turned to see a cloaked figure with a staff leaping away from a half-undressed woman spinning hoops around her waist.

"That's the Thorn!" one of the Knights shouted.

The Thorn was backing away when another figure—a blonde woman dressed far more sensibly, at least for the purpose of fighting—came out of an alley and threw a dart at the Thorn, which barely missed. The Thorn ran over and jumped up onto the stage.

"My apologies, Reverend," he said as he changed weapons to a bow, "but I need the stage."

Pemmick wasn't sure what to make of this. "I don't understand, son, but perhaps . . ."

"Get him to safety!" the Thorn shouted, and Pemmick immediately realized that this was directed to the Knights. They were already getting in front of the congregation women, drawing out their knives.

"No weapons!" Pemmick shouted.

The Thorn took aim at the blonde woman, who threw another dart. He fired, and in the same moment, shoved himself against Pemmick. It took a moment for Pemmick to realize that the Thorn was struck in the arm, and that the dart might well have hit him instead.

"Son—" the reverend started, before the Thorn grabbed him by his cassock and pulled him down behind the stage. Another *dektha* flew past them.

"This isn't the place, I know," the Thorn said as soon as they hit the ground behind the stage. "I wasn't given much choice."

"You're in no state—"

"I'm aware of that," the Thorn said, drawing out his arrows. The dart was still lodged in his arm, blood gushing. The two women shouted taunts, and the air was pierced with Constabulary whistles. "Tell the saints I'm coming sooner than I'd hoped."

Then he jumped up, a higher, faster jump than any man could naturally make, and landed back on the stage with his bow drawn back.

Suddenly, up there, with the glare of the sun forming a halo around him, his bow, and his billowing cloak, Reverend Pemmick saw the Thorn in the image of Saint Benton.

It only lasted for a moment, but it burned an idea into Pemmick's heart. He knew, as surely as if God himself had spoken to him, that he must help the Thorn in any way he could. This was Pemmick's penance.

The Thorn fired.

The Rabbits on Orchid were dispatched in short order. There had been little fight to them, it was almost embarrassing. They left the bird alive—arm set, shivering in a cold sweat—so she could limp back and spread the word that Orchid was purely Prince territory. The sew-up ended up being perfectly accommodating, and as far as Colin could tell, the folks at the secretarial were thrilled to have the Rabbits out of their basement.

There wasn't much else to it. The two holdings served little purpose beyond giving the Rabbits a toehold. Plenty of space in the basement, so it might have been they were to use it for storage.

Now the Princes would.

"So now what?" one of the bruisers asked as Colin walked out of the secretarial shop. Feckie, probably the sharpest tool among the lot.

"Now I buy some cheese, head back to the bosses and tell them what's up. You and Ment will keep an eye on these two new flops with the rest of the boys."

"For how long?"

"Until you hear otherwise, get?"

"Got," Feckie said. He scowled for a moment. "Mind if I claim the secretarial basement? That sew-up's office smells like bleach and vomit."

"Fair enough. I'll make sure you all don't sit too long. I know—"

Whistles blew—Constabulary whistles. A lot of them, at that. Something was going on, not too far away.

"Something's happening," Colin said.

"Best get out of sight," Feckie said. "They've been lockwagoning Princes and anyone else like crazy."

"Right," Colin said. "But I need to get back to the bosses. So you all sit tight here."

"Fine by me," Feckie said. "I don't want any trouble with the sticks." He went back inside.

Colin tore off toward the whistles. It might be that Jutie was caught. Or Veranix. Either way, he needed to know, no matter what the bosses would do to him.

The Ceremony of Letters was held in the Haveldale Center, a venue that was used for convocations, sports, theater—anything where a large audience was desirable. The whole day would be devoted to presenting finishing students with their Letters of Mastery in front of friends, family, and peers. This was academic regalia at its highest form, and the stands would be filled with people.

"There's a loading passage on the south side," Kaiana said as they approached. "There're tunnels and storage halls under the center that the ground staff uses." Master Jolen's own offices and quarters were down there.

"You think that's where he's going?"

"Makes more sense than crashing into the front entrance." Not that she had any real idea. Perhaps this time Cuse Jensett wanted his show. But she was betting that whatever he was doing required setting up, and was going to be big enough that he would want to get far away before it went off.

"It's in there somewhere, I can tell you that," Delmin said. They came up on the loading passage, where there were conspicuously no cadets on guard.

"All right," Kaiana said, steeling her courage. "Go find Phadre and Jiarna. I doubt you could get much closer."

"What are you going to do?"

"With any luck, find Cuse and crack his skull open before he gets started."

"You can't go down there alone."

"No other choice. Go do your part." She went to the passage.

Delmin took a few steps away, then turned back. "You think Vee . . . he'll be able to . . ."

"I don't know, Delmin. But we can't worry about that now."

She went in and only hoped it wouldn't be the stupidest thing she'd ever done.

So much about Veranix made perfect sense to her now.

As soon as she was inside, the first thing she saw was a pile of dead cadets. No tricks or gas or anything like that—just dead bodies with several stab wounds.

Farther down the tunnel she heard voices and noise. Someone giving instructions, things being moved. She crept closer and saw the wagon. A man stood on the top and shouted another order to one of the Rabbits, telling him to bring a barrel down a different passage.

That was Cuse Jensett.

She snuck closer, trying to think of the best way to move in. She was still in the shadows, hadn't been spotted yet. If she could get him first, then no matter what happened next, his magical-chemical whatever couldn't be launched. The other Rabbits might beat her to death, but they wouldn't be able to get his true plan started.

Her foot hit something soft and wet. She looked down and saw another body.

Master Jolen.

She never liked the man. In fact, she hated him, and she was pretty sure he hated her as well. But he had been her father's friend, and kept her employed for her father's sake. And the bloody shovel in his cold hand showed he hadn't gone down without a fight.

She pulled the shovel free. If she had made noise grabbing it, none of the Rabbits noticed. Cuse was now doing something with powders in a vial, and putting them in place in a contraption he had set up in the back of the wagon.

There was only one Red Rabbit left with him now. A big bruiser of a Rabbit.

The Rabbit asked something, to which Cuse replied derisively about not being bothered. The Rabbit shrugged and wandered a few paces away.

This was as good a moment as Kaiana was ever going to get.

Resisting the urge to cry out while she did it, Kaiana stormed at the wagon, raising up the shovel. Cuse looked up and shouted something, but it didn't save him from having the shovel smashed across his knees. He dropped like a sack of potatoes. She delivered another solid slam of the shovel on his back, and raised up to give him another when the Rabbit came at her.

The bruiser wasn't too fast, and he came over to grab her in a bear hug. Kaiana dropped to the ground and rolled under the wagon. She got away from his grasp, but dropped the shovel in the process. His meaty hands were already coming after her, so she didn't have a chance to get hold of it before she had to scramble away. She was almost out from under the wagon when his hand wrapped around her ankle.

She slammed her other foot into his face repeatedly. While doing so solicited grunts of pain and a liberal flow of blood from his nose, it didn't diminish his zeal for trying to pull her toward him.

"I'm going to tear you apart, you crazy Napa!"

Kaiana pulled the spade out of her pocket. There was no good way to get a solid hit in with it, and her continued kicks weren't slowing him down. If she moved in to stab him, all she'd do was give him greater purchase to maul her.

Driving her heel into his face once more, she glanced around for anything else she could use. Then she spotted it: the wagon horses were standing in place, but clearly were a little out of sorts. It shouldn't take much to spook them.

She threw the spade at the closest horse's flank as hard as she could. It struck true, and the horse reared up.

The wagon surged forward, and Kaiana gave a hard kick to the Rabbit's hand as the wheels came on him. He screamed and let go, giving her the moment to scurry away while the wagon went over him.

"Stupid . . . blazing . . . Napa . . ." he wheezed out. She grabbed the shovel off the ground and slammed in onto his face before he said anything else.

That seemed to do it.

Then she went back to Cuse.

He was still lying on the wagon, though he had propped himself up on his elbows, chuckling through shallow, pained breaths.

"I've already triggered the catalyst," he said. "There's nothing you can do now."

Chapter 25

"**T**ELL THE SAINTS I'm coming sooner than I thought."

He tried to sound light, but he doubted he was fooling the reverend at all. Because he knew he was going to die, today, in Cantarell Square. If he was lucky he could stop one of these two Deadly Birds before the other killed him. But that meant there was nothing to keep in reserve. Nothing to hold back anymore.

With a wisp of *numina* he jumped back up onto the stage while nocking three arrows at once. He drew back and took the first shot he had, which was Bluejay. The arrows sang out across the square, and she quickly shifted her hoops to protect her chest, shredding two of the arrows before they reached her.

The third arrow landed squarely in her thigh.

Magpie had jumped up onto the stage in the meantime and delivered a kick to his stomach that he had no chance of dodging. He went down hard and managed to roll onto his back to see her foot about to drop onto his face.

"Rose Street!"

The foot flew out of sight as a blur shot past Veranix's field of vision and tackled Magpie.

Veranix used the moment to get back on his feet, despite the pain. Jutie was locked in a furious struggle, wrestling with Magpie, trying to get his knives buried into her chest. She wasn't giving him any chance to do that, holding his arms back. Despite being on top of her, he couldn't press any advantage. She twisted enough to force his knives into the stage floor. As soon as they weren't a concern, she twisted her arm through his and jerked. Jutie screamed, and a sickening crack came from his arm.

She knocked him off of her with a combination of elbows and fists, then leaped on top of him and pummeled his chest, until Veranix took the moment to bash her across the back with his staff, right where she was cut from Bluejay's blades.

"I thought you wanted me," he taunted with as much bravado as he could muster. The last thing he wanted was another of Colin's Princes dying to help him. He jumped off the stage and backed away into the street.

Magpie hopped down. "We were commissioned to give a show," she said. "I'd hate to disappoint."

A whirring sound to his right confirmed that Bluejay was still on her feet. She limped forward slowly, spinning the two hoops on her hands in whirling death.

Veranix kept backing off, holding his staff defensively as they approached. They were boxing him out, forcing him into a corner, and there wasn't much he could do about it. He hadn't even realized how far back he had gone until he bumped into a building.

They had him now, pinned against the Trusted Friend.

"I'm telling you," Jensett said through bloody teeth. "It's already started. You cannot stop it."

Kaiana answered with another punch in the face. Then she crawled up on the wagon, looking at the large triangle of glowing objects. She reached to grab one, and got a sharp charge up her arm for her trouble.

"Told you," he chuckled. He was making no attempt to fight or stop her. Of course, she had probably broken his leg and some ribs, so he didn't have much ability to fight back.

She picked up the shovel. "Then I'll get your men and their barrels."

"Pointless. Further catalyzers that have already done their job. Want to know a secret?" He laughed and coughed up blood. "The real reactant is the limestone and iron used to construct this building. You going to get rid of that?"

"So what's it going to do?" she asked. Since he seemed to be interested in talking, maybe she could get something meaningful out of him.

"Already doing it. Feel a little warm in here to you?" It was.

"It's building, slowly at first. A few more minutes and the heat will be nearly impossible to bear. But then it will feed into itself, and soon this whole building will burn like the sun!"

"The whole—"

"Frankly, I didn't do the calculations with this much power. It's not impossible it would ignite the whole campus."

"Or the whole city." Delmin was being carried by Jiarna and Phadre, his body shuddering. "You really are insane, Jensett."

"No argument on my end, friend," Jensett answered, craning his neck to see the other three.

"What is this?" Phadre asked.

"It's quite impressive," Jiarna offered, pulling a monocle out of her pocket and looking through it. "I mean, the power levels alone."

"It makes my teeth hurt," Phadre said.

"It makes my everything hurt," Delmin moaned.

"I don't care how impressive it is," Kaiana said. "How can we stop it?"

"Is it warm in here?" Jiarna asked.

Cuse laughed and coughed up blood.

"Everyone in this building, on campus, will die—"

"Be incinerated," Cuse offered.

"If we don't stop it. And if the two of you can't manage it—"

"Right, right," Phadre said. "All right, those are clearly some form of *numinic* storage devices, charged with an absurd amount of *numina*. On the order of kilobarins."

"And look at the web of the flow patterns," Jiarna responded, still looking through her monocle. "It's creating convergences that build off each other . . ."

"Probably some kind of harmonic expansion . . ."

"Because, of course, there are twenty-seven of them. Three to the third power."

"That's brilliant."

"Stop it!" Kaiana snapped. "Don't marvel at it. Just make it stop."

"Well, what is it doing?" Jiarna asked. "The energy is feeding into the building itself."

"Oh, she's getting it," Cuse said. He was chuckling maniacally, while blood kept coming from his mouth.

"He could use medical attention," Phadre said.

"I am not getting him a Yellowshield," Kaiana said. "Now what can we do?"

"Nothing," Jiarna said. "The energy is already flowing, and some sort of reaction is happening in the—"

"It is definitely getting hot in here."

"Iron and limestone. The reaction is . . . it's being sustained by the *numina* flowing from here, but it's already linked. We can't disrupt the link just by moving the wagon out of here."

"And you can't move the devices themselves out of position," Kaiana said. "I tried. But what can we do?"

Phadre and Jiarna looked at each other blankly. Finally Phadre said, "We would have to break the link of the *numinic* flow."

"But there isn't a good way to do that," Jiarna countered.

"Maybe with dalmatium?"

"No, those storage batteries likely use a dalmatium compound, plus some sort of release catalyst. That's really ingenious."

"Thank you," Cuse gasped out. Kaiana kicked him in his broken ribs.

"We are going to die," Kaiana said. "Everyone is going to die unless you come up with some way to stop it, block it, disrupt it—"

"Redirect it!" Phadre said.

"Yes!" Jiarna shouted. "The *numina* is going to flow out, so if it's sent somewhere other than the building's foundation . . ."

Cuse whispered out a taunt. "There's no way to do that."

"Well, practically, no," Jiarna admitted.

"What do you mean, practically, no?" Kaiana asked. She was now soaked in sweat, as was everyone else, and she wasn't sure anymore if it was the heat or raw panic.

"I mean that, in theory, it could be done, but—"

Phadre stepped in. "In theory, if you had a way to draw the *numina* off its current path, you could funnel it to a new target, far away."

"Right, but there's no way we could do that," Jiarna finished.

"Why not?" Kaiana asked.

"For one, we don't have anything we'd need."

Kaiana wanted to scream. She hadn't done this much, come this close to quit without a fight. "What would it take? This place is filled with storage, maybe there's something—"

"Kai, I'm telling you, it isn't even—"

"Just tell me!"

"Fine," Jiarna said. "You would need something that could overcome both the catalyzed dalmatium compounds and the synergetic reaction with the iron and limestone. The only thing I can even think of that could do that is—again, theoretically—napranium."

"Napranium?" Kaiana asked. Could they be that lucky?

"Two sources of napranium, ideally," Phadre said. "The second some distance away to receive the redirected *numinic* flow."

"Preferably somehow attuned to each other?" Delmin offered weakly, the slightest smile crossing his face.

"Well, yes, and given how extraordinarily rare napranium even is—" Phadre started.

Cuse cackled. "You might as well ask the saints themselves to stop it!"

Kaiana gave him a smack and opened up her shoulder satchel. She pulled out the rope and handed it to Jiarna. "Here. We'll be sending it about a mile away in Aventil. Do we need to aim it somehow?"

The entire group was dead silent, faces in complete shock.

Finally Jiarna managed some inarticulate gibbers.

"Imminent death if we don't do this," Kaiana said.

"Right, right," Jiarna said, taking the rope. "Of course, someone will have to be conduit. I . . . I don't know what that will do to them."

"I can try," Phadre said, stepping over to the cart. He held his hand a few inches from the rope. "I mean, it's me or Delmin, and I don't think he's in any condition to do it."

"You'll need something—someone—to anchor you," Jiarna said. "I'll be right here."

"Good, because . . . oh, to blazes with it." He wrapped his hand around the back of her head, and kissed her. Jiarna, for her part, responded eagerly.

Kaiana wished she was surprised by that, but it really was to be expected. She couldn't begrudge either of them, even in the dire circumstances.

Delmin wasn't as forgiving. "Enough already!"

Phadre grabbed the rope, while not letting go of his embrace of Jiarna. His whole body buckled, but she held him up, and then the rope moved, forming a coil around the two of them. Then it glowed bright, too bright for Kaiana to look at. She moved away, over to Delmin, who had fallen over.

"Is it working?" she asked him, pulling him on his feet.

"It's doing something," he said. "We'll know soon enough. So will Vee."

If he was still alive.

Magpie was taking her time advancing, presumably to let Bluejay keep pace with her. Both of them looked like they were eager to savor the kill.

"Somebody help him!" Jutie was shouting from the stage, barely able to get on his feet. His arm was twisted in utterly inhuman ways. "Is there a Prince worth his arm here? You bleeding Knights, Orphans? Someone!"

No one moved, save Magpie and Bluejay.

"Or you damned sticks? I see you over there, cowering! Come and take me, but save the Thorn first!"

Veranix kept his staff in a defensive posture, not that he would be able to hold either of these Birds off. "Don't bother, Prince. I don't want anyone else hurt because of me."

"So noble," Magpie said. Her fingers danced along her bandolier, but she seemed to be out of darts. That was only a small blessing delaying his death by a few moments.

"We shouldn't drag it out," Bluejay said. "Not too much. But I owe him some pain."

"I charge you to step away," a voice boomed out. "On your very souls, ladies, you are charged by God and the saints to leave this man."

The reverend had come over, arms wide. His face was full of fear, but he stepped forward anyway.

"This soul is long lost," Magpie said.

"As long as you draw breath, your soul can be absolved," he said. "Please."

"Reverend, don't—" Veranix started. "I'm not worth it."

"Every soul is worth it," the reverend said, stepping even closer. For just a moment, Magpie's guard softened. The reverend took the opening, and reached out to her shoulder.

She reacted hard and violent, a palm heel heading for his face. Veranix thrust a jab at her, forcing her to miss the reverend. Magpie shifted and sent a kick at Veranix, and at the same moment, Bluejay swung one of her hoops over her head and prepared to bring it down in a lethal spinning strike. The reverend pulled himself in, as if he intended to take the blow for Veranix.

And then the world stopped.

Something else hit Veranix, but it wasn't a fist, foot, or blade.

It was pure *numina* suddenly flooding his body. It came without warning, ferociously, and the raw power of it made everything slow to a halt.

The world became a still tableau, utterly clear. Bluejay's blade, inches away from his face. The sweat on Magpie's brow, hovering on the verge of dripping off her pale skin. The reverend, reaching inside the scrum. In the distance Veranix could see Jutie on the stage, clutching his arm. The Knights of Saint Julian frozen in their dash to help the reverend. The pair of Constabulary officers, pointing at Jutie. Even far off he could see Colin, just coming into the square. Shock and determination on his face, as plain as if he were right next to Veranix.

The energy was more than his body could ever handle, ever hold. It would tear him apart in a moment if he didn't channel it, shape it. Even with the world frozen, he didn't have any time to spare.

With the slightest push—Veranix wasn't even sure if it was with magic or his hand—he sent the reverend out of harm's way, into the arms of the Knights. Then he channeled some of the *numina*, only as much as he could manage to wrestle a hold over, and formed a shell between himself and the rest of the crowd. He didn't want anyone innocent getting hurt.

Bluejay and Magpie he kept inside. He wasn't going to worry about their well-being right now.

Then he just let it all burst out of him, everything that he had but couldn't hold, everything that was still careening into him.

And then the world was light and thunder.

Chapter 26

OLIN ROUNDED THE CORNER to Cantarell Square, but the place was already in a state. People were running and panicked, and a few Constabulary were working their way over to the stage. There was a Rose Street Prince screaming on the stage—Jutie. That's where the sticks were going. But that wasn't even the center of action in the square. That was in the far part of Carnation and Bush, in front of the Trusted Friend.

Veranix was there, with two Deadly Birds moving in on him.

Even if Colin ran at a full sprint, he wouldn't be able to save either of them, let alone both.

He still went in. It was the only thing he could do. He had failed his vows to both of them. These boys were his to look out for, and they were both going down at the same time.

Colin didn't get more than three steps when the world lit up. Veranix became imbued with light, which expanded off of him in a deafening blast.

Colin found himself on the ground when his eyes and ears cleared. He quickly pulled himself up and started running again. The people in the square were now all in disarray, most of them on the ground, but no one truly hurt as far as he could tell. He wasn't hurt.

But where Veranix had been there was now only rubble. The Trusted Friend had collapsed.

Colin doubled his sprint, passing by the dazed crowd. He reached the fallen awning of what had been the Trusted Friend, and fought to get it off the ground. As he strained, another pair of hands joined him. The reverend.

"Put your back in it, Prince!" he shouted.

With a strain, they pushed it off, to see Veranix and the two Birds lying unconscious on the ground, nowhere near as injured as they should have been.

A thin sheen of violet light was draped over the three of them, but then vanished once Colin touched it.

"A miracle," Reverend Pemmick whispered.

"The miracle is getting him out of here," Colin said, while a plan formed in his head. He grabbed the cloak off of Veranix, as well as the bow and the staff. "I'm going to put it on you, Rev."

"Son—"

"Reverend," Colin said, putting his hand on the priest's arm. "I swear to you on the saints and Rose Street that I will take whatever charge you put against me, but I beg that you get him to safety."

"But why—"

Colin pulled him closer. "I say this under Absolution, hear? He is my cousin. Hold that with sanctity."

The priest nodded. "I will want to speak more later. Come to my chambers below the church when you can."

Colin threw the cloak over his shoulders and pulled up the hood. People were still getting their own bearings in the square; the only ones truly on their game were the sticks.

The sticks grabbing and ironing Jutie.

Colin glanced back at Veranix as the priest picked his limp form up. He was out of arrows. The only arrow left was in the one Bird's leg.

Colin pulled it out, which woke the Bird up with a scream. Not that he cared.

He drew back the bow and took a shot at the stage. Of course, he only hit one of the set walls, having barely ever fired a bow before. That got the sticks looking at him.

"Thorn victorious!" he shouted. Hopefully no one was paying enough attention to notice the discrepancy in height, build, and clothing.

The sticks did take notice of him, and shouted for someone to grab him. Colin gave a glance back at the reverend, taking Veranix out of the square. At least he'd saved one of them. But he was in no position to save Jutie without getting caught himself, with the Thorn's gear at that. Too much risk for himself, and for Veranix. He had to run.

"Nobody catches the Thorn!" he cried out, and ran down an alley. One that would, conveniently enough, with a couple of turns, lead him to the back entrance of the sew-up.

The whole time he prayed that Jutie never saw that he had abandoned him.

The light surrounding Phadre and Jiarna dissipated, and they collapsed to the floor. Footsteps came from down the causeway, and Kaiana grabbed the rope before anyone else spotted it.

"Is it over?" Jiarna gasped. "Did that do it?"

"The energy is gone," Delmin said. "We're . . . we're all right."

Phadre didn't speak, but just fell over onto Jiarna.

"No," Jensett moaned. "It's not possible."

"Sorry to disappoint you," Kaiana said as she shoved the rope into her bag. She saw him struggling to take something out of his pocket, but she wasn't about to let him try any further tricks. She grabbed his wrist and yanked it out, squeezing it with all her strength for extra measure. He cried out—whimpered, really—and she hauled him onto his feet. He wasn't capable of standing, as she had broken his knee earlier, so she leaned him against the cart and used his own belt to tie his hands behind his back.

"You're all right," Jiarna whispered to Phadre. "You did it."

Kaiana took a good look at Phadre. Whatever he had done had had a cost. Shocks of his sandy blond hair had turned white, and his face had become drawn and gaunt.

"Let's get him moving," Delmin said. Now that the energy was gone, he seemed fine. He might even be the one in the best shape of any of them at this point. Kaiana herself was now feeling all her aches and sores, not to mention that gash in her arm.

The footsteps were now a large, rushing group, which included several cadets, a few school officials, and Professor Alimen. He looked the most disturbed. Kaiana wondered if he had experienced part of what Delmin had, or at least had sensed what Phadre had done.

"What is going on here, exactly?" one of the officials asked.

Kaiana, despite exhaustion setting in, dragged Jensett over. "This man is the . . . Prankster who has been attacking the University. He almost caused further destruction to the Ceremony of Letters."

"And you caught him, miss?" the official said skeptically.

"Is that hard to believe?" Phadre was the one who said it, despite still being curled into Jiarna.

"Not at all," Professor Alimen offered. "I can confirm that . . . something of a magical nature was occurring here not too long ago. But it appears to have been disrupted."

"Magic and science combined," Jensett wheezed. "Alchemy."

"Hmm," Alimen said. "I have a vague recollection of you, son."

"I remember you very well."

"Enough," the official said. "If he's the one, we'll take him."

Two cadets grabbed Jensett. Another picked the Rabbit off the ground, who was also in no shape to fight back.

"There are a few more of those around here," Kaiana said, indicating the Rabbit. "You might need to round them up."

The official whistled and gave some of the cadets hand signals, and they went running off. As Jensett was dragged off, he started screaming. "I can tell you who the Thorn is! I know who he is!"

Kaiana's heart froze.

"What's a Thorn?" the official asked.

"Some guy in the neighborhood," a cadet offered. "Sort of a folk hero or something. Constabulary wants to bring him in."

"And I'll tell you!" Jensett shouted, despite blood dripping from his mouth. "Because he's a magic student here!"

Alimen stepped toward him, signaling to the official to hold. "Tell me who."

"If I—"

"Tell me now."

Alimen said it with such force of authority, Kaiana almost confessed herself.

Jensett sneered. "Fine. His name is Tyson."

Alimen chuckled. "There is no magic student by that name."

Kaiana found that she could release the breath that she was holding.

"I'm telling you, he's a mage named Tyson!"

"Take him away," Alimen ordered, and the officials wasted no time following the directive.

"Now, Mister Golmin, Miss Kay," Alimen said, crouching down to Phadre and Jiarna. "You had already received your Letters. There was no need to show off."

"Just trying to impress you, sir," Phadre said weakly.

"Color me impressed," Alimen said. "I don't know if I'd have been capable of dissipating the *numina* fueling this . . . alchemical reaction. But it seems the two of you have a far greater understanding of alchemy than I could hope to."

Jiarna looked like she was about to say something, but then simply nodded her head.

"And you, Miss Nell," he said. "You seem to find yourself in the middle of crises."

"Lucky, I suppose, sir."

"Perhaps of the poor variety," Alimen said. "But twice now lucky for me, and lucky for all the campus that you are able to handle yourself in such an admirable manner. I will definitely make sure the administration is aware of that."

Delmin had helped Phadre up. "Perhaps some lunch is in order for you."

"Yes, I think so," Phadre said.

"Indeed," Alimen said. "In fact I believe I will treat you all to one of my favorite little places just outside the west gates. Hardly a sufficient reward, I'm aware, but . . ." He glanced around at the four of them. "It seems someone is missing from our assembly of heroes here."

"Veranix is—" Delmin offered, though he then clammed up. Knowing Delmin, he probably was incapable of coming up with a believable lie.

"It is of no moment. I'm sure he was busy celebrating his successful completion of his third year. If he is not on hand to join our celebration, that's his loss."

Kaiana hoped that was the only thing that was his loss. "Sir, I should probably get cleaned up before I join you."

"Oh, of course," Alimen said kindly. Then he really looked at her. "Miss Nell, perhaps you should even visit the hospital ward." He glanced about again. "I am a foolish old man. You all probably should do that first. Our celebration can wait. Perhaps by that time Mister Calbert will have crawled out of whatever hole he is in and be in a state to join us."

"I sincerely hope so," Kaiana said.

Alimen looked at her, and for just a moment she swore she saw a sparkle of understanding in his eye. Then he winked and said, "We can taunt him for missing the excitement. Now let us get out of this dismal place."

Every bit of his body hurt. Every muscle and down to the bone. Even his hair hurt, somehow.

That was how Veranix knew he was still alive.

He was in a bed—not much of one, but an actual bed—in a small, secluded room. At least, it had no windows and was lit only with a few candles. His first instinct was that he had been captured, held locked away in some private cell where he'd never see the light of day again. This didn't look like a Constabulary holding, though. It was simple, but it had a humble warmth to it. Which meant that it likely wasn't Fenmere who had him either.

Plus there was the fact that his clothes, including his cloak and weapons, were in a neat pile in the corner of the room.

His scrapes and wounds had been tended to, clearly by someone who knew what he was doing. He felt well enough to get on his feet and get dressed. Wherever he was, however long he had been there, Jensett was still out there. He might have already released whatever horror he had planned.

Two men were talking outside the door. Veranix wondered if he should go for his staff. Of course, if they meant him harm, they hardly would have healed him. Not to mention, he wasn't in much condition to fight back if they intended that.

The door opened and Colin was there with the reverend from the square. Veranix was so surprised by that he dropped back down on the bed.

The reverend came in. "You'll forgive me that I did not warn the saints of your impending arrival. Your worldly time hasn't ended."

"And I imagine I have you to thank for that," Veranix said.

"I did what I was called to do. I saw a soul in need, and I tended to it."

"I helped," Colin said.

"Well, I—" Veranix stumbled as he got to his feet. "Thank you. But I have to go—"

"Hold on," Colin said, pushing Veranix back onto the bed. "Where are you going?"

"Campus. Jensett may have struck, and if he did—"

"Easy, easy. Everything is fine there. Jensett and a bunch of Rabbits were hauled off campus in irons."

Veranix sighed and relaxed, if only a little. He had no idea what state Kaiana or the rest of his friends were in. "I can't stay long, though. I have to . . ."

"Patience, son," the reverend said. "We'll get you back home to campus shortly."

"I don't really know—" Veranix stared. Then he looked back at the priest and his strangely serene smile. "How much do you know about me, Reverend?"

"Like all servants of God and the saints, I have accepted secrets under the rite of Absolution. And I am bound by my oath to keep silent or face the cost on my own soul."

Veranix looked to Colin. "You performed Absolution? To help me?"

"I . . . I did what I had to do. I have my own oaths, you know."

"Mister Tyson and I will still have long discussions about penances."

"And me, Reverend?" Veranix asked. "Do we have a long discussion ahead of us?"

"If you wish, son. But I will tell you plainly. This church is, right now, a safe haven for you. And I am here for you. I don't . . ." The reverend paused, looking for the words he wanted. "I am still praying for guidance in reconciling the things that you've done in your . . . mission. I am troubled by them. But this city, this neighborhood is troubled, and perhaps . . ."

He trailed off.

"Many saints faced trials to do what was needed," he said finally. "And when I saw you today—"

"I am not remotely a saint, Reverend."

"No, truly. But I think trials are coming; we all may need the Thorn before they are over. Do you understand?"

Veranix didn't, and said so.

The reverend chuckled. "I don't either, to be honest. I just know that for months I have been asking the saints for strength, for a sign, and they showed me you."

Veranix mused, and nodded at Colin. "Usually when I asked the saints for help, they just send him."

"And he's a better soul than he would admit."

"Hush, would you?" Colin said. "Can we have a minute?"

The reverend nodded. "This place is yours, Thorn." He left.

"He was helpful," Veranix said.

"I may have pointed out where the large deposits in the collection boxes were coming from," Colin said.

"You were there, in the square at the end," Veranix said. The haze of the final moments of his fight against the Birds was coming together. "I—I'm not even entirely sure what happened."

"Don't ask me," Colin said. "Some crazy magic something, and then you blew up the Trusted Friend."

"And your Prince, Jutie. Is he all right?"

"Nah," Colin said, his lightness an obvious front. "He got nabbed by the sticks."

"I'm sorry, Colin, that's my fault—"

"No, it ain't. It ain't, at all. He'd killed a stick the night before, so they were coming for him one way or another." He took a moment, staring at his boots. "It's probably for the best things went the way they did. He'll go to Quarry, he'll be alive. Things could have turned left, and he could have ended up at the wrong end of a crossbow."

Veranix didn't think for a moment that Colin believed that, but he didn't say anything.

"So you pass your exams?" Colin asked.

"At least half of them," Veranix said. "But I think so."

"Good. Your pop made me promise a lot of things, but one was to make sure you finished Uni. You get kicked out, Fenmere's the last of your worries."

"All right," Veranix said. "Are you going to be fine?"

"Fine enough," Colin said. "But I owe the rest of my crew the truth about Jutie. You should probably wait a little while before heading out of here. We need to be a bit more careful about being seen together."

"That Red Rabbit boss knew who I was," Veranix said. "Who I really am. If he talks . . ."

"Don't worry about that." Colin didn't sound too convincing.

"I'm sure some old Princes could do the same if they got a good look at me."

"And they . . . they're sniffing in that direction," Colin said. "They've got your bow. Your father's bow."

"Got it," Veranix said. "I'll stay out of Aventil for a bit. Focus on bringing the fight to Fenmere again."

Colin's face fell. "Saints, Vee, you . . . you need to be smarter than that."

"That's what everyone keeps telling me."

Suddenly Colin grabbed Veranix and took him in a tight embrace. "I'm saying I need you to be smarter than that, cousin. Get?"

Veranix hugged him back. "Got."

"All right." Colin released and stepped away. "I've got some drumming I've got to take, I'm sure. Give me a few clicks before you go, hear?"

"Heard," Veranix said. Colin went for the door. "Colin?"

"Yeah?"

"Thanks. For being there."

"It's family, Vee. It's what it's for."

Chapter 27

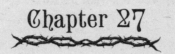

LIEUTENANT BENVIN should have been elated. Arch's killer—Juteron Higgs—was in the station, ironed and locked. Case was barreled up. City Protector had no beefs. Kid was going to Quarrygate.

On top of that, they had grabbed a few Red Rabbits, and between the wrecked bar and shredded brewery, there was more than enough evidence that they had been developing this Red, which his examinarium boys confirmed was worse than *effitte*. That was kept off the streets before it really got out there.

And the final success, they had hauled in Miss Magadina Kend, known in some quarters as Magpie. An actual saints-be-damned Deadly Bird. Kings' Marshals were coming to claim her, and Benvin had the feeling he didn't even want to know what would happen next to her.

It should have been a good day.

But it didn't sit right, and not just because Arch was lying in the examinarium down in the basement.

Not even because the kid—that blasted Prince— stood in front of him in his cell with a look on his face like he had won, despite his arm mangled beyond any chance of it healing right. Though that irritated the blazes out of Benvin, that was for certain.

It was the Thorn.

The Thorn was the reason they had the Red and the Deadly Bird, and he had gotten away. First time he had shown up in broad daylight, and he still slipped off into the shadows. Benvin was of half a mind to knock every patrolman who had been in Cantarell onto their backside and put them on night shift filing for a month.

Far as he could see, the Thorn was nothing but a menace.

And the best lead he had to the Thorn stood smirking in the cell.

"Give me a name, Mister Higgs," Benvin said. "Give me a name and maybe you'll get out of Quarrygate before you need a cane to walk."

"That's what he's worth to you?" the Prince said. "You'll put a stick killer on the streets a few years early for the Thorn's name?"

"I'll see what I can do."

"I don't whisper," Higgs said. "I don't tell anyone's secrets to the sticks. Not mine. Not Princes'. And not the Thorn's."

"So you know something."

"I only know he's doing more for Aventil than anyone in this building," Higgs said. "I heard you talking about the Red, Left. And why do you have that?"

"Shut it, Higgs," Benvin said. "Enjoy the 'Gate."

He stalked back off to his offices, where the rest of his crew were finishing their filing. Arch's coat and crossbow were laid over his chair there, in respect. Benvin wondered if they'd ever find someone else to fill that chair. The stationhouse was filled with incompetents and corrupted souls, save the boys in the room with him.

"So that's it for the Red Rabbits," Tripper said, hobbling over to the slateboard. "There's still a handful of them out there, but between their favorite holes being flushed, half the captains being locked up, and old Gabe Jensett being strangled, there's not much center to them."

"Don't count them out yet," Benvin said. "But they're the least of our worries."

"Princes and Orphans next?" Pollit asked. "We've still got the lead on that cider ring. We could—"

"We're not going to waste our time with a cider ring," Benvin said. He grabbed a cloth and wiped the slateboard clean. "Right now we've got one thing at the top of our list."

He wrote in big letters across the top half of the slateboard: THE THORN.

"He's always been part of the list," Wheth said.

"As of now, he is the list."

"You're sure about that, sir?" Jace was the one who said it. "I mean, it seems he's not—"

"The Thorn caused destruction of two buildings, I don't know how many deaths, chaos and confusion throughout the neighborhood. And people cheer him!"

"Well . . ." Jace stammered.

"He is not above the law," Benvin said. "Mal, I want you and Wheth to get a Writ of Arrest approved for him."

"Under what name?" Mal asked.

"Under the Thorn. Put the word out through the station that every blasted stick on foot or horse should try to arrest him on sight. We're not going to stop until we have him ironed and celled. Am I clear?"

Everyone nodded, save for Jace. He just stared at the floor. But he was a kid. He still had plenty to learn.

"Good," Benvin said. "Let's get to work."

Colin had left the church, and was only about a block into Prince territory when he was approached by three heavies, led by Hucks. "Bosses want a word, Tyson."

Colin held out his arms wide. "That's where I was going, Hucks. No need to make a thing about it."

Hucks just narrowed his eyes.

"Swear on the street, Hucks. You don't need to do anything . . . additional to bring me along."

"That's smart of you, Tyson." Hucks and his two friends almost looked disappointed, though. Colin made a point not to do anything to give them an excuse to exercise discretion on how to handle him. He walked at a brisk pace to the basement offices, no sudden moves, keeping his hands in plain sight.

They still brought him in with a little bit of shoving—mostly because they wanted to shove someone around, he figured.

The whole gang of minor bosses were at the table, no cards or anything else. Just the five of them staring at him. Nints got up and pounded on the inner door and sat back down.

"Gents, I don't know what you're clearly worked up about," Colin said. "I did a good job over on Orchid. If anyone has cause—"

"Shut it, Tyson," Giles said.

Old Casey came out of the back room, pulled a chair over and indicated for Colin to sit down.

"Colin," he said softly. "I'm going to ask you a few questions, and I want you to swear on Rose Street and your father's good name that you'll tell me the truth."

"Yeah, of course," Colin said.

"Swear it!"

"Swear on Rose Street. And my father's good name." Such as it was among this crowd. Of course, he wasn't sure what he was going to be asked, and what he'd have to tell. They made him swear on Rose Street, and lying under that oath . . . it wasn't something he wanted to do.

"All right. Do you know if your uncle Cal is still alive?"

That he could answer truthfully. "No, he's dead. I'm sure of it."

"Fine. Did he ever come to you and introduce you to his son, perhaps?"

"No." Strictly speaking, that was the truth. Cal never introduced him to Veranix; he only told him that Veranix was on the campus.

"And did anyone ever approach you and claim to be his son?"

"No." Again, in the strictest sense, true. Veranix didn't tell Colin that. If anything, Colin had explained it to him when they first met.

"Do you think the Thorn could be Cal's son?"

Colin thanked the saints for the phrasing. "I'd be lying if I said that I hadn't considered it."

Casey backed away for a bit, pacing the room. "So here's the thing, Colin. I understand. I get if you were thinking that, you'd be inclined to trust him. Blazes, plenty of Princes would, not just you. So I need to know, did you tell any of the rest of your crew what you thought?"

"No, never," Colin said.

"Good, good," Casey said. His energy turned nervous, hands shaking. "I know you've got a Prince's heart, Colin. I know those stars belong on your arm, hear?"

"Heard," Colin said, not sure what was happening now.

The door opened, and Vessrin came out with Deena. Deena had stars on her arm, fresh and raw.

"Did you ask him?" Vessrin said.

"I did."

"All right," Vessrin said. "Girl, tell him what you told me."

Deena looked nervously to the side, and then said, "This morning, I was keeping lookout at the lockdown basement." She meant Colin's flop. "So this Napa girl and a Uni kid come sniffing around. Then Jutie jumps out at them."

"Jutie was there?" Colin asked.

"And that Napa girl was the same one who you talked to the other day."

Colin had no response to that.

"Then she was saying she was looking for you. Jutie recognized her, and she said she was working with the Thorn, and she and Jutie went off together."

"So, Colin," Vessrin asked. "Is the Napa the Thorn's messenger girl? Runs back and forth between you?"

"She's with him, yeah," Colin said. "But it ain't like that."

"Thorn hammered the Red Rabbits. And Gabe Jensett, that wormy bastard, is dead. So how far is it going, Colin?"

"How far is what going?" Colin asked.

"The Thorn, is he coming for me next?" Vessrin asked. "He taking over all of Aventil?"

"That ain't . . . from what I know, it's all about the *effitte* for him. That means Fenmere, and it meant the Rabbits because they got messed up in it. I don't . . ."

"You don't what?"

"I don't think he cares about doing anything to you, sir," Colin said. "At least, that's what I think."

"Nah, nah," Vessrin said. "If he is Cal's son, if he's, god and saints damn it, if he's your rolling cousin, Colin, then *of course* he wants to take me down. What else could he possibly want?"

Colin didn't have an answer, but Vessrin wasn't looking for one. He stormed around the room, and then to the beer taps. He poured one for himself and slammed it down his throat. "I'm putting this on you, Casey. You hear? You say he should keep his stars, I'll listen. For now." An accusing finger was jammed in Colin's face. "But one toe out of line, hear?"

He stormed off.

After a moment, Casey sighed. "So this is how it's going to go, Colin. You've done good work on Orchid today."

"Damn right I did," Colin said. "I don't deserve this damned sewage!"

"Right, so those boys you've got over there, they're your crew now. Holding on to Orchid is your main concern."

"Wait, what?" Colin asked. "What about . . . what about Jutie and Tooser?"

"Jutie is gone," Hotchins said. "And you should really ask yourself why."

"And Tooser will stay with his new captain in the lockdown flop," Casey said, giving a nod over to Deena.

Giles got to his feet. "So Orchid Street. Why don't you and I take a stroll over there. I hear there's an excellent cheese shop."

Colin gave a last glance at Deena, who had the decency to look sheepish. He didn't blame her, though. She made a smart choice, and got her stars. Tooser would be good to her. She was getting a good reward for her loyalty there.

And while Colin wasn't losing his stars, they were clearly pissed with him. That's what knocking him out of the lockdown flop meant.

He'd take it, though. He'd take whatever they, or Fenmere, or the rest of the damned city would throw at him.

He was a Rose Street Prince.

Moreover, he was Colin Tyson, son of Den Tyson. That was something he was damned proud to be, and they couldn't take that away.

Concern was shown upon Bell's return. Most of that concern came from Gerrick, who had the decency to send for one of the doctors Fenmere kept in his pocket. A real respectable man with a practice, not some sew-up. But Gerrick brought Bell into the sitting room to meet with Fenmere once it was clear that his injuries were not life-threatening.

"Red Rabbits did this to you?" Fenmere asked.

"Led by one of the old bosses."

"Rabbits only really have the one left, Reb's little brother Gabe," Fenmere said. "None of the rest of them is old guard."

"Well, they don't have him, neither," Bell said. "I snapped his neck."

"Good," Fenmere said. He leaned over to Gerrick. "Even still, have a few gents round up some Red Rabbits tonight and make a spectacle of them."

"Speaking of spectacle, sir," Corman said, standing by Fenmere's chair. "The, um . . . Owl is still waiting to see you."

"How long has she waited?" Fenmere asked.

"Over an hour."

"Good. Send for her."

As Corman left, Fenmere leaned in to Bell. "Now tell me about what you saw of the Thorn's fight with the Birds."

"Well, I didn't see much. They were both, you know, making a show of it, while he was doing his damnedest to keep them off him. I mean, he's a scrapper, and he's got moves, but it was like a cat fighting two snakes. Then one of them got a little sloppy—"

The Owl walked in carrying a valise, and despite her age she moved with nothing but grace. She had an air about her like she could still knock out the throats of every man in the room if it suited her.

Fenmere laughed—a large, jovial laugh, as if he was really enjoying Bell's story. "Which the Thorn took advantage of, right?"

"He did, right, sir. Twisted her around so she got hit by the other one. Gave him a moment to blast some magic or something, and dash out of there. And the girls, see, they still acted like they were doing a good job."

"They tell you that?" Fenmere asked.

"Cocky as anything. Marched out right after him."

"Cocky as anything," Fenmere repeated, and then turned his attention to Owl. "And yet, and yet. The Thorn, victorious. I hear he actually shouted those very words in the street while your girls lay on the ground."

"Sadly, true," Owl said. "I've brought your returned funds. Doubled, as per the agreement." She slid the valise over.

"Well, at least I have that to comfort me," Fenmere said. "Corman, do take that, please. Unless it's worth our while to reinvest in the Birds."

"No," Owl said. "If a contract fails with an engagement in the assigned time, we do not take it up again. That is our rule."

"Really? I would think that you would be itching for another shot at the Thorn."

"That's not how we operate, Willem," she said. "Vengeance makes for bad business."

"But this wouldn't be vengeance."

"Willem, let me make it clear what this venture has cost me. I have one girl who was arrested. I have two who are injured, and quite possibly neither of them will be capable of taking further work. In addition, I got to pay you for the privilege." She stood up and brushed off her skirt. "I know when to walk away from a bad investment. Consider the same."

With a curt nod, she walked out of the sitting room.

Fenmere leaned back in his chair. "Thorn victorious," he said idly.

Corman picked up the valise. "Shall I start making inquiries about other professionals?"

"Not yet," Fenmere said. "Let's put that money aside for some good investments. I trust you can do your magic there, Corman, but keep it isolated. Some ventures that will pay off by summer's end."

"So you won't be addressing the Thorn issue over the summer?" Gerrick asked.

"Not personally, no. Blazes, it's the summer, and I will go down to my house on the coast, like I do every year. I'm not going to let the Thorn ruin that for me. Not after having such a good week."

"Good week, sir?" Bell asked, before he even realized the words came out of his mouth.

Fenmere turned to him, a bemused look on his face. "Let me make something clear, Mister Bell. Failure is a choice. I don't own this neighborhood because I'm the kind of man who chooses it. We've weeded out some of the sewage from old crews, we've slapped the Thorn around, and because of him, an actual threat that the Red Rabbits posed has been neutralized. Including that chemist who robbed us."

"All of the Aventil gangs have been weakened, sir," Gerrick added.

Fenmere continued, shaking his meaty finger at Bell. "Red Rabbits most notably. No small part thanks to you, Bell. You contributed to that and I won't forget it. And according to my information, there is plenty of resentment in the neighborhood for the damage the Thorn caused. Including—and this is quite delicious—the most pure and incorruptible Constabulary man in the neighborhood has all but declared war on the Thorn." He patted Bell on the side of the face. "Fenmere victorious. Never forget that."

"You think we don't have to worry about him anymore?" Bell asked.

"I'm saying we can focus on other business for the time being, including my vacation. Besides, we have special projects in the works, Bell. Fingers in pies all around the city. And since I am feeling magnanimous, Mister Bell, I think you might get to taste one of those pies."

"Thank you, Mister Fenmere, sir," Bell said. "I won't let you down."

Fenmere got up from his chair and put a hand on Bell's shoulder. "You probably will. But the world brings us pleasant surprises."

He walked off, issuing orders to Gerrick and Corman regarding travel plans.

Veranix had limped his way back to the flop over the laundry press, using the cloak to magic his appearance into an old man, so no one would think it was strange he was walking so slow. Once there he had stashed away his cloak and weapons—such as they were, given that he had no arrows—under the bed. He had changed back into his regular clothes and made his way back to campus.

Things had been afoot, that much was clear. Cadets and Yellowshields walked about, but without any sense of urgency. An emergency had come and passed, and the emotions were ones of relief, not tragedy.

Veranix was torn about where to head first, but chose the carriage house. No sign of Kaiana or anyone else.

Next he went to Almers, where he was approached by Rellings on the walkway before he even got to the door.

"Calbert, there you are," he said. A phrase Veranix had often heard from Rellings, usually with an edge of accusation to it. This time, it had no edge. Rellings, dressed in smart traveling clothes, looked calmer than he'd ever seen him. "Didn't see you around at all last night. Nothing too rough, I hope."

"No, Rellings," Veranix said, not sure what to make of this. "I'm not in trouble, I presume."

"Not with me. As of the noon bells, my tenure as a prefect ended. I performed one final duty this morning, delivering examination marks and completion of year notifications. Yours are on the desk of your room."

"So I passed," Veranix said idly. "Saints be praised."

Rellings looked back up at Almers, sighing ruefully. "Oddly, I'm going to miss the old girl. You ready to be one of the tall men on the third floor?"

"Tall men" were what they called fourth-years, at least the kind of fourth-years who looked out for the underclassmen around them. The kind of fourth-years who never called those under them "kish."

"As long as they don't try to make me the prefect," Veranix said. "Saints preserve us all from that."

"I don't know," Rellings said. "You might rise to it."

"So where to for you?" Rellings had now earned his Letters of Mastery in Law.

"North side," Rellings said. "I've a cousin who's arranged a clerkship for one of the City Aldermen."

"Then good luck in that, Rellings." Veranix extended his hand, almost surprising himself how sincerely he meant the sentiment.

"And good luck to you." Rellings took the hand and shook it warmly, and walked off leisurely.

Veranix went up to his room, the whole while passing other young men who were in the process of packing off and leaving. Before he reached his room, he spotted Delmin, coming back from the water closet, dressed almost as smartly as if he had been in dress uniform.

"Veranix!" Delmin almost shouted when he spotted him. "You ... you're ..." He had no more words, and grabbed Veranix up in an embrace.

"You were sure I was dead?" Veranix asked with a grin, keeping his voice low.

"The thought crossed my mind."

"And is ... anyone else?"

"No," Delmin said. "Though it was pretty strange for a bit. But, yes, we're all fine: me, Kaiana, Phadre, and Jiarna."

"Why them?" Veranix asked.

"Oh, right, you don't know. We wouldn't have stopped Jensett without them."

"Huh," Veranix said. He glanced around the hall, making sure no one was marking them too much. "Let's talk in private, hmm?"

"Yes, well, just ..." Delmin said quickly, but Veranix had opened the door to their room before he finished his thought. It was immediately clear what he was about to say, though.

"Professor Alimen," Veranix said blankly. "What a surprise to find you in my room."

"As pleasant a surprise, I would hope," Professor Alimen said, as he sat idly at Veranix's desk, "as it is for me to actually see you here. I was wondering what you had been up to."

"I've been, you know . . ." Veranix stammered. At this moment he couldn't even think of a lie.

"Celebrating and carousing?" Professor Alimen offered. He held up the marks report. "You did pass everything, after all."

"Yes, yes," Veranix said. "Lost myself in my cups and only just now . . ."

"Sewage, Mister Calbert. Rutting fetid blazing sewage."

Veranix actually took a step back. "Really, sir, I don't think—"

"Mister Calbert, please have some respect for my intelligence. Do you honestly think I would believe that somehow Mister Sarren here, as well Mister Golmin, Miss Kay, and Miss Nell, would all be involved in apprehending the culprit behind these attacks, and yet you were off carousing? I do not believe you would abandon them like that. You have numerous faults, Mister Calbert, but that sort of callous disregard is not one of them."

"I am quite capable of callous disregard, sir," Veranix said. "Just the other day—"

"The other day he used my towel and left it on the floor," Delmin offered.

"Mister Sarren." Professor Alimen raised an eyebrow, silencing Delmin. "Please go to the courtyard and wait for the others."

Delmin nodded and walked off. Professor Alimen got up from the chair and shut the door.

"Professor, sir, whatever you're thinking . . ."

"I think you're an emotional young man who leads with his heart. I know perfectly well you went charging off after the culprit—what was his name?"

"Jensett," Veranix said before he caught himself.

"Yes, that was it," Alimen said. "You tried to get him after the dinner, and I imagine you tried again last night. He caught you and used your power to fuel his plans. Am I correct?"

"Sir, you have to—"

"Veranix." Alimen's voice was somehow both tender and curt at the same time. Rolling up the sleeve on his left arm, he displayed the tattoo for Lord Preston's Circle. "There is one thing I have to do. Teach you how to use the gifts you have so that you can earn this, and be safe to . . ." He trailed off, and then grabbed Veranix in an embrace. "I don't know what I would have done if you had been hurt, my boy."

"I'm fine, sir," Veranix said, barely able to find his own voice.

"And you will stay that way. At least while you are my student." Alimen let go. "The University will officially commend Delmin, Phadre, Jiarna, and especially Kaiana for their efforts. Though I imagine that their efforts would have been futile if you hadn't been involved somehow." He raised up his hands. "I am happier not knowing details. But while you will not receive any official commendation, you have my thanks right now."

"I appreciate that, sir."

"You should, Mister Calbert, since right now my thanks includes an invitation to Hightower Club." He went to Veranix's wardrobe and pulled out a suit. "This won't do, I think." With a rush of magic, the suit shifted in style, suddenly become far more impressive.

"Thank you, sir." Veranix took the suit and started changing. "Am I staying here for the summer, sir?"

"Here in third floor Almers?" Alimen gave a doddering look around. "I imagine that would be for the best. Unless I had you stay in Bolingwood Tower with me."

Veranix halted. "I don't . . . I mean . . ."

"We'll see what happens, Mister Calbert. Hurry up and come along."

Changed and looking rather smart, Veranix followed Professor Alimen down to the courtyard between the dormitories. Delmin was waiting with Phadre and Jiarna, who were sitting on a bench and engaged in an intimate conversation. It was clear, whatever they had done to stop Jensett had taken its toll on Phadre. He was now as gaunt as Delmin, and half his hair had turned white. Despite that, he looked jubilant, especially when looking at Jiarna. Delmin waited there with patient frustration.

"Mister Calbert is joining us," Alimen said. "We're almost all assembled?"

"Almost," Phadre said. He got up and shook Veranix's hand, and Jiarna did the same.

"Good to see you, Calbert," she said. "You . . . had us worried."

"I was worried as well."

She leaned in close. "I noticed that something of yours was damaged. I might be able to do something about that."

"I'm not sure—"

She mouthed the words: "A rope?"

"Yes, of course," Veranix said. "If you could . . ."

"Might," she emphasized. "But worth a try."

"I'd be grateful."

She shrugged, and then wrapped her arm around Phadre's elbow. "The least I could do for . . . someone so helpful."

Kaiana approached the group, again in her yellow dress. Veranix noticed right away that her arm was bandaged—the dart she had taken from Magpie.

"You—how are you?" she asked hesitantly.

"Surprised to be surrounded by the heroes of the hour," Veranix said. "I understand you're getting especially commended."

She smiled. "I'm not sure what that means, exactly. But it sounds good."

"Let us go, all," Alimen said, and he led the walk toward the western gates. Delmin walked with him, and Phadre and Jiarna followed behind them, arm in arm. Veranix hung back just a bit and Kaiana kept pace with him.

"So, did everything turn out . . . all right?" she asked him. "Obviously, you aren't dead."

"Somehow, I think I have you all to thank for that," Veranix said. "It was on the edge of the razor for a bit."

She smiled, warmly and sweetly. "It felt pretty good to really help you, you know."

They walked silently for a bit, and then Veranix nodded over to Phadre and Jiarna. "And how do you feel about that?"

"They're good for each other," she said. "I can't argue with that."

Her tone was neutral, but there was a hint of . . . something else. Veranix couldn't quite figure out what. And possibly it was for the best that he didn't. "I suppose not."

"And how do you feel right now?"

Veranix thought about that for a moment. The past few days he had been attacked, one way or another, more times than in the rest of his life. He was tired, down to his bones, from everything he had been through. And after it all, nothing he had done had gotten him any closer to stopping Fenmere.

But still, here he was, walking and breathing. He had passed all his exams, and was being taken to a celebratory dinner with his best friends in the world.

"Lucky, Kai," he finally said. "I feel *damn* lucky."

Appendix

Calendars and Astronomy

The year of *The Alchemy of Chaos* is 1215 by the Druth calendar. The calendar's first year marks the end of the Rebellion from the Kieran Empire and the coronation of King Maradaine I, forming what was called at the time the Great Kingdom of Druthal. Druthal went through many changes over the next twelve centuries, including breaking into smaller kingdoms and then re-unifying centuries later in its current form.

The Druth calendar has its roots in classical astronomy, which is tied to the era when Druthal was part of the Kieran Empire. Therefore the classical Kieran names for astronomical bodies remain in Druth scholarship. The sun is officially "Canus," and the world "Tovara," though these terms are almost never used outside of academic settings. The world revolves around the sun every 362 days. The two moons are Onali—the larger white moon—and Namali—the smaller red one. Onali has a thirty-two-day cycle, and Namali a nineteen-day cycle. There are also thirty-six official constellations of "constant stars," and seven planets ("inconstant stars" in the old Kieran). The planets are Enevium, Kioxu, Acalsa, Ghenix, Miersum, Renyla, and Lemeschi.

The Druth calendar measures the year with twelve

months that range from twenty-six to thirty-two days*. The calendar begins with the month Keenan, which has thirty-two days. Keenan first is also called New Spring and is the vernal equinox. The remaining spring months are Maritan (thirty days) and Joram (twenty-six days). The summer months are Erescan (thirty-one days), Letram (thirty-two days), and Soran (thirty days), with the summer solstice on Erescan fourth. The autumn months are Oscan (thirty-two days), Poriman (thirty-one days), and Alasim (thirty days), with the autumnal equinox on Oscan second. The winter months are Nalithan (thirty-two days), Maleman (thirty days), and Sholan (twenty-seven days), with the winter solstice on Nalithan first.

The Druth calendar also notes a seven-day week, which has its origins in ancient Kieran religious practices that do not apply to modern Druth life. The days are Lemes, Ene, Kio, Acal, Ghen, Mier, and Ren. The primary social distinction of the Druth week is most civil employment pays weekly on Ren, especially for the city positions in Maradaine: Constabulary, Fire Brigade, Yellowshields, River Patrol, Sewer and Pipemen, and so forth. Every day of the week is a workday in Druthal, but there are twenty-four Saint Days over the course of the year which are observed as holidays to varying degrees. The most important of these Saint Days are Fenstide (The Feast of Saint Fenson), Terrentin (Saint Terrence Day), and Quiet Night (Saint Jasper Day, also the winter solstice). There is one national holiday as well:

---

*Ancient Kieran calendars originally had twelve thirty-two-day months and, as more accurate measurements were made, the calendar was corrected by dropping days off some months. Legend has it that Joram became the shortest month because King Bintral IV (674–684) wanted to irritate his cousin, whose birthday was Joram twenty-seventh.

Reunification Day, celebrated on Erescan thirty-first, which commemorates the unification of the ten arch-duchies under the Druth throne and the newly formed Parliament in 1009. Parliamentary and local election results are traditionally announced on Reunification Day.

Satrine Rainey...

Former street rat. Ex-spy. Wife and mother who
needs to make twenty crowns a week to support
her daughters and infirm husband. To earn that,
she forges credentials and fakes her way into a
posting as a constabulary Inspector.

Minox Welling...

Brilliant Inspector. Uncircled Mage. Outcast of
the stationhouse. Partnered with Satrine because
no one else will work with "the jinx."

Their first case together
—the ritualized murder of a Circled mage—

brings Satrine back to the streets she grew up on,
and forces Minox to confront the politics of mage
circles he's avoided. As more mages are found
dead, Satrine must solve the crime before her
secrets catch up with her, and before her partner
ends up a target.

A Murder of Mages
by Marshall Ryan Maresca
978-0-7564-1027-8
